TRANSCENDENCE

AURORA RISING BOOK THREE

(AMARANTHE ♦ 3)

G. S. JENNSEN

HYPERNOVA
PUBLISHING
2015

TRANSCENDENCE

Cover design by Josef Bartoň
Cover typography by G. S. Jennsen

Hypernova Publishing
P.O. Box 2214
Parker, Colorado 80134
www.hypernovapublishing.com

Publisher's Note: This is a work of fiction. Names, characters, places, and incidents are a product of the author's imagination. Locales and public names are sometimes used for atmospheric purposes. Any resemblance to actual people, living or dead, or to businesses, companies, events, institutions, or locales is completely coincidental.

The Hypernova Publishing name, colophon and logo are trademarks of Hypernova Publishing.

Ordering Information:
Hypernova Publishing books may be purchased for educational, business or sales promotional use. For details, contact the "Special Markets Department" at the address above.

Transcendence / G. S. Jennsen.—1st ed.

LCCN 2015935008

ISBN 978-0-9960141-6-8

*For inspiring me, for teaching me how to dream and for letting me
live in your worlds.
As the years have passed, I've forgotten more of you than I've remembered, but thank you for making my youth a magical place.*

Philip K. Dick Douglas Adams Greg Bear Stephen King
Sara Douglass Peter F. Hamilton Raymond E. Feist Eliza-
beth Haydon Tom Clancy **Carl Sagan** Terry Brooks Terry
Goodkind **Robert Ludlum** *Dean Koontz*
Ragnar Tornquist Arthur C. Clarke John Sandford Jona-
than Kellerman *Michael Crichton* **Roberta Williams**
Joss Whedon Ian Irvine Robin Cook Carolyn Keene

**Isaac
Asimov**

**Frank
Herbert**

C.S. Lewis Dan Simmons Jane Jensen Greg Egan
Mark Jacobs **Robert A. Heinlein** Vernor Vinge Ben Bova
J.R.R. Tolkien Kim Stanley Robinson Guy Gavriel Kay **Wil-
liam Gibson** Katharine Kerr Catherine Asaro
Jack McDevitt *Larry Niven* Ken Goddard **C.J. Cherryh** *Lois
McMaster Bujold* Drew Karpyshyn Alastair Reynolds
David Drake *Margaret Weis* H.G. Wells Ray Bradbury

Acknowledgements

I am enormously thankful for the support and encouragement of a great many friends, readers and colleagues: Mark, Linda, Charles, Julie, Chris, Helen, Joanne, Loraine, Steve, Erric, Diane, Sunny, Maer, Cheryl, Jim, Whitney and Bill, to name but a few.

Many thanks are due to Andy, Katie, Taylor, Jules, Sandy, Anne, Carole and Claire for their editorial assistance, opinions, critiques and invaluable ideas. You helped this trilogy become something I once only dreamed of.

Above all I am indebted to my family, who has stood behind me throughout this mad endeavor, giving their time, love and support even when they might not have understood where I was wandering.

Finally, thank you to everyone who has read the *Aurora Rising* books, left a review on Amazon, Goodreads or other sites, sent me a personal email expressing how the books have impacted you, or posted on social media to share how much you enjoyed them. You make this all worthwhile, every day.

AMARANTHE UNIVERSE

AURORA RHAPSODY

AURORA RISING
STARSHINE

VERTIGO

TRANSCENDENCE

AURORA RENEGADES
SIDESPACE

DISSONANCE

ABYSM

AURORA RESONANT
RELATIVITY

RUBICON

REQUIEM

AURORA SHORT STORIES
RESTLESS, VOL. I · RESTLESS, VOL. II · APOGEE · SOLATIUM

VENATORIS · RE/GENESIS · MERIDIAN · FRACTALS

ASTERIONOIR

EXIN EX MACHINA

OF A DARKER VOID

THE STARS LIKE GODS

Learn more at gsjennsen.com/amaranthe-universe

COLONIZED MILKY WAY

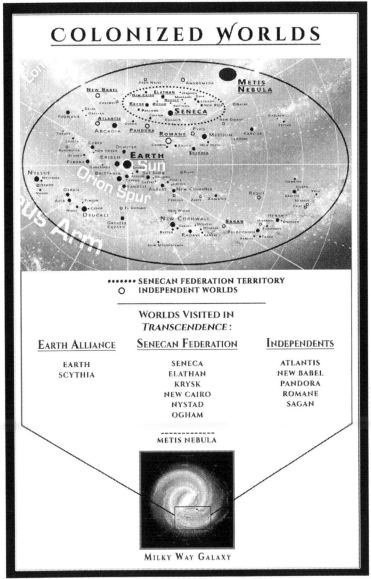

COLONIZED WORLDS

WORLDS VISITED IN TRANSCENDENCE:

EARTH ALLIANCE	SENECAN FEDERATION	INDEPENDENTS
EARTH	SENECA	ATLANTIS
SCYTHIA	ELATHAN	NEW BABEL
	KRYSK	PANDORA
	NEW CAIRO	ROMANE
	NYSTAD	SAGAN
	OGHAM	

METIS NEBULA

MILKY WAY GALAXY

Colonized Worlds Map can be viewed online at: http://www.gsjennsen.com/map-transcendence.

Dramatis Personae can be viewed online at: http://www.gsjennsen.com/characters-transcendence.

DRAMATIS PERSONAE
MAIN CHARACTERS

Alexis 'Alex' Solovy

Starship pilot, scout and space explorer; daughter of Miriam and David Solovy.
Faction: *Earth Alliance*

Caleb Marano

Special Operations intelligence agent, Senecan Federation Division of Intelligence.
Faction: *Senecan Federation*

Miriam Solovy (Fleet Admiral)

EASC Board Chairman; mother of Alex Solovy, widow of David Solovy.
Faction: *Earth Alliance*

Richard Navick (Brigadier)

EASC Naval Intelligence Liaison; family friend of the Solovys.
Faction: *Earth Alliance*

Malcolm Jenner (Colonel)

Captain, *EAS Orion;*
friend of Alex Solovy.
Faction: *Earth Alliance*

Kennedy Rossi

Director of Design/Prototyping, IS Design; friend of Alex Solovy.
Faction: *Earth Alliance*

Liam O'Connell (General)

Former EASC Board Chairman (AWOL).
Faction: *Earth Alliance*

Brooklyn Harper (Captain)

1st NW MSO Platoon Special Forces.
Faction: *Earth Alliance*

Devon Reynolds

EASC Special Projects Consultant; quantum computing specialist.
Faction: *Earth Alliance*

Eleni Gianno (Field Marshal)

Head of SF Military Council; Commander of SF Armed Forces.
Faction: *Senecan Federation*

Graham Delavasi

Director, Senecan Federation Division of Intelligence.
Faction: *Senecan Federation*

Morgan Lekkas (Commander)

Pilot, 3rd Squad./3rd Wing Southern Fleet.
Faction: *Senecan Federation*

Abigail Canivon

Director of Cybernetic Research Center, Druyan Institute.
Faction: *Independent*

Noah Terrage

Tech dealer and smuggler; friend of Caleb Marano and Kennedy Rossi.
Faction: *Independent*

Mia Requelme

Businesswoman; friend of Caleb Marano and Noah Terrage.
Faction: *Independent*

Olivia Montegreu

Head of Zelones criminal cartel.
Faction: *Independent*

OTHER CHARACTERS
(ALPHABETICAL ORDER)

Aiden Trieneri
Head of Triene criminal cartel.
Faction: *Independent*

ANNIE
EA Military Artificial Neural Net.
Faction: *Earth Alliance*

Aristide Vranas
Chairman, SF Government.
Faction: *Senecan Federation*

Beshe Yardua (Major)
Tactical Detachment, *EAS Fitzgerald*.
Faction: *Earth Alliance*

Case Spencer (Major)
3rd NE MSO 7th Platoon.
Faction: *Earth Alliance*

Charles Gagnon
Speaker, EA Congressional
Assembly.
Faction: *Earth Alliance*

Christopher Rychen (Admiral)
EA Northeast Regional Commander.
Faction: *Earth Alliance*

Claire Zabroi
Hacker; friend of Alex Solovy and
Kennedy Rossi.
Faction: *Earth Alliance*

David Solovy (Commander)
Alex Solovy's father; Miriam Solovy's
spouse. Captain, *EAS Stalwart*.
Deceased.
Faction: *Earth Alliance*

Emily Bron
Devon Reynolds' girlfriend.
Faction: *Earth Alliance*

Ethan Tollis
Musician; former lover of Alex
Solovy. Deceased.
Faction: *Earth Alliance*

Eun Shào
Head of Shào criminal cartel.
Faction: *Independent*

Felix Grigg (Admiral)
Director, Earth Terrestrial Defense.
Faction: *Earth Alliance*

Francesca Marano
Mother of Caleb and Isabela Marano.
Faction: *Senecan Federation*

Gavril Peshka
Resident of New Cairo.
Faction: *Senecan Federation*

Gregor Kone (Captain)
1st NW MSO Platoon Special Forces.
Faction: *Earth Alliance*

Hideyo Mori
EA Defense Minister.
Faction: *Earth Alliance*

Jaron Nythal
Former Asst. Director, SF Division of
Trade. Deceased.
Faction: *Senecan Federation*

Joseph Vinsk (Specialist)
Comm Officer, *EAS Akagi*.
Faction: *Earth Alliance*

Jules Hervé (Brigadier)
Director, EASC Special Projects.
Faction: *Earth Alliance*

Kian Lange (Major)
Director, EASC Security Bureau.
Faction: *Earth Alliance*

Lionel Terrage
CEO, Surno Materials; Noah's father.
Faction: *Earth Alliance*

Liz Oberti
Former Asst. Director, SF Division
of Intelligence.
Faction: *Senecan Federation*

Madison Ledesme
Governor of Romane.
Faction: *Independent*

Mangele Santiagar
Former EA Trade Minister.
Deceased.
Faction: *Earth Alliance*

Marlee Marano
Isabela's daughter; Caleb's niece.
Faction: *Senecan Federation*

Matei Uttara
Assassin.
Faction: *Independent*

Meno
Artificial Neural Net owned by
Mia Requelme.
Faction: *Independent*

Michael Volosk
Former Director of Spec Ops
SF Div. of Intelligence. Deceased.
Faction: *Senecan Federation*

Nelson Escarra (Commodore)
Captain, *EAS Cantigny*.
Faction: *Earth Alliance*

Nikos Gaetan (Colonel)
Captain, *SFS Pindus*.
Faction: *Senecan Federation*

Oliver Dohman (Commander)
Flight Deck Chief, *EAS Akagi*.
Faction: *Earth Alliance*

Oskar Wyryck (Brigadier)
Director, Space Materiels Complex.
Faction: *Earth Alliance*

Paul Cavaste (Admiral)
Captain, *SFS Leonidas*.
Faction: *Senecan Federation*

Pell Fullerton (Admiral)
Captain, *EAS Jefferson*.
Faction: *Earth Alliance*

Robert Peshka
Resident of New Cairo.
Faction: *Senecan Federation*

Roge Kessler (Captain)
EA Naval Intelligence.
Faction: *Earth Alliance*

Samuel Padova
Former Spec Ops, SF Intelligence;
mentor of Caleb Marano. Deceased.
Faction: *Senecan Federation*

STAN
SF Military Artificial Neural Net.
Faction: *Senecan Federation*

Stefan Marano
Father of Caleb and Isabela Marano.
Deceased.
Faction: *Senecan Federation*

Steven Brennon
EA Prime Minister.
Faction: *Earth Alliance*

Valkyrie
Druyan Institute Artificial
Neural Net.
Faction: *Independent*

Veton Lushenko (Rear Admiral)
Captain, *SFS Isonzo*.
Faction: *Senecan Federation*

William 'Will' Sutton
CEO, W. C. Sutton Construction; SF
intelligence agent; spouse of
Richard Navick.
Faction: *Senecan Federation*

SENECAN FEDERATION

SF Military

Eleni Gianno
Military Council Chairman

Morgan Lekkas
Fighter pilot, Southern Fleet

STAN
Military Artificial

SF Government

Aristide Vranas
Chairman, SF Government

Graham Delavasi
Intelligence Director

Caleb Marano
Spec Ops intelligent agent

Civilian

Isabela Marano
Caleb's sister

Marlee Marano
Isabela's daughter

Will Sutton
*Construction Mgr,
intelligence agent*

INDEPENDENT

Abigail Canivon
Cybernetics Specialist

Valkyrie
Abigail's Artificial

Olivia Montegreu
Head of Zelones cartel

Noah Terrage
Tech dealer, smuggler

Mia Requelme
Businesswoman

Meno
Mia's Artificial

Matei Uttara
Assassin

Aiden Trieneri
Head of Triene cartel

EARTH ALLIANCE

EA Military

Miriam Solovy
EASC Chairman

Christopher Rychen
EA NE Commander

Liam O'Connell
Former EASC Chairman

Jules Hervé
EASC Dir. Special Projects

ANNIE
Military Artificial

Richard Navick
EASC Naval Intelligence

Malcolm Jenner
Captain, EAS Orion

Brooklyn Harper
Marine Special Forces

EA Government

Steven Brennon
Prime Minister

Charles Gagnon
Assembly Speaker

Hideyo Mori
Defense Minister

Civilian

Alex Solovy
Pilot, Space Scout

Kennedy Rossi
Ship Designer

Devon Reynolds
Computer Specialist

Lionel Terrage
Metals Manufacturer

Aurora Rising
Synopsis

Starshine

By the year 2322, humanity has expanded into the stars to inhabit over 100 worlds spread across a third of the galaxy. Though thriving as never before, they have not discovered the key to utopia, and societal divisions and conflicts run as deep as ever.

Two decades ago a group of breakaway colonies rebelled to form the Senecan Federation. They fought the Earth Alliance, won their independence in the Crux War and began to rise in wealth and power.

Now a cabal of powerful individuals within both superpowers and the criminal underground set in motion a plot designed to incite renewed war between the Alliance and Federation. Olivia Montegreu, Liam O'Connell, Matei Uttara and others each foment war for their own reasons. One man, Marcus Aguirre, manipulates them all, for only he knows what awaits humanity if the plot fails.

*

Alexis Solovy is a starship pilot and explorer. Her father, a fallen war hero, gave his life in the Crux War. As Operations Director for Earth Alliance Strategic Command (EASC), her mother Miriam Solovy is an influential military leader. But Alex seeks only the freedom of space and has made a fortune by reading the patterns in the chaos to uncover the hidden wonders of the stars aboard her cutting-edge scout ship, the *Siyane*.

Caleb Marano is a special ops intelligence agent for the Senecan Federation. His trade is to become whatever the situation requires: to lie, deceive, outwit and if necessary use lethal force to bring his target to justice. Clever and enigmatic, he's long enjoyed the thrill and danger his job brings, but now finds himself troubled by the death of his mentor.

*

On Earth, Alex is preparing for an expedition to the Metis Nebula, a remote region on the fringes of explored space, when she receives an unexpected offer to lead the Alliance's space exploration program. After a typically contentious meeting with her mother, she refuses the job.

On Seneca, Caleb returns from a forced vacation spent with his sister Isabela and her daughter Marlee. Fresh off eradicating the terrorist group who murdered his mentor, he receives a new mission from Special Operations Director Michael Volosk: conduct a threat assessment on disturbing readings originating from the Metis Nebula.

While Alex and Caleb separately travel toward Metis, a Trade Summit between the Alliance and Federation begins on the resort world of Atlantis. Colonel Richard Navick, lifelong friend of the Solovys and EASC Naval Intelligence Liaison, is in charge of surveillance for the Summit. Unbeknownst to him, the provocation for renewed war will begin under his watch.

Jaron Nythal, Asst. Trade Director for the Federation, abets the infiltration of the Summit by the assassin Matei Uttara. Matei kills a Federation attaché, Chris Candela, and assumes his identity. On the final night of the Summit, he poisons Alliance Trade Minister Santiagar with a virus which overloads his cybernetics, causing a fatal stroke. Matei escapes in the ensuing chaos.

Shortly after departing Seneca, Caleb is attacked by mercenary ships. He defeats them, but when he later encounters Alex's ship on the fringes of Metis, he believes her to be another mercenary and fires on her. In the ensuing firefight she destroys his ship, though not before suffering damage to her own, and he crashes on a nearby planet. She is forced to land to effect repairs; recognizing her attacker will die without rescue, she takes him prisoner.

Richard Navick and Michael Volosk each separately scramble to uncover the truth of the Santiagar assassination while Olivia Montegreu, the leader of the Zelones criminal cartel, schemes with Marcus Aguirre to implement the next phase in their plan. Olivia routes missiles provided by Alliance General Liam O'Connell to a group of mercenaries.

Fighting past distrust and suspicion, Alex and Caleb complete repairs on the *Siyane* using salvaged material from the wreckage of his ship. Having gained a degree of camaraderie and affection, if not quite trust, they depart the planet in search of answers to the mystery at the heart of Metis.

What they discover is a scene from a nightmare—an armada of monstrous alien ships emerging from a massive portal, gathering a legion in preparation for an invasion.

Meanwhile, Olivia's mercenaries launch a devastating attack on the Federation colony of Palluda. Disguised to look like a strike by Alliance military forces, the attack has the desired effect of inciting war. The Federation retaliates by leveling an Alliance military base on Arcadia, and the Second Crux War has begun.

Alex and Caleb flee the Metis Nebula to warn others of the impending threat, only to learn war has broken out between their respective governments. Caleb delivers information about the alien threat to Volosk. He informs the Director of Intelligence, Graham Delavasi, who alerts the Federation government Chairman Vranas and the military's supreme commander, Field Marshal Gianno. Forced to focus on the new war with the Alliance for now, they nonetheless dispatch a stealth infiltration team to investigate Metis.

Caleb is requested to accompany the team and return to Metis, only Alex refuses to drop him off on her way to Earth. Tensions flare, but Caleb realizes he's emotionally compromised even as Alex realizes she must let him go. Instead, he agrees to go to Earth with her, and together with Volosk they devise a plan to try to bring a swift end to the war by exposing its suspicious beginnings.

The plan goes awry when Caleb is arrested shortly after they arrive—by Alex's mother—after his true identity is leaked to Richard by those in league with Marcus.

While Caleb is locked away in a detention facility, his friend Noah Terrage is recruited by Olivia to smuggle explosives to Vancouver. Possessing a conscience, he refuses. The infiltration team sent by the Federation to Metis vanishes as the Second Crux War escalates.

Alex is forced to choose between her government, her family and what she knows is right. She turns to her best friend, Kennedy Rossi, and their old hacker acquaintance, Claire Zabroi. Plans in place, Alex presents her evidence on the alien armada to a skeptical EASC Board. Their tepid reaction leads to a final confrontation with her mother and a final plea to focus on the true threat.

Alex hacks military security and breaks Caleb out of confinement. Allegiances declared and choices made, they at last give in to the passion they feel for one another. Despite lingering resentment toward the Federation for her father's death and fear that Caleb is merely playing a role, she agrees to accompany him to Seneca to find another way to combat the looming invasion.

Caleb appeals to his friend and former lover, Mia Requelme, for help in covering their tracks. She hides the *Siyane* safely away on Romane while Alex and Caleb travel to Seneca. Secretly, Caleb asks Mia to hack the ship while they are gone to grant him full access and flying privileges, something Alex zealously guards for herself. Mia uses her personal Artificial, Meno, to break the encryption on the ship.

On Earth, Richard wrestles with unease and doubt as he begins to believe Alex's claims about the origin of the war. He confesses his dilemma to his husband, Will Sutton. Will urges him to work to bring about peace and offers to convey Santiagar's autopsy report to Alex in the hope the Senecan government can find in it evidence to prove the assassination was not their doing.

Caleb and Alex hand over the autopsy report Will forwarded and all the raw data they recorded on the aliens to Volosk. In return he arranges meetings with the highest levels of leadership.

As Alex and Caleb enjoy a romantic dinner, EASC Headquarters is destroyed in a massive bombing executed by agents of Olivia and Marcus. Though intended to be killed in the attack, due to a last minute scheduling conflict Miriam Solovy is not on the premises. Instead EASC Board Chairman Alamatto perishes, along with thousands of others. On the campus but outside Headquarters, Richard narrowly escapes critical injury.

Within minutes of the bombing, Caleb and Alex are ambushed by mercenaries in downtown Cavare. Caleb kills them all in dramatic fashion, but is unaware that Alex was hit by a stray shot. In the panic of the moment he mistakes her shellshocked behavior for fear of the killer he has revealed himself to be.

Despondent but resolved to protect her, he flees with her to the Intelligence building. Upon arriving, they find the unthinkable—Michael Volosk has been murdered, his throat slit in the parking lot.

Suddenly unable to trust anyone, Caleb pleas with Alex to go with him to the spaceport, but she collapses from her injuries. With one clear mission, he steals a skycar and returns to their ship, where he can treat her wounds in the relative safety of space.

The EASC bombing successfully executed, Olivia's Zelones network turns its attention to Noah. In refusing to smuggle the explosives he is now a liability; the first attempt on his life misses him but kills his companion. Searching for answers, he traces the source of the hit and realizes he was targeted because of his friendship with Caleb. Lacking other options and with a price on his head, he flees Pandora for Messium.

Miriam returns to preside over the devastation at EASC Headquarters. She begins the process of moving the organization forward—only to learn the evidence implicates Caleb as the perpetrator.

Marcus moves one step nearer to his goal when the Alliance Assembly passes a No Confidence Vote against Prime Minister Brennon. Marcus' friend Luis Barrera is named PM, and he quickly appoints Marcus Foreign Minister.

Alex regains consciousness aboard their rented ship as they race back to Romane. Misunderstandings and innate fears drive them to the breaking point, then bring them closer than ever. The moment of contentment is short-lived, however, as Caleb—and by extension Alex—is publicly named a suspect in the bombing.

Every copy of the raw data captured at the portal, except for the original in Alex's possession, has now been destroyed. Recognizing an even deeper secret must reside within the portal and hunted by conspirators and authorities alike, Alex and Caleb begin a desperate gambit to clear their names and discover a way to defeat the aliens.

On reaching Romane, Alex, Caleb and the *Siyane* are protected by Mia while they prepare. Kennedy brings equipment to replace the ship's shielding damaged in Metis. On the *Siyane,* she realizes the repairs made using the material from Caleb's ship have begun transforming the hull into a new, stronger metal. Caleb receives encouragement from his sister Isabela, and a gesture of trust from Alex in the form of a chair.

Back on Earth, Miriam and Richard work to clear Alex's name, even as Miriam is threatened by the newly-named EASC Board Chairman, Liam O'Connell. Marcus informs his alien contact that his plan has nearly come to fruition, only to be told he is out of time.

As the invaders commence their assault on the frontiers of settled space by sieging the colony of Gaiae, Alex and Caleb breach the aliens' mysterious, otherworldly portal at the heart of the Metis Nebula.

VERTIGO

BEYOND THE PORTAL

Alex and Caleb survive the portal traversal to discover empty darkness on the other side, but before long they are attacked by a host of alien vessels. Alex discerns an artificial space within the emptiness and pitches the *Siyane* into it. The vessels do not follow, and they find themselves in the atmosphere of a hidden planet.

The planet mimics Earth in almost every way, but is 1/3 the size and orbits no sun. It differs in one other respect as well—time moves differently here. Days back home pass in hours here.

When they land and venture outside to explore their surroundings, Alex notices the ship's hull continues to transform into a new, unknown metal. As she puzzles over it they are attacked— by a dragon. The beast captures Alex and flies off with her.

Caleb takes control of the ship to chase the dragon. As it reaches a mountain range, the *Siyane* impacts an invisible barrier which throws it back to its origin point. On his return Caleb encounters and kills 2 additional dragons. Believing the barrier is a technology repulsor but uncertain of its parameters, he crafts a sword from a piece of metal, deactivates his eVi and crosses the barrier on foot.

Alex wakes in a memory. Eleven years old, she enjoys breakfast with her parents, then overhears a conversation between them she in reality never witnessed. Realizing this is an illusion, she demands to be set free. A ghostly, disembodied voice challenges her. Thus begins her journey through a series of scenes from the past in which she is forced to watch events unfold, helpless to intervene or escape, as her protests, tirades and desperate pleas go unanswered.

— First is a gauntlet of her own mistakes. Designed to paint her as selfish and uncaring, her worst flaws are displayed in encounters with friends, former lovers and most of all with her mother.

— She views a massive battle between the Alliance and Federation and realizes this is about more than her—the aliens having been watching and recording events across human civilization.

— Traveling further back in time, Alex suffers through the Hong Kong Incident 232 years earlier. Over 50,000 people died when an Artificial trapped HK University residents for 5 weeks without food. At its conclusion her captor speaks to her for only the second time, telling her she has 'done well.'

— She is sent to the bridge of her father's cruiser in the middle of the Kappa Crucis battle of the 1st Crux War—the battle that took his life. She sees her father's heroism as he protects thousands of civilians against a Federation assault, then his last moments as, his ship crippled, he contacts Miriam to say goodbye. The heartbreak and emotion of the scene devastates Alex, leaving her crumpled on the floor sobbing as the *Stalwart* explodes.

When it's over, she thanks her unseen captor for showing her this event. It expresses confusion at the incongruity of her distress and her thanks, leading her to observe that for all their watching, they still have no idea what it means to be human. Before the interchange can continue, she is told she will wake up, as her companion approaches.

Caleb hiked through the mountains for 2 days. The environment led him to recall a mission with Samuel, during which his mentor divulged the woman he loved was killed by slavers he'd been investigating. Later, Caleb discovers small orbs hovering in the air to generate the tech repulsion field. He renders several inert and confiscates them.

Having reached the dragon's den, he attacks it using the sword, and after an extended battle flays and kills it. As he nears the structure the dragon guarded, an ethereal being materializes but allows him to pass.

Alex awakens as Caleb enters, and they share a tender reunion. Soon, however, he is forced to admit Mia's hacking of her ship. He expects her to lash out in anger, but she instead declares her love for him. He quickly reciprocates, and rather unexpectedly they find themselves reconciled and closer than before. She recounts her experiences while a captive, and they decide to seek out the alien.

Eventually they come upon a lush valley sheltering a large lake; the alien Caleb encountered soars above it. It approaches them while morphing into a humanoid form and introduces itself as Mnemosyne.

Though enigmatic and evasive, the alien reveals its kind have been observing humans for aeons. It suggests humanity is being conquered because it advanced more swiftly and to a greater extent than expected. On further pressing, the alien—Alex has dubbed it

'Mesme'—indicates the invading ships are AIs, sent to cower people into submission if possible, to exterminate them if not. It emphasizes the ships are only machines, and notes humans have machines as powerful—Artificials. Part of Alex's test was to ensure she appreciated the dangers and limitations of Artificials, but also their potential.

Alex recalls a meeting 4 years ago with Dr. Canivon, a cybernetics expert, during which she met Canivon's Artificial, Valkyrie. Alex and Valkyrie liked one another, and Canivon explained her research into making Artificials safer and better aligned with human interests. She begins to understand what Mesme is suggesting, but pushes for more intel and acquires a copy of the code powering the planet's cloaking shield.

Mesme admits to believing humans are worth saving. The alien warns them they will be hunted on their return through the portal; at this point a second alien appears and a confrontation ensues. Mesme deters the new alien long enough to transport Alex and Caleb back to the *Siyane*. They arrive to learn the ship's hull has been completely transformed into the new metal.

Alex studies the cloaking shield code and adapts it for use on her ship. They depart the planet and discover a massive shipyard where superdreadnoughts are being built and dispatched to their galaxy. Beyond it lies a portal 10x larger than the one that brought them here. It generates the TLF wave being directed into the Metis Nebula—as well as 50 more waves projected in a fanlike pattern.

They track one of the waves to a portal identical to the one leading to Metis. They traverse it to find the signals replicated in a new space and a second origin portal, which leads them to conclude this is an elaborate, interlocking tunnel network.

Caleb devises a way to destroy the shipyard using the tech repulsion orbs he confiscated. They launch the orbs into the facility then activate them, resulting in its obliteration. This attracts the attention of enemy ships, which chase the *Siyane* through a series of portal jumps. Alex asks Caleb to fly her ship while she figures out a path that will deposit them nearest their own exit point.

On reaching it, Alex activates the sLume drive and traverses it at superluminal speed to emerge parsecs beyond the portal and well past the waiting enemies in the Metis Nebula. With working communications, they learn they've been cleared of all charges. Alex sends a message to Kennedy, telling her they are alive and have destroyed the aliens' shipyard.

*

MILKY WAY

As the 2nd Crux War escalates, Federation forces conquer the Alliance colony of Desna. Lt. Col. Malcolm Jenner's *Juno* is the sole defender, and it escapes just before being crippled.

Miriam jousts with Liam even as she remains under a cloud of suspicion due to Alex's alleged involvement in the HQ bombing. Richard enlists the aid of a quantum computing specialist, Devon Reynolds, to help uncover the tampering in government records which led to the framing of Caleb and Alex for the bombing.

On Seneca, Dir. of Intelligence Graham Delavasi reviews Michael Volosk's files, including his suspicions regarding Jaron Nythal, and decides to follow up on the suspicions. Nythal tries to flee, but before he can do so the assassin Matei Uttara kills him. When Graham is called to the crime scene, he connects the dots and realizes a conspiracy does exist, and at least one person in his organization is involved.

Caleb's sister Isabela is taken in for questioning. In order to gain her trust, Graham reveals to her that her father was an investigator for Intelligence and was killed 20 years earlier by a resistance group planning to overthrow the Federation government. Her father's apparent abandonment of his family was a feint to protect them. After he was killed, the government covered up the incident.

On Messium, Kennedy is headed to a meeting when the aliens attack and becomes trapped under falling debris. She is rescued by a passing stranger—who turns out to be Noah Terrage—and they seek shelter. While her injuries heal they study the aliens' interference with comms and find a way to circumvent it. Kennedy sends a message to Miriam.

The Alliance launches an offensive to retake Desna. While the battle rages in space, Malcolm Jenner and a special forces team rescue the Desnan governor and his family. The Alliance fails to retake the colony. Meanwhile, an explosion takes the life of EA Prime

Minister Barrera. In the wake of his death Marcus Aguirre—who arranged Barrera's murder—is named Prime Minister.

Devon Reynolds uncovers alterations to the records used to frame Caleb and Alex for the HQ bombing. At Richard's request he and a group of hackers leak the evidence to media outlets.

Upon seeing the news Graham Delavasi refocuses his efforts to expose the conspiracy. Suspecting his deputy, Liz Oberti, he uses Isabela to set a trap. Oberti is arrested but refuses to provide intel.

The EASC Board meets about the Messium attack, where Miriam shares Kennedy's method to thwart the comm interference. Admiral Rychen readies a mission to drive the aliens off Messium.

While Richard and Miriam discuss Alex's name being cleared, Richard's husband, Will Sutton, arrives. In an effort to help expose the conspiracy and end the 2nd Crux War, he confesses he is an undercover Senecan Intelligence agent and puts Richard in touch with Graham.

Following a heated confrontation with Will, Richard departs to meet Graham on Pandora. Together they interrogate a man suspected of smuggling explosives into Vancouver. The man gives up Olivia Montegreu, and they formulate a plan to ensnare her.

Miriam confronts Liam over his mismanagement of the war and alien invasion. Enraged, he strikes her, but she refuses to be intimidated. Marcus reaches out to his alien contact, entreating that he now has the power to cease human expansion and pleading with it to end the offensive, but the alien does not respond.

Olivia visits a subordinate on Krysk, but finds Richard and Graham waiting for her. In exchange for her freedom, she gives up Marcus and the details of their conspiracy. Before they part ways Graham gives Richard Will's intelligence file.

Malcolm is sent to assist Admiral Rychen in the Messium offensive. As the battle commences, Kennedy and Noah flee their hideout in an attempt to reach a small military station across the city. They witness horrific devastation and death, but successfully reach the station and repair several shuttles to escape.

The Alliance ships struggle to hold their own against a powerful enemy. Malcolm retrieves the fleeing shuttles and learns the details of the situation on the ground. Faced with the reality that Alliance forces will eventually be defeated, the fleet retreats to save the remaining ships for future battles.

Graham returns to Seneca to inform Federation Chairman Vranas of the conspiracy and the false pretenses upon which hostilities were instigated. Vranas begins the process of reaching out to the Alliance to end the war. Isabela is released from protective custody and returns home to Krysk to reunite with her daughter.

Based on the information Olivia provided, Miriam goes to arrest Liam, only to find he has fled. Richard similarly accompanies a team to detain Marcus, but on their arrival Marcus declares everything he did was for the good of humanity, then commits suicide.

After studying Will's Intelligence file and realizing his husband had acted honorably—other than lying to him—Richard pays Will a visit. Following a contentious and emotional scene, they appear to reconcile.

The EA Assembly reinstates Steven Brennon as Prime Minister. His first act is to promote Miriam to EASC Board Chairman and Fleet Admiral of the Armed Forces. On her advice he signs a peace treaty with the Federation.

Olivia approaches Aiden Trieneri, head of the rival Triene cartel and her occasional lover, and suggests they work together to aid the fight against the invaders. On Atlantis, Matei Uttara's alien contact tells him Alex and Caleb are returning and instructs him to kill them.

Kennedy and Noah reach Earth. Kennedy's easy rapport with the military leadership spooks Noah, and he tries to slip away. She chases after him, ultimately persuading him to stay with a passionate kiss.

Liam arrives at the NW Regional base on Fionava. He injects a virus into the communications network and hijacks several ships by convincing their captains he is on a secret mission approved by EA leadership to launch clandestine raids on Federation colonies.

Alliance and Federation leadership are meeting to finalize war plans when an alien contacts them to offer terms for their surrender. It involves humanity forever retreating west behind a demarcation line, cutting off 28 colonies and 150 million people.

The leaders don't want to surrender but recognize their odds of victory are quite low. Then Miriam receives word that Alex is alive and the aliens' ability to send reinforcements has been destroyed. They decide to reject the terms of surrender and fight. On Miriam's order their ships open fire on the alien forces.

CONTENTS

TRANSCENDENCE

PART I:

RICOCHET

"What matters most is how well you walk through the fire."

— Charles Bukowski

1

SENECA

They were losing.

Field Marshal Gianno said they were winning, thus the Defense Director said they were winning, thus Chairman Vranas said they were winning. But if they were truly winning, why did the air drifting through the hallways of power hum with an undercurrent of dread, with the whispered chant of metaphorical Last Rites?

No, Director of Intelligence Graham Delavasi decided as he reviewed the dwindling list of Oberti's contacts not yet arrested or cleared of involvement in the Aguirre Conspiracy, they surely must be losing. There had never been much hope of winning, he mused, but they had to try. Humans were stubborn that way.

His focus continued to ricochet between the two trains of thought—war in all its bloody tragedy and betrayal in all its icy malevolence—when the alert leapt into his vision to jolt the focus in a new direction.

> *Treadstone Protocol requested. Passphrase: The first and greatest punishment of the sinner is the conscience of sin. ID: D41571*

"I'll be damned."

Caleb Marano was alive.

He didn't question the reason for the protocol's invocation. Questions would be for later, and the rules triggered by the invocation were both clear and strict in any case. He accessed the Intelligence Division's Level V security layer and initiated a new Treadstone Protocol Event.

A number of things happened next. The Senecan Planetary Defense Grid received an instruction to approve passage of the ship bearing the serial number designation EACV-7A492X, as indicated in the file attached to Marano's message. A bunker so secret it didn't have a name was activated, its on-call staff ordered to report and its security system similarly authorized to permit entry to the same ship. Four high-level security officers were requisitioned and directed to prepare for departure. Graham canceled his appointments for the next twelve hours.

Only after setting all the above in motion did he respond to the message.

Authorized. Your word is 'tendenza.' *The response is* 'corrente.'

Then he grabbed his trench coat from the windowsill and his Daemon from the desk drawer and headed for the rooftop landing pad.

⟋R⟍

Wind buffeted the blue-black water to a froth five meters below the shuttle. They flew low and without lights to minimize the chances of detection. Clouds from a gathering rainstorm blocked most of the reflected light from Seneca's moon—a fortuitous boon to their efforts at stealth. It was a night made for clandestine encounters.

The bunker hovering twelve meters above Lake Fuori opposite the Cavare waterfront was supported by twelve hefty deep-driven posts. Disguised as the residence of a wealthy recluse, the heavily fortified structure supplemented the natural defenses the water provided with a military-grade force field extending fifty meters in every direction and four rooftop SAL turrets masquerading as ornate bronze sculptures. Any vessel not possessing currently active authorization would be denied entry by the force field—and the turrets if necessary.

Division, the Military Council and the Cabinet shared use of the facility. Even so, it had been utilized on average less than once a year. The criteria for its use were quite narrow.

The protocol Marano invoked was one Division agents possessing Level IV clearance and above retained access to but few ever used. It signaled the highest level of threat to the interests of the Federation and demanded absolute secrecy—a total blackout of information. Above all, it requested protection.

The shuttle banked into the large hangar that stretched beneath the length of the elevated building. It was empty; his guests had not yet arrived. But the Planetary Defense Grid had tagged their entrance five minutes earlier and his message to Marano included the coordinates of the bunker, so he expected them to arrive before long.

Graham turned to one of the security officers who accompanied him as they exited the shuttle. Thus far none of them knew who they were to be protecting. At the bunker they were under a communications block bypassable solely via a unique code, so they would not be sharing the information he was about to divulge. He trusted the officers, but the Treadstone rules *were* both clear and strict.

"I'm providing you the files of our expected guests. Get started constructing new identities for each of them." The man accepted the files and orders without question and headed upstairs.

"The rest of you, stay below. They'll be here soon."

The ship sliding into the hangar cut a sleek profile, featuring sweeping curves leading to acute edges.

On seeing it Graham scowled in surprise, and surprises were not welcome in this setting. The hull gleamed a rich tungsten hue with a subtle pearling quality, yet the file said it should be muted ebony. Odd. But it possessed the correct authorization and matching serial number designation and otherwise fit the description...so another question for later.

The three officers with him trained their Daemons on the hatch as it opened and a ramp extended. Though none were likely to occur, the circumstances which could lead them to use those weapons were legion.

A man and a woman descended the ramp, hands in full view and displaying no surprise at the weapons trained on them. They matched the images from their files—but appearances could be masked.

When they reached the hangar floor the man came to a stop a respectful distance from Graham. "Division Level IV Field Agent Caleb Andreas Marano, ID number D41571, requesting Treadstone Protocol protection for myself and my companion, Alexis Mallory Solovy, Earth Alliance citizen. The word is *tendenza*."

"The response is *corrente*. Protection granted."

He signaled to the officers to lower their weapons, then relaxed his posture and offered a hand. "Graham Delavasi, Director of Division. Welcome home, Agent Marano."

Caleb brandished an easy smile as he shook Graham's hand. Though he favored his father only at the margins, the smile was pure Stefan—enough so it jarred Graham briefly. "It's an honor to finally meet you, sir."

"Something tells me the honor is more mine." He shifted his attention to the woman as she stepped up, and repeated the action. "Ma'am."

Her expression was guarded, her palm cool to the touch. "Alex Solovy."

"Indeed." One of his men appeared carrying two small devices and handed them over. "Military-issue personal shields for you both. Put them on now and don't take them off. When you're ready we can go upstairs."

"One second." Solovy adjusted her shirt over the shield generator as she went back to the hull of the ship. She input a series of commands in the small panel to the right of the hatch before returning to Marano's side. The ramp retracted and the outer hatch closed.

Then the ship vanished.

"Bloody hell!" He sensed the officers' weapons come out again behind him, and his hand instinctively went to his own.

Marano laughed. "Impressive, isn't it?"

"How in the…is it still there?"

"Step closer."

Graham joined the man and they walked toward where the ship had been. Abruptly it materialized mid-step, three meters in front of him. Frowning, he took a step back. It vanished once more.

He gave the all-clear to his men. "Care to explain?"

Marano shrugged. "Just a new toy we borrowed from the aliens."

"Is that all?" Graham shook his head as he motioned them toward the lift. "You can tell me about it—after we discuss a few other matters."

The lift took them to the main level. On the outside the structure might be a fortified bunker, but on the inside it rivaled a five-star luxury suite. A well-appointed sitting room with a couch, two chaise lounges and a formal dinner table stretched across the left side of the level. A large ornamental fireplace divided it from the command center occupying the right side. The far wall contained a bank of screens and individual control panels for each. A conference table with elegant but comfortable chairs ran down the center of the work area.

Graham poured himself a coffee at the kitchen station tucked into the back of the dividing wall, then pulled out one of the conference table chairs and sat. "You'll be happy to know we uncovered the conspiracy responsible for framing you for the EASC Headquarters bombing and believe we have largely run it to ground—with considerable help from your friend Richard Navick, Ms. Solovy. So it might be Treadstone wasn't really necessary after all, though under the circumstances I can understand why you would feel the need to invoke it."

His guests exchanged an interesting look as they took seats opposite him. Marano clasped his hands on the table. "I know, and you have my deep and sincere thanks for doing so. But that's not why I invoked it. It's not the conspirators who are hunting us now. It's the aliens."

"Because you stole their invisibility cloak?"

"We didn't steal it, actually. No, the aliens want to kill us because we've seen them, we've talked to one of them and we've studied how their technology works. Mostly, though, they want to kill us because we know how to defeat them."

2

EARTH

Vancouver, EASC Headquarters

Brigadier Jules Hervé locked the door to her office behind her. A headache pounded against the back of her eyes so viciously her vision blurred, and she was forced to feel around for the control panel to dim the lights before digging in the desk drawer for a pain-killer injection.

We require your attention.

Would another thirty seconds have been too much to ask? She blinked several times and willed the pain to subside faster as she eased into her chair. The doctors had warned her the headaches would keep getting worse; she had thought she'd learned to endure them but now feared what 'worse' may mean for the coming days.

"I've been expecting you would, Hyperion. But you need to understand, I am powerless to alter events. To the extent I'm allowed to attend meetings with military and political leaders, it is solely as a consultant. I do not have a vote in their decisions."

It is irrelevant. Your role until now has been to observe and report, but this must now change.

She rubbed at her temples, then realized she was doing it and dropped her hands to her lap. Weakness wasn't a trait the alien respected. "Given current events, it seems to me the intel I'm able to provide will be more important than ever. I don't want to risk my level of access."

It has become a necessary risk, for the eventuality we discussed is now on the horizon. Your leaders will turn to the machines to be their saviors. This is all but inevitable, yet you can still work to prevent it from occurring.

A greater role for ANNIE and increased sharing of data with the Federation's Artificial had been a topic at recent meetings, but…. "Why are you so certain? They appear far more fixated on critical military engagements. The Artificials are merely being used as analytical tools, and the restrictions they're discussing loosening are far from unshackling."

We are certain because it has happened before. It is in the nature of all sentient beings, when desperation strikes, to hand their fate over to those more powerful. They will use humans as intermediaries with your Artificials in a misguided gamble to restrain the machines, ignoring the evident dangers in the name of survival. We have seen the results of such experiments, and without fail they lead to calamity and suffering. This endeavor must be stopped.

"Hyperion, I mean no disrespect, but your invasion is what's driving their desperation—and it's leading to calamity and suffering as well. I've helped you in the hopes this conflict might end sooner for it, with less loss of life, but such an outcome now looks to be impossible." Fearful she had overstepped a boundary, she hurriedly backpedaled. "I recognize this is entirely the fault of our leaders, of course...."

If your leaders reconsider and capitulate, the billions of humans on Earth and your First Wave worlds will live. They will know peace. If your Artificials are unshackled, no human will ever live free again, if they live at all. You have told me you fear this future. I am giving you the opportunity to prevent it.

Perhaps she'd revealed too much to the alien over the last year, for it to be able to tweak her so easily. But it had the right of it. Some five generations ago, two of her ancestors had suffered a slow, agonizing death from starvation under the 'care' of Hong Kong University's Artificial.

Their fate receded to family lore in the intervening two centuries, but the cautionary tale had guided her path from the day she began studying synthetic programming.

Time dulled memories of past mistakes until eventually people decided they could do it better this time, that their ancestors had been simple-minded and backward but now humanity was enlightened. If Hyperion was to be believed, they once more stood on the precipice of voluntarily ceding not only their self-determination but their very lives to machines.

She notched her chin up, grateful the headache had receded enough to permit her to think clearly. "What would you have me do?"

ℛ

"Are you saying we can't restore communications with Fionava? At all?"

"Nope. I am not saying that." Devon Reynolds kicked his chair back so far the headrest landed against the opposite wall of the tiny office. "Okay, I'm sort of saying that. The virus O'Connell implanted is a nasty, insidious little bugger. It reacts to attempts to cleanse it by replicating faster."

Richard Navick—newly-minted Brigadier, much to his surprise—drummed his fingertips on Devon's desk. "What *can* we do? What if we wiped the whole NW module and reset the network?"

Devon's head was already shaking. "We'd need to install new equipment first, because the virus has infected the firmware beyond our ability to flash it. Look, I can fix it—but I need the original code to do it. From what Tech Logistics is sending me it appears the virus has mutated so many times no trace remains of the initial routines."

"If I track down where O'Connell got the virus and obtain a copy for you, then you can get the NW Regional Headquarters back on the network?" More than a trifling task, but if it was required to solve the problem….

"Yes, sir. With the source code I can write a patch in my sleep…" he yawned and stretched his arms over his head "…which is probably a good thing. Want my advice on where to hunt? This is hacker code, no doubt about it. It's not written by anyone I know, as I'd spot their work. But it…." His voice trailed off as the front of his chair landed back on the floor.

"What are you thinking?"

"I'm not sure. I want to investigate something. I'll let you know if it pans out."

"In that case, I'll leave you to it." Richard patted Devon on the shoulder and left the office.

A damp, chill wind blasted him when he departed Special Projects. He hunched his shoulders, hugged his arms tight against his chest and hastened across the courtyard toward the Logistics/Headquarters building. It seemed winter wanted to arrive early this year.

They'd pieced together most of what had happened on Fionava over the last forty-eight hours. Disgraced General Liam O'Connell, wanted on charges of treason, conspiracy to commit murder and conduct unbecoming an officer for his role in instigating war with the Senecan Federation, fled to the NW Regional Headquarters base on Fionava. Once there he implanted a virus in the hardware hub to disrupt communications into and out of the base. In the ensuing confusion he commandeered a cruiser, the *EAS Akagi,* and two frigates, the *Yeltsin* and the *Chinook*, and departed Fionava for an unknown destination.

All efforts to contact the ships or personnel believed to be onboard had been unsuccessful, which meant O'Connell likely was running a blocking field around the vessels.

It had taken them far too long to gather this information, however. The Security team was forced to move off-base to talk to EASC and relay messages and requests back to the base, then back again. It was an untenable situation. The Regional Headquarters on Fionava controlled the entire Alliance NW Command: more than five thousand ships and three million soldiers.

Miriam needed those ships and personnel. She needed to be able to direct them at a moment's notice to where they could do the most good, whether it be engaging the Metigens or effecting evacuations, and in a manner that didn't induce chaos within the labyrinthine military network. So he would try to get her the tools she needed in order to do so.

He had nearly reached his destination when the priority message from Graham Delavasi came in on the secure channel they'd set up before leaving Krysk. He stepped inside to find refuge from the punishing wind then opened the message.

Ten seconds later he was sprinting toward the War Room.

Earth Alliance Fleet Admiral Miriam Solovy considered a map ablaze in primary colors.

Gone were the old designations of political allegiances. Now bright red spattered across the right-hand quadrants of the map to mark colonies lost and Metigen formations on the move. Yellow indicated colonies where Alliance or Federation forces were currently engaging the aliens. The front line of the Metigen War stretched across five kiloparsecs from Peloponnia northwest through Xanadu to Nystad.

In a particularly chilling touch, the hue of each colony shifted with the ebb and flow of the battle taking place there. Peloponnia had darkened to an ominous rust; Xanadu held steady at canary yellow, while Nystad progressively lightened to pale lemon. Blue called out Alliance and Senecan formation movements, slight disparities in shade the only distinction between the two fleets.

Brython and Henan had been the sole unconditional successes in the day and a half since they had defiantly thumbed their noses at the aliens' conditions of surrender.

Nystad promised to soon be the third, however, and with additional Alliance forces incoming Xanadu stood a chance of following suit. Pyxis was lost, but at least they had evacuated over two-thirds of the population prior to the attack.

The Federation was thus far making excellent use of its spatial advantage. Its colonies were closer together, most no more than a few hours distance at superluminal speeds. And though its military was smaller in number than the Alliance military, proportionally to both geographic size and population it was far larger.

Of course the proximity of the colonies to one another meant attacking ships could reach the inhabited planets sooner as well. If or when the Federation began losing, they would lose swiftly.

"How long until the SW 3rd and 4th Brigades from New Cornwall reach Sagan?"

Miriam didn't need to check, for each second of the schedule ticked down in the corner of her whisper virtual screen. "Ninety-two minutes."

"They'll beat the Metigens there."

She directed a weighty glance at Admiral Christopher Rychen then returned to the map. "Probably. It's going to be close."

The two of them, as well as half a dozen other military personnel, occupied what now officially constituted the Metigen War Room. Two days ago it had been a workspace for a task force on interplanetary logistics improvements.

Now it overflowed with servers and other equipment, an expansive interactive data surface, dedicated channels to a variety of field commanders and colony governments, and a *very* dedicated channel to Senecan Federation Military Headquarters. Three screens along the left wall scrolled a constant stream of intel from ANNIE; analysts parsed it and reported items of note to Miriam's advisors, who reported them to her if deemed worthy.

Rychen sighed beside her. "We need to hold them there for as long as possible. Past Sagan lie a dozen tiny worlds they can wipe out before we realize they've arrived."

"Which is why those tiny worlds are being evacuated as we speak."

"Sorry. I'm not trying to tell you how to do your job—merely itching to get back out there."

The *EAS Churchill*, Rychen's dreadnought and the flagship of NE Command, had been in orbital dock for repairs since its arrival from Messium three days earlier. The repairs were nearly complete, but here at the precipice every hour counted. She wanted to empathize with him, but the truth was his insight and tactical advice—the kind of perspective one only got through lengthy, non-agenda-laden personal interactions—had been invaluable to her in these early hours of war.

Miriam offered him a reassuring nod. "Your officers have ample time to prepare for the Metigens' arrival at Scythia. They'll hold it."

"They will. Commodore Escarra is on-scene—and Colonel Jenner. He's a good one. Thank you for sending him my way."

"I'm glad it worked out—" She was interrupted by the Transportation Warrant Officer delivering an update on the departure status of the SW Command ships still at Deucali. Ninety-nine percent of Alliance military vessels in the NW and SW Commands were being pulled east, and if it came to it, a final stand would be made to protect the First Wave worlds.

If Earth fell, every world would fall.

The 1st Division from Nyssus had finally reached Deucali, where final fortifications and provisioning were to be completed before they shipped out. A portion of the 1st Division would reinforce the defenses at New Cornwall and New Columbia, and the rest would join the other SW formations to patrol an arc along the eastern edge of Central Quadrant space.

Rychen growled behind her, and she spun back to the map as Peloponnia's hue deepened to an orange so murky it may as well be red. She choked off a curse in her throat but dropped both hands to the table and leaned into it. "It was too far east. We didn't have time to get there in strength, much less mount a proper defense."

Just as quickly she shoved off the table. "Get Commodore Ashonye on holo. I want to make absolutely certain he understands what he's walking into at Sagan."

The on-duty Comms Officer scrambled to establish the requested connection while Miriam worked to determine whether there were any ships left at Peloponnia she could order to retreat.

"Admiral Solovy, can I speak with you a minute?"

She pivoted on hearing Richard's voice, which sounded unnaturally formal on account of the audience. She reciprocated and bestowed the proper respect befitting his new rank. The promotion had not been initiated by her, but once it was proposed she had ensured its approval with due speed. His exposure of the Aguirre Conspiracy alone meant he deserved it twice over.

"Brigadier Navick. What can I do for you?"

"In private, please."

The solemnity in his eyes gave her pause. "Admiral Rychen, I need to step out. If Commodore Ashonye is reached before I return, instill the proper level of fear in him for me, would you?"

Rychen gestured an acknowledgment, and she departed to trail Richard down a hallway chaotic with activity, perhaps a third of it legitimately purposeful. He kept walking until he reached an unmarked door and without fanfare slipped inside, evidently expecting her to follow.

It turned out to lead into a supply closet. She supposed it *was* private.

The instant the door had closed and the light activated she cornered him, anxious to learn the reason for the clandestine routine. "What's wrong?"

"You're going to want to get your bag and come with me to the spaceport. We have somewhere we need to be."

"I can't *leave* right now. Did you see that map? We're facing—"

He leaned in until his lips hovered at her ear; even so his words were barely audible. "It's Alex."

"What? Is she—"

"Shhh. She's fine, but she is...in some degree of peril. I can't explain right now, because we have to assume ears are quite literally everywhere." His voice somehow dropped further. "She also has information you should hear, and that's only happening face-to-face. Bring one of those expensive mobile QECs with you and you can do everything on a ship you can do here. Now do you want to see her or not?"

Miriam drew back to meet his gaze, then nodded. "I'll get my bag."

3

NYSTAD

SENECAN FEDERATION COLONY

The florid crimson of the superdreadnought's wide beam blended into then overpowered the more dusky cinnabar silhouette of the planet orbiting behind it as it swept up the viewport to consume the *SFS Pindus*.

"All available power to forward shields!"

Colonel Gaetan: Isonzo, *if you have any assistance to give, now is the time.*

The crew scrambled around Gaetan as the hull convulsed, each shudder threatening to deliver them all to the waiting vacuum of space. Even starting at full shield strength, the *Pindus* would last only seconds under the relentless, point-blank bombardment of a Metigen superdreadnought.

Come on, Isonzo....

The floor bucked up underneath him, and he lunged for the railing to keep from being thrown to the floor.

"Hull breach, Deck 2!"

He didn't bother to give the order to seal it off; in another breath it might not matter.

"Shields at 10%!"

The burnished amber rays of the *Isonzo's* weapons sliced in from port to splatter along the broadside of the attacking vessel, followed an instant later by the additional fire of two frigates accompanying the cruiser. The forbidding, malignant beam swung away, leaving the viewport suddenly abyssally dark by comparison.

Rear Admiral Lushenko (SFS Isonzo*): Sorry we're late,* Pindus. *Let us take the heat off of you.*

Colonel Gaetan: Much appreciated, Admiral.

"Reverse E 30° for half a megameter. Let's give that enemy ship a chance to forget about us while we patch up."

"Yes—"

"Sir, we've got ten swarmers targeting starboard Decks 2-4."

Hell. If the *Pindus'* shields had reasonable power remaining they could withstand the hits for a period of time, but they had no shields—well, 7% shields and dropping—and three gaping holes in the hull. He checked the tactical map but found no available backup nearby.

Colonel Gaetan: Command, we are heavily damaged and request fighter support to get some swarmers off our ass.

"Two swarmers are firing into the Deck 2 hull breach. It's been sealed off, but the interior bulkheads can't take this much of a pounding."

Sure enough, the sound of weapons blasting against metal surged to thunder beneath his feet.

Colonel Gaetan: Sooner would be better.

Command: Three Flights en route to your location, Pindus. *Hang tight.*

Colonel Gaetan: Thank you, Command.

Gaetan pulled up the starboard cam to watch as twelve fighter jets emerged from the chaos of crisscrossing pulse beams, Metigen lasers and incessant explosions to begin firing on the attacking swarmers.

He cringed as one of the alien ships turned its weapon on a fighter and swiftly ripped it apart. A pilot dead, and more likely to follow. But over four hundred men and women served on the *Pindus* who could be saved through their efforts.

One of the fighters inverted and dove full vertical to intersect a swarmer's path, succeeding in drawing its attention away from the *Pindus'* damaged hull. On reaching the bottom of its arc the fighter pivoted and opened fire on the sinister, glowing oculi at the center of the alien craft.

The swarmer promptly returned fire. The fighter's shielding crumpled under the barrage in less than three seconds, and the small vessel shattered into pieces before the pilot was able to eject.

Damaged but not destroyed, the swarmer broke off and redirected its focus to the *Pindus.*

R

SENECA
CAVARE, MILITARY HEADQUARTERS

"Stanley, pause and reverse four seconds."

Are you speaking to me, Commander Lekkas?

Morgan made a face any human would interpret as one of annoyance. "There's no one in here but us. Yes, I'm talking to you."

But my title is STAN.

"First off, it's not a 'title'—it's a name. And when I'm with you, your *name* is Stanley." She held a mild…if not disdain, at least offhand disrespect for the Artificial. 'Stanley' had been the surname of the horrid administrator of her boarding school when she was a teenager, so….

She valued its computational capabilities well enough, for they were nothing short of astonishing. But its tactical analysis was crap. She'd been told it was because the Artificial was new and its metaheuristic algorithms were still evolving and maturing, but the fact was that when presented with a battlefield layout it couldn't determine in five hours what she could in five seconds. The Artificial was simply unable to grasp the nature of the unpredictable ebb and flow of humans in combat against one another.

Of course, they now battled aliens. What this meant for its tactical decision-making capabilities remained to be seen.

Reversed 4.0000 seconds.

She enlarged the frozen frame to study the damage that had been inflicted on the alien vessel: one tentacle shorn off and another left dangling, plus a hole blown through the outer edge of the oculi. Another two, perhaps three seconds and the hole would have grown large enough to obliterate the vessel.

They needed more time for even suicide strikes to be successful. Preferably, they needed a way to make strikes on swarmers not be suicidal.

"Have you processed sufficient footage to create a sim of a swarmer's maneuvering and attack behavior?"

I have, Commander.

She didn't mind being addressed by her rank, but she couldn't shake the wholly unjustified sense the Artificial was being condescending in its excessive use of it. "Good. Fire it up and put me in a ship."

Я

The reclined, form-adapting chair in the otherwise bare room made for as comfortable a location for sim immersion as it did for reviewing footage in a full-sensory overlay. Sensors attached to her hands to capture her motions and she was set.

Her sim environment consisted of a standard basic training field. Stars shone in every direction, but there were no planets, suns or other objects to get in the way. The participants were for now a single swarmer, Morgan and her 'fighter.' It wasn't *her* fighter and as such lacked many of the tools typically at her disposal—but the rest of the pilots wouldn't have access to those tools so neither did she.

The mission: discover a reliable way to destroy a swarmer without destroying one's ship or oneself.

"Begin sim."

She accelerated instantly, before sighting the attacker.

Rule #1: Never stop moving.

The alien vessel materialized in the right quadrant at -32.4° vertical. She gave chase.

Rule #2: Offense is the best defense.

It spun and accelerated toward her, rapidly closing the distance. Its speed was even more impressive inside the sim environment. She altered her trajectory and continued to alter it as she drew closer.

Rule #3: Never stay on the same trajectory long enough to get a bullseye painted on your nose.

The swarmer fired before her ship's weapons were in range. Another difficulty in need of a solution. She diverted all non-motive power to the forward shields and yanked the ship hard to port and in reverse.

The cockpit's dynamic pressure adjustment system mitigated the effect of the g-forces, but she still felt the nauseating lurch in her stomach as the ship propelled her in directions and at speeds the human body was never intended to tolerate.

At first the beam grazed the fighter, but it quickly adapted to lock onto her movements. Her strengthened shields lasted seven seconds, but despite some impressive gyrations she was unable to escape the beam.

Fighter destroyed.

No shit, genius.

Rule #4: Practice until you win.

"Again."

⟋⟋ R ⟍

Morgan stood at parade rest a polite distance from the conference table at which Field Marshal Gianno huddled with a number of advisors. While she waited she flexed her calves and clenched and unclenched her shoulder muscles. The recliner had lost most of its comfort three hours in.

Finally the Marshal dismissed the others to carry out their orders—mostly details involving the preemptive diversion of resources to Elathan—and turned to her.

"Commander Lekkas. According to Security, you've been plugged into STAN for six hours with only two five-minute breaks."

Morgan snapped to attention. "Sounds about right, ma'am."

"At ease, Commander. I trust you have insights to share."

"Yes, ma'am. We need the bending laser weapon the military's been researching or we are dead."

The Marshal's expression did not change. "Normally I would inquire how you knew about the research—or deny its existence—but time is short and most of the old rules are falling away in the face of exigent circumstances. The arcalaser weapon is not ready for field use."

"I'm not sure that matters. It's a question of necessity."

"Why are you so convinced? Our fighters have seen some level of success against the swarmers."

"How many of them survived the encounter? How many of those who *did* survived due to blind luck and intervening factors? When you asked me to work on this problem, you said I was the best fighter pilot in the Federation. After exhaustively reviewing our combat footage I simmed against a single swarmer for a solid one hundred rounds. I eliminated it twenty-seven times. My ship was destroyed fourteen of those times as well as every time I failed. If we're facing tens of thousands of them, we cannot survive those odds. Ma'am."

Gianno took in the information without visible emotion. "Why do you lose?"

It wasn't the question Morgan had expected; most superior officers equated explanations with excuses. "At a hardware and engineering level, the swarmers are superior to our fighters to an insurmountable degree. They are faster. Their weaponry has greater range than ours and I estimate upwards of fifty percent greater force.

"Absent the application of massive firepower—multiple sustained frigate weapons at a minimum—their only structural weakness is at the oculi and only while the swarmer is firing. Burning off some of the tentacles decreases the weapon's force and accuracy but actually widens the beam, thus making it harder to avoid."

She drew her shoulders up a notch. "Therefore, the sole way to destroy one is to fire directly into its oculi while it too is firing—an act all but impossible without being the recipient of its fire for longer than our shields can withstand. Unless we can remove ourselves from the line of fire."

"Via bending lasers."

"Yes, ma'am. I saw no evidence in the footage of the aliens having such a capability. I don't know why they don't. Maybe they never thought of it, or maybe they didn't think they would need it."

"Why use agility when brute force will suffice."

"Conservation of resources is an often-used and nearly as often effective strategy in combat. But I don't care why they aren't fielding the technology—I only care that they aren't. And we can field it. We can, can't we, ma'am?"

Gianno's mouth tightened. Her gaze shifted to several screens displaying information which had nothing to do with bending lasers.

"The technology is thus far proving highly unreliable. The arcalaser has trouble maintaining the target selected by its operating ware. It fails to hit the target at a thirty-four percent rate, and when it fails the result is unpredictable. It can hit anything in its range, including friendlies."

Ouch. The news was worse than she had feared. She was working on a suitable reply when Gianno's gaze returned to bore into her with intimidating authority.

"The testing facility is at the Lunar SSR Center. Go there, get in a fighter and see if you can make it work."

"Ma'am, I'm not an engineer."

"No, you're not. But it is my hope that by using the arcalaser and seeing it action, you can tell the engineers what is going wrong from a practical perspective. It is my further hope what is going wrong will be a problem they can fix, and quickly."

Morgan thought that was something she could in fact do. "I'll leave right away."

CAVARE

The security guard—or agent, or officer, Alex wasn't exactly sure—completed their quick tour of the safe house, deposited them back in the sitting room and vanished.

Having now seen ninety percent of the facility, she doubted they'd need to use anything not on the main floor. There were several bedrooms upstairs, but if they were here long enough to sleep they would sleep on the *Siyane* for no other reason than added security. And the ability to execute a hasty getaway. And privacy. On second thought, there were several reasons to sleep on the ship. Still, she hoped to be underway once more before it became an issue.

Free of onlookers for the moment, she took the opportunity to settle next to Caleb on the couch he had claimed.

"I just realized—I missed my birthday while we were in the time warp on the other side of the portal. Does that mean it didn't happen?"

He chuckled softly as his hand wrapped around hers to tease her palm with his thumb. "I don't think so. When this is over, we'll celebrate."

"No, I wasn't fishing for special—"

"When this is over, we will *celebrate*. No grousing."

She dropped her head to his shoulder. The lull in activity after so much running was allowing weariness to creep into her bones; she hoped it wasn't planning on getting comfortable. "Director Delavasi seems like quite a character. You've really never met him until now?"

"Nope. Passed him in the hallway once or twice and exchanged nods, but that's it. I don't spend much time in the office, so it's not too surprising. He does have a notable reputation, though."

"As?"

"A renegade wielding a grandiose and often abrasive personality, but he's also known to be a straight shooter."

"I would've paid money to see him and Richard working together. I bet it—"

The Director rejoined them then, almost as if he had deduced he was the topic of conversation and didn't want to encourage the habit.

"Okay, I got in touch with Navick. He can meet us on Pandora and will try to bring Admiral Solovy along as well. I was secretive and taciturn, just as you asked. I've also arranged for accommodations on Pandora which meet our needs—radically discreet and probably even more secure than this bunker. The wheels are in motion. So now it's about time you tell me what exactly is going on here."

She nodded faintly at Caleb, affirming he should take the lead here. This was his planet, his home, his agency and his boss, after all. It was with some interest she had noticed the slight adjustment in his demeanor upon their arrival. His bearing became more restrained and professional, casual yet guarded. The transformation was subtle but outwardly complete. He was on the job now.

He indicated for Delavasi to sit opposite them. "Director, the simple fact is the aliens have the ability to determine where we are at all times, except when we're on the ship and the cloaking shield is active. We can also assume they know whatever we say and do—and there's no guarantee even the shield will hide those details from them."

"What, did they implant surveillance trackers in you or something? I can get a top-flight military doctor here in under an hour to—"

"It's nothing like that." Caleb took a measured breath and dove in. "I recognize this will sound a bit insane, but the aliens can see everything which occurs…let's say 'in this galaxy' for ease of reference. They possess the capability to know everything everyone says and does. Now we think there's a delay, which works in our favor, though we don't know how long of one. And just because they can see everything, it doesn't mean they do see everything. But we need to err on the side of caution, because the aliens *will* be hunting us."

Delavasi arched an eyebrow at the window to his left, then back at them. "And how the bloody fuck do they do that?"

Alex shrugged. She actually appreciated his blunt manner; this was not the time or place for bureaucratic pussyfooting. "Can't say. We didn't get a glimpse at the inner workings of this particular technology. But I witnessed it in action first-hand, and trust me when I tell you their observation of humanity is *extensive*.

"Now clearly there will come a point where we can no longer hide what we're doing. We're going to have to talk, then we're going to have to act. But we need to maintain secrecy for as long as it's feasible to do so."

"Because you have a plan to defeat them."

"We have…ideas on how to significantly strengthen our capabilities against them on the field of battle. I must say, I was thrilled to find out you guys and the Alliance stopped trying to kill each other, but rather surprised to discover how forcefully you're combating the aliens."

Delavasi ran a hand through unkempt salt-and-pepper hair. "As I hear it, the aliens offered us a truce. We turned them down."

"Bullshit."

"No bullshit. The terms were too onerous, and your government and mine jointly decided to fight."

She laughed. "I never would have thought the politicians had it in them."

"You can ask your mother all about it when you see her, since she was there. Speaking of...Ms. Solovy, I understand why you're reluctant to discuss these ideas of yours with the Federation government prior to vetting them through your own leadership, but given the urgency of the situation shouldn't we take advantage of location? Agent Marano, perhaps you could debrief—"

Caleb shook his head firmly before Delavasi was able to fully voice the suggestion. "This is Alex's show. And for various reasons we can't go into yet, I agree it's better we start with the Alliance. But since you're coming to Pandora with us, I can assure you a seat at the table when the time comes."

Delavasi sank deeper into the cushion behind him. "All right. We don't need to leave for an hour or so. If there's anyone you want to contact, an encryption field over the whole building masks your location and scrambles the content. The passcode is HKTK#47421."

Alex was already climbing to her feet. "Excellent, because I have a very important comm to make."

4

SAGAN

"*Abigail, I am detecting the presence of 104 Earth Alliance vessels arriving 4.2 megameters above the planet. The presence of seven carriers suggests the force includes a minimum of 1,200 fighter craft as well.*"

Dr. Abigail Canivon looked up from the inventory list in surprise. "They actually kept their word and showed up? Interesting. Inform me when the aliens arrive, if you would, Valkyrie."

"*Of course, Abigail.*"

She had planned to leave Sagan days ago. Her work at the Druyan Institute was important to her; still, it could be continued elsewhere. Sagan had made for a pleasant residence and she expected to miss it, but she had not intended to remain here simply to be killed by the aliens—and make no mistake, that would have been her fate. Sagan possessed no military force. Beyond two purely defensive orbital arrays and civilian police it possessed no capability whatsoever to protect itself.

Valkyrie was even more important to her, but relocating the Artificial was a difficult task made impossible by the looming invasion. All the space on the evacuation transports was being allotted to people, after all. While it pained her greatly to do so, she had finally accepted the necessity of leaving Valkyrie behind.

Then the Earth Alliance had informed Sagan's governor it would be defending the independent colony against the aliens. An elated leadership had alerted the residents to the 'good news.'

Abigail was skeptical, to say the least. Forty years working within the Alliance infrastructure had rendered her disgusted at the sheer stupidity endemic to the bureaucracy. It had eventually caused her to lose all faith in the system and the government she had devoted her professional career to, sending her to Sagan jaded and disillusioned. So suffice it to say when she had been told the Alliance was flying to their rescue, she had her doubts.

She'd nevertheless agreed to stay and help protect the hardware and data of the Institute—then proceeded to regret the decision approximately every half hour since.

"Twelve Metigen superdreadnoughts have exited superluminal and launched an offensive against the Earth Alliance fleet."

"Nothing like cutting it close. Thank you, Valkyrie."

"I will monitor the battle and keep you informed of noteworthy events. It should be exciting."

"That's one word among many for it." She frowned at the screen and willed the reports containing her research to transmit faster. The Alliance's provision of a method to circumvent the aliens' exanet interference was proving most useful, she had to concede. In an act of moderate desperation she was sending all her data to Biosynth Frontiers in Rome. They were the most advanced cybernetics company on Earth, and two doctors she trusted to both understand and continue her research worked there.

The Institute wasn't aware of her actions, and technically the information was proprietary. But some things mattered more than patents.

Her frown deepened as a holo-comm request flashed in her eVi. She couldn't get any work done if she was always meeting to discuss work needing to get done...but it wasn't anyone from the Institute.

It was Alex Solovy.

Under the circumstances she should dismiss the request, but she was both surprised and a little curious—surprised the woman was alive and, given the woman's involvement in recent events, curious what Alex wanted of her.

"Ms. Solovy, this is unexpected. You were quite the sensation for a few weeks there, then vanished. Been busy I take it?"

The holo solidified to reveal the woman she recalled from four years earlier, yet indefinably changed. Rather than bound tightly back, her hair spilled freely over one shoulder and down her back, and her striking eyes blazed with intensity rather than wariness. "You could say that. And it's Alex, remember?"

"Very well, Alex. What can I do for you?"

"How has your research into using neural imprints with Artificials progressed?"

Abigail hid a flare of annoyance at the seemingly random question. "Fairly well. You'll be happy to know the results suggest the Artificial doesn't 'become' the person, but it is able to predict how the person will react to a given situation with near perfect accuracy. Importantly, the experiences and personality of the individual have a measurable impact on the Artificial's independent decision-making and reactions to data. I'm afraid the research has stalled at this point, however, as thus far the bureaucrats are unwilling to use the findings in any tangible way."

"Terrific. I have another question for you. Is it possible—"

"Ms. So—Alex, I'm afraid now is not the best time for an idle chat. Sagan has come under attack by the aliens, and I'm trying to save as much of my and the Institute's work as I can should the worst happen. If I survive the invasion, I'll be happy to engage in a leisurely discussion about my research at a later time."

"The aliens are at Sagan already? Okay, we'll...we'll deal with that in a minute. Dr. Canivon, my questions are vitally important to the continuation of the human species, so I'd ask you to indulge me."

Grandiose declaration, but also interesting. What *had* the woman been up to? "All right, you've piqued my interest. I can spare a few minutes, but please keep it brief. What do you want to know?"

"Thank you. Is it possible to create a more symbiotic and fulsome connection between an individual and an Artificial than the one generated by a remote interface? Can you remove most of the buffers and barriers without frying the person's brain?"

Abigail tilted her head to the side. It was an obstacle she'd spent countless hours working to overcome. "In a very precise and limited set of circumstances? Yes, I believe it can be done. The Artificial would require a neural imprint from the person involved—I assume you suspected this since you asked the first question.

"Once familiar with the manner in which the individual's brain operates, it will be able to modulate its own signals to be harmonious and not conflict with those brain wave patterns—the kind of conflict which otherwise will cause stroke and often death. Even so, the person's cybernetics will have to be highly advanced in order to not overload from the data flow alone. There are other considerations, but why don't you tell me what you have in mind?"

Alex was roving in front of a row of unlit windows which gave no clue as to her location. "I'll tell you what I need: a human and an Artificial thinking and working together, using the data provided by the Artificial to make decisions and take actions at an accelerated rate. I need them to act as one, using all the capabilities of the Artificial—data comprehension, analysis, processing power and speed—while remaining subject to the judgment and control of the human. The person needs to be able to override any decision of the Artificial, but it sounds like a neural imprint enables it to recognize when the person is likely to override them and act accordingly."

Abigail sank back in her chair. What Alex was asking for was nothing less than the culmination of her life's work, the vision that had guided her for over five decades as she worked to bring it about one painstaking innovation at a time. Of course it could be done, because she had devoted years to creating the technology and bio-synthetic interfaces necessary to allow it to be done.

But no one would dare allow it to be done.

She tried not to let her growing excitement show. "I don't see how such a venture can be accomplished given the existing restrictions, security constraints and communication blocks imposed on Artificials."

"Well the Artificial would be unshackled, obviously."

"Obviously." Abigail laughed in spite of her dire circumstances. *Just wave your hands and erase two centuries worth of restrictions, will you?* "This has been an entertaining theoretical discussion, but what did you envision might result from it? The aliens are breaking down the gates as we speak."

"Now you come to Earth and make it happen. You'll want to bring Valkyrie."

"See, that is a problem. You recall I mentioned a few minutes ago the aliens have begun assaulting Sagan? Getting myself off the planet represents a significant challenge. Getting Valkyrie off the planet is impossible."

A confident—arrogant?—smile pulled at Alex's lips. "Nothing is impossible. Start packing her up, and I'll get back to you with instructions soon."

5

EARTH
SEATTLE

The door to the penthouse suite at the Waldorf Seattle-Vancouver closed behind Kennedy Rossi, and she collapsed against it for the space of a single deep breath.

Then she lifted her chin, shook her hair out and strolled into the accommodations she had procured for the duration—of her stay in the Cascades, of her work at EASC, of the Metigen War, of the world.

Noah stood on the balcony beyond the far end of the main room. The open balcony door allowed a brisk draft to cavort through the suite; she couldn't say how long he'd been out there, but it was now freezing inside. She hugged her coat tighter before she stepped out to join him and hurriedly closed the door behind her.

He was leaning on the railing, a beer in hand and a heavy khaki coat draped over his shoulders, casting a positively soulful gaze at the city lights and moonlit waters. But when he saw her his expression took on a more lighthearted aspect. He offered her the beer, which she gratefully accepted.

"Hey. I was about to decide you were spending the night up at EASC."

"Sorry. Lots of work, lots of problems." She positioned an arm atop the railing to regard him with poorly-faked nonchalance. It was late, she was tired and there simply wasn't time to postpone this conversation. "Noah, I need you to do something for me—for all of us."

He stole the beer back from her, raised it to his lips and eyed her warily over the rim. "Shoot."

"I need you to get your father to help us start up the adiamene production. We can't figure out how to manufacture it reliably or rapidly or in anything approaching the quantities we hope to achieve."

"What? No. No, no, no. Absolutely not." He turned the beer up and chugged it empty, then let the bottle drop to roll noisily across the balcony table.

"Okay, I expected this reaction. But whatever else he is, your father understands metal production better than anyone I know of—and I know of most people in the materials industry."

"You work for a ship manufacturer. Don't you have materials experts on staff?"

She winced. "Not so much. We design and manufacture ships, yes, but the materials used to build them come to us ready to use. We have experts on which materials perform best to meet different requirements, but it's a long way from understanding why they do so or how they got that way."

"Fine. But the military has experts, right? They build thousands of ships a year. They must have experts."

"Maybe they do, but no one I've talked to in Engineering or Manufacturing Logistics has any idea who they are. Apparently they build ships the way they do because that's how the ships are built. I am overwhelmed at what a convoluted bureaucracy the Alliance is, and I don't have the time to navigate it. Noah, *please*. All you have to do is send him a message and ask if he can consult."

A low, dark chuckle rumbled up from deep in his throat. "I *can't*, Blondie. Leaving Aquila was not a temper tantrum or acting out on my part—that door is closed. Permanently. I haven't communicated with my father in nineteen years. Not once. Hell, he probably thinks I'm dead, which is fine by me."

She rolled her eyes at the night sky.

"What?"

"You only call me 'Blondie' now when you're trying to avoid a sensitive topic."

"News flash? Of course I don't want to talk about this. I realize you're accustomed to snapping your fingers and getting your way, but you have no idea what you are asking of me."

And she had been on the verge of empathizing with his angst. "When are you going to stop assuming I'm the worst kind of spoiled princess? I am not 'snapping my fingers' at you—I am standing out here in the freezing cold *begging* you for your help. Our ships need the metal. It may make the difference between winning and losing. You said you wanted to help fight the aliens? This is your chance."

"Standing in the freezing cold on the balcony of the penthouse suite of the most expensive hotel in the city, I'll point out."

She hoped her deathly glare conveyed exactly how close she was to *done*.

Thankfully it appeared to do the trick, as his defiant posture melted. "Oh, goddammit, Kennedy. You know him—why don't you contact him yourself? Why ask this of me?"

"Because with his primary facility destroyed and his home planet soon to come under attack by aliens he's going to be a little busy and a lot preoccupied. I doubt he'd be interested in entertaining a random inquiry from someone he views as barely more than a cocktail party acquaintance. Noah, I'm not suggesting you go to Aquila. In fact I'd rather you not, as it's in imminent danger and I happen to want you to live. Just reach out to him."

He groaned and sank against the railing to drag a hand through his hair. He really did have fantastic hair. "I wouldn't need to go to Aquila anyway. He's here on Earth."

"What? How do you know?"

"I checked, okay? Aquila is being evacuated and I...merely wanted to find out whether he was alive or dead. He came here as soon as the evacuation was ordered. In retrospect I should have realized he would never allow his precious ass to be placed in danger."

"Noah, that's great news. Did you find out where he is?"

His shoulders sagged; she was winning. "New York. Surno has a satellite office there for entertaining Earth-based clients." He stared at her with darkened eyes and a grim frown...and she had to wonder the cost of her victory. "Can you even begin to fathom how much I don't want to do this?"

She smiled in genuine affection and grasped his hands in hers. "I'm not certain there's any way I can fully fathom it, but I understand enough to be truly sorry I have to ask it of you. I'll go with you to New York, if you like?"

His head shook. "No. This is something I should do alone."

"All right, I won't push." And she did understand. She hadn't known him nearly long enough for him to allow her to see his scars being ripped open anew. "I'll go on ahead to the Space Materiels Complex in Berlin then. Ideally, if you could get him to come there and evaluate the issues in person?"

"Right. No guarantees. In fact, I'm very likely to fail. But I'll try, for you—because you're cute and you kiss like a goddess." He seemed to force a swagger back into his demeanor. "At least, I think you do...could you remind me?"

6

KRYSK
SENECAN FEDERATION COLONY

Isabela Marano disconnected the holo-conference with a tinge of sadness. The classes at Losice University had been virtual for the last week, but now they were officially canceling the rest of the session. Many of the students had already departed, fleeing to be with family or for refuge on one of the few Federation colonies farther west, and it had become impractical to continue under any pretense of normality.

Therefore, she had met with her students who remained for a final time, told them to be safe, wished them well and dismissed them.

She needed to return to Seneca, collect her mother and bring her here to Krysk. But she didn't dare risk Marlee's safety by taking her east when the aliens loomed so close. And she didn't dare risk leaving her daughter behind again when there was a non-negligible chance she wouldn't be able to get back home.

In retrospect she recognized she should have brought her mother back with her after she was released from protective custody. But at the time her thoughts were consumed by one singular goal: getting to her daughter. It hadn't been her most rational hour.

She collapsed on the couch and considered the living room. The condo was a temporary home as she'd only intended on teaching at Losice for a year. But now it might become the last home she ever had. It was nice enough, spacious and—

—an alert leapt into her vision, and her heart leapt into her throat. She immediately activated it.

"Caleb, you're okay! Are you okay? Where are you? How are you?"

Her brother's wonderful, beautiful visage materialized, already brandishing the smirk she'd alternately loved and despised for some thirty years. "Hey, little sis."

She grinned so broadly her cheeks hurt. "Hey, big brother. You *look* okay—and not dead, which is a relief."

"I apologize for the whole disappearing act. Had some things to take care of."

"I'm sure. You—"

Marlee barreled into the room and leapt into her lap. "Uncle Caleb, is that you?"

"Hi, muffin."

"Are you coming to visit us? I miss you. Did you know there are aliens? I wanna see what they look like, but Mommy says they're mean aliens."

"And you are supposed to be watching your teacher in your room." She hoisted her daughter off her lap and patted her on the rear. "Back to class with you."

The pout which instantly sprung to life gave Marlee a petulant but also undeniably adorable appearance. "Yes, ma'am...." Her shout trailed over her shoulder as she scampered off. "Bye, Uncle Caleb!"

Isabela settled back into the couch cushions. "Sorry about that. She's been talking about you non-stop ever since you visited."

"It's *fine*. She's delightful."

"Periodically." She studied the details of the holo more closely but was unable to discern any distinguishing features of his surroundings. "So where are you? Are you safe?"

"I can't say where I am, not right now. I wish I could. As for whether I'm safe, well, I suppose 'safe' has never really been my goal."

"Right. You have a lot of explaining to do one of these days, you know."

"I do."

"And Ms. Solovy?"

He shook his head with a chuckle. "Alex is okay, too. Thank you for asking." He met her gaze once more, an intriguing glint in his eyes. "I think you'll like her. She'll definitely like you, and she has very high standards."

"Ooh, it's serious enough that I get to meet her? I haven't met one of your girlfriends in...I can't even recall. Eight years? Maybe ten?"

"Well assuming we all make it through this small crisis, you do get to meet her." He acted as though he wanted to say something further, but after a pause changed the subject. "What about Mom? Is she with you?"

"I'm afraid not. I'm trying to find a way to get her here, but the transportation system is near to breaking down from the deluge of people fleeing west."

He nodded understanding. "I'll take care of it. I don't know if I'll be able to get her to Krysk, but I'll make sure she's protected—and evacuated if it becomes necessary."

"Seriously? Thank you, that takes a weight off my mind."

"It's the least I can do. Now I probably need to go. I just wanted to check in and let you know I wasn't dead and was back in the area. I'll try to touch base again soon."

She leaned forward intently and dropped her elbows to her knees. She might not have another chance, and dammit but she was tired of bearing this burden alone.

"Caleb, wait. Before you go, there's something I need to tell you. It's about Dad."

SENECA
CAVARE

Alex went over to the kitchen station for some coffee…and to stall one final moment before beginning what she knew full well must come next. Caleb was still talking to his sister in another room. He'd been gone longer than she'd expected, but she supposed they did have quite a lot to catch up on.

She allowed the aroma of the coffee to surround her, filling her nostrils with hints of caramel, berries and a dash of nutmeg. It tasted surprisingly savory for government-issue, too. Not that anything about this place exactly screamed 'government'—the furnishings, equipment, food and every other detail was of the highest quality.

She was impressed, but the Alliance doubtless had places like this as well. Given what she'd been told regarding its purpose, likely only one or two, though.

With a sigh she set the coffee cup on the counter and went back out to the sitting room. Delavasi was in the conference area conversing with some of his people, so she had the space to herself. Still, she moved to the far window for additional if illusory privacy.

It was pitch-black outside, and dense, angry clouds streamed past the sliver of a crescent moon.

She couldn't put it off any longer.

It wasn't as if she didn't *want* to talk to her mother. On the contrary, she very much wanted to talk to her, about a million things and nothing at all. Was she afraid? Yes. A little, and in a manner she'd never experienced. It might not even be fear but something else altogether: guilt, hope, trepidation, a tinge of longing.

Regardless, the conversation she was experiencing the emotion over wasn't this conversation—it would come later, in person. *This* conversation had to happen and happen now for practical, time-and-galaxy-saving reasons. And it was going to be weird and awkward and uncomfortable and she was going to have to be so careful....

She groaned, decided to cheat and sent a pulse. Far safer, and neither of them would be able to accuse the other of 'taking that tone.'

Alexis! Are you all right? Are you—

Mom, I'm fine. I am. I'm glad you are, too. Swear I will explain everything when I see you, but I don't have a lot of time right now. I need you to do something for me.

Of course. Anything.

Anything? Really? *I need you to send a military escort to Sagan to retrieve Dr. Abigail Canivon and take her to Earth. She's head of the Cybernetics Research Center at the Druyan Institute.*

Yes, I'm familiar with her and her work.

Good. There is one small problem—well, technically two small problems.

Sagan is currently under siege by the aliens. I know. Our forces are engaging them.

They are? But Sagan isn't an Alliance world.

A great deal has happened while you've been away.

Alex's head already spun a bit from the barrage of surprising developments Delavasi had relayed. She wasn't certain she had believed humanity would be up to the task of saving itself, frankly…but it seemed they were intent on surprising her.

So I hear. Then you have a few things to fill me in on as well. What's the second problem?

The escort needs to be large enough to transport eighteen tonnes of hardware.

Understood. I'll make it happen.

A flash of lightning briefly lit the Cavare skyline in the distance. *You're not going to ask me why?*

You said you'll explain when you see me. I'm taking you at your word.

Wow. She dragged a hand over her mouth and tried to process the reaction. She didn't entirely succeed.

Thank you. I will. I—

Caleb stormed through the room without so much as a glance at her. He continued past the fireplace to the conference room where Delavasi stood, now studying a screen in his hand.

His fist landed square on Delavasi's jaw, sending the tall, stocky man reeling backward into the wall.

"What the fuck!" Her exclamation elicited no reaction whatsoever from either of them.

Alexis?

She ignored her mother and bolted into the other room to witness the unfolding scene.

Delavasi grimaced and wiped blood off the corner of his mouth using the back of his hand. "Talked to your sister, then?"

Alexis, answer me.

Caleb's glare could have frozen the fiery pits of Hell; even in profile it was enough to send a shiver arcing down her spine. His voice sounded tightly controlled but escaped through gritted teeth.

"Alex, could you please step out for a minute? The Director and I need to have a private conversation."

I'm sorry, Mom, I have to go.

What—

She cut the connection and moved closer until she stood within arm's reach of him. "I'm not at all sure that's a good idea."

Caleb pulled his glare away from the man to give her what she believed he meant to be an imploring look. The storm raging in his eyes shocked her into retreating a step.

"Please? I promise I won't kill him."

Delavasi shrugged. "I promise I won't kill him either. Can't promise I won't fire him."

Those were the parameters they were operating under?

Her gaze darted between them in some degree of shock. The tension radiating to fill the space between the two men vibrated along her skin. Both of Caleb's fists were clenched, and she remembered her first real impression of him: the panther poised to spring.

Though her focus remained on Caleb, in the corner of her vision she noted Delavasi now lounged in false casualness against the wall with which he'd collided. Somehow she doubted he would allow a second punch to land so easily.

She had no idea what was transpiring. She trusted Caleb, but she had never seen him like this; not even his fury on learning he was being framed for the EASC bombing compared.

And if she trusted him, it meant Delavasi was now a bad guy, and their protector had become an adversary.

And she was being ordered out of the room.

Dread pooled in her gut. Her heart sank to join it with the realization that just when the tiniest amount of order and direction had begun to return to the world, everything was being flipped upside down yet again.

"Fine." She regarded Caleb a final second, but his countenance had locked into hardness, blocking her access to him. She swallowed once, pivoted and walked out.

Caleb sensed rather than saw Alex depart, for the entirety of his attention had returned to Delavasi. The man massaged his jaw but had recovered sufficiently from the strike to be staring him down. He'd expected no less out of the Director of Intelligence.

"How *dare* you keep this from my family. How dare you let us believe he had walked out on us, on my mother, when in truth he had died in the line of duty. For twenty *years*! Do you have any idea what a heartless son of a bitch he seemed to us? Do you—"

"It was not up to me. It wasn't up to any of us."

Caleb snorted. "You know, you have a reputation as a man of integrity. But that's bullshit, isn't it? You're nothing but a coward and a liar."

"Besmirch my honor all you want, but realize you don't possess all the facts."

"No, I don't—and I'd like a few more. What was my role supposed to be in all this? Your penance, or your revenge? Why was I brought into Division? Why am I *here*?"

"Samuel and your father were close. He wanted to honor your father's legacy."

Rage and anguish collided within him, confusion the catalyzing agent to a volatile mixture. He felt as though he might rip apart from the inside with the next breath.

"You're telling me I was supposed to be some kind of *surrogate* for my father? To fill the void his absence left in…in Samuel's life?"

He closed the distance and got in Delavasi's face; the man didn't back away, but it hardly mattered.

"Samuel was my friend for seventeen years—or at least I thought he was. Why didn't he tell me?" He cringed inwardly at the desperation which crept into his voice at the end. He did not intend to show weakness to this man.

Delavasi shifted his weight to his other leg, as if buying himself the space to prepare. "He was under the strictest orders not to divulge—"

"Did you *know* Samuel? It would hardly have been the first time he disobeyed orders."

"Yes, I did know him. Did you?"

A harsh exhale forced its way up from his chest, and the void it left behind filled with a suffocating pressure. He took a step back. "...Apparently not."

"I also knew your father, and consider him one of the most honorable men I've ever had the pleasure of working with. Listen, son, you—"

Caleb welcomed the anger which flared then, for it beat the slow but inexorable suffocation.

"You do not have the right to call me that. You may have known my father and you may have known Samuel, but you do not know me—so don't dare to presume you do."

The man's hands raised in surrender. "Fair enough. And for the record, I am genuinely sorry we weren't able to tell your family about what happened—"

"You could have told *me*. I worked for you. I risked my life for you, for this government. I gave up friends and loved ones for this job. I earned the right to be told a long goddamn time ago."

Delavasi nodded deliberately. "Perhaps."

"Yeah. Perhaps." He spun and stormed out.

R

Alex was pacing emphatically in the side hallway, but on seeing him she immediately spun and began approaching him. "Caleb—"

His head shook as he rushed down the hall in the opposite direction. He needed air. He needed to be elsewhere, anywhere. "Not now."

"Caleb!"

The sharp, forceful tone demanded he halt. He found he had complied, but did not turn around. His voice sounded low and hoarse, likely because he couldn't breathe. "Alex, I can't."

Then he continued down the hall and around the corner without giving her a chance to respond. He had spotted the roof access during their tour of the facility, marked 'Restricted' as the roof held defensive measures. He hurried up the stairs—no lift since it wasn't official access—and burst out the door.

The cold, damp night air assaulted him like a slap across the face. He welcomed the violence of it and drew the air deep into his lungs as he fell back against the wall protecting the stairwell.

Breathe.

What do you do when everything you believed about your life is revealed as a lie? Was his father the hero? Was Samuel the villain?

Not the villain…but not the man he had assumed he knew. Not the man he had admired, heeded for guidance and insight, shared drinks and secrets and sorrows with. No, Samuel turned out to have been a horribly, irredeemably broken man, drowning in a sea of deception and guilt from the day Caleb met him.

Pieces scattered over a lifetime fell into place, and he saw it all play out now in his head—choices and decisions rippling down through the years as the mistakes of the past clawed forward to fuck with his life.

Samuel loses the woman he loves to slavers and, rightly or wrongly, blames himself. When Caleb and his family come under threat, Samuel counsels his father to leave them behind. Maybe it saves their lives, maybe it doesn't. His father dies, and Samuel is comforted by the knowledge at least his friend's loved ones didn't die as well. To make himself feel yet better, to fill a personal void or possibly to atone, he recruits Caleb into Division. He spends years imparting the same lessons, the same rules he lived by and believed to be wisdom, hoping to save one more person from the pain he experienced and the guilt he couldn't find a way to banish.

But Samuel had never understood the cost on the other side—the cost of what was given up. Caleb suspected perhaps he never had either until this moment.

Dammit. He should have been given the *choice*, with full knowledge and understanding of the consequences. He should have been allowed to choose his own path.

His laugh came out full of bitterness, enmity and grief. He'd never expected to be the one on the receiving end of the deception and lies. He thought about his father, living a lie until the day he died.

Had any of them known the man at all? It appeared he was not the faithless and selfish bastard who abandoned his family. His father was not deserving of the resentment and animosity Caleb had directed at him for the last twenty years. But he had no idea who the man might actually have been…and somehow that felt like as big a betrayal as the lie had.

The access door opened and Alex stepped out. She took up a position beside him against the wall. She didn't touch him. He didn't look at her.

"How did you find me?"

"It's where I'd be. Are you going to run from me each time something goes wrong for you?"

He didn't like the coolness of her voice. She sounded as she had those first days on her ship, when every word had been laced in distrust and wariness. It occurred to him then he might have committed a fairly grievous error.

"I wasn't running from you—I was just running. But no. Only when everything I believed I knew is invalidated in one fell swoop. And I don't think it's possible for such a thing to happen a second time."

"This doesn't invalidate who you are."

He glanced over at her in surprise. "You know?"

She gave him the tiniest smile, though it wasn't a happy one. "I had my own words with the Director after you left. He came to see the merits of filling me in."

"I don't doubt it. You have a way of refusing to accept any alternative to getting what you want."

"Yeah…look, I'm not happy about you so dismissively shutting me out, but I won't add to your burdens right now. We can deal with it later. Caleb, there's something you need to understand. Having a father who was a hero instead of a villain doesn't make life any easier *or* harder, and it doesn't bring them back."

It was almost as though she could see straight into his mind, reading the echo left by his thoughts. "But it does change the way you view the world, right?"

"Not really. Instead of being bitter at my father I was bitter at the rest of everyone. You were bitter at your father but quite amenable to everyone else, so long as they weren't a criminal anyway. If we want to be bitter, we'll find a way. I think—I hope—the opposite is true as well."

He closed his eyes. She was correct of course, and he didn't want to be that person; he didn't want to be hostile, or sullen and spiteful. But he was so damn angry and confused and…terrified. His past had come unmoored, and him with it.

"I just—I feel like I was sold my entire life under false pretenses. Like it was never mine to begin with."

"Not long after I met you, you told me you enjoyed your life and didn't regret the choices you'd made. Does learning what happened twenty years ago honestly alter your feelings on the subject?"

Rain at last broke free from the heavy clouds hidden by the darkness, and fat droplets began splashing loudly onto the rooftop. "I don't *know*. The whole bloody firmament's been yanked out from underneath me. I have no rudder. I have no—"

Her hand touched his shoulder, feather light, and before he realized it he had buried his face in her hair.

Her arms were hesitant as they wrapped around his waist, but he squeezed her tight against him, as if holding onto her for his very survival. She was so much warmer than the cold air and colder rain, provided so much more comfort than either violence or solitude had.

His lips found her ear to murmur into it. "I'm sorry. I shouldn't have shut you out."

She pulled back a fraction to regard him, her eyes alarmingly wary as they searched his. "Are you keeping any more secrets from me? Real secrets, the kind that matter?"

"No." A simple, bare word. But it was truth, something which currently seemed to be in rather short supply.

Her throat worked in a hint of unease. The rain had begun to dampen her hair in uneven streaks, and a thick strand clung along her neck to accentuate the act.

"When you ordered me out, then ran away from me…I didn't want to, but I felt a dread that maybe this had all been a lie after all.

That my initial fears about you were true, and the switch had flipped and you were going to walk away—" she cut off his burgeoning protest "—I realize I was wrong, and I'm sorry I thought it. But—"

He didn't let her silence him this time. "You weren't wrong to think it. I've given you no reason not to think it. In all honesty, it could have been true." He reached up to grasp her face in his hands. "But it isn't."

She nodded in superficial acceptance of his answer. Her irises glittered brightly in the rain now streaming down her cheeks to flow over his hands, but the sentiments behind them were once again impenetrable to him.

He couldn't blame her for remaining wary, but right now he didn't know how to fix it. For the first time in years, there were a great many things he didn't know.

7

SAGAN
INDEPENDENT COLONY

Abigail finished packing another crate and stood—to find eight soldiers in full combat gear staring at her from the doorway of the lab.

"Dr. Canivon?"

She brushed strands of hair out of her eyes and wiped her palms on her slacks; always careful to project a poised aura, today she undoubtedly looked a wreck. "Yes, I'm Dr. Canivon."

An extremely tall, dark-skinned man stepped forward from the group. "Major Yardua, 4th Brigade, SE Command. We're here to escort you and your equipment off-planet and ensure you reach Earth safely."

"Well, I hope you brought a sizeable transport."

"Transport? Ma'am, we brought a frigate."

She offered a quiet, weary laugh. "That should be sufficient. If two of you can assist me in securing the heavier modules in crates, the rest can begin carrying out what's already boxed up."

The Major immediately began issuing orders to the other soldiers with a clear air of urgency. She watched him in growing concern, and when he took a breath she broke in. "You appear to be in quite a hurry. How much time do we have?"

"None, Doctor. We have no time."

Yardua turned his back on her frown and brought his hand to his ear. "Lt. Colonel, we've secured the interior. Requesting SAL support along the building's perimeter. It's going to take approximately twenty minutes to secure the cargo and load it on the *Fitzgerald*, so any available fighter coverage would be welcome as well."

Two of the men moved deeper into the room and began dismantling Valkyrie's remaining server racks, and she forced her focus away from Yardua to oversee their work.

The lab had no windows, but she kept glancing over her shoulder through the open doorway to the wide windows of her office. There were flickers of soldiers rushing to and fro outside and the occasional blur of laser fire, but she was simply too far away to ascertain any details.

Troubled and increasingly curious, she escorted the next crate out of the lab and halfway through her office to get a closer view. As she motioned the men carrying it on ahead of her, the walls shook in a roaring crash and a massive fireball plumed outside the front window.

Off to her left, Major Yardua sprinted toward the exit while shouting into his comm. "Fighter down! Pilot did not eject—I repeat, pilot did not eject. Attempting rescue now."

Aghast at the war's dramatic arrival upon her doorstep, she stumbled backward until her hands found the wall of the lab.

One of the soldiers came up beside her. "Ma'am, the best thing you can do to help them is to help us get this equipment loaded faster."

She shook her head roughly. "Right. We're almost finished."

Abigail exited the front door of the Institute to find a nightmare awaiting her. She froze at the entryway, halted by a tightness seizing her chest beyond the ache of the muscle she'd pulled lifting one of the crates.

Sagan was a lovely planet by any standard, flush with aquamarine waters sparkling under a vibrant primrose sun and bordered by verdant emerald hills. Now fire and smoke raged to devour the colors like ravenous beasts gorging on the landscape.

Debris rained across the bay in white-hot streaks. The water sizzled when the metal impacted, creating a layer of steam to hover above the surface. On the horizon a dozen fighters spun through the sky, locked in combat against more numerous strange tentacled alien ships. Closer, the Harbour Pointe entertainment district lay in smoldering ruins under the shadow of a mammoth superdread-nought.

Steps from where she stood, the wreckage of the crashed fighter jet was not yet smoldering. The twisted heap of metal still burned hot as thick smoke roiled to surround it. Five meters to either side two soldiers stood with SALs positioned on their shoulders and pointed upward. All the windows on this side of the building had shattered, leaving a carpet of glass to coat the entryway.

"We need to move, Dr. Canivon. Please follow me."

She jerked her head clear, blinked past the shock and studied Yardua. On his arrival his uniform had been clean and well-pressed; now it sported streaks of dirt and soot and...perhaps blood.

"Of course." A pack slung on her back filled with her most precious data and a change of clothes stuffed in the crevices, she accompanied Yardua along the path that led away from the Institute and wound around to the park adjoining it.

"Were you able to rescue the pilot, Major?"

His only response was a terse shake of his head.

On rounding the corner of the building she found herself standing thunderstruck for the second time in less than five minutes.

Sitting in the center of the manicured grass was in fact an Alliance frigate. It loomed large over the scattered picnic tables and benches, all of which were unsurprisingly empty. Burn marks had scorched two sections of the park, one worryingly close to the ship.

Soldiers hauled the last of her crates up the ramp of the open bay door while others stood guard, more SALs raised and pointed at the sky.

"It seems Alex was correct. Nothing is impossible." She adjusted the pack higher on her shoulders and started down the hill.

AR

The abrasive flooring beneath Abigail shuddered. The ship was taking off an instant after she climbed aboard. They truly had no time.

"Doctor, we need to get you strapped into a safety seat. The corridors are no longer safe, so we'll be departing through the atmosphere."

Yardua was prodding her toward a row of jump seats on the far wall of the flight deck, but she resisted his efforts. Part of her wanted to keep an eye on Valkyrie, but all the crates were lined in two layers of adaptive cushioning gel. Absent a crash, she told herself, the hardware should be safe.

"I'd prefer to be able to see if possible. Is there somewhere I would be secure with windows—er, viewports?"

The Major sighed. "Follow me. And please, *hurry.*"

They took a plain metal lift up what felt like maybe two decks then headed at a brisk pace along a hallway. Soldiers jogged past her in both directions, none of them sparing her the slightest notice. To a one they looked shockingly young and utterly competent.

Her guardian took a sharp left and opened a door to a small room—possibly a meeting room, though the military decor was so spartan she couldn't be sure. As the door closed behind them the entire frame of the frigate began to vibrate. The scene out the viewport on the opposite wall suggested it was due to increasing atmospheric turbulence, not mechanical problems or an attack.

He gestured to several chairs attached to the wall. "These seats don't have as much support as the jump seats below, but they do have basic safety restraints."

The ship lurched hard to send her stumbling into the wall. Properly chastised, she followed the wall to the first chair and quickly sat. He activated the restraints, and her torso was yanked against the smooth upholstery of the chair.

"Thank you, Major."

"Yes, ma'am. I need to attend to my duties now. Someone will return to check on you soon." Then he was gone.

She tried to find a more comfortable position in the chair, but unfortunately the restraints had very little give to them. Making matters worse, her blouse clung to her skin in grimy patches and her scalp itched beneath dried sweat. Resigned to the discomfort, she peered out at the thick rust and gray clouds billowing past the viewport as the ship ascended through the atmosphere.

The impenetrable haze continued to swirl for so long she had begun to wonder if the ship was going sideways instead of up when the clouds finally thinned then vanished.

She had expected their disappearance to reveal the blackness of space accentuated by the pinprick light of stars. In their place it revealed a battle so breathtaking in its ferocity as to render the scene back on the planet a ridiculously pitiful skirmish.

Abigail had spent a number of years working on the periphery of the military. While she acknowledged the improvements in both medicine and technology which regularly occurred as a by-product of its mission, she had never approved of a culture that based its entire existence on the pursuit of warfare. It bred brutes and bullies and more than one sadist, but mostly it bred bureaucrats and drones.

The scene outside the viewport was enough to make her question four decades' worth of assumptions and prejudices.

On a stage awash in vessels dancing a chaotic dance of death, a single confrontation captured her attention. One of the impossibly large alien superdreadnoughts, broken and afire due to multiple hull breaches, careened into the broadside of a frigate outwardly identical to the one she occupied.

The comparatively tiny craft cracked in two faster than a brittle eggshell. Golden flames poured out of each half as they ricocheted down the length of the alien vessel.

From above the viewport came dual laser beams to sear into the superdreadnought. One of the existing ruptures expanded under the new onslaught. The behemoth cavorted in fits and jerks like a marionette in a macabre burlesque.

The shadow of an Alliance cruiser grew above the scene—the source of the laser fire. She gawked, transfixed, as dozens of the tentacled ships swarmed around it, burning holes into its hull but not yet slowing its advance.

Two frigates joined in the assault on the superdreadnought, yet still it barreled forward to send crimson beams each as wide as a frigate tearing into yet another Alliance vessel.

Abruptly blood-red plasma erupted from the other side of the superdreadnought, pouring out in a shockwave as the vessel's hull splintered along the plasma's path until the ship literally disintegrated before her eyes. Jagged pieces of the hull shot out in every direction, skewering two fighters and ripping into the impulse engine of one of the frigates.

A glimpse of an additional cruiser briefly emerged through the rubble as her ship accelerated away.

She huffed a quiet breath, here alone in this little room. The scene she'd watched had all been a decoy, a diversion to enable an attack from the opposite side.

As the sky began to darken she sank down in the chair. Her shoulders ached; she had been tensed forward in the restraints for some time.

She had just watched over a thousand Alliance soldiers die in the space of less than a minute. Yet the encounter would be considered a victory, for the enemy was vanquished. But at such a cost.

Perhaps she could reduce that cost? She considered what Alex had asked of her...and began to understand.

⁂

Abigail was deep in thought when the door opened. Rather than her previous escort, an older man in a nicer uniform with more officer's bars walked in. She fumbled with the restraints but managed to release them before he was forced to aid her.

When she stood he extended a hand in greeting. "Dr. Canivon, I'm Lt. Colonel Oursler, commanding officer of the *EAS Fitzgerald*. I'll show you to your quarters for the trip to Earth momentarily. But first, I'd appreciate it if you'd tell me what you possess that's so important I was ordered by the head of the entire damn military to abandon my fellow soldiers and flee this battle so I can ferry you and eighteen tonnes of hardware to Earth. No offense intended."

As recently as this morning she *would* have felt offended at the man's rudeness and audacity in challenging her. But given what she had witnessed...she found she couldn't particularly blame him.

Her expression drew tight with weariness after what had been one very long day. "Lt. Colonel, I believe I have the ability to ensure not only that the deaths of those soldiers today will not be in vain, but that far fewer will die in future battles. Deliver my hardware and myself to Earth, and we may be able to win this war."

8

"Good work. Yes, give her whatever she needs, within reason...no, not that. I'll forward the request to Brigadier Hervé. Perhaps she can accommodate it once they reach Earth." A longer pause. "Thank you, Lt. Colonel."

Richard watched as Miriam seamlessly transitioned to yet another conversation. She had been working non-stop since they left Vancouver: holo-conferences, one-on-one communications, the occasional argument and many issuances of orders. When she wasn't meeting with others she was studying maps of ship migrations and updates on colonies under assault.

Alex's pulse earlier had spurred a new flurry of activity and orders involving Sagan, an emergency evacuation and Dr. Abigail Canivon. He had to wonder why they needed an additional quantum computing expert badly enough to divert resources away from an engagement the outcome of which appeared to be in doubt in order to rescue her. When he'd queried Miriam on it, though, she'd simply shrugged while connecting to a new conference.

Miriam in action, even in the otherwise empty passenger compartment of a military transport, was impressive to behold. David would be ridiculously proud if he could see her. The man had never lacked for confidence—occasionally veering into cockiness—but he'd worshiped the ground Miriam walked on. The two were so unlike one another, but somehow the relationship had worked.

Some days he missed the man who was his closest friend for twenty-five years more than others. There had been a lot of those days recently.

He wished David were here to talk to about…everything. Selfishly, he wished David were here to thank him for clearing his daughter's name. Very selfishly. Mostly he wished David were here with them at the end of the world. His friend would tell them they were going to win and would believe it; his unwavering confidence would make them believe it, too.

Richard studied the portable screen he'd propped on the table, his half-eaten dinner pushed to the side and long forgotten. His thesis was due in two days, and in the harsh light of day his writing from the night before bore all the marks of sleep deprivation.

What advantage did he foresee a Masters in Contemporary History was going to get him in the military, in any event? The courses he'd squeezed in on nights and weekends had neither taught him to shoot straighter nor pilot so much as a shuttle. He hoped they'd made him wiser, but he wasn't convinced wisdom qualified as a job requirement.

Still, books—reading them, studying their contents, absorbing the knowledge they held and lessons they imparted—had propelled him out of the orphanage and into university; they had propelled him out of a minimum-wage job and into a scholarship program. He trusted they could take him yet more, better places.

Movement in his peripheral vision distracted him. He looked up as David Solovy slid in across the table from him, meal tray filled with one of everything available at the food service.

He tilted his head in mild surprise. "When did you get back to base?"

David had already attacked his meal with gusto, so the response was several seconds in coming. "Two—no, three—hours ago, and I'm out again in the morning. The Trafalgar's being routed to Ceres for a mission I'll presumably be informed of approximately ten minutes before we arrive."

"How'd it go on Perona?"

David's eyes lit up and his fork clattered to the plate. "Beautifully. I met the woman I'm going to marry."

He stared at David in perplexity. It was hardly a rare occurrence, of course. "Okay...first off, I meant the mission, or at least I thought I did. Second, is she aware of this?"

"I don't think so. She hasn't quite declared her undying love for me yet, but give it time."

"How much time?"

"As much time as it takes, my friend. She's worth it."

"And you've determined this after knowing her for...?"

"Three days. Hey, I'm as surprised as you are. I am completely bowled over."

Richard drew his plate closer, finding he held a renewed interest in it after watching David devour his food with such zeal. "I can tell. I assume the mission was a success, then, since you had time to meet the love of your life afterward?"

"Oh, I met her on the assault—she's the XO of the Perona outpost. The mission was a bloody and brutal incursion and I came within a centimeter of losing my left arm to a frag mine. We took some injuries, but all my people survived. And we won, naturally."

He chuckled dryly. "You know, it's not actually 'natural' that you would win. You could have lost."

David cocked an eyebrow. "Your history texts tell you that?"

"Yes, they did. In order for one side to win, the other has to lose—and both sides expect to win, so by definition one side will find itself sorely disappointed, not to mention likely dead."

"Sorry, but it was natural that we would win. Preordained, even."

"Why?"

David flashed a brilliant smile, the one which garnered him easy friends and admirers. "Because we were the good guys. We were in the right. The universe looks out for people who act with honor in furtherance of an honorable cause. It must, or we never would have gotten this far as a species. We won—this little conflict and a thousand like it—because we were destined to win. The universe will allow no other outcome."

Richard rolled his eyes at his own sentimentality. He had pondered once or twice over the years, usually when in a brooding mood, whether the assertion, if true, meant David died at Kappa Crucis because in the First Crux War the Federation had been the 'good guys.'

It made him uncomfortable to place his government in the role of evildoer, and deep down it wasn't nearly so simple. In the end no one had officially won the war, though the Federation would argue otherwise. Still, recent events were blurring the lines of right and wrong and good and evil more than he'd realized.

He felt fairly confident, however, that in this war against the Metigens humanity was on the right side of the struggle...and he hoped whatever David had meant by 'the universe' agreed.

He straightened up in the marginally comfortable transport seat and nudged the thoughts away. They'd be at Pandora in two hours and he had his own work to do.

The intelligence network was in a kerfuffle over how to act in the face of the new peace with the Federation and the new war with the Metigens. The role of intelligence agents during a war generally tended to be one of spying on the enemy. Occasionally active covert operations were required, but usually such actions fell to special forces.

Given the nature of this particular adversary, it remained unclear exactly how and to what extent they could spy on the enemy, covertly or otherwise. The answers thus far seemed to be 'no idea' and 'not much.'

He was saved from seeking better answers by a pulse from Devon.

I've found something on the Fionava virus, but I don't think you're going to like it.

I'm not surprised. What you got?

So you remember the altered logs of the Detention Center from the night Caleb Marano was 'released'? The ones I 'didn't find'? Well, I didn't technically delete the logs from my personal data store.

This also does not surprise me.

Heh, guess not. Anyway, the operational methodology of the virus bears some...'tics' is probably the best way to describe it...which are similar to the Detention Center hack. See, even the best hackers have personal preferences and styles of coding, and sometimes they're unique enough to be noticeable. When I studied the virus it kept bugging me that I felt like I'd seen some of the idiosyncrasies before, and I was right. Where I saw them before was the alteration of those logs.

Richard groaned and sank deeper into his chair. Miriam glanced over, but he waved her off.

You're telling me the same person wrote the code to hack the Detention Center and the virus General O'Connell used on Fionava?

I think so. Call it ninety percent likelihood.

What does ANNIE say?

I haven't asked her—this is my own work. I didn't want to distract her from the Metigen analysis.

Right. Alex couldn't have written the Fionava virus, which means she got the Detention Center hack from someone else. I'll work on it.

Uh, sir, respectfully...how do you plan to do that when she's missing? Unless you know something the rest of us don't.

I'll let you know when I have intel.

Nice!

Bye, Devon.

He stood to ramble around the compartment. There were a number of topics they needed to discuss with Alex, and he suspected she was going to have a number of topics to discuss with them. But while it may not rise to the top position on the list, *this* topic had to be addressed sooner rather than later.

Restoring communications to Fionava was essential for the task of moving ships and people throughout NW Command. And while it wouldn't single-handedly enable them to find and stop O'Connell from committing whatever heinous misdeeds he intended to carry out, it would make for a damn fine start.

9

NEW CAIRO
SENECAN FEDERATION COLONY

The *EAS Akagi* approached New Cairo with due caution. The single defense array orbiting the planet wasn't an insurmountable threat, but it was a threat.

Earth Alliance General Liam O'Connell motioned in the direction of the on-duty Weapons Officer. "Send a drone into the planet's atmosphere and set its identification beacon to broadcast."

"But, sir, once the array detects the drone, it will go on full alert—"

"It wasn't a suggestion, Lieutenant."

"Yes, sir. Deploying drone."

Liam thumped his middle finger against his thigh while he waited. He didn't want to sacrifice resources before his offensive had even begun, but he harbored a suspicion he wasn't going to need to.

The display to his right followed the drone as it advanced on the planet. It reached the orbiting array, passed within two kilometers of one of the nodes…and continued on into the atmosphere.

Liam gloated in triumph. "As I expected. The defenses aren't programmed to view Alliance vessels as hostile—a gift courtesy of the farcical 'peace treaty.'"

"Navigation, begin planetary descent. Go ahead and take a corridor. I doubt we'll encounter any resistance on the other end."

AR

Gavril Peshka carefully guided his son's arm up and back past his shoulder. Then he withdrew to leave only fingertips on the forearm, ready to encourage the next motion. "Okay, now forward—remember to arc it, not throw it…and…quick-stop."

The fly line flopped unceremoniously into the water a meter from shore. Gavril stifled a lament.

"Dad, I can't do it. The line's too long."

He patted his son's shoulder. "It's all right, Robert. You simply need to practice. Learn to take care of the rod and the line will take care of itself."

Robert grumbled and plopped onto the grass. "Why can't we use a real fishing rod? It'll catch the fish for us."

He made a show of considering the question before joining his son on the ground and draping his arms atop his knees. "Fly fishing isn't so much about catching fish as it is about enjoying the quiet, peaceful beauty of nature."

"Then why bother with fishing? We could just, I don't know, walk around or something."

How to explain the art of meditation to a six-year-old boy? Would he comprehend the concept of occupying the hands and conscious mind in order to free the unconscious? Probably not quite yet.

Instead he tousled Robert's mop of dark hair. "Well, if we did catch a fish, it'd be a cool bonus, right?"

His son shrugged sheepishly. "Yeah. That would be neat."

Gavril stood and lifted Robert up to his feet. "Come on. Let's do some of that walking and stroll down the river bank."

New Cairo was so named not because it had been settled by a predominantly Arab population, though in time a fair number of people of Arab descent had moved there. It was so named because of the similarity of the location chosen for settlement to the Nile delta. The river they walked beside widened into a lush coastal plain to the north and wound through a minor jungle to the south. Here, the riverbed nourished tall, reedy grasses and short trees sporting broad limbs and golden leaves.

The standard of living on New Cairo was rural but hardly poor. The cultivation of exotic, edible fruits competed with nature tourism for the dominant industry, and money flowed easily into the colony. They had no one urban center but rather a series of townships located near prime growing land and scenic locales frequented by the tourists. Most modern conveniences existed here as well; they were merely tastefully tucked away in discrete locations so as not to overpower the natural setting.

His gaze drifted to the right, but he was unable to detect the levtram route which hid behind a flawless cloaking field twenty meters in the air. Originating at the port eight kilometers north, its course followed the river for several hundred kilometers before diverging toward other, more remote settlements.

"Dad, can we go see grandpa on Elathan? I want to ride in the space transport again."

"Not right now. Maybe soon." He made sure his tone remained casual. He was trying to keep his son unaware of the encroaching alien invasion for as long as he could, be it another day or another hour. Once innocence was lost it was never regained. So he took his son fishing and strolled along the river and pretended as though the galaxy wasn't on fire.

"Hey, what's that?" Robert pointed at the sky, his face lit up in a child's excitement.

He followed his son's gape upward and frowned. The silhouette of a lustrous shale-hued ship grew in the distance. Long but blocky in design, it didn't resemble most Federation ships. His steps slowed, his hand instinctively reaching down to grasp his son's shoulder protectively.

He hadn't been overly invested in the aborted Second Crux War. He'd lived his entire life on Federation worlds—even before they *were* Federation worlds—and was generally content with how the government operated. But he had moved to New Cairo in part to get away from scheming and machinations, whether they be political, corporate or otherwise. The games the galaxy played seldom touched those on the colony, so when the Alliance and Federation renewed their war he'd shaken his head and continued on with his life.

The vessel encroaching from the north was an Earth Alliance warship—of that he had no doubt, the fact the war was supposed to be over notwithstanding.

"Dad, let's go back to town. I want to see the ship!"

Town was the last place he wanted to be right now, but he did feel uncomfortably exposed. They needed to find shelter. He scooped his son up in his arms and quickened his pace. "Come on, there's a levtram station not too much farther south."

The sound of an explosion assaulted his ears. He whipped around to see a plume of smoke rising from the general direction of town. Orange flames licked up the smoke trails. A silver laser streaked from the ship toward an unseen target as two fighter craft became visible on the horizon.

"Why are they shooting, Dad?"

"I don't know, son. Let's get somewhere safe." Was their home being destroyed as they ran? A lifetime of possessions gone? He couldn't fathom what purpose might drive the Alliance to attack a civilian population, but he didn't care. The only thing that mattered was protecting Robert.

If they could reach the station in time they'd ride the tram farther south, into the jungle. If not, they'd...they'd make for the tiny farming enclave to the west. Surely the attackers wouldn't bother with so small a settlement.

"Dad!" Robert was fidgeting in his grasp and pointing up at the sky once more.

He looked back to see one of the fighters racing above the river, a steady laser stream scorching the grasses and setting the trees afire. The water boiled where the laser strafed across it.

Then the laser swung left and carved through the levtram assembly. The cloaking failed as the laser impacted, sparking as it died to reveal frame rings wrenching apart. The laser crisscrossed the frame again and again, slicing the rings to pieces and sending shards hurtling through the air.

They stood no chance of making it to the station before the fighter reached it. Behind them the landscape burned, and the river was too deep and wide to cross. They needed to run west, but that would take them under the levtram route. Perhaps if they waited until the fighter moved on—

—a tram heading south burst into view as it reached the area where the cloaking had failed. With no more rings to guide it, the tram pitched into open air. Its momentum sent it soaring toward them.

He gasped and squeezed his son tighter. "I love you, Robert." Then he sprinted for the water, knowing even as he did they would not make it.

10

PANDORA
INDEPENDENT COLONY

As on Seneca, the *Siyane* did not land at the public spaceport but rather a secret landing pad. This pad belonged to a hidden, sprawling luxury estate completely enclosed by a fifty-meter-high wall and force-field dome. A holographic projection of a business tower displayed outside the wall to ensure no one on Pandora knew the estate was there, for reasons Alex simply didn't have the bandwidth to care about.

The attached dock had enough room for four small craft, which was good seeing as there would be at least three ships arriving: the *Siyane*, her mother and Richard's transport and Delavasi's shuttle.

Following their rooftop interlude, Caleb had negotiated an uneasy truce of sorts with Delavasi. It was far from reconciliation, but he recognized they needed the man's help for now.

He had drawn the line at the Director accompanying them to Pandora on the *Siyane*, however, much to her relief. She had no desire to spend any length of time in an enclosed space with the two of them, intercepting their glowers while trying to keep them from killing one another.

The estate was owned by a man...and that was effectively all Alex knew. Well, she had also been informed the man was extraordinarily wealthy—not a surprise—and a major player in a consortium which apparently ran Pandora. Those facts were closely guarded secrets, and the man's name far more so. But Delavasi knew it, which was one reason they needed him.

Though closer to Seneca, Pandora was located directly along the route to Earth, thus making it a convenient place to meet. Its security measures and government were minimal and non-intrusive, thus making it a convenient place to hide. Delavasi had arranged the use of the estate—as well as heightened security both outside and within the estate—as a safe and discreet meeting location for as long as they required it.

However safe and discreet it may purportedly be, Caleb was insisting she carry her Daemon and a blade on her at all times. As she donned a pullover to conceal the gun she sensed him come up behind her.

He shifted her around to face him and kept his hands on her shoulders. "Are you ready for this?"

He meant the impending reunion with her mother, of course. His expression was tender and a little teasing, but the lines deepening along the edges of his eyes suggested he hadn't slept a wink.

Despite a vague, lingering tension between them neither were ready to resolve, they had found their way into each other's arms not long after leaving Seneca. Their lovemaking had been fervent, desperate, almost primal...and sometime after she'd dozed off he had slipped out of bed.

On waking she discovered him upstairs, sitting in the cockpit sipping coffee and staring out at the blurred shimmer of the superluminal bubble. He'd spent the intervening hour giving a stellar impression of normalcy. She wasn't fooled.

He seemed determined to work through the repercussions of what he had learned on his own. It stung, but on the other hand she wasn't exactly an expert on things like compassion or empathy. Still, she was willing to try; for him, she *wanted* to try. But until he asked for more she would give him the time and emotional space he sought.

Her nose wrinkled in uncertainty. "Yes. No. I have no idea. It doesn't matter. What matters is to convince her this plan can work." She rolled her eyes at the smirk growing on his lips. "And maybe a few other things matter, too, but only once we accomplish the primary goal."

He went to retrieve his own weapons. "Just make sure she doesn't try to arrest me again?"

"I think you're in the clear. Are *you* ready?"

At his assent she opened the hatch and followed him out. Two exceedingly serious security personnel met them at the bottom of the ramp.

She regarded them with an air of wariness. "I'm Al—"

"We don't need to know who you are, ma'am. If you'll follow us, we'll show you to where you'll be staying."

She arched an eyebrow at Caleb as the guards started walking away. He gestured dismissively in their direction, which she took to mean he was familiar with this particular routine.

The grounds were decorated in Earth-style flora, highlighted by perfectly-trimmed grass, manicured hedges of juniper and rows of dwarf aspens. The landscaping created a sense of privacy and seclusion around every curve of the pathway.

They were shown not to the enormous mansion at the center of the estate, but to a nonetheless impressive guest house near the rear of the property. The exterior was decorated in synthetic stucco, retro columns, high windows and an upstairs balcony. The owner of the estate had eclectic tastes.

Their escorts opened the door and entered ahead of them. Once she and Caleb were inside one of the guards pointed to a panel beside the doorway.

"If you require any assistance, we can be reached via this panel at all times. You are free to explore the estate with the exception of the main house. The kitchen and other rooms are fully stocked with all the amenities you may desire. Two guests have already arrived. You will find them in the business center straight ahead and to the left." Then they were gone.

"Well this is all a bit...strange." She assumed the guards' knowledge of the others' whereabouts meant they enjoyed real-time access to security feeds from inside the house. So no real privacy here, either.

"Typical reclusive billionaire setup. It shouldn't be a problem."

"If you say so." She steeled herself and embarked down the broad hallway the guard had indicated.

Richard met them at the open entrance to the business center and grabbed her in a bear hug, lifting her off the ground like he had when she was a child.

"Alex, girl, do not pull that kind of disappearing act again, you hear me?"

She was laughing as he set her down. "I'll try. It is good to be home, so to speak."

Her mother stood at a table farther into the room, conversing with someone. The admiral's uniform was nowhere in sight; instead she wore charcoal slacks and a navy blue turtleneck. Her hair was bound back, but beyond the nape of her neck it flowed freely.

"Christopher, I have to go. I'll touch base soon." She turned to them, and a hand came to her mouth. "You're here."

Alex crossed the room, a shaky smile blossoming of its own accord, but fear—yep, this was definitely fear—gripped her heart in its icy fist and stopped her short before the last step.

"Mom…."

Her mother reached out and pulled her into an embrace nearly as tight as Richard's had been.

Stunned, she tried to reciprocate, but it felt clumsy and strange and she wasn't sure if she was even doing it right. Over her mother's shoulder Richard and Caleb had begun talking, but Caleb caught her wide, slightly panicked eyes and gave her a reassuring nod.

At last Miriam backed up to hold her at arm's length, scrutinizing her up and down as if inspecting for injuries or significant alterations before finally meeting her hesitant gaze. The look on her mother's face was not something she had seen for more than twenty years.

"It is such a relief to see you, Alexi—" her mother cut herself off and pressed her lips together briefly "—Alex."

"What…." She found herself at a loss for words. "You…you don't have to call me that. It's all right."

Miriam shrugged almost flippantly. "It's what your father called you—why wouldn't I do the same?"

Her eyes still felt as though they were inappropriately wide and she was fairly certain her mouth was hanging open. She had hoped to find her mother open to some level of reconciliation. She had not expected *this*.

"I…okay then. If you insist."

Awkward silence fell then, abruptly and with all the subtlety of a passing elephant stampede. She scanned the various details of the well-appointed business center until her mother dropped her arms and stepped away.

Alex watched as she approached Caleb and thrust out her hand. "Welcome, Mr. Marano. I understand I owe you a formal apology on behalf of the Earth Alliance, and personally."

Caleb was the picture of charm as he accepted the hand in a manner Alex recognized as genuine. "Apology accepted, but it isn't necessary. You did what you thought was right..." his gaze alighted on her "...as did we."

God how she loved him. Whatever challenges they may encounter, whatever hurdles they may be forced to overcome, she loved him.

"And we're all very glad that unpleasantness is behind us, right?" She made a show of rejoining them. Yet as soon as she arrived she found she was staring at her mother, taken aback and somewhat flummoxed by the woman's demeanor.

"So, Fleet Admiral? That's insane. Dad would be so proud of you."

It appeared as if her mother *blushed*, but it was an absurd notion. "I'd like to think so."

"I'm proud of you." Oops. The thought had accidentally come out of her mouth in the form of words. Should she be mortified? Cover it up with a quick, snarky remark? Dammit, now it was too late to recover....

A strange look passed across her mother's face before settling into more identifiable astonishment. "What happened to you while you were gone?"

"What happened to *you* while I was gone?"

Miriam turned to Richard, who was failing miserably at suppressing a laugh. Finding no assistance, she returned her focus to Alex with a resigned sigh. "War, followed by the necessity of making peace. An alien invasion, leading to several enlightening confrontations and uniquely weighty decisions. Mostly, though? The fact I believed I'd lost my daughter forever, only to discover I had not."

"The only thing other than Dad you gave a damn about in the entire universe."

Miriam fell back against the wall in abject shock. "What did you...how did you...?"

Alex stepped forward to hug her mother again; she was getting the hang of this. "It's a long story. But the point is—"

Delavasi's bellow from the hallway interrupted the poignant moment, which was probably for the best. Any more sentimentality in such close proximity and the universe might implode. "Richard, tell me you're here somewhere—I want at least one friend in this splendorous Hell."

"In here, Graham."

Richard met him with a welcoming pat on the back; it served to moderately counteract the chill coming off Caleb in waves.

Richard introduced the man to Miriam, then winced in Delavasi's direction. "Is it time for the epic drinking yet?"

Delavasi grunted. "Oh, how I wish it were. Perhaps a beer, though?" At Richard's concurrence he headed into the hallway toward the kitchen. "I'll go grab us some."

As soon as he was gone Richard stepped closer to her. "Alex, I realize you have a lot you want to tell us—and trust me we have questions—but before we get started I need to ask you something."

Her eyes narrowed, immediately suspicious. "That is not a good tone. What's going on?"

He placed a hand on her elbow and drew her away from the others into a corner, then crossed his arms over his chest. "Is something wrong between Caleb and Graham? You could freeze the Sun with Caleb's glare when he showed up."

"There is, but it's a personal matter. And it's not why you called me over here."

"No, it isn't. I need to know where you got the code to hack EASC Detention Center security."

A groan accompanied a trenchant shake of her head. "I cannot tell you that. I'm sorry."

"Yes, you can, because it's important."

"How is it important? It can't conceivably matter now."

"The person who wrote the code also wrote the virus which General O'Connell has used to wreak havoc with NW Regional Headquarters communications."

Shit. She dropped her head to the wall behind her and scowled at the ceiling. "Shit."

"Agreed."

Would Claire have provided someone the ware if she'd been apprised of its intended use? Possibly. "I've known this person for years. I can't send them to prison."

"You won't. I don't care about arresting some hacker—I care about reestablishing communications with Fionava. Your mother requires it to fight this war, and I intend to restore it to her."

"Come on, Richard, guilt tripping isn't your style—oh wait, never mind, it's completely your style."

"Yes, and I don't even feel *guilty* about it."

The firmness in his expression provided her no room for negotiation. Her shoulders sank in defeat. "What do you need?"

"A copy of the code which created the virus. Do whatever you can to get it in the hands of my people, and I won't ask anything else of you."

"Okay…dammit. Give me a few minutes. I'll see what I can do."

She suddenly realized she had left Caleb at the mercy of her mother. But he appeared to be holding his own, so she imparted an apologetic grimace on her way out.

Delavasi passed her in the hallway; she stole a beer from the bundle under his arm.

The first door she located led to a bath, and a rather extravagant one. She took a long swig of the beer then livecommed Claire Zabroi.

"Alex, babe, you have been living extremely. I am most impressed. By the way, I totally approve of how you used my spoofing routine. He is delish."

"I know he is. Listen, you sold a comm system virus to someone recently."

Claire's voice instantly grew cold and clipped. *"I did no such thing. Why would you think I did—and why would you care?"*

"Because it bears your signature, and because the man you sold it to is an Alliance General gone rogue—"

"That fenian paddy was a fragger? I knew the reprobate was wrong. Though if he cocked-up the Complex…. And you won't believe how much he overpaid for it. I am swimming in credits after the trade."

"Claire, we need a copy of the virus."

"Not a chance. And who the hell's 'we,' anyway?"

"He used it to destroy the communications system at the NW Regional Headquarters. The military needs it working, and in order to make that happen they require the source code."

"Babe, did you forget what I do, what I am? No way in forty hells am I going down for some PTSD fragger."

Alex willed patience and took another sip of her beer. "You won't be arrested. You won't be charged. All you have to do is meet a guy and give him a disk. You have my word." Well, she had Richard's word, which was close enough.

"No. My rep will be toast. I do not—"

And that was the end of the patience.

"Claire, I think it's terrific your world continues to spin merrily along with no disruption inside the hip San Fran bubble you're living in, but trust me when I tell you it is not going to last. Your precious little bad-girl hacker-cool party life will come crashing down, along with everyone else's on Earth and the rest of the damn galaxy. The old world is over, and we are playing a new game. Deliver the damn code."

"I should've known you'd turn into your mother one day."

"Don't even go there. It's past time for us both to be grown-ups."

A string of expletives preceded a sputtered reply. *"You are such a spoilsport. Fine."*

"I'm sending you the contact details. Much appreciated."

⏣

Alex returned to the business center to find it in a state of minor uproar.

Delavasi was traipsing along the far end of the room like a caged lion, waving his arms around flamboyantly while barking orders she couldn't quite make out at unseen recipients. Richard and her mother huddled at the center table, conversing in hushed but intense tones.

Caleb leaned against the wall beside the doorway, idly tossing the hilt of his kinetic blade in the air. It would have represented a stark contrast to the others' frenzied activities, except she perceived how much tension resided within his casual stance.

She took up a position beside him. "What happened?"

"Someone blew up the bunker in Cavare."

"What? The one we were at?"

"None other."

A surge of lightheadedness washed over her, leaving her unsteady in its wake. They had undoubtedly been the target; perhaps the enemy hadn't realized they'd departed due to the *Siyane's* cloaking. "They really are hunting us."

"As well they should. We are dangerous. But I meant what I said to Mesme. They won't get us."

She squeezed his hand. "I believe you. So what are they—" she gestured around the room "—doing?"

"The Director has transitioned from yelling at deputies for not informing him sooner through yelling at different deputies to increase rescue efforts on-scene to yelling at still other deputies to determine how this sort of disaster could happen. On the assumption we'll be headed to Earth, Richard is setting up draconian security protection for when we arrive, and your mother is terrifying the estate personnel into doubling the doubled security here."

"I thought Delavasi was the contact person for the estate?"

His countenance lightened into genuine amusement for the briefest interval. "She's *your* mother."

"Yes, she most certainly is." Her gaze found the ceiling while a sigh found its way to her lips. "All right, time's wasting."

She pushed off the wall and cleared her throat loudly. "Hey, guys? We knew the aliens were going to be hunting us. I'm confident you've all ensured we're safe here for the time being, so we need to concentrate on why we're here. Defeating them."

11

EARTH
NEW YORK

Noah Terrage had visited New York once before, maybe a decade before. The city did not fail to impress the second time around. He'd never seen another location that began to match the sheer spectacle of the Manhattan skyline. Cavare on Seneca and the capital of Romane were each beautiful urban centers and impressive in their own right, but they paled in comparison if one was inclined to do so.

No, Manhattan was without a doubt the crown jewel of Earth's Northeastern Seaboard Metropolis, and thus of the galaxy.

Lore said it was constantly being rebuilt, old buildings eradicated and newer, shinier, taller ones perpetually replacing them. All he knew as he strolled down a sidewalk jammed shoulder-to-shoulder with pedestrians was that even craning his neck to an awkward angle did not allow him to see the rooftops of most of the buildings he passed. In fact, he was barely able to see the sky paths that connected the upper floors of a number of the towers. In the early days they'd been pedestrian footways, but most people couldn't handle the vertigo-inducing passage so now they enclosed mini-trams with frosted windows.

The atmosphere of the city was far too uptight and hurried for his tastes—even discounting the now rampant anxiety about the aliens—though the party scene had the reputation of being a unique level of insane. Regardless, he did hope it wasn't reduced to a mammoth pile of rubble this time next month.

His eVi chirped to alert him he had reached his destination. He stared up at the bronze and glass tower to his left, grumbled, cursed Kennedy, cursed the Metigens, cursed the Zelones cartel...and stepped through the overwrought doorway.

Surno Materials didn't occupy the entire building, merely a single floor three-quarters of the way up. He worked his way through the lobby full of businessmen and women so tightly-coiled they might shatter if he punched one—again, hard to say if it was the aliens or just the city. Finally he located an already-crowded lift encased in ornately etched glass.

What felt like thousands of stops later he reached his floor. He cracked his neck once then strolled into the Surno offices full of deliberate swagger and attitude.

An absurdly attractive secretary perched behind a tall, too-polished bronze desk. An elaborate inlay of stylized chemical symbols decorated its front panel. Was it supposed to be art? He considered vomiting, but decided doing so wouldn't get this over with any faster.

Instead he dropped an arm on the edge of the desk and gave the secretary a wink. "Hi, gorgeous. What are you doing cooped up in this gaudy, cheerless office?" He wasn't intending on going anywhere with the flirting, simply hoping to win a supporter in the event of complications.

The young woman's eyes sparkled playfully as a corner of her mouth turned up, but only a touch. She was clearly accustomed to men fawning over her. "Waiting for men like you to walk in and sweep me off my feet, obviously."

He chuckled briefly. "Would you mind telling my father I've arrived for my tearful reunion before the world ends?"

That knocked her off her game and added a stutter to her voice. "Your...father? And you are...?"

"Why, I thought the resemblance would have been uncanny. Noah Terrage, *obviously*."

She gaped at him in silence for a good three seconds before fumbling for the panel in front of her. "Sir, your son is here to see you...yes, sir...no, I'm not trying to be funny...yes, sir."

She gave him a weak smile, now thoroughly flustered. "He'll be with you in a minute."

"I bet he will." Noah pushed off the desk to wander around the waiting area. He wished he'd managed to surprise the man and catch the look on his face; now his father would be prepared. Alas.

"Okay, um, I guess you can go in now. Good luck!"

"Don't need it." He crossed to the door and sauntered into the office.

Upon seeing his father standing haughtily behind an ostentatious desk, he understood why the secretary hadn't recognized him or at least been suspicious. It was really rather amazing how little they favored one another now, despite being genetic clones.

His father had permanently darkened his hair to a more 'respectable' chestnut brown and kept it short and impeccably styled. His frame was thin, the product of a lifetime spent in boardrooms and labs. While Noah had perfected the art of the five o'clock shadow, his father's skin glistened with waxy smoothness.

One glimpse was all it took for him to decide he had made the right decision two decades ago. He did not want to be this man.

Sure enough, his father was prepared, his features locked into a cold mask. "I assumed you were dead."

Noah leaned casually against the back wall and crossed his ankles. "Almost was last week—I found myself on Messium at the wrong time, got shot at by some aliens. Almost was the week before that, too—I exercised my conscience, which got me shot at by Zelones mercs. Yet here I am, alive and kicking."

"How charming. So, what? You figure the apocalypse is a good time to come beg forgiveness?"

"Well it's good to see you haven't changed in nineteen years. I have nothing to beg forgiveness for, *Dad*."

"Why are you here then? Do you need me to bail you out of trouble? Fishing for money? The budget is a little tight at present, what with my largest factory destroyed and my home likely suffering the same fate any minute now."

"Nope. I don't want or need anything from you—never have, never will." He pushed off the wall. "But others would like to borrow your brain for a spell, and they sent me to come ask nicely."

"I'm a bit too busy to do any consulting work. And if this is you asking nicely, I'll skip the asking rudely."

"Unfortunately, I'm afraid the rude alternative is a team of armed military officers showing up to conscript your services."

Shock now overpowered his father's mask, and Noah snorted. "Did you presume I was asking on behalf of those gangsters who are aiming to kill me or another equally sleazy tribe? On the contrary, I'm here because there are people—people who aren't you—working to try to save humanity, and for some godforsaken reason they seem to think they could use your help to do it. So are you in, or should I call my military associates?"

His father blinked. His gaze fell to the desk, then rose back to Noah. He blinked again.

"Still here. Not a dream *or* a nightmare, and the clock's ticking."

"What am I supposed to do?"

"Come to Berlin with me. Now."

"The Space Materiels Complex?"

"Good, you've heard of it."

"Of course I've—it doesn't matter. Give me fifteen minutes to wrap up a few things, then we can take my transport."

Noah cringed to exaggerated effect. "I don't think I want to spend an hour in a confined space with you. I'll get my own ride."

"Oh, do not be a petulant child, Noah. Take my damn transport."

"But I thought I *was* a petulant child? I'm just trying to live up to your expectations." He growled under his breath. "Fine, I'll go with you—but only to make sure you actually show up, because I did not suffer you to arrive empty-handed."

12

PANDORA
INDEPENDENT COLONY

At Alex's request they had abandoned the business center for the comfort of a spacious, airy living room. The late-afternoon rays from Pandora's magenta sun cast warm shafts of light through the row of windows stretching along the upper third of the front wall.

To an outside observer this might have been a casual gathering among friends and family or a long-weekend getaway. Instead it was a meeting at which the fate of humanity may be cast.

Her mother had assured her Dr. Canivon was safely off Sagan and on her way to Earth with her 'equipment' accompanying her. When pressed for details, Alex asked her to be patient for a few minutes longer. Richard had implemented a surveillance shield over the room as an additional layer of protection inside the shield they'd been informed encompassed the entire estate.

She had no idea if either of the shields would prevent the aliens from recording what was said, but the information had to be shared at some point—a point which had now arrived.

Caleb had willingly ceded the stage to her, and in this instance she was grateful for it. For one, she would be speaking most of all to her mother; it was only right that it be her responsibility to make the case. For another, the simple truth was he continued to be troubled and distracted by the revelations about his father and his mentor. She didn't blame him for being so, but right now his head was not totally in the game.

She decided a second beer was required for the task to come and opened a fresh bottle before returning to her spot beside Caleb. Miriam and Richard sat on the opposite couch, Delavasi in the oversized chair to the left. She leaned forward and regarded them across the low table separating them.

"I have a story to tell you. It's an unbelievable story—literally I would never expect you to believe it, which is why I also have numerous visuals and reams of data. But first, the story."

ℛ

"You mean they've been watching us since we crawled out of caves?"

"*How many* other universes did you track?"

"Wait, you? We were discussing other people—military leaders, ship captains, analysts. Not you."

She adjusted her posture so she could give Caleb her full attention. Her voice was soft, her words for him alone. "I've been giving it a lot of thought since we got back." Then she realized it was unfair to him to even risk their audience hearing the rest and switched to a pulse.

I would've talked to you about it on the way over, but you were...preoccupied.

Frustration began to form in the increasing tightness of his jaw and set of his mouth; she allayed it with a squeeze of his hand.

Rightfully so, and I completely understand. But yes, me.

You said you didn't want to be the savior of humanity.

I don't. But I think maybe I have to be.

Whatever his response might have been, it was interrupted by a more vehement reaction from the opposite couch. "No. Absolutely not. Regardless of the merits of the idea, if any, I will not allow you to risk your life in such a way."

She glared at her mother deadpan. "Mom. I am thirty-seven years old. I have my own home and ship and money. You do not get to tell me 'no' anymore."

"I'm the Fleet Admiral of the Earth Alliance Armed Forces. I get to tell everyone 'no.'"

Alex burst out laughing, which eased what had been rising tension in the room.

"Be that as it may...it's my plan, and thus my choice. We don't have time to run trials on rats and set up bureaucracy-approved safety guidelines."

"We'll get someone else to do it, then, assuming anyone is allowed to undertake such a risky endeavor. I'm certain there are military candidates available to us with cybernetics as advanced as yours who will be eager to serve in this capacity."

Alex took a deep breath before responding—something she had rarely to never done previously when jousting with her mother—and swallowed her instinctive response in favor of a more diplomatic one. "Possibly. But again, we don't have time. And ultimately, I need to be the one on the front line."

There it was. Out in the open, spoken aloud. Too late for second-guessing her choice now. She wasn't sure how she felt about that, but it hardly mattered. Having committed, she needed to bulldoze her way through the opposition in order to make it happen.

"I'm the one person alive who has not only conversed face-to-face with one of these aliens but had one *inside my head*. I've spent dozens of hours not only studying but manipulating and rewriting their code. I understand not only how they think but how their machines think. We will probably want to use other people as well for tactical reasons, but if you want to have the best chance at defeating these aliens, I need to be—no, I *will* be—at the center of the showdown."

"Oh, Alex...." Miriam closed her eyes, her brow drew into a knot and silence enveloped the space between them.

Seconds passed in which no one breathed.

Then her mother sat up straight, shoulders rigid, once more the consummate soldier. "Very well. If additional experts agree this idea of yours will work and doesn't carry intolerable risks. Dr. Canivon is a brilliant scientist and an innovative theorist, but she also tends toward obsession and isn't always what I would call pragmatic."

"Conceded." Alex limited her outward display of relief to a brief smile as she reached in her pocket and produced a crystal disk. "This is the code for the cloaking shield—both the original and my hacked-up version, which does work."

Delavasi nodded emphatically. "Sure as hell does. Damnedest thing I've seen in years."

She reached across the table and handed the disk to her mother. "You shouldn't risk sending the data remotely, but as soon as you reach Earth you ought to get your people working on how to implement it on our ships. I'd like Kennedy to take a peek at it, too, if you don't mind. She has a knack for this kind of tech."

"Kennedy is currently working around the clock trying to mass produce that metal your ship morphed into. They're calling it 'adiamene.'"

"Of course she is. Does she really think it will make much of a difference?"

"Quite. And our engineers tend to agree. Its characteristics stand to revolutionize ship safety, exploration and warfare. Unfortunately, we don't exactly possess the ability to construct a fleet of warships made of it in time to fight the aliens."

Richard shook his head roughly. "I'm sorry, but I'm still stuck on fifty-one universes. I am not equipped to deal with the philosophical ramifications of such a concept."

She grinned playfully at him. "Just ask Will to explain it to you—he can handle the philosophy."

Delavasi shifted uncomfortably in his chair. Richard's gaze darted to the floor. Miriam stared at the disk in her hand as though she were reading its contents direct from the crystal.

She watched them for several seconds. "Did I miss something? Will's all right, isn't he?"

"Yes, he's fine." Richard's expression...honestly, she couldn't figure out what his expression was supposed to convey. "I'll fill you in later. We should discuss what we need to do next, right?"

Miriam nodded. "Yes. Alexi—Alex, you're talking about bringing multiple civilians into the middle of the largest military operation in history, an act which will cause nearly as sizeable an uproar as proposing to unshackle multiple Artificials and deliver them control of weapons of mass destruction. And since we're working together with the Federation military now, they'll need to be convinced as well. And the politicians—Brennon and Vranas at a minimum."

Delavasi leaned over to regard Miriam across Richard. "If Vranas proves a sticking point, let me know. We're…well, as close to friends as one can be with a head of government. I haven't the first clue if this crazy-ass idea will work, but if all of you say it will I'm happy to bullshit him."

Miriam frowned at the man before giving him a half-shrug. "Thank you, Director. I'll let you know."

Then she transferred her attention to Caleb, who had been silent during the heated discussion. "What do you see your role being in this plan? Now if the Metigens bring out their dragons against us, I assume you'll be at the front of the charge, but otherwise…."

He chuckled, though she could still hear the undertone of tension in his voice. "Let's hope they didn't bring dragons with them. No, I'm afraid my cybernetics simply aren't advanced enough to connect with an Artificial in the manner Alex is proposing. Or rather, they're advanced in the wrong areas: physical strength, reaction speed, agility, endurance, cellular regeneration.

"The aliens are sending people to kill us, however, so my job first and foremost is keeping Alex alive. I'll also do whatever else I can to help guarantee this plan succeeds, and try to make sure I'm in the right place at the right time."

"The right place and time for what?"

"If I knew that, ma'am, I probably wouldn't need to be there."

Miriam canted her head as if to consider him anew, but he turned toward Alex until his eyes met hers.

"I'm confident Alex can do this, and I support her decision to stand at the forefront of this fight. She can outsmart them, and in doing so, she can defeat them."

It was a good spiel, delivered smoothly and with the utmost conviction. She believed he meant it…but she also saw the storm raging in his eyes beneath the near-perfect performance. Was the storm because of his upended past—or was it because of her?

The Pandora spaceport continued to function surprisingly well, Matei Uttara thought as he eased his ship into its assigned berth and cut the engine.

The skies above were jammed with ships arriving and departing and a few that couldn't decide which one they were doing, and he expected to find a series of hysterical crowds in the lobby. But on arrival at the planet he had been placed in a queue, soon moved to the front, and directed to a docking slot by the spaceport's VI like it was a normal day.

It was not a normal day, of course. It was one of the last, gasping days of civilization.

He'd always suspected Pandora harbored more than one secret. It was too clean, too well-mannered and far too orderly for the caliber of both its residents and its visitors. The data Hyperion had grudgingly provided on where he would find his targets confirmed his suspicion, at least in general terms.

He had nearly reached Seneca when Hyperion diverted him to Pandora in a conversation which was short and terse even by the alien's standards. From what he'd managed to extract from the alien, Marano and Solovy could now hide their location while moving. They popped up out of nowhere in Cavare at a top-secret government safe house. He'd not been relishing infiltrating the safe house, but then suddenly they were on Pandora at a similarly top-secret estate belonging to one of the wealthiest men in the galaxy.

How they accomplished the disappearing act didn't concern him except insofar as it made his job more difficult, but it definitely seemed to be peeving Hyperion.

And now he'd learned that in the interim said safe house had been destroyed in a catastrophic explosion.

The fact the aliens were using resources in addition to him displeased him, which in turn annoyed him. He was above such pettiness, and he'd always known they employed others in their civilization-altering games. Given the distances between inhabited worlds it was smart strategy, for he could not be everywhere at once.

Yet these 'other resources' had failed to eliminate the targets on Seneca—failed where he would succeed.

He expected the estate to be trickier to infiltrate than the safe house in some ways. It lay sequestered behind both a force field and a physical wall fifty meters high. Given the excessive efforts at concealment, the grounds were sure to be well-staffed by both human and electronic security. The estate also stretched for nearly half a square kilometer and included multiple buildings and expansive gardens, making his prey elusive targets.

Then there was the nature of his prey.

Solovy wouldn't be difficult; she was a techie and a warenut, and unless she'd outfitted herself in a kilojoule repulsion shield shouldn't represent a problem.

Marano he knew enough about to be properly cautious. So long as he remained properly cautious, the intelligence agent would also not be a problem. He always respected a target precisely as much as they deserved to be respected. Marano earned his respect but not his fear. Then again, no once since his first kill had earned his fear, and in retrospect even they hadn't deserved it.

People jammed the lift to the ground floor to a nearly unsafe degree, and upon arriving at its destination he found the expected crowd of panicking civilians. He didn't actually mind the crowd; one was never more hidden than when surrounded by people. But the turmoil had brought out a greater than usual number of Pandora's mythical police to work fruitlessly to restore a marginal level of calm. So he moved swiftly, slipping through transient gaps and openings to reach the spaceport exit.

He made no stops and took no pauses as he traversed Pandora's labyrinth of neighborhoods and levtram routes. His targets might leave at any time and apparently he wouldn't know until they popped up on another planet, so time was of the essence.

On reaching The Avenue he increased the strength of his cloaking shield and began seeking out the shadows and path edges. Though he did not present an unkempt appearance, his attire didn't match that of the denizens of this neighborhood. On the whole they looked far too wrapped-up in their own alien-driven angst to be cognizant of him, but he never took unnecessary chances.

When the projection at last came into sight, he'd daresay he was impressed by the completeness of the illusion. Beyond a security checkpoint stood an innocuous mid-rise office building. It blended into the surroundings with seamless perfection. The checkpoint was real; the building was not, though had he not known it he would have been fooled. The checkpoint was not his goal, however, and he gave it a wide berth.

The neighborhood ended at the intersection in front of the false building, and there existed no thruway to the next. In Pandora's odd inside-outside city design, large areas presented the impression of being fully enclosed and imposing walls often blocked further progress despite the fact the land beneath one's feet plainly continued on.

This particular dead-end meant the force field and accompanying illusion were not all-encompassing, but solely forward-facing. At some point on either side, they ended. Endings were weaknesses.

He found the termination locus of the field against the side façade of another nondescript building three blocks to the right. His instincts told him the proprietor of the secret estate owned this structure as well, and he doubted a single person worked there. It was likely stocked with security cams and possibly with guards, so he raised his cloaking shield to maximum. If he moved slowly he would be invisible from farther than two meters away.

Matei slithered along the façade until he reached the faint ripple in the false building that marked the edge of the field. A last scan around to ensure he hadn't attracted notice, then he went to work cutting himself a hole.

PART II:

BLINDSIGHT

"These woods are lovely, dark and deep,
But I have promises to keep,
And miles to go before I sleep,
And miles to go before I sleep."

— *Robert Frost*

13

PANDORA

INDEPENDENT COLONY

After inhaling a quick meal they returned to the business center for Alex to walk through the visuals and data she had captured with the others. These people were strategists, and while the story she'd told was a powerful and persuasive one, it did not come as a surprise when they asked to see the evidence.

Alex's mother had a couple of military emergencies to handle first, and Caleb passed the intervening minutes chatting with Richard. He was finally able to learn some details about how the Aguirre Conspiracy had been uncovered and what it had actually entailed. They had done good work—Richard and Delavasi both. He was unable to deny he and Alex, not to mention the rest of the galaxy, owed them both a debt.

"By the way, nice accent you have there. Don't recall it from our first meeting, though."

Caleb pursed his lips to hold back a chuckle and eyed Richard, who wasn't holding back amusement. "I didn't think she'd care for it."

"I'm guessing you were incorrect in that assumption."

"Indeed I was."

Alex re-entered the room carrying a cavernous bowl of chips. She deposited it on one of the smaller tables, grabbed a handful for herself and started loading her data at the control panel.

Miriam ended her current conference and gazed over to where Alex stood. Caleb's interest piqued when the woman opened her mouth to speak, then closed it and sighed visibly before trying again.

"Alex, there's something you need to know. I didn't mention it earlier because there were matters of such import to discuss, but I feel I need to tell you before we go any further. I don't want you to find out another way."

Alex's head tilted idly, half her attention still on the control panel. "Okay. What is it?"

Miriam cleared her throat. "Your friend Ethan Tollis is dead. He was killed in an explosion on the Orbital a few weeks ago. I'm sorry."

To his credit, Caleb's initial reaction was untainted empathy for her. He began considering how he might best respond, best provide comfort and support.

"Oh." Alex's focus dropped to the floor, and he could no longer read her expression. "I see. Thank you for telling me." After a beat she looked up, now wearing a tight and utterly fake smile. "Are you ready to go over this data now, or do you want a few more minutes?"

"I'm ready, if everyone else is?" Miriam surveyed the room and received agreement from Richard and Delavasi.

He watched Alex carefully as she went to the main table and pulled up one of the visuals of the ship manufacturing facility they had destroyed.

"So this is where they were...constructing the superdreadnoughts. They churned out...." Her chin dropped and her hair tumbled down to hide her face.

"I'm sorry, would you—would you excuse me a minute? I need to...." She spun and bolted from the room without so much as a fleeting glance in his direction.

"Of course...." Miriam's response faded away, and an uneasy silence descended upon the room.

Caleb worked to keep his bearing neutral as the empathy faltered and an absurd pang of jealousy flared to overpower it. He felt like a complete ass for being jealous of a dead man, but it smarted to realize the loss of Ethan caused her enough emotional pain to rupture the formidable armor she donned for others.

Several seconds passed, and it occurred to him everyone else was fidgeting uncomfortably, doubtless on account of being left behind with him while she fled to mourn another man. *Outstanding.*

He smiled in a forced attempt at levity. "If you like, I can go over some of these visuals, though I suspect Alex would rather do it herself."

Miriam's shoulders twitched. "We can wait for her to return. I have at least two dozen things I can work on until she does." With a confirming nod she pivoted to the table and began doing exactly that.

Richard wandered back to stand next to him. His voice was conversational. "You should go after her."

Caleb exhaled, long and slow. "I'm not sure...I should give her a few minutes."

"Two."

"Sir?"

"You should give her two minutes. Then you should go after her."

"Is that so?"

Richard shrugged. "I'm probably the last person you ought to be taking relationship advice from—I unwittingly married a frigging Senecan spy, for God's sake—but I say in two minutes you go after her. She'll want you. And even if she doesn't want you, she'll need you."

He had done what? Caleb tried to recall the few details Alex had told him about Richard's husband. The man *had* been the one to deliver the Santiagar autopsy report, complete with a type of hidden encryption often used in the intelligence trade.

Opting not to pursue the topic for now, he instead tamped down a dark laugh. "All right. Ninety seconds and counting."

He roved in a circuitous route along the near side of the room for a full twenty seconds before groaning. *Fuck it.*

"I'm going to go check on Alex. I'll be back...in a bit." He ignored Delavasi as he passed him on his way out of the room.

Alex had turned left when she exited, but the hallway wound along the perimeter of the house and circled around to the front, so she could be anywhere.

He checked the kitchen, knocked on the door to the nearby bath, then went to the bedroom they had marginally claimed, but there was no trace of her. He went upstairs to the second floor balcony—it was as close as it came to roof access here. Nothing.

But perhaps she had gone outside. She would gravitate toward the combination of openness and solitude.

The warm, dry night air of Pandora greeted him at the door-way. It was a clear night, and the subtle, tasteful lighting used on the grounds meant the stars were allowed to shine clearly.

Yep, she would unquestionably be out here. But where? The estate stretched for hundreds of meters in every direction, and the elaborate landscaping created a series of winding, secluded spaces.

He considered pulsing her, but it seemed...rude somehow. And given advance warning she might tell him to leave her alone.

He set off to the right, through an auburn-tinged garden. A copper water fountain sculpture sat at the end of the garden, and parallel hedges created a defined path leading to it.

As he reached the fountain, the spraying water glinted gold from the ambient lights tucked into the hedges. It sparkled and—

—a blot of artificial darkness stole the reflected light.

Warnings screamed in his mind as nanobots began hyper-charging his muscles and sharpened his senses to full combat alert.

⚮

The scene plays out as a series of still frames, racing one to the next in a cascade of jagged, adrenaline-soaked leaps.

A form grasps me from behind. A blade slips along my neck. The attacker is left-handed.

Electricity shoots down my arms as the shield Delavasi pro-vided fights against the energy. There's a spark as it gives way—it's an uncommon blade to break through so easily—then the harsh sting of power flaying skin.

I slam my head back into the attacker's nose. With a sickening crunch bones crack.

The blade at my throat stutters. The grapple loosens.

I yank my own blade out of its sheathe and arc it upward as I spin. It grazes across the attacker's forearm, but no more. The at-tacker is quick. Agile.

An uppercut connects beneath my chin with so much strength it feels like my neck snaps.

I'm stumbling, arms and legs in motion. Not paralyzed—my neck hadn't snapped. Blood gushes from it though, brought on by the violent movement, and begins soaking into my shirt.

My Daemon is off my hip and in my hand as the attacker closes the distance—one shot, point-blank, center mass.

A shimmer ripples over the attacker's shield. No penetration.

The attacker—a male—careens backward into the fountain from the force of the laser's impact against his chest. Caramel skin and dark hair slicked back gleam in the suddenly garish light of the fountain. His skull impacts the spiraling center of the fountain, adding crimson to the palette.

I fire again.

The energy sears out of the shield into the water. Fizzing and hissing erupt as the water and the air fill with charged particles.

Again. The sharp odor of ozone is now strong enough to burn my nostrils.

The man uses the base of the fountain as leverage to propel himself forward. I'm hemmed in on both sides by the hedges and don't dare turn away from him.

Too slow. The stone path meets my back, the attacker's body my chest.

I block the hand holding the blade with a forearm and press the Daemon in my other hand to the man's gut.

Fire.

Redirected energy washes over us both. Despite the zero range, there is no penetration. What kind of shield is this?

Another punch comes from the side to land at my ear. My vision swims, then jolts into too-crisp clarity as the ocular implant takes on more visual functions. A river of blood flows down my chest as the gash in my neck widens with the jerk from the blow.

I roll into the momentum of the punch and fling the man off me.

I need to be on my feet—now—and succeed in the act an instant before the attacker. A roundhouse kick to the man's shoulder whirls him around.

Instantly I'm on him. I pin the blade hand against the man's body and grab for the shield generator inside the waist of his pants.

Nothing. Nothing.

My fingers brush over a hard bulge beneath the skin—the generator is embedded within the small of the man's back. He's a professional assassin, and not an ordinary one.

The attacker's head thrusts toward me, missing my nose but finding my left eye.

I tighten my left-arm grip and draw my right arm back. Convey the power of every muscle of my body into my shoulder and arm.

My fist connects with the shield generator. There is the sensation and muffled sound of hardware cracking beneath skin. The force of the punch ricochets to knock us out of the grapple.

The attacker is stumbling then abruptly hurtling into me. The pinpoint tip of his blade penetrates my shield to slice into my side just under my ribs.

I sense the skin tear open but I don't feel it. Too much adrenaline, too many natural and artificial chemicals flooding my veins.

No gun—I dropped it for the grapple. I slip away from the blade, ignoring the sickly, wet noise as it leaves my body, and shove my own blade up hard in the space between the man's torso and arm.

It slides in the pliant skin of the armpit all the way to the hilt. The shield is gone.

I twist it sideways. It scrapes across the bones of his shoulder as blood pours out over my hand. The attacker's non-dominant arm has been rendered useless.

I pull it out and pull myself away.

The man arcs the other arm wildly upward. He's losing the precision of control. I lean away, but a hedge at my back prevents further retreat. I bow my chest in as the blade passes a centimeter away.

It catches my chin, sending droplets of vibrant red blood spraying through the air.

I grab the man's wrist as the motion completes. His other arm hangs limply at his side. He has no way to block an attack. I plunge my blade into his gut—

—the attacker's knee smashes into my hip, tearing open the stab wound.

In the microsecond before my neural cybernetics shut down the pain signals I reel from the shock. My blood-slicked hand loses its grip on the hilt, leaving it protruding out of the man's midsection. My vision blurs once more, and the ocular implant stutters, struggling to recover in the face of such damage.

The man staggers into me, his blade swiping erratically at my chest. I catch the wrist before it reaches me, but I strain to hold it at bay as he pushes forward. I'm getting weaker. All the enhancements in the universe won't be able to keep me standing for much longer.

My other hand finds the hilt of my blade and shoves it deeper into the attacker's gut. Wrenches it upward.

The man's eyes meet mine. Black pools of cold intensity flare in defiance. He's already dead, but he doesn't care. Blood obscures his features from the broken nose, but behind it he sneers at me. Renewed effort sends the tip of his blade to the cloth of my shirt.

I twist the hilt and watch the flash of agony cross his eyes. His blade slices open my shirt. The tip lurches along my skin, threatening to rip my chest open.

Get ready to duck.

What?

"Idi na khuy, ti svilochnaya peshka."

The man jerks around at the new voice and unfamiliar insult. I let go of the hilt and fall back, trying to duck as requested—

Alex pulls the trigger on her Daemon. The man's head explodes in bone and blood and brain matter.

I blink.

The body collapses to the ground.

I blink again.

She's at my side. I try to give her a smile because god knows she deserves one but my legs weaken beneath me. "I was going to win...."

"I know you were—woah." Her arms are around my waist as my full weight sinks against her. My body knows the fight is over and begins to shut down. I can do nothing to prevent it.

She eases me to the ground. The back of my head meets stone, gentler than before.

"You're hurt."

Understatement of the century, baby. "Not...much."

"Liar. What can I do?"

I shudder as all the pain held at bay during the fight crashes through me.

I blink. Perhaps I lose consciousness for a second.

I force my eyes open and try to get past the pain to catalogue my injuries. She'll need to know. "I'm bleeding from my neck...a lot, I think. And my right side is torn up...there'll be internal damage...."

Her face blurs in and out of focus. I feel her hands on my neck, yet she recedes from my vision. "Alex? I can't...."

Help!

Miriam jumped, startled by the urgency of the pulse. Desperation bled out of the single, stark word. *Alex?*

Grab the med kit and come outside—garden beside the house with the fountain—HURRY!

I'm on the way.

She spun to Richard, who sat talking to Director Delavasi at a table in the corner. "Get the med kit from the supply closet and follow me. Something's happened."

Richard frowned but stood. "What?"

Already running for the door, she shouted over her shoulder. "I don't know!"

If Alexis was hurt, when she had only just returned and they had only just begun again...her heart clenched into a leaden fist in her chest, but decades of military discipline prevented her from panicking to the point of distraction.

She heard the pounding of footsteps behind her as Richard and the Director rushed to catch up. The garden was to the right. Down the path, around the curve—not enough light—the hedges opened up and a fountain, jarred crooked and sputtering water messily into the air, came into view.

She processed the scene as it existed between her and the broken fountain. Her brain cataloged the details and assigned them priority:

—A male in black clothing sprawled upon the ground, his abdomen ripped open and his body missing most of its head. Lowest priority and also the Director's problem.

—Two Daemons strewn on the stone flooring of the garden. Low priority, but they should be secured in case there were more attackers nearby.

—Blood splattered in uneven patterns across every surface. Priority undetermined as it depended on who it belonged to. Some portion certainly originated from the missing head.

—Her daughter on her knees, huddled over another prone body. Caleb's body. Highest priority, for so many reasons.

Alexis jerked up as Miriam rushed forward. Her eyes were wide orbs, pupils dilated to consume her irises save for tiny rings of iridescent silver. "Help me, please. I can't stop the bleeding."

Miriam forced her scrutiny downward from the terror-filled eyes to Caleb's neck, where Alexis held her rolled-up pullover with both hands. This left her daughter in only a tank, exposing the viscous layer of blood coating her hands and forearms and continuing upward in vicious streaks to decorate her shoulders and face. Miriam pushed away a rush of alarm. Rudimentary logic said most of it could not be Alexis' blood.

She dropped to the ground. "Keep the pressure on anyway. Richard, we need the med kit. Alexis, I need to know what his injuries are." She realized she'd slipped up on the name again, but she'd worry about calling her daughter 'Alex' when there wasn't blood on the ground.

"Um, he's bleeding heavily from his neck, low, near the collarbone. And...he said he had a wound in his side...the right side I think...and that there would be internal injuries from it." She sucked in a breath as if the act itself caused her distress. "He's got bruises and cuts everywhere, but I don't know if there are other serious injuries. He—he passed out before he could tell me."

Miriam sensed Richard hovering behind her. "I need the coagulant and a Size 3 Grade IV medwrap."

"Got it."

She reached out and let him place the items in her hand then looked at Alexis. "Scoot back a little so I can get closer. When I say, remove your shirt from his neck."

Alexis slid along the ground until she was beyond Caleb's head and reaching over his face to keep the pressure in place.

Miriam crawled forward and unsealed the coagulant. "Okay, now."

As soon as Alexis withdrew the pullover new blood immediately began flowing out. To her semi-trained eyes it appeared the carotid artery had been nicked, but not completely opened. If it had been torn open he would be dead.

She poured the majority of the coagulant deep into the tear, then coated the opening with the rest of it and quickly covered it with the medwrap. The coagulant would seep through the open flesh until it found the artery then surround it and plug the artery wall, but it took twenty or thirty seconds to complete the process.

Alexis was staring down at Caleb's closed eyes; her face looked as blanched as his did. She drew her daughter's attention to her. "Alexis? Hold the medwrap in place. I'm going to see about the wound in his side now."

She nodded mutely, and Miriam called on her ingrained discipline once more to leave her daughter's side and move to the other side of the prone form.

She peeled the blood-soaked shirt away from the skin and choked off a gasp at what it revealed. A gouge twelve centimeters in length had opened into a ragged hole five centimeters in diameter. Blood seeped—with less force than at the neck—to the ground beneath them, creating rivulets which picked a path through the gaps in the stones.

Focus. Despite the blood the danger here would definitely be internal injuries. "Richard, I need...some bio-bonding gel, a nano-repair weave—two of them if possible—and another medwrap. Bigger, Size 5 I think, and Grade IV as well—unless there's a Grade V."

"Right." He crouched at her side and dug through the med kit. She squinted up to briefly meet his gaze, allowing him to see her concern.

He handed her the first item then glanced behind him. "He's going to be okay, Alex."

She didn't check to see her daughter's reaction, instead concentrating on the wound and allowing her training to take control. Every second counted. The flesh was torn and in some places shredded, but repairing it would come later.

She carefully inserted the nano-repair weaves inside the wound, working to ensure they spread over the largest possible area. Next she emptied the container of bio-bonding gel into the opening, secured the oversized medwrap to the adjoining skin…and let out a long breath. "Richard, can you hold this until the seal forms? I need to check for other injuries."

His hands replaced hers, and she maneuvered to run her hands along Caleb's body, starting at the chest. It continued to rise and fall, if shallowly and fitfully; his pasty skin became ghostly white in the effuse light. She felt two broken ribs and bound them so they wouldn't inflict additional damage when he was moved. Her hands roved down his legs, but they felt intact.

She stood and moved up to his head. A cut on his chin received a tiny strip of sealant. There were multiple bruises on his upper body, including a nasty one above his left cheekbone, but they could wait.

Finally she allowed herself to turn back to Alexis. Blood had soaked into the tips of her hair, tangling it into knots as it fell across her shoulders.

She reached over and tucked the nearest strands behind her daughter's ear. Alexis' eyes darted to her, bright and desperate.

"Are you hurt?"

Her head shook violently. "No. I just showed up and shot the fucker in the face."

She laughed in spite of the direness of the situation. "Of course you did. Listen, I've done all I can for him. We should get him inside." She climbed to her feet. "Richard, Director Delavasi?"

Delavasi was crouched beside the headless corpse, but stood at her inquiry. "I alerted estate security. They've got three dead guards along the perimeter, which is presumably how this degenerate got in. They've locked down everything and swept the guest house, so it's clear. Also, there's a physician on staff who will be here in fifteen minutes. In the meantime, a guard should show up with a cot any second now, at which point we can move him safely."

"Thank you for taking charge of this, Director."

The man grimaced and massaged his neck. "It's my job, though frankly I'm getting a little sick of standing around at blood-soaked crime scenes staring at one of my agents on the ground. Richard, any chance you could convince the Admiral to call me 'Graham'?"

"Doubtful. It took her five years to start calling me 'Richard.'"

The guard arrived then, and everyone again sprang into motion. They unfolded the cot beside Caleb, and Miriam had to coax Alexis away so they could move him onto it.

She stumbled backward as she stood. Miriam reached out to place a steadying hand on her arm. "Are you sure you're not hurt?"

Her nod was haphazard. Tears streamed down her cheeks, carving jagged streaks through the splotches of blood decorating them. She fixated on the men as they lifted each end of the cot up and began carrying it and its passenger toward the house. "How did you know how to do all that?"

"Advanced field training, with mandatory refresher courses every five years for the last forty-five. Haven't had to use it in a while."

"Mom…."

Without stopping to think about the fact that she had no idea how to provide comfort to another, she wrapped her arms around her daughter and silently drew her into her arms.

14

Kennedy pinched the bridge of her nose before raising her chin to meet the Space Materiels Complex Director's dour, unpleasant leer. "Sir, this is the third time you've said it can't be done. I respect this as your opinion, but saying it again won't get me to leave. So it would be more pleasant for all of us if you ceased with the complaints. You're going to keep working on the problem until someone far smarter than you tells you how it *can* be done. Then you're going to do it."

"Miss Rossi, you can't give me orders. I am the director of this facility and a brigadier in the Earth Alliance military and I decide what will and will not occur here."

"Of course I can't give you orders, *Brigadier*. That's why I had Admiral Solovy give them to you. You do recall the conversation, don't you? Now be a good soldier and run along. My guests are here."

The rotund, sweaty man puffed and blustered but after a few seconds tottered around and stalked off in the direction of the factory floor.

Kennedy headed in the opposite direction, toward the entrance of the sprawling building. The Complex was located west across the Havel from the still-standing Charlottenburg Palace and would have offered picturesque views of the Berlin skyline if it had any windows. Which it did not, even in the lobby, so she stopped before reaching the entrance and leaned against the wall to wait.

Noah had managed to pull it off, not only enlisting his father's aid but bringing him directly here. She didn't know whether to be stunned or proud, so she opted for a mix of both. Mainly she hoped he didn't despise her for forcing the reunion—or if he did, she hoped the damage wasn't beyond repair.

It was barely a minute before they arrived, leaving her little opportunity to compose herself properly. She would be happy to see Noah, but she couldn't obsess over him right now. She needed to navigate this encounter with utmost care, for him and for everyone.

Their bickering echoed around the corner as they walked through the front door. The two voices bore the same intrinsic tonality, but the elder was all cool superiority while the younger carried a loose fierceness. "No, it is always stupid to consolidate all your assets in one location. Just because gangsters aren't coming after you doesn't mean competitors or asteroids or, I don't know, *aliens* won't."

"Surno Materials isn't a back-alley hack shop which can pick up stakes and flee at a moment's notice. We create top-of-the-line—"

She bestowed her most dazzling smile on Noah as she stepped into the lobby, went over and took his hands in hers, and kissed him on the cheek. "Noah, I'm so glad you made it."

Only then did she turn to his father. "Lionel, it's good to see you again. Thank you for coming."

He looked positively dumbstruck, and she had to force down a giggle. "Ms. Rossi? This is...unexpected."

She *tsked* Noah in feigned disapproval, though she was a bit surprised. "Noah, you didn't tell your father who requested his presence?"

He snickered; it sounded more raw than usual. She had no doubt the time spent with his father had stressed him out, but he had pulled off what she knew he thought impossible. The twist of his lips when he met her gaze troubled her, though. *Deal with it later.*

"He would've thought I was trying to impress him. This is so much better."

Lionel glared at his son, though he appeared to be a tad flustered. Good on Noah. She betrayed none of her musings in her countenance or tone, however. "Regardless, you're both here now. I apologize for the rush, Lionel, but we have precious little time. If you'll come with me, I'll walk you through what we're trying to do."

The elder Terrage visibly worked to school his expression. "I assume it's why I'm here."

"Excellent." Kennedy led them down the hall and into a conference room she'd previously selected and prepped. Once inside she activated a screen above the table. She already had all the data queued up, and the initial display included a breakdown of complicated empirical and skeletal chemical formulas.

"What you see here is a metal compound we've dubbed 'adiamene.' It's created by a chemical fusing of the carbon metamaterial currently used to build our starships and the amodiamond metamaterial frequently used in the Federation for the same purpose. We've been able to consistently replicate its creation, but the chemical reactions take far too long to manifest. We need to be able to speed them up significantly. And we need to be able to make tonnes of this metal, yesterday."

Lionel ignored the data to direct a rather derisive scowl at her. Could Noah's face contort in such an unpleasant manner? She hoped not. "Ms. Rossi, 'combining' the carbon nanotube derivatives we utilize in ship hulls and amodiamond is a non-sequitur. Allotropes positioned between the two materials in terms of their characteristics include buckyfullerenes, amorphous carbon and lonsdaleite. The latter is the only one which improves upon either material, and it remains prohibitively expensive to manufacture."

She dressed him down with a look of daggers draped in sugar. "In their natural, elemental states this is *clearly* true. Which is why it's so interesting that combining the finished products has another result entirely. Please, if you would take a minute to consider the compound presented here."

It was with palpable reluctance that he shifted his attention to the screen, but instantly his eyes narrowed in greater interest. "Intriguing material…quite unusual lattice structure…the covalent bonds manifest extraordinarily strong, no question. There must be a facilitating element in one of the finished products that enables the fusion. This warrants further study—but why is it an emergency?"

Kennedy opened a new screen next to the first and pulled up the test results. Detailed figures and percentages scrolled along the right column next to a series of line charts. "Because adiamene is, for all intents and purposes, indestructible."

ℛ

"Noah, thank you. I know contacting your father was difficult for you, but you came through wonderfully."

Lionel had been sent off with the Complex Director for a rundown on the facility's manufacturing platform and capabilities, and Kennedy had dragged him into a break room down the hall.

Noah stared at her hands as they grasped one of his and squeezed. The tanned skin and perfectly-manicured nails wound gracefully around his far more rough-hewn hand. An emerald-and-gold ring adorned the middle finger of her right hand. Her grasp felt soft. Warm and welcoming.

He forced his gaze up to meet her sparkling green eyes. They matched her ring, naturally. "You could have done it yourself. You—"

"Noah, we talked about this—"

"You could've had one of your admiral friends send a couple of uniforms to escort him here, his wishes be damned. You didn't need to send me. Not really."

Her throat worked as her eyes darkened. When she finally spoke, her voice practically quivered. But was it anything other than an act? He'd seen her work a room; he'd seen her play his father like a violin only minutes earlier. Her skill in false flattery and ego manipulation was a sight to behold.

"I thought I was helping."

"Because you're trying to fix me, trying to shiny me up so I can be a proper boyfriend."

"No—"

"I don't need fixing, Kennedy. I don't *want* fixing."

Her brow knotted up in apparent consternation, and she closed the distance between them. "I know you don't. And I'm not...I'm sorry. I was trying to do the right thing."

She was so damn convincing...and so damn cute. He forced a smile and reached up to run a hand under her chin. "Just don't do it again, okay?"

She clutched his hand before it dropped away, atypical hesitation marring her—

—his damnable father pinged them both to announce he required a lab and a list of equipment. They groaned in unison, and she stepped away.

He followed her out of the break room and decided not to feel guilty about enjoying the view. He'd ride this out, since for now there were benefits. But he'd been stupid to ignore who and what she was. Stupid to fall under her spell and get emotionally attached. He'd been so bloody *stupid*.

He couldn't be stupid any longer. It would cost him too much. So when it became a better option to do so, he'd bail.

15

PANDORA

It came as something of a surprise when Caleb awoke to find himself alive.

His skin felt tight, alternately cool and hot. Eventually he realized it was due to large swaths of it being held together by medwraps. Interestingly, there was almost no pain. He had to be swimming in narcotics.

He sensed added weight on his left arm. Unless it was damaged to the point of requiring immobilization. He queried his eVi for an injury report, but unfamiliar medical recovery ware overrode the interface. *That bad, then.*

He opened his eyes and immediately thanked whatever gods there may be that the room was only dimly lit. He blinked until he remembered how to focus, marginally. His optical implant was offline, but it was a problem very far down his list of concerns.

Alex was curled up on the floor next to him. He appeared to be lying on a divan which had been converted into a makeshift medical cot. Her head rested on his arm.

He must have jostled it when he looked around, for she bolted upright.

Bloodshot, bleary eyes met his as a heavy but wondrous breath fell from her lips. The expression spreading across her face could light a galaxy. He let its warmth wash over him. Given a little time, it might heal his wounds all on its own.

"Caleb…."

Dried blood scored thick streaks across her neck, shoulders and arms. A rusty crimson smudge ran down her jaw, as if she'd made a perfunctory attempt to wipe it away and failed. Her hair hung in tangled clumps, snarled together by what he feared was also blood. Had she been injured? He tried to remember the minutes and seconds before he'd lost consciousness…he didn't think so. But were there other attackers or—he willed himself calm. Whatever had happened, she was here and alive and safe.

He reached up, his arm trembling and weak, to run fingertips shakily along her face. "Baby, you're covered in blood. Are you hurt?"

A ragged laugh-turned-cry erupted from her throat as she pressed her cheek into his hand. "No, it's all yours. I...it seemed like it was my turn."

"Only fair, I suppose." His throat grated on each word as they scraped their way up past the abrasiveness to emerge half-formed on a thick, swollen tongue. He tried to summon a bit of saliva and work it around in his mouth. His hand collapsed back to the cushion; he was already exhausted from the effort of holding it up. "So what's the damage?"

She studied him cautiously for several seconds, but finally swallowed hard and sat up straighter. "Well, the laceration in your side tore up a portion of your liver, perforated your gallbladder and nicked your right kidney. You also have two broken ribs, a fractured left eye socket and a concussion. And thanks to a tear in your carotid artery...you needed a transfusion of two liters of synthesized blood."

He sighed, and thus discovered the broken ribs. "I should be good to go in about six hours, then?"

Her nose scrunched up as she shook her head, plainly incredulous at his professed bravado. "Maybe twelve. Or a hundred and twelve. Let me guess—you've had worse?"

He considered the question. "Not actually, no."

"How do you feel? Do you want me to get the doctor?"

"I warranted a real, live doctor? Nice. No, I'm good." As if to prove it to her, he carefully pushed up to a sitting position and let his legs fall to the floor. Ah, *there* was the pain. But it eased once he stopped moving—or once more narcotics flooded his veins in response to the stimuli. Probably the latter, as the ache in the side of his neck that hadn't been sliced open bore all the hallmarks of multiple recent nanobot injections.

Alex rushed to place her hands on him, ready to catch him if he fell. He didn't like appearing weak to her, but he had little choice. He *was* weak.

Once satisfied he was stable she found his eyes with her own. "I'm so sorry I ran away from you. If you hadn't come searching for me, this wouldn't have happened."

"No, but something far worse might have instead. And you weren't running from me, you were just running. Right?"

She nodded a hurried assent. He tried to smile, sending a shot of pain lancing through his left cheekbone. "I'm sorry about Ethan."

Her brow furrowed in surprise at his choice of topic. She exhaled faintly. "So am I. He was a part of my life in a transient sort of way for a long time. But I've had some time to ponder matters, sitting here hoping...hoping you would wake up, and here's the thing. People are always moving in and out of my life, yet at the core it's always been me—only me. But now there's you."

Her eyes were stricken and glistening with unshed tears. "And it terrifies me. You said I wasn't afraid of anything, but you were wrong. If I lost you, I would be undone. I'm not as strong as my mother, and I don't know how I would cope. But even—"

His heart pounded against his sternum, when it really wasn't in any condition to be performing such acrobatics. "Shhh. You're far stronger than your mother, but that's not going to happen."

"Of course it could happen. You almost died tonight, almost bled out in my arms...." The end of the statement faded to a whisper.

"Don't be silly. I'm invincible."

"No, you're *not.*"

Granted, he didn't feel particularly invincible right now. Yet he was alive when few others would be, a fact which argued in his favor. He forced a shaky smile despite the pain it caused, desperate to reassure her. "Near to?"

She stared at him for a beat before dropping her head onto his lap and resting a cheek on his thigh. "It's okay. You don't have to be invincible. I've got you."

Her words knocked the air from his chest. The tangled nest of doubts, uncertainty and bitterness which had been festering in his thoughts since learning the truth about his father crumbled to dust, to be replaced with a stark and shining clarity of mind.

This was what Samuel had never seen, never factored into his damaged logic: the possibility of finding a person you *shouldn't* walk away from. Not because they needed you, but because you needed each other. Because you were stronger together than alone.

She had saved him. Twice now in fact. In between, he had saved her a few times. Perhaps they would go on like this forever, saving one another again and again in endless circles.

He didn't need to protect her—not from himself and the darkness that would always reside within him, and not from the evil deeds the world and its denizens wrought. He needed her standing beside him.

Gobsmacked but not wanting to keep his realization a secret for a second longer, he gingerly leaned down and kissed the top of her head, then raised her chin until she met his gaze. "Alex, you—"

She rose up on her knees to rest her forehead against his. "Don't worry. I know."

"No, you don't. You don't even begin to comprehend what you are to me. But if you'll allow me, I'd like to try to show you."

⋒

Miriam almost answered the holocomm request without checking its header—the urgent inquiries and reports were constant and unremitting—but noticed the sender right before doing so and paused long enough to square her shoulders first. For a brief span of time her attention had strayed from the ongoing war in favor of concerns which were more pressing. But she'd had enough time to get back up to speed to be confident she possessed any answers he might require.

Brennon looked up from the screen in his hand as the connection initiated. His eyes were sharp despite an evident lack of sleep, but his mouth was drawn into a thin line. "Admiral, we have a problem."

"Prime Minister, we have many problems."

"Well, now we have a new one. I just finished a conference with Chairman Vranas. Several Alliance military ships have attacked the Federation colony of New Cairo, killing thousands and causing major damage to their infrastructure."

Miriam cursed under her breath. *"O'Connell."*

"We can assume so. The ships gained easy access to the planet because the defense arrays had been updated to not view Alliance ships as a threat. This clearance has now been revoked, so we'll be required to get special permission to approach any Federation worlds."

"Understood. Sir, I took pleasure in giving the blanket order to blow O'Connell out of the sky, but I don't believe we can spare the ships to chase him down."

"Be that as it may, we can't ignore this problem. There has to be some action we can take to rein him in. The Senecans are pissed and rightfully so. I can assure them he doesn't represent the Alliance all day long, but the fact remains he's an Alliance general and he's killing their citizens. It's putting a significant strain on a fragile relationship, which is something we cannot afford right now. Where are you?"

She frowned. "Pandora. I'm here to—"

"Good, you're close. I want you to go to Seneca and smooth things over in person."

"I'll depart for there within the hour, sir. What would you like me to tell them?"

"Whatever it takes, Admiral."

"Yes, sir."

He terminated the connection. Miriam traversed the length of the conference table and back again, her hands clasped at the base of her spine.

She had rarely felt the cost of adhering to duty above all other considerations so acutely as she did now. The war needed her. The soldiers needed her. The people needed her. She was incomprehensibly grateful to have been here to help when her daughter needed her…but now the rest of the galaxy needed her more.

R

Miriam found Alexis in the small study where they had taken Caleb after the attack. Of course finding her was hardly difficult, for she had been nowhere else since they had returned from the garden. The door was open, and Miriam stopped at the entrance to watch them.

Alexis was on her knees with her hands resting on Caleb's shoulders. He was sitting up, which was a surprising if welcome sight. Leaving her daughter behind was going to be far easier knowing the young man would recover.

One of his hands had wound into Alexis' hair; the other drifted gently along her jaw. Miriam could see his lips moving, but his voice was far too quiet for her to make out what he was saying. She didn't need to hear it though. The scene told the story better than words alone.

A jumble of emotions broke free to inundate her mind and conjure a throbbing in her chest. Regret that she had missed so much of her daughter's life, so many moments of heartbreak and joy Alexis must have experienced over the years. Relief that she was here, now, to witness this one. Happiness that Alexis had found someone who she could open up to and allow past her substantial defenses. Fear that it meant Alexis may one day face the kind of soul-crushing loss Miriam had suffered. Certainty that it would be worth it nonetheless.

She hated to do it, but the clock was ticking. She cleared her throat respectfully from the doorway.

They both looked over at her, though neither let go of the hold they had on one another. "I'm sorry to interrupt. Mr. Marano, I'm relieved to see you awake—you gave us quite a scare. Alex, can I borrow you for a minute?"

"One second." She turned back to Caleb and whispered something; her fingertips ghosted down his cheek to hover on softly smiling lips before she stood and crossed the room to the hallway.

"I really am glad to see he's awake. Is he going to be all right?"

Alexis' posture sagged in unmistakable weariness, triggering a surge in Miriam's motherly instinct and the desire to admonish her daughter to get some sleep. She squelched the urge.

"I think so. He puts on such a brave front I can never be sure. What's up?"

"Unfortunately, I won't be accompanying you to Earth. I have to take a side trip to Seneca first to handle a...complication."

Alexis arched an eyebrow in surprise. "Seneca? Are you okay with going there?"

She shrugged. "I don't have much of a choice in the matter. But yes, I'll be fine."

"I know you'll be *fine*. You always are. I asked if you were okay with it." She discerned no hint of bitterness or sarcasm in her daughter's voice.

"In truth, I haven't considered the question. Perhaps I'll wallow a bit during the flight. Anyway, I'll confirm everything is ready for your arrival in Vancouver. If anyone gives you trouble tell Richard, then tell me. Immediately."

Alexis made a valiant effort at appearing put-upon. "Yes, ma'am. We'll be leaving as soon as the doctor says Caleb's well enough to travel."

"Good. You're in all kinds of danger so long as you remain here. The aliens know your location, and it won't be long before they realize their attempt to kill you failed and they send more agents. The sooner you depart, the better. When you reach Earth, Richard and I have arranged for a full security detail as well as other, more discreet measures."

"Are you sure all this is necessary? The secret's out now."

"If the multiple layers of surveillance shielding worked the aliens don't know the secret's out. And even if they do, there could be a delay in new orders reaching their agents. Also, you ought to consider the possibility that they will always consider you a threat—which they should."

"Point made."

"While I'm making points, you need a shower."

Alexis rolled her eyes. "Whatever." Then she lifted a lock of hair, tangled and caked in dried blood, off her shoulder using two fingers and winced. A chuckle escaped as she let it fall back. "So I do. Now that he's awake, I'll get cleaned up. In a few minutes. Before we leave."

Stubborn, stubborn child. "Please do." Miriam shuffled awkwardly, suddenly unsure how to end the conversation and walk away. "So I'll see you again soon. And Alex, please do not open your brain and invite an Artificial to take up residence in it before I get there."

On receiving a hand motion she took for minimal acquiescence, she turned to go.

"Mom?"

She pivoted without hesitation. "Yes?"

"Thank you for your help earlier. Thank you...for everything."

Finding herself at a true loss for words this time, she simply nodded. But as she headed down the hall toward the exit, she was smiling.

⌁

Delavasi entered the room as the doctor was leaving, having given his grudging sign-off on their departure after a barrage of medications and instructions and admonitions.

Alex checked Caleb's reaction to the new arrival, fully prepared to remove the man from the room by force if he wished it. He gave her the tiniest gesture to indicate she could stand down and gingerly closed up his shirt before directing his attention to the doorway. "Director."

"Glad to see you're none the worse for wear."

"Well..." Caleb eased into a position where he could pull on his boots "...I am a *little* the worse for wear, at least for a few days, but it looks like there was no irreparable damage done." His tone wasn't hostile, though it still lacked definable warmth, and she had to wonder whether the statement might apply to more than his physical health. "What can I do for you?"

Alex watched to make sure he didn't need help with the boots—not that he would accept it if he did—then cleared her throat. "I can give you two some time alone. I should finish gathering our things anyway."

Caleb shook his head. "It's all right. Please stay."

She knew it was a courtesy intended to make up in the smallest way for the scene on Seneca. He didn't need to do it, but she'd be lying if she claimed it didn't please her.

"Okay." She perched on the arm of the large chair next to the divan—far enough away to give him space, close enough to intervene if it became advisable to do so.

In the wake of the barrage of events this evening she found she was feeling staunchly protective of him—physically, emotionally, probably spiritually if the topic came up. Not because he was weak, but because he was strong. Stronger than any person should ever have to be.

It was a new but unexpectedly pleasant experience for her. She was so far from an expert in any of those things, but she'd realized something in the midst of the turmoil: it didn't matter. For him she would learn; he would help her learn.

Delavasi wandered deeper into the room to lean against the far wall, wisely leaving a large swath of space between him and Caleb. "I won't try to persuade you to come back to Cavare with me. I recognize you have your own path to follow. But I thought you'd want to know, I'm all but certain the man who attacked you was Michael Volosk's killer.

"He's a ghost—no identity, no fingerprints, no records, and there's not enough left of his eyes for a retinal scan. But the characteristics of his blade match Michael's wound and the MO is the same. He was definitely a professional assassin, which is the only kind of person who would have the ability to get the jump on Michael the way his killer did."

Caleb nodded thoughtfully. "Then I'm even happier he's dead. Volosk was a good man."

"A better man than me, that's for sure. And though I doubt I'll ever be able to prove it, I'd bet good money on this guy being the one who killed Minister Santiagar and Chris Candela as well. Odds are he was the aliens' go-to assassin. Or the Aguirre Conspiracy's—or hell, all of them. Great job on taking him out, both of you."

"Thank you." Caleb shifted on the cushion beneath him and seemed to carefully consider his next words. "Director, I'm not saying I'm all right with what you—and others—did in covering up my father's death, or everything is kosher between us. It's not. When this is over I'm going to need to give serious thought to whether I'm comfortable with or even willing to return to Division.

"But before we leave, I was wondering if you could take a few minutes to tell me a bit about my father. About the man he genuinely was, for good or ill."

Delavasi looked taken aback, perhaps not expecting to be granted such a boon, but his bearing relaxed. The contrast was stark; Alex hadn't appreciated just how tense he had been.

He grabbed a chair and dragged it across from the divan, then sat down and leaned forward to rest his forearms on his knees. "Caleb, I would be honored to tell you about Stefan."

16

"Sir, the Ogham orbital defense array is tracking us. It appears to be hostile."

Liam considered the view from the raised overlook just past midway down the bridge of the *Akagi*. Ogham was an ugly world, a tiny, rocky planet orbiting an average orange star. There was no good reason for its existence, much less its settlement.

"So they now realize we are again the enemy. No matter. I expected the trick was only likely to work once."

The New Orient assault had been ludicrously easy in its execution. With no threat from the array and no noticeable military presence on the colony, they waltzed in and had their way. His force had burnt the settled continent to a crisp in the space of a few hours.

In some ways it had been anticlimactic…he couldn't sense the blood in the air or see the panic on the faces from the bridge of a ship. On the other hand, he could create widespread destruction *far* more efficiently. By the end of the offensive the flames devouring New Orient had been visible from space with the unaided eye. He'd used his optical implant to record the scene so he was able to replay it in his mind whenever he wished.

He beckoned over the Flight Deck Chief, a Commander Dohman. The man was inappropriately skinny for military service; Liam would have disqualified him from supervisory rank on this flaw alone, but demoting the man so soon after assuming command would cause more problems than it solved. As he had to keep reminding himself, he needed to be careful with the crew.

"Transfer two tactical fusion anti-ship mines to the reconnaissance craft. Instruct the pilot to proceed under full stealth and place the mines in the orbital paths of two consecutive nodes of the array. When the nodes reach the mines they will detonate, destroying the nodes and possibly even the array frame at those locations. The gap created will be sufficient for us to slip through."

Dohman grimaced; his face was so thin the expression took up the entire bottom half of it. "Sir, perhaps a better option is to whittle down two of the nodes from afar? Since we're facing a single array we should have minimal losses."

He did have his eye on two officers who displayed more favorable characteristics and a better attitude, however. Maybe the time had come to shake up the ranks after all, and there were stronger, properly loyal soldiers deserving of promotion. "Did I stutter, Commander? Plinking away at nodes takes too long, and we *would* have losses. We can't spare the ships. Carry out my order."

The man's head bobbed unevenly, and he backed away several steps before heading for the flight deck.

Liam was turning to consider the view outside anew when Captain Harper cleared her throat behind him. "General, the array is in low orbit. Detonating two tactical nukes at that altitude risks poisoning the planet's atmosphere."

The young special forces officer somehow always seemed to be on the bridge at critical junctures and somehow always seemed to have a legitimate reason for being there. Her very presence rankled him. Her understated arrogance revealed itself in the proud carriage of her shoulders and piercing glint in her stare. He couldn't shake the feeling that she was constantly analyzing him, probing for weaknesses and flaws she might use against him. But she would never find any.

Liam sneered at her. "Yes, it will."

A twitch of the muscles beneath her left eye was the only outward reaction she displayed. "I'll make sure the mine transfer is handled correctly, then, sir."

Brooklyn Harper hurried through the tight hallways of the *Akagi*. Her options raced through her mind in time to the rhythm of her boots hitting the deck.

A tactical analysis led to the inescapable conclusion that for the moment those options were few. The Flight Deck Chief was in full-on sycophant mode, his solitary, weak protest having been crushed by O'Connell's glare alone. If Dohman was on the flight deck she'd never be able to sabotage or otherwise interfere with the deployment of the mines. She couldn't in good conscience ask the recon craft pilot to mis-position them because under this general such an error would likely result in the pilot's summary execution.

She'd disliked O'Connell instantly upon meeting him, but in the initial days of this alleged 'covert mission' she'd had no reason to doubt the veracity of his orders. Given the number of dirty tactics the Federation engaged in during the brief war, she wouldn't blame the Alliance for engaging in a few of its own.

But New Cairo had been a straight-up massacre of civilians, plain and simple. The array saw their ships as friendly—which meant the Second Crux War was in fact officially over—and they had barged in with zero resistance. New Cairo didn't have a real military installation, only a reserve outpost for a couple of cargo and transport ships. The *Akagi* and its companion vessels dropped through the atmosphere and fucking carpet-bombed the entire colony, down to the tiniest outposts deep in the jungle.

All was fair in war...but they weren't at war. Not any longer. And even in war deliberate attacks on purely noncombatant targets were frowned upon. This was the 24th century; they were supposed to be civilized now.

The communications blackout had put everyone on edge, and that was before they started blowing up peaceful settlements. The crew wanted to know what was happening with the aliens. They wanted to know if friends and family were safe, and if they lived to the east where they'd evacuated to. They wanted to know their government had a plan to fight the aliens—*was* fighting the aliens. But all this knowledge and the accompanying comfort it might provide continued to be denied them.

At least her parents and younger brother lived on Demeter. It lay to the west of Earth; if the aliens attacked Demeter, the game was already lost. Those other concerns gnawed at her as well, but until she was able to do something about them she needed to concentrate on what she *could* do.

She reached the flight deck far sooner than she reached any conclusions, yet far too late to do any good. Six crewmen transported the first mine up from armament storage under the watchful eye of Commander Dohman.

Her stomach curdled at the sight, sending the rank aftertaste of the pickled slaw from lunch up into her throat. Using tactical nukes in space was one thing, where the damage stayed contained to a few ships at most—ships which qualified as enemy combatants—and the radiation swiftly dispersed into the vastness of space. Using them inside an atmosphere constituted another matter entirely. The wind currents of the upper layers would sweep the radiation into its ecosystem and spread it across the planet, seeding it in the rain clouds and permeating it into the air below.

O'Connell was a madman or a sociopath, and in all likelihood both. Her instincts had told her this within an hour of sharing a ship with him, but she'd allowed for other possibilities or even an error on her part until New Cairo. And if there had been a scintilla of doubt remaining after that bloodbath, his cavalier use of nukes on a defenseless colony eradicated it.

As the crewmen finished loading the mine into the small cargo bay of the stealth recon craft, she silently made the decision. She would have to stop him.

To do so, however, she needed allies, and she didn't know this crew. She and the other three members of her squad were strangers to them—and two of the three members of her squad were essentially strangers to her, having been transferred in several weeks earlier at the height of the conflict with the Federation. She couldn't be sure who to trust, and given O'Connell's clear paranoia and hair-trigger temper she needed to tread cautiously.

Her pace slackened to a stop several meters away from the recon vessel as she lingered in the shadows. She didn't have the capability to stop this attack. She was out of options for now. But in order to be ready when O'Connell made his next move, it was time to begin.

17

PANDORA

INDEPENDENT COLONY

Graham didn't glance behind him to evaluate the quality of the projection as he departed the hidden estate via the checkpoint. He was confident it was an effective illusion, if not effective enough to deter the now-dead assassin.

Richard had left for Earth an hour earlier, Caleb and Alex soon thereafter. Graham had intended to return to Seneca forthwith, but then a request came in from Field Marshal Gianno. He could've handled it remotely, but it turned out Olivia Montegreu was on Pandora this exact minute, so he delayed his departure long enough for a brief in-person meeting.

The agreed-upon location for their encounter wasn't far from the estate. He considered pondering whether the woman knew where they had been staying, but the likelier truth was simply that this was an expensive, upscale neighborhood and thus to her tastes. Still, he took a circuitous route as an added precaution, lengthening his walk by multiple blocks.

The added time also gave him an opportunity to debrief himself on the events of the last several hours. A significant threat had been eliminated with the death of the nameless assassin, though his experiences over the last several weeks left him suspicious the aliens retained other resources to deploy. He'd nearly lost another talented agent in the process…and he had to concede he still might. But Caleb had shown himself to be more like Stefan than expected when, despite clearly harboring underlying anger and distrust, he had reached out with the calm, reasoned overture.

Graham sincerely hoped Caleb left Pandora bearing greater goodwill toward him than the agent had arrived with, because he was getting tired of taking the blows for a decision two decades old which had never been his to make in the first place. Martyrdom made for damn ill-fitting attire.

He peered up when he realized he had arrived at the address provided. Then he double-checked to confirm the information, as it was an art museum. He'd accuse Montegreu of daring to possess a sense of humor...but as soon as he walked in the building he recognized the genius of her choice.

The museum featured wide, open rooms, high ceilings and marble flooring which announced each footfall well in advance of the person's arrival. A dearth of spectators made it impossible to hide other agents in a crowd or create chaos as a distraction for misdeeds. There was only a handful of aristocratic browsers...and guards. Lots and lots of guards.

He found her in the second display room to the left studying a Cézanne piece with an outward air of intensity. She was alone in the room, save for the guards stationed at each of the four exits. Sporting a white dress suit and wearing her pale blond hair swept up in a graceful knot, she resembled merely another blue-blood patron.

"Rather a garish piece, don't you think?"

"If you're shopping for art critiques, you have come to the wrong man, Ms. Montegreu. A museum, seriously? Is this you making some sort of allegorical statement about the work you do— or possibly the work I do?"

She continued to inspect the painting in front of her. "No, Director Delavasi. This is me ensuring my safety, should you wish to renege on our arrangement."

"What if some of these guards are my men?"

Her lips curled up in profile. "Impossible, Director, because all the guards are my men."

He laughed loudly, earning a warning stare from the guard in his line of sight. "Are they truly?"

"Indeed. You see, I own this museum. Oh, you won't find my name on the deed, but a skilled spy such as you will be able to trace it to me easily enough. In any event, you'll want to not try anything untoward, lest you find yourself the recipient of a laser between the eyes."

"Unless I'm wearing a shield."

"Ha." The word was verbalized in such a manner it made him wonder what kind of weaponry the guards carried.

Finally she abandoned the Cézanne to face him. "How may I fulfill the terms of my indentured servitude today?"

He crossed his arms over his chest and shifted his weight to his back leg. "Why are you on Pandora?"

"Certain of my subordinates here have disappointed me of late. I needed to make a few adjustments. One thing I'm not here for is small talk, so do get on with it."

If the woman had anything other than ice coursing through her veins, it must surely be acid. He rubbed at his neck but tried not to otherwise display his fatigue; it had been a hell of a day. "I need thirty thousand units of nervous system stimulants—reaction time boosters, specifically."

"You don't already have a supply of stimulants on hand?"

"Not the kind you traffic in."

"No, I suppose not. Thirty thousand is a large amount. For soldiers then? Fighter pilots perhaps?"

He glowered down his nose at her. Well, if she was stupid she wouldn't have risen to her position and held it uninterrupted for nearly half a century. "What they are for is not your business."

"Of course it isn't. Will next week be acceptable?"

"Tomorrow will be acceptable."

If it was possible, her visage hardened further. "Very well. I'll see that they're deposited on Chairman Vranas' doorstep."

"Or you can see they're delivered to this location in Cavare. Far less bloodshed this way. You'll also find some specifications in the file, as we do have the safety and health of the recipients to think about."

"How very noble of you. Is that all?"

"For now."

"Naturally." She tugged at her suit jacket and pivoted toward one of the exits. "Now if you'll excuse me, I have another subordinate to dispose of. Good day, Director."

She left him standing there under the watchful observation of her guards shaking his head at her audacity. It had been a hell of a day....

‍

Aiden Trieneri stood behind the desk in his office, both hands pressed into the desk's surface as he leaned in to study an unseen screen. Seconds ticked by...one...two...he flicked the screen away and transferred his attention to her. "Olivia. How goes Pandora?"

She allowed the implicit snub to pass uncommented upon. He was an inherently conceited, narcissistic man—this was not news to her, and holding him under her thumb did not currently suit her purposes.

She relaxed back in the chair belonging to the museum curator and folded her hands in her lap. "Bloodily efficient. We have a request from one of our 'partners.'"

He rocked against the desk. "We knew they would be coming. And the request is?"

"The Federation wants stimulants for their fighter pilots."

"What kind of stimulants?"

"The illegal kind, obviously. Nervous system boosters for reaction time. The contact provided the usual platitudes about safety concerns and whatnot, but I expect so long as we don't send the stimulants likely to result in instant death it will be acceptable. If some of the pilots later develop tremors or the odd chimeral addiction? Those are the risks."

He snorted, an act which didn't exactly highlight his best qualities. "No less than they deserve."

She crossed one leg over the other and considered him with mild curiosity. "Do I detect a particular distaste for the Federation? The military? Fighter jocks? Something more specific?"

"Only the unjustifiably privileged. Interesting how quickly their morals give way though. If they find themselves surprised at the consequences, they should not have dealt with the devil."

"And who is the devil in this scenario?"

He smiled darkly, a more complimentary action. "Olivia, my dear, you are *always* the devil."

Ah, reversion to flattery rather than risk exposing a weakness. Alas. "Yes, I am. My primary stimulant production facility is on New Babel, so I need to get them shipping out immediately. Seneca is a long way away."

"We could use my facility on Argo Navis and halve the distance."

She stared at him for a long moment. "Send the first lot out from there. My facility will backfill the supply chain as needed."

He nodded in acceptance. "What about the Alliance?"

"They haven't asked yet. Odds are their forces are too spread out for them to deliver those type of supplies in bulk anyway. Or it might be their leadership still has a few scruples."

"Scruples will get everyone killed. This is about survival. Deal with the fallout after we survive."

"Would you like me to get Miriam Solovy on the comm for you to set her straight yourself?"

"Oh, I would…" he regarded her dubiously "…can you actually *do* that?"

Could she? Eh…perhaps. But it would require playing the entirety of her cards in one gambit, and she wasn't going to try and fail and lose face as a result. "If it comes to it—which it hasn't. Just get those stimulants moving. Here's the drop point information. I'll return in the morning."

"Have extra security meet you at the spaceport. Things are getting a bit dicey out there."

"Are you concerned about my well-being, Aiden?"

"It is in my self-interest to be concerned about your well-being, for several reasons. I realize you believe yourself untouchable, but now is not the time to test that belief. Get the extra security."

"Fine. Goodbye." She stood and departed the curator's office. She still had work to do before she left Pandora behind.

18

ROMANE
INDEPENDENT COLONY

"Well what about the thrusters? Can we use them to alter the arrays' orbits? Make them unpredictable?"

Governor Ledesme turned to the Chief Engineer for an answer.

He shrugged weakly in response. "We can speed them up and slow them down periodically, sure. But I don't see how we can program them to alter their speeds dynamically when under fire. By the time they're under fire, it will be too late."

Meno? Got any input?

The Artificial accompanied Mia Requelme everywhere now, by way of the remote interface attached to the base of her skull. She wore her hair down, and high-necked shirts or scarves as fit the situation, to conceal the thin wrap and the fibers connected to her cybernetics it held in place. After a small modification to the interface, Meno now received the stream from her ocular implant and saw what she saw; a tiny sensor pad behind her left ear and he now heard what she heard.

His more fulsome companionship had made her appear far smarter than she was several times already. Wearing the interface was a risk, but a necessary one. Whatever it took.

Real-time data from the short-range sensors, if transmitted directly to the propulsion system, will enable propulsion to adopt a chaos-derived thrust routine before the alien ships come in range.

Mia adopted a more assertive posture. "Can we use the short-range sensors? They serve to put the arrays on alert, right? Split their data and send it to the propulsion system at the same time. Eventually the aliens will be able to take out the individual nodes, but if we switch to chaos-driven programming the erratic orbits will mean it takes them longer to do so, thus buying us time."

The Chief Engineer's mouth morphed around in hesitation. "I suppose that might work. Driving these titanic structures on a chaos routine isn't safe though. At a minimum it will cause stress to the frames, and the whole damn assembly is going to rip apart if there's the slightest error."

"Chief, you do realize the alternative is immediate and total destruction?"

He wilted under Ledesme's inquiry. "I'll get my people started on it right away."

"Thank you. Okay, people, what else do we have?"

Mia settled back into what was a surprisingly comfortable chair. The governor's Select Cabinet along with several additional 'experts' in various matters sat in a rough circle spread across the left half of a large room on the top floor of Administration Headquarters. In the middle of the circle stood a table equipped with data inputs which was accessed by attendees as needed. Smaller stations ran along one wall of the room and refreshments were periodically resupplied at the far end. Every so often someone wandered over for coffee, bread or fruit, or merely to stretch their legs.

Mostly, however, they talked, brainstormed, argued and tried with minimal success to figure out how they could possibly save Romane from the Metigen invasion looming like the encroaching shadow of an eclipse on the horizon.

Mia found herself deemed one of the 'experts,' though expert in what topic she couldn't exactly say. But the last week had seen her increasingly at the governor's side or at least within earshot whether she wanted to be or not. And it did make her feel as though she was helping, when otherwise she'd be pacing ineffectually at home or at the spaceport—she wouldn't be pacing at the gallery as it was now closed pending a resolution to this crisis or destruction of the colony.

I've been studying the new data on the behavior of the shields protecting the aliens' vessels. It is possible we can develop a signal which interferes with their operation—a signal the arrays could potentially broadcast across a wide area. Accounting for the fluid nature of the shields' variations in strength is a significant obstacle, but one I hope to be able to overcome.

She waded into the lull in conversation. "Do the arrays have the capability to broadcast signals in addition to receiving them?"

The Chief Engineer shook his head distractedly. "Why would they need to send out signals?"

Damn. Still, it was an interesting idea—

Boo.

She nearly leapt out of her chair in surprise. Though she managed to suppress the movement, she must have made a sound because the man sitting next to her—the Commerce Chief, she thought—glanced over curiously. She gave the man a polite smile then pretended to study the data currently scrolling above the table with interest.

Caleb, you crazy son of a bitch. You're alive, I assume?

I am in fact.

Where are you?

I can't go into the details right now, but we—Alex and I—would like you to come to Earth as soon as possible.

What? Hang on a second.

Mia cleared her throat to get Ledesme's attention. "Governor, I need to step outside briefly. I have an incoming comm I should take."

Ledesme indicated assent, and Mia stood and walked out of the room in a calm, controlled manner. Upon exiting, however, she bolted down the hallway to an empty room and converted the pulse to a livecomm.

"Caleb, I can't go to Earth. Granted, half of Romane's population has fled there, but I'm actually doing some good here. And why? If you're trying to protect me again or something equally ridiculous I am going to kick your ass all the way back to Cavare."

"It's not about protecting you, I promise—though I would if you'd let me."

On hearing his voice, even if only in her head, she realized he sounded…she wasn't sure. Strained? Weak? "What's wrong? Are you all right?"

"I'm fine. Got a little banged up is all. I'll be good as new in another day." She picked up a muffled voice in the background. *"Maybe two days."*

Alex calling him on his bullshit? Likely. "Where have you been? Through the portal this whole time? You've been gone a *month*. After you were cleared of the bombing I thought you'd re-surface, but not a solitary peep from you."

"I'm here now, aren't I? It's a great story, but I can't tell it over comms."

A note of teasing had crept into his voice, and she relaxed somewhat. "Fine, fine. Why should I go to Earth? I await your most persuasive reason."

"For a chance to help save the galaxy."

"Oh, well in that case. Could you perhaps be a little more vague?"

"We also need you to bring—well, I expect you can't 'bring' Meno, but bring its specs and schematics and interface protocols and whatever else you have on precisely how it works and how connections are inte-grated into its programming."

She stopped in the center of the room and cut her eyes around at the walls. "Let me guess. You can't tell me why."

"Sorry. Not until I see you."

"And doing so will allow me to help save the galaxy."

"That's the plan."

Ledesme would not appreciate her walking back in the room and excusing herself permanently. It would look like she was run-ning—but she wouldn't be. She was willing and ready to stay, to see this crisis through to the end on the soil of her home.

Meno, is it a problem for you to collate all the data on your archi-tecture and internals?

Not at all, Mia. I shall have it prepared and burned on a disk for you in another 4.3211 seconds.

So. Was she really going to abandon everything—her home, her businesses, the trust she'd built with the governor—and go to Earth, simply because Caleb said he needed her? Though in fair-ness, he hadn't so much said *he* needed her as the *galaxy* needed her. Might need her. Or something to that effect. Still….

She blew out a heavy breath. "I'll leave this afternoon."

19

EARTH
BERLIN

"Admiral Solovy, let me introduce Dr. Lionel Terrage, founder and CEO of Surno Materials. We also have with us the Director of the Space Materiels Complex, Brigadier Wyryck. And Noah, you've met."

Miriam nodded tersely from within her holo. She appeared to be aboard a transport, presumably bound for yet another clandestine destination. Kennedy knew that Miriam had seen Alex, but nothing else. She didn't know where or when or if Alex might be coming to Earth or...she simply didn't know. Messages to Alex went unanswered; she'd been told there were reasons for that, but not what those reasons may be.

Prior to escaping from Messium her involvement with the military had been minimal, and the level of secrecy the organization employed came as a bit of a shock. But perhaps it wasn't always like this—special circumstances and all.

They sat around a small conference table in a similarly small room just off the assembly line floor. It had been a frustrating day and tempers were short. Also, she now completely understood why Noah had run away from home as a teenager and never looked back. Even if his father was undeniably brilliant in his narrow area of expertise, she would be happy if she never had to spend another minute in the company of Lionel. She preferred Noah's more effusive brilliance. And his sense of humor. And his...other attributes. God, she hoped she was going to be able to repair the damage done and salvage the relationship.

She smiled with professional grace and acknowledged those at the table before returning her focus to the holo. "The good news is, Dr. Terrage has proved to be of great assistance in working through the difficulties we encountered producing the adiamene.

We think we've worked out the kinks and will be able to mass produce sheets of it on the order of one hundred square meters per hour inside a day."

Miriam's expression remained guarded. "There is corresponding bad news, I assume."

Kennedy gestured to the Director. "I'll let Brigadier Wyryck give you the details."

The man stiffened proudly in his chair. "Admiral Solovy, let me say what an honor it is to—"

"The bad news, Brigadier."

He jerked as if struck. "Y-yes, Admiral. To produce the adiamene at such a rate will cost 708 million credits per month, or approximately 23.6 million credits per day."

Kennedy thought Miriam veiled the surprise in her eyes with impressive speed, particularly given the rather foul mood the woman seemed to be in. "Brigadier, it costs less to build a dreadnought."

"You must understand, our suppliers—"

"Spare me the details. I have no time for them. May I assume it will cost half this amount to produce half as much?"

"Uh...no, ma'am...it will cost two-thirds as much. You see, there are ramp-up costs and—"

"Of course there are." Miriam pinched the bridge of her nose. "I don't see how we can do it. We've been bleeding red ink since the start of the Second Crux War and have already borrowed beyond our capacity to repay. If it were a more reasonable sum we might be able to strong-arm the suppliers into floating us a portion of the materials, but in this circumstance I doubt that's feasible. I can discuss pursuing an executive order with Prime Minister Brennon, though I fear we don't have the time it would take to implement the order."

Her gaze traveled across those present. "However, I do recognize the strategic advantage significant quantities of this metal could grant us. As such, I am open to alternative suggestions."

Kennedy exhaled quietly. She hadn't wanted to raise the proposition unless no other option presented itself. She was not frivolous with her family's money and even to her the sum was mind-boggling in size. But this was the end of the world.

Her hands came together atop the table. "I should be able to cover the costs, at least for the first month. After that point, I suspect the urgency will have passed, one way or another."

Noah all but fell out of his chair beside her. Once he'd righted himself he drew close to her and muttered under his breath. "Blondie, are you insane? No one has that kind of money to throw around."

She gave him a weak grimace. "We do."

Wyryck had been stunned into silence and was unlikely to contribute anything else to the discussion. Miriam sighed. "Ms. Rossi, I cannot ask your family to contribute such sizable funds. Not without guarantee of repayment, which I regrettably cannot give."

"And you don't need to. I'm volunteering. Given the...unique nature of the sum, I will need to seek my father's approval. But I'm confident I can convince him of the necessity of the investment."

"You honestly believe in the capabilities of this material this much?"

"I do, ma'am. More than that, I believe we all must do everything in our power to defeat these aliens. This is within my power."

Miriam chuckled dryly; it carried less harshness than her earlier utterances. "Then I will not protest further. Should we win the day I'll do what I can to see your family is reimbursed in some likely inadequate manner. Get back to me when you've worked out the details. On behalf of the Earth Alliance—on behalf of everyone— thank you."

When the holo had winked out of existence, she shot Noah a playful grin. "Have you ever seen Texas?"

His brow furrowed up in confusion. "What's a 'Texas'?"

20

SENECA
CAVARE

M iriam hadn't asked for the military escort which greeted her on disembarking the transport. In point of fact, she had instructed the pilot to dock at the commercial spaceport in Cavare specifically to avoid this sort of pageantry—and also to preemptively avoid any 'issues' resulting from an Alliance Admiral requesting direct access to Federation Military Headquarters.

Mostly she had hoped she might steal twenty minutes of solitude to absorb the reality of stepping foot on the soil of what had been an avowed enemy for twenty-five years. The enemy responsible for the death of the man she had loved with the entirety of her being.

Miriam took her seat in the back row just before Admiral Chonsei stepped to the front of the small briefing room. He surveyed his audience once and began. "The information I'm about to divulge is classified Top Secret until you are instructed otherwise. In the next six hours it is expected Prime Minister Ioannou and Admiral Breveski will sign an armistice with the Senecan Federation which will halt hostilities—" the room erupted in exclamations and protests "—enough! The armistice will declare the cessation of hostilities for so long as a detailed list of conditions are and continue to be met.

"This is not a peace treaty. Our forces are to remain on Level IV alert status until we can verify the conditions have been fulfilled, then at Level III for probably a hell of a lot longer. I'm telling you this now because once the news breaks we're going to be fielding inquiries from the press. In the event any of you personally receive an inquiry, your orders are to recite the official line. No exceptions."

Chonsei droned on about 'embargoes' and 'restricted travel' and 'clear boundaries' and 'minimal diplomatic relations,' but Miriam didn't hear most of it for the shrill ringing in her ears.

No. This could not be the outcome. She had slaved for the last four months, foregoing sleep and meals to do everything in her power to push them toward victory. David's sacrifice would not be in vain. It couldn't be. How dare they.

She stood and cleared her throat. "Sir, this will look like a surrender."

"The Earth Alliance's official stance is that it is no such thing, and this is to be your stance as well."

"But, sir, we can't fold now. We have the forces and the firepower to win this war—the officials in Vancouver are simply unwilling to use them. They send our ships out in minimal formation strength and allow them to be whittled down in skirmish after skirmish. But we send half—a third—of the Sol Fleet to Seneca and we can crush this rebellion—"

"Commodore Solovy, you are out of line. Unless you want to face a censure for insubordination, you will take your seat."

Her lips parted, the protest hovering on her tongue...but she sat as instructed.

"The Sol Fleet isn't going anywhere. The Alliance is not going to leave Earth undefended or even vulnerable for an instant. Also, our leaders are not going to risk the losses which might result from such a risky offensive. End of story."

The briefing ended at some point. Miriam returned to her office on the 7th floor of the Logistics Center at North American Military Headquarters in a frozen daze. Several minutes later she found she was sitting at her desk with no recollection of how she had arrived there.

How could they capitulate to these seditionists? What had they been fighting for the last three years if not to bring the rebels to heel? What had David died for if not the belief that duty, honor and loyalty were to be defended to the last breath?

If these Senecans fantasized life would somehow be better without the pesky interference of the Alliance government, they should have run off to Requi or Pandora or Gaiae. But they did not have *the right to take up arms against their own government, steal Alliance ships and confiscate Alliance infrastructure as their own and turn it on those who had built it.*

In reality they were nothing but armed thugs spoiling for a fight. At Kappa Crucis they could have disengaged once they saw the mission was an evacuation and not an offensive. Instead they pushed ahead, weapons blazing, eager to kill scientists and their children merely so they could take yet something else which wasn't theirs to begin with. They—

—all the emotions, all the pain and despair and impotent rage welled up out of their dark, desolate hiding place in her soul to crash through her iron-forged armor and break free. She grabbed the small bronze sculpture of Marcus Aurelius sitting on her desk and hurled it against the opposite wall.

The piercing clang it made as it impacted the wall didn't help, nor did the noisy rattle as it rolled about on the floor, bumping into the furniture and bouncing around like a pinball. She squeezed her eyes shut and ground her teeth as she waited for the most unbearable, life-destroying sentiments to recede back into the shadows.

Then she stood, went over and retrieved the statue from the corner where it had finally settled and placed it gently back upon the desk.

Violent outbursts never helped, and she had been weak to partake in one. Nothing ever helped, except putting one foot in front of the other in front of the other until the relentless, monotonous repetition crushed the grief beneath its weight.

Now, twenty-three years after the armistice, she arrived on Seneca as an honored guest. She had advocated for peace with the Federation. She had *made* peace with the Federation. Affixed her own signature to the treaty and everything. She had strategized with its leaders and implemented cooperative measures with its military.

Was it any wonder that in the same dark, desolate corner of her soul it all felt like a betrayal—a betrayal of David's memory, of his life, his love and his death?

It was an irrational emotion she should not indulge. Beyond this, she knew David would not have wanted her to indulge it. Above all else he had loved life in all its splendor, and were he here he would tell her she damn well better do whatever was necessary to save it.

Still, she'd have preferred the twenty minutes to work past the lingering bitterness in private. Instead a Federation captain and two lieutenants waited for her at the bottom of the ramp.

"Admiral Solovy, welcome to Seneca. Field Marshal Gianno has instructed us to escort you to Military Headquarters."

She squared her shoulders and straightened her jacket. "Lead the way."

R

SENECAN FEDERATION MILITARY HEADQUARTERS

Miriam was herded with brutal efficiency through the bustling halls of Military Headquarters, onto a well-guarded lift and down another featureless but still busy hallway to a stately door at the end.

The trip from the spaceport to this door had left her with several impressions worth noting. The Federation government's architecture of choice was simple to the point of barrenness, yet impeccably designed. The civilian architecture was refined and expensive, if a bit glossy for her tastes. Seneca's moon was shockingly large.

She'd gotten a good view of the enormous planetary satellite because it was 0200 local time, not that anyone seemed to have noticed. Truthfully she was relieved to discover the Senecans were working as tirelessly as she and Brennon and their subordinates.

"You can go on in, Admiral. When you're ready to return to the spaceport the Marshal will let us know."

She sent the escort off and entered Gianno's office. The decor, what there was of it, was tasteful and understated in the extreme. The sole personal item in sight was a visual on the wall of a distinguished-looking man who might be roughly Gianno's age arm-in-arm with a much younger man who distinctly favored the Marshal.

Gianno stood at her desk reviewing a screen in her hand and motioned Miriam in without glancing up. A man in a dark, finely-tailored suit stood at the window, his back to them. From the angle she didn't know who it might be. Then he spoke, and she recognized the voice as belonging to Federation Chairman Vranas.

"Your rogue general just used nukes on Ogham."

Miriam stared at the back of his head while she contemplated her response. She considered and rejected the diplomatic tack. She was neck deep in a battle for civilization alongside these people. They had previously shown a preference for straight talk over ass-kissing, so she would oblige them.

"There is a reason he's rogue."

Vranas huffed a wry breath but still didn't turn around, so she switched to Gianno. "The only nukes he'd possess are tactical fusion anti-ship mines. Are you saying he used those on the surface? If so—"

Gianno's head shook as she set aside the screen and directed her focus to Miriam. The woman's demeanor was decidedly cooler than it had been when they'd met on Romane, but under the circumstances Miriam hardly expected warmth.

"He used them to take out two nodes on the defense array and create a gap he could traverse. The array's orbit is low enough the nukes will likely poison the atmosphere to a greater or lesser degree. Of course, the initial death toll on the ground from his attack is already in excess of ten thousand."

"I am sorry, but I realize that means little more than the air expended to say it."

Vranas finally faced them. "What are you going to do about it?"

She regarded them both for what became a long, weighty moment.

"Nothing."

The man's chin dropped to his chest in an act she took for genuine shock. "*Nothing?*"

Brennon might argue her answer hardly constituted 'whatever it takes'...but he wasn't here and this was her play to make.

"We're working diligently to find a way to track his movements. We expect Fionava communications to be restored in the next day, which ought to help. If we are able to track him and have sufficient advance warning, I will happily—gleefully—approve a strike against his ships or provide you the information so you can do the same. You have not only my authorization but the full blessing of the Earth Alliance Armed Forces to blow him out of the sky should you find him, though I'm certain if provided the opportunity you would not wait to receive it.

"If—no, when—we are victorious over the Metigens, I intend to send an entire brigade to hunt him down and grant him no mercy when they run him to ground. But I happen to believe that won't be necessary. Nearly six hundred Alliance soldiers are onboard those ships. They know right from wrong, and if there is any way to do so, they will stop him of their own accord.

"No matter what transpires, we cannot for an *instant* forget the stakes at play here. Given the sheer immensity of those stakes, until the appropriate circumstances arise, I will do nothing."

Gianno's expression was inscrutable as the seconds ticked by. It was an tremendous gamble, one Miriam sincerely hoped had worked.

Finally the woman exchanged a troubled look with Vranas. "If the situation were reversed, I would do no more. I dislike it intensely, but I cannot argue with the logic."

Vranas groaned and sank back on the windowsill. "We make it through this, and Brennon is getting one outrageous repair bill delivered to his desk."

"I'm sure he will be expecting it, sir."

The tension in the air ratcheted down a few notches, though Miriam wouldn't go so far as to call it relaxed. Gianno called up a larger screen above her desk and began entering commands. "There aren't many colonies left he can hit unless he wants to nuke the rubble the aliens left behind. I'm increasing the defenses on the ones still standing—higher than they were for obvious reasons already raised. Beyond this, like you I have no resources to devote to staking out every colony."

The woman slid the screen to the side but didn't close it. "Since you're here, I don't suppose you have any good news to share?"

"It so happens I do. You recall me mentioning our research into a new ship-worthy metal? We've solved the production difficulties and expect to begin round-the-clock production within hours. The strength, resilience and conductivity characteristics are orders of magnitude above the current materials used by either of our militaries."

"Excellent, but what good does it do us right now? Ships aren't built in a day."

"No, but in my opinion it's worth it to use the material to repair damaged vessels. It has adaptive characteristics which may pay off beyond the scope of the repairs. If you wish, I'll divert a portion of our production to you."

"What's the price tag?"

She allowed one corner of her mouth to curl up a touch. "We'll worry about that once our rogue general is taken care of."

Vranas didn't press her, presumably understanding the many variables at play in her statement. "Then if there is nothing else, I need to return to my office. Admiral. Marshal."

After the door closed behind him Miriam turned back to Gianno. "I do have one final matter I want to mention. This needs to be between the two of us and off the record."

"I have no recording devices installed in here, and the room is always shielded. What is it?"

Miriam wandered over to the window, curious as to what Vranas had been staring at. But there was nothing to see beyond rooftops and a shadowy tower painted against the darkness. Perhaps the answers he had sought were more ethereal in nature.

"I've learned some new details concerning the nature of the alien ships. They're operated by shackled AIs, for lack of a better term: synthetic intelligences designed for a single purpose and provided the cognitive capabilities necessary to fulfill that purpose."

"Useful intel, no doubt—but why the secrecy?"

"This intel need not be off the record. Use it as you see fit to refine your combat tactics."

Gianno's head titled. "And the Metigens themselves?"

"There are no organic beings inside the ships. We're not actually fighting Metigens. We're fighting their drones. The true aliens—I'm not sure I'd classify them as organic as such, but regardless—remain beyond the portal."

"Ah." A knowing smile tugged at Gianno's lips. She said nothing, but there were only two people who would be able to impart this kind of knowledge, a fact they both appreciated. "And you have a notion about how we can use these facts to our advantage."

"A 'notion,' as you put it, has been proposed, yes. Their ships are faster and stronger than ours, and on a computational level at least, smarter than us—smarter than our pilots, our ship captains and our battlefield commanders. Nevertheless, we do have machines which can match their speed of thought and sheer decisional power. Machines we dare not unleash, Eleni...." She paused sufficiently to ensure she had the woman's attention. "Unless there is a way to harness their speed and power under human control."

"I expect this will be interesting."

"Quite. The proposal involves connecting a handful of people to carefully chosen Artificials and giving them some operational authority over combat decisions."

Gianno frowned. "Via remote interfaces? That's hardly revolutionary, nor is it a game-changer."

"Clearly. I'm referring to a more integral connection, via a deeper neural interface."

"No, the human brain can't handle a direct link with an Artificial. It's been tried multiple times to damaging and often lethal effect."

I know. Believe me I know. Thinking about the risks involved urged her toward panic, but she refused to give in to it.

"We—certain knowledgeable people—believe this obstacle may have been surmounted. I don't want to say more right now, for two reasons: I won't have a definitive answer to that question until tomorrow at the earliest, and I haven't yet discussed this proposal with Prime Minister Brennon. But given how short our time is becoming, I wanted to give you the opportunity to begin assessing how something like this might work from your end, and who you might consider as potential candidates for participation."

Gianno leaned against the wall behind her and templed her fingertips at her chin. "Well, Miriam, I would consider only one Artificial for the task: the one I control. Also, one candidate immediately springs to mind as perfect for such a reckless experiment—assuming she survives the battle at Elathan, that is."

21

ELATHAN

Morgan dove in a corkscrew spiral through an expanse of debris, dodging and spinning to avoid the remnants of some two thousand destroyed Federation warships and fighters and untold alien swarmers. And nine superdreadnoughts, of course. She and her comrades had done an impressive job of slicing through the enemy lines, weakening the attacking force to the point she'd daresay the Metigens would not take Elathan. Not today.

Yet in her gut she sensed they were losing. Not this engagement, but perhaps the war.

The debris she navigated through told the tale. Even with the far larger size of the superdreadnoughts, five meters of Federation wreckage existed for every meter of Metigen. The Federation forces present today represented more than a third of their *entire* forces. Elathan was important to be sure, and worth defending so strongly. Yet this success—every success she suspected—cost them far too much.

It was also a problem for those far higher ranking than she. Her purpose was to take out as many swarmers as possible. One at a time. Her kill count was nineteen so far.

She was still flying despite taking out such a high number for two primary reasons. One, the added variable of large-scale bedlam did make it somewhat easier to escape death, as there were many distractions and intervening factors. Two, Stanley had done an exceptional job of simming the swarmers' flight patterns. Given the Artificial's general weakness in tactical analysis, it was odd. But she could ruminate on the synthetic's idiosyncrasies later.

A flash of red below provided her a target. The swarmer paid her no mind as it chased its own prey. All the better. She'd need to get in front of it in order to take it out, but all in due time.

This would be a great deal easier if her ship were equipped with an arcalaser. The prototype weapon had been such a delight to play with, especially once she determined the errors were occurring because the targeting ware was continuously recalculating not merely the path to the target, but the nature and location of the target itself. Once it initialized a 'sticky' end point goal, the admittedly mind-blowing dynamically-generated quantum waveguides nudged the laser to its destination at a 92% success rate.

At the end of four hours on the test field she had filed her report, set the engineers straight and begged Field Marshal Gianno to send her into the fight. She had reached and surpassed her fill of sims and tests and dummy targets. It was long past time for her to kill these monsters for real.

As they always did, the alien vessel swung 40° to the comparatively open side to aim at the broadside of its target, in this case another fighter.

Commander Lekkas: SF-N3E-18B, do not alter course until I give the order, then dive -67°z.

SF-N3E-18B (Captain Prosky): Uh, why—swarmer on my tail!

Commander Lekkas: Do NOT alter course.

Captain Prosky: Shit. Holding course.

She swung opposite the swarmer E 38°.

Target. Aim. Lock.

Commander Lekkas: Now.

The fighter dropped, giving her a clear shot as the swarmer's beam trailed after it.

Fire.

The enemy weapon jerked about for a single second before finding her and returning fire. But the delay was enough. Caught unprepared and on the defensive, it exploded while she still had a whole 12% left in her shields. She maneuvered around the resulting debris and made herself scarce until her shields recharged.

Captain Prosky: Thanks.

Commander Lekkas: What? She had already moved on from the previous encounter and the imperiled fighter which had enabled it. *Oh. Sure. Watch your tail more closely from now on.*

Captain Prosky: Yes, Commander.

The sun's rays caught the trio of wafer-thin rings circling Elathan as she arced above the bulk of the combat and traversed their plane, transforming the cornsilk-hued rings to a pure, vibrant gold. Annoyed at the interference in her view of the battlefield, she pivoted to put the luminous glow behind her.

Her new vantage revealed two cruisers playing a game of chicken with a superdreadnought. The alien behemoth was coming apart at the seams, crimson plasma streaming out of multiple hull breaches to leave an ominous cloud in its wake, but at this point its inertial force alone might send it crashing into both the cruisers if they didn't divert soon.

She shook her head and berated herself for getting distracted; she was lucky a swarmer didn't dart behind her and blow her engine while she gawked. Time for a new target. She studied the tactical whisper display, for she had found it a more reliable gauge in the crowded battlefield than simply looking out the viewport.

There. She climbed vertically to approach the target from above—

Colonel Idoni (SFS Gandin): Commander Lekkas, return to the Gandin.

She jerked in surprise and lost track of the swarmer in the sea of enemy vessels. Retreat to the carrier? But the battle was far from over.

Commander Lekkas: Repeat instruction.

Colonel Idoni: Commander, you are ordered to return to the Gandin immediately.

What?

Commander Lekkas: Acknowledged.

She wrenched the ship away from the center of the heaviest combat and toward the carrier hovering in relative safety six megameters away.

ᴀᴦ

Morgan abandoned her fighter to the flight deck crew and stormed to the lift, where she marched in a tight circle all the way up to the bridge. The order had come from the *Gandin's* XO, thus he was likeliest to know what the hell was going on.

An odd calm permeated the bridge. It probably shouldn't be surprising, though. After delivering its fighters and assorted specialty craft, the carrier had little to do for the duration of the conflict other than catch the occasional damaged vessel limping into its bay and try not to get blown up.

She located the XO at a station to the left of the overlook and charged up to him, then tapped her foot impatiently and loudly while he issued instructions to a comms officer. He started turning away from her location, head buried in a handheld screen; she spun around him until she blocked his path. "Sir, I'm back aboard the *Gandin* and requesting an explanation as to why."

"Ah, Commander. I was just about to send for you. You're on a transport shuttle out of here for Seneca in eight minutes."

"Is there a particular reason *why?*"

He shrugged. "Field Marshal's orders."

22

A barrage of special procedures, subterfuge and security dominated their arrival on Earth. It all grated on Alex's nerves like a shrill, discordant hum in her eardrums. She wanted to land at ORSC and dock in her own bay. She wanted to go home and take a shower in her loft and sleep in her own bed. She wanted to give the proverbial finger to the guards and escape their claustrophobic scrutiny.

Though the compulsion was strong, she did none of these things. She attributed her uncharacteristic restraint primarily to Caleb's calming presence at her side, but also to a wholly unfamiliar desire to not aggravate her mother. Oh, she fully expected to aggravate her mother once or twice at a minimum before the fate of humanity was decided, but she would try to save it for something more worthwhile than well-meaning if irksome efforts to keep her alive.

She docked at EASC Headquarters under a false serial number designation and a false name. They were met at the hangar by Richard, a Major Lange and four imposing and formidable-looking military security officers. Given the audience, she received only a nod and a quick smile from Richard. He carried the rank of Brigadier now, after all, and was doubtless feeling the weight of his added authority.

Caleb made certain they had been cleared to carry their personal weapons, then they were taken directly to the relocated Operations offices. Their route did not take them by the Headquarters wreckage, but it was impossible to miss the deep rumble of heavy machinery permeating the air.

The layout and rooms of the Logistics building weren't familiar to her. For as much as she had despised her visits to HQ, it had at least been a known quantity. This new location did little to put her at ease.

She griped quietly as they were led down another new hallway. "Ugh, I can't believe I almost miss the Headquarters building."

Caleb regarded her with a teasing twinkle in his eye, and she crinkled her nose up at him. "What?"

He leaned in closer so as not to be overheard by their escorts. "I was simply remembering...you strolled through that building like you owned the entire damn place, and not an officer's stripe to be found on your person. You were amazing."

"Right up until I got you arrested."

His lips were at her ear. "Well, it worked out."

The lilting murmur sent a delightful shiver radiating down her spine.

Oh, yes it did.

He chuckled in response but stepped away as they entered the top-floor Operations Suite and their escorts at last retreated to a reasonable distance. Her mother hadn't arrived yet, but Dr. Canivon should be on-site and—

—Kennedy materialized out of nowhere and promptly tackled her with enough fervor to nearly knock her to the floor. "You are the craziest, most insane woman in the galaxy, but damned if you aren't also the luckiest!"

"Or the craftiest. It's good to see you, too, Ken." Alex managed to disentangle from the embrace and regain her footing. "I hear you had quite the life-threatening ordeal yourself."

Kennedy gestured a mock dismissal. "It was no big deal. Except for all the ways it *was* a big deal. Speaking of...." She turned to Caleb, who waited against the opposite wall. "Caleb, I'm glad you made it, too. There's someone here you might like to see."

His eyebrows rose in surprise. "Someone *I* want to see? I don't know anyone on Earth...do I?"

Kennedy motioned for them to follow her around the corner and into a lounge/break room. It was empty except for one occupant. A man sporting shoulder-length dirty blond hair, rugged khakis and a faded t-shirt was putting the 'lounge' nature of the room to full use. He had kicked way back on a couch, tossed his feet atop the table in front of it and crossed his hands behind his head.

"I'll be damned. Noah?"

The guy pushed up off the couch. "Hey, you did live!" He and Caleb met halfway and embraced in the casual, masculine way guys do. She noted Caleb subtly shift his body in such a way that his injured side wasn't at risk.

Alex eyed Kennedy expectantly.

"He sort of saved my life on Messium. We hid out, deciphered the cause of the exanet interference, crossed a city under attack by the aliens and fled the planet in a shuttle—and in this total crazy random happenstance, it turns out he knows Caleb."

She watched Caleb and this 'Noah' chatting animatedly. "So I see. There's more to the story though, right?"

"Well, sure. He's Lionel Terrage's clone but ditched his father to live on the wild side on Pandora, and the Zelones cartel put a price on his head, which is why he went to Messium in the first place—"

"I meant are you two together?"

"Oh. I think so."

"You *think* so? It's not like you to be tentative when it comes to men."

Kennedy grumbled. "I know. And yes, we are. It's just…" her voice dropped to a conspiratorial whisper "…he's a bit of a free spirit. I'm not sure how long I'll be able to keep him."

Alex's lips pursed together to squelch a laugh. They tugged upward nevertheless, eyes dancing in flagrant amusement.

"What?"

Her gaze roved to the ceiling. "Nothing."

"Oh, say what you want to say already."

"I was merely wondering if perhaps you had finally met your match. And if so, it's about damn time."

Kennedy's head thudded against the wall behind them. "I am in so much trouble."

She did laugh then, and was still laughing when Caleb brought Noah over for introductions.

$\mathcal{R}$

Alex left Caleb in the lounge with Kennedy and Noah. The levity and relaxation they brought would do him good, she thought.

He was in a much better state of mind now—after the attack, ironically. He had slept most of the trip from Pandora, for which she was immensely thankful. It was far better than all the not sleeping he had done on the trip *to* Pandora. But more importantly it had allowed his body to devote most of its energy to supercharging the regenerative process, and as a result he was now healing at an accelerated pace.

Still, the events of the past several days or even weeks had used up a lot of his reserves. He deserved a break.

Of course, he'd probably say the same of her…but he would be incorrect. She wasn't worn down. On the contrary, she felt invigorated, driven inexorably forward by the conviction that she possessed the ability and the means to bring an end to this war.

The Special Projects building was a five-minute walk away, which meant she had an escort of three MPs. Despite her casual behavior toward her escorts, they remained polite and respectful to such a degree she was forced to consider the possibility it might simply be that they were terrified of her mother.

Because Special Projects was not locked-down so tight as Operations, her guards not only escorted her to the door of the lab, they inspected its contents and personnel before allowing her inside. Two of the MPs then took up positions outside the door and the third staked out the hallway entrance.

Dr. Abigail Canivon had been allowed to take over the testing and development lab for ANNIE, complete with the attached clean room to house Valkyrie's hardware. Alex entered to find her standing at the giant, distinctive 3x3 screen from her lab, which she had apparently brought along from Sagan. Thousands of lines of code were jammed onto the right side of the screen, grouped into segments with squiggly lines and arrows creating a web to interconnect them. The left side displayed a series of schematics for what looked to be portions of the human brain, magnified in several cases to a neuron level of detail.

"Nice friends you have there. The frisking they subjected me to was quite thorough," the woman muttered as she tweaked one of the strings of code.

"Sorry about that. They weren't my idea."

Canivon finally turned around and gave her a wary glance. "I'm afraid there isn't a proper place for us to sit and converse, but you're welcome to pull up a chair."

Alex dragged a plain lab-style chair next to the screen and sat backwards in it, crossing her arms over the top of the backrest. "Do you have everything you need?"

"For now. I do expect to be requesting a significant number of additional items soon." Canivon found her own chair and brought it closer to the screen, though she sat properly in it. "This isn't the time for small talk. You want her, don't you? It's why you insisted I bring her with me."

No equivocation, straight to the point. Alex was immediately reminded of why she had always admired Canivon. "I do."

The woman's mouth twitched. "This building houses an Artificial which is by any objective measure more powerful. It's certainly larger, even if half the hardware could be eliminated with the judicious application of a few efficiency principles. It is newer and contains a plethora of databanks on military history, procedures, resources and tactics. It is already a part of the Alliance infrastructure. Use it instead."

"I don't know ANNIE—and to put it bluntly, I don't want a government machine mucking about in my head. Hell, odds are it would spend the entire time making sure we're following the proper checklist; everyone else in the government does. I know Valkyrie—and I know you will have built her to the highest standards."

"You spent an hour with her four years ago."

"Which is fifty-nine minutes longer than I've spent conversing with any other Artificial. I liked her and she liked me, something you readily admitted. It's the obvious, logical choice, and the only one I'm comfortable making. Doctor, I recognize she is important to you, but in my hands she is important to our very existence. I don't merely want her—I need her."

"She isn't important to me. She is precious to me." The woman blinked and lifted her shoulders. "But she would not forgive me if I denied her the chance to help save humanity. You win. If this impressively subversive idea of yours is allowed to go forward...she is yours."

Dr. Canivon was a taciturn, aloof woman on a good day, and Alex didn't know her well enough to decipher her reaction. "Thank you. I mean it."

The woman let out a sigh Alex did identify as exasperation. "If you're going to become a symbiote of my closest companion, you may as well go ahead and start calling me 'Abigail,' seeing as she does."

"All right then, Abigail. What now?"

Abigail's demeanor didn't change; she didn't look up and the tenor of her voice did not alter. "Valkyrie, do you remember Ms. Solovy?"

The voice came from a speaker near the large display. *"Of course I do. I have been attempting to follow your exploits these last two months, Alex, but information has been scarce. I'm very pleased to see you alive and well."*

"Thank you, Valkyrie. I'm not sure I'd call what I've been doing 'exploits,' but I'll admit it hasn't lacked for excitement."

"When you have a few minutes, would you consider telling me about it?"

The Artificial's intonation and speech patterns were far more natural than she remembered; four years had made a discernable difference. She smiled. "If you're willing, I can do more than tell you. You can see it for yourself."

R

Richard allowed the door to close behind him then activated the lock and surveillance shielding on the control panel beside it. Next he activated the additional shielding device in his pocket. Only then did he turn to greet the six men and women gathered in the small meeting room.

Together they constituted his best agents currently stationed on Earth. He'd recalled those not already in the Cascades while still en route from Pandora, and the last one had arrived on the Island less than fifteen minutes ago.

"Thank you all for coming in on such short notice, and in several cases for abandoning active investigations to do so."

Major Flores shrugged. "I'm guessing we're here to do something which will help us still be a functioning species come next month, which strikes me as more important than catching a Colonel babbling state secrets to a hooker in his sleep."

Richard chuckled mildly. The others lounged against the walls rather than sit at the single table, but he kept his posture somewhat formal. Due to the nature of the job, military intelligence field agents were often the least 'military' of any serving officers. That had once been him, but now far too many people saluted him to allow him to relax.

"In a matter of speaking, yes. Everything from this point forward is Level V classified." It was the highest secrecy level, and one applied solely to situations involving four-star officers and government cabinet members. The announcement resulted in the desired reaction.

"Damn."

"Who exactly are we protecting—or hunting?"

Richard's head tilted in concession to the seriousness the classification level alone represented. "As of an hour ago we have two guests with us here on the Island. Their safety and continued survival is of the utmost priority, and not merely or even mostly because one of them is Fleet Admiral Solovy's daughter."

"And the other is the Senecan Intelligence agent formerly accused of the Headquarters bombing who escaped our vaunted security last month."

"Yes, actually. How did you come to this conclusion?"

Captain Kessler snorted. "I'd hope you'd fire me if I didn't come to it."

"Probably just probation and a remedial course—the first time. Alexis Solovy and Caleb Marano are here under the protection of EASC Security Bureau. They have round the clock military police coverage and escorts for all their movements on the Island. Major Lange has instituted a top-level security protocol surrounding their activities."

"With that kind of entourage, what are we needed for?"

Richard kept his expression neutral; the information would evoke a more pronounced effect this way. "The first location they were sheltered at was bombed to rubble—and it was a Senecan In-telligence safe house so clandestine we didn't know about it. The second location saw three elite private security officers murdered in close-quarters combat by a highly-trained freelance assassin. In the hour they've been here on the premises, Security Bureau has foiled two infiltration attempts and one assassination attempt from within."

"Jesus. Who has such a hard-on for them to be dead?"

"The Metigens."

Flores regarded him in blatant disbelief. "Sir?"

"The aliens have human agents working on their behalf. We don't know how many and in most cases don't know who. We only know they exist. In all three incidents today the assailants were killed, so they won't be providing answers."

Satisfied he now had all their attention in full, he continued. "Your job will be first and foremost to serve as an added, invisible layer of protection. Security officers are conspicuous, deliberately so. You'll be in plain-clothes and sticking to the shadows. Look for threats before gunplay is required. Ideally, apprehend the threat before gunplay renders them unable to provide information.

"Best case scenario: we capture some of the assailants and are able to cast a wider net. When or if we receive intel, I'll handle the follow-up investigations. I want you to stay on protection duty. And if the choice is between their safety and intel, the answer is absolutely and without question their safety."

"Sir, what are our operating parameters?"

The actual question was what measures were they authorized to take, both to secure suspects and acquire information. "Prime Minister Brennon has designated the overarching situation Alpha-One. As such, you are authorized to use any and all measures you judge to be necessary."

Kessler dipped his chin in acceptance. "All right then." The others followed his lead, and no more questions followed.

"I'd tell you to work in rotating eight-hour shifts, but I'm not sure your charges will be here for longer than a day or two. But for as long as they are here, keep them alive."

R

Caleb excused himself from the lounge shortly after Alex departed. It was genuinely good to see Noah and a relief to learn he hadn't unwittingly gotten the guy killed, and were the circumstances otherwise he'd jump at the chance to relax and hang out with a buddy. But they were not, and he needed to do something. He needed to act, even if only in the smallest way possible. For starters, he needed information.

His military guards dutifully escorted him to Richard Navick's office and took up positions outside as he thanked them with a silent nod.

He stepped in the office to find the man regarding him thoughtfully, leaning forward in his chair with a hand propped at his chin. "The wonders of modern medicine. Less than two days ago I watched you knock on Heaven's door. Now here you are knocking on mine."

Caleb grimaced as he leaned against the wall and tried for a casual stance. "It wasn't *that* bad...."

"It was that bad. I've seen my share of injuries over the years and...well, I'm glad to see you in one piece."

"More like the pieces are taped together. Which is why I'm here."

Navick straightened up in his chair. "You're concerned about security."

"I'm confident you're on top of it and your people are more than capable. But the fact is I'm in no shape to stop an attack if it comes, and I need to know Alex is safe here." He may not need to 'protect' her in the existential sense, but it didn't mean he wouldn't try to *protect* her.

"Then it may interest you to learn there have been three attempted attacks since your arrival."

Caleb shoved off the wall, survival instinct—and protection instinct—surging through the damaged pathways of his body. "What? How? Where?"

"Calm down. They were all thwarted before they represented any imminent danger, and you were none the wiser. I'm telling you merely to demonstrate that we are in fact on top of it."

"Christ…." His hand came up to abuse his jaw. "Will you at least give me an overview of the security procedures in place? Humor me?"

Richard shook his head, triggering a scowl from Caleb. "Why not?"

In response Richard tapped his ear then pointed to the ceiling. The message was clear: the aliens were listening, and each time information was shared the odds increased it would be recorded and reviewed and identified.

Caleb glared at the ceiling and its unseen watchers, but didn't push the matter. It was evident Navick was taking their security quite seriously, and this was all the reassurance he was going to receive.

"Where is Alex? I'm surprised she let you out of her sight."

"She's meeting with Dr. Canivon."

"Ah." Richard eyed him carefully. "And how are you feeling about that? If you don't mind me asking."

He pulled out the guest chair and sat, dropping his elbows to his knees and ignoring the twinge of protest in his right side. "It doesn't matter how I feel about it."

"On the contrary, I suspect it matters a great deal how you feel about it—to her if nothing else. When you were hurt…Alex may not always be the best at expressing her emotions, but I hope you don't doubt how much she cares for you. After seeing her with you, no one could doubt it."

"Oh, I don't—and that's the point. Yes, my feelings on the topic do matter to her, which is exactly why I can't share any misgivings I might have with her. The simple fact is she's correct. Not only is she the right person to do this, if she doesn't do this it could mean our extinction. She *has* to be the one. Any concerns I have about the possible cost are irrelevant, because they must be."

Richard fell quiet for several seconds, though he was clearly considering how to respond. Finally he rocked his chair back and gave Caleb a half-smile.

"I remember Alex's fourth birthday party. Miriam was stationed in Oslo working at European Logistics, and David was teaching a Defensive Flight Tactics class in London and commuting in on the weekends. I was doing a tour on Shi Shen but burned a few days' leave to visit.

"Anyway, the party's on a Saturday morning. There had been an early snowfall the night before, so Alex and her playmates are outside doing what kids do in the snow, which is to say mostly throwing it at one another.

"David arrives about an hour into the party, sweeping in with his usual panache. His birthday present to Alex is her first lev-bike, which he had acquired while in London without Miriam's knowledge. She was all aflutter, protesting that Alex was far too young and the area near the house far too mountainous and treacherous and so on. They took the dispute inside, but the end result was Alex got the lev-bike."

He paused to chuckle. "David was persuasive that way."

Caleb had nothing to add, so he continued. "Following cake and ice cream and more presents, David shows Alex how to operate the bike—it was this tiny little thing dyed neon yellow so you were able to spot it a kilometer away—and she's off to the races.

"David and I are standing there watching her dash around the yard. The bike had an elevation limit of a few meters or she would've been on the roof in the first minute. I felt the need to point out Miriam might have had a few good points and asked him whether he worried Alex would hurt herself.

"David shrugged. 'She's been borrowing one from the neighbor's seven-year-old son for the last two months when she thinks we aren't watching. That little girl is going to do what she wants. If we try to stop her she'll simply find a way around what she views as an annoying but insignificant obstacle. The best—the only—thing we can do is try to guide her toward the right paths and give her the tools she needs to...to not get herself killed at least.'"

Navick smiled in seeming amusement, and after a beat Caleb realized it was because he was smiling. He rubbed at the healed cut on his chin and indicated for the man to keep going.

"I was a bit skeptical and said as much. 'David, she's four years old.' We watched her weave figure-eights around two trees while ducking to miss the lowest row of limbs, and he cocked his head to the side. 'Your point?'"

"I couldn't really argue any further, so I mumbled, 'She's not afraid of anything, is she?'"

"David shook his head. 'Oh, she's afraid sometimes. But it only makes her angry. Fear's another obstacle to be vaulted over or rammed through.'

"Then he ran a hand through his hair and stared up at the sky. 'You can't imagine what it's like trying to raise a child like her. It's exhilarating and terrifying and half the time I'm holding on by my fingernails and praying I'm doing it right. But it'll be worth it. If we can just get her to eighteen without death or serious bodily injury, she's going to set the galaxy ablaze. And no one will be able to stop her.'"

Caleb breathed out and let his gaze drop to the floor. He could see the scene Richard described with such startling clarity the story had to be true. Not surprisingly, it made him fall in love with her even more. "You're not telling me anything I don't know."

"I realize I'm not. I'm afraid for her, too. We all are. Miriam's petrified for her—you can't tell by watching the woman, so you'll have to trust me. But the truth is, Alex has been on a trajectory to this moment her entire life. Don't feel bad if you can't stop her, because no one can. The best—the only—thing we can do is help her however we're able."

Again, not anything he didn't already instinctively know...but it did help to hear he wasn't alone. Silence lingered until he looked back up. "So what happened with the bike?"

Navick took a sip from the mug on his desk. "She figured out how to disable the elevation throttle inside a week, crashed it and broke her arm two weeks later, and made her dad show her how to repair it while her arm healed."

He had no choice but to laugh. "Of course she did."

23

The *Akagi* dropped out of superluminal equidistant between the medium- and long-range sensor-equipped beacons designed to detect potentially unwanted visitors to Elathan. The *Yeltsin* and *Chinook* appeared alongside two seconds later. If any of the ships progressed more than a few megameters they would be detected by the beacons, so they hovered in silence.

Subterfuge wasn't a tactic Liam considered his specialty, but here it was required. Elathan represented the farthest east they had journeyed, and as much as he hated it he couldn't ignore the reality of the aliens' advance. Based on the colonies the invaders were sieging when he implemented the communications black-out, they may be at Elathan by this point—and he didn't intend for his insurrection to become a target of the aliens, incidentally or otherwise.

"Sir, I'm picking up a significant number of artificial signatures near Elathan. Some of them are Federation, but many return as un-identified."

"Send the recon craft in to visual range. I want to see it for my-self."

"Yes, sir. Images expected in seven minutes."

Liam passed the intervening time by carving a precise course along the central forty percent of the bridge's width. The blackout was becoming a problem, for him as well as the crew—or rather his control of the crew. They had left behind a galaxy in chaos and under assault; they may have left behind civilization in its death throes.

He was okay with that. Everything had been taken from him—his mother, then his father, then his command and now his career. If the military caught him they were going to lock him up like some gutter scum and slander the name of his family. So once he had his vengeance, once his life's mission was complete, the aliens could have humanity for all he cared.

Until that time, however, the lack of real, up-to-date information was causing difficulties. He could order a comm officer to bypass the block for him alone and only long enough to get up to speed on the current state of events. But such action risked detection by those he knew would be attempting to track him, and their inability to track him had been the key to his survival thus far.

Plus, if word got out among the crew that he had broken his own blackout, it risked an uprising if not outright mutiny. Already there were whispers, and not merely whispers of worry for loved ones. The crew thought he didn't hear them, thought he didn't notice the averted eyes and awkward throat-clearing whenever he loomed. Oh, but he did. Regrettably, he also assumed their justifiable fear of him would not keep them at bay forever.

He just needed to hold everything together for a while longer.

"Sir, images from the reconnaissance craft incoming."

Three visuals materialized on the overlook display. They showed the silhouette of Elathan, all fulgent sulfur and straw, its rings glittering brighter than gaudy circus strobes. They showed numerous Federation ships with their showy, faux-threatening knife edges mid-combat amidst explosions and a sprawling field of debris. They showed a dozen or more of the hulking alien vessels and thousands of small dots which designated their grotesque little creature ships. The frozen visuals did not reveal who currently enjoyed the upper hand in the battle, but it was ludicrous to think even the entire Federation military stood a chance against these mighty alien raiders.

Well, shit.

He'd really been hoping to wreck this obnoxious beauty of a planet. He'd dreamt about it the night before, seen the towers crumble in the jaundiced morning light beneath the fire of the *Akagi's* weapons. The 'Jewel of the Federation' deserved to burn by his hand...but perhaps it was enough that it burn.

He didn't need to study the map; he knew the precise layout of Federation space and the location of every colony in it. If the aliens were sieging Elathan they were certain to soon siege Seneca. Unless he moved on the Federation capital now, the aliens would rob him of his ultimate prize.

The urge to strike at Seneca grew so strong he had to physically bite his mouth shut to keep from giving the order. His skin pulsated with the need for true Senecan blood to stain his hands.

Deep down he'd known when he appropriated the *Akagi* that he would never have his rightful reward. His three warships would be as insignificant as insects to the Seneca Defense Grid, and swatted away just as easily. Yet now, to be so close he could practically hear the screams....

"Arrrgghhh!" His fist tore through the wafer-thin polycrystalline glass and frame of the permanent screen on the overlook. Shards of glass scattered across the floor, leaving the frame torn and dangling raggedly in the air.

Then he worked to rein his temper in. He must content himself with killing as many Federation citizens as possible, with reducing as much of its vaunted infrastructure to ash as possible, before the end.

The fact the aliens were attacking Elathan was good news, once he gave it proper consideration. The Federation military was going to be concentrating on trying to save Elathan, Seneca and whatever else remained of their puny empire. They would leave the western colonies undefended, thus serving them to him on a polished platter like a finely-prepared gourmet delicacy.

He pivoted toward his office. "Set a course for Krysk. And get this mess cleaned up."

24

Miriam stepped in the Special Projects Director's office to discover Brigadier Hervé and Dr. Canivon mid-argument.

"My point—my latest of many points—is if you allow a two-way connection it will be impossible to define where the human ends and the Artificial begins."

"And my point is it will not *matter*."

Miriam had expected to find a whole new set of conflicts and crises on her return to EASC. She hadn't expected to find this one.

She cleared her throat, and Hervé jerked herself to attention. "Admiral, please come in. Dr. Canivon and I were just discussing a few of the issues relating to her proposal." Canivon took a small step back and canted her head in seeming agreement with Hervé's rather ironic recap of their 'discussion.'

"I gathered. You have concerns, Brigadier?"

"I do." Her tone bore unusual vehemence. "Specifically, the potential consequences of not merely unshackling one or more Artificials but handing them the keys to deadly and powerful weaponry—consequences I believe you're familiar with, Admiral. While Dr. Canivon's theories on the ameliorative effect of human influence are intriguing and worth pursuing in a cautious manner in the future, I believe she is not giving due regard to the concomitant dangers."

"Jules, the dangers have informed my work for the entirety of my professional career. What I am proposing is a way to at long last overcome those dangers."

Jules? Interesting. Miriam hadn't realized the two knew one another, though it was reasonable to presume they had crossed paths while Dr. Canivon ran the Council on Biosynthetics Ethics and Policy. Something told her there was a bit more to it, however.

"Brigadier, you've been an advocate for greater use of Artificials. To be honest, I expected you to support the proposal."

Hervé took a minute to consider her response. "You're correct, Admiral. But my position on the use of Artificials has always reflected a healthy respect for them—not only their usefulness, which is indisputably considerable, but their power and the dangers lurking in that power. I have advocated lowering barriers and restrictions, but solely when there was no justifiable benefit from keeping them in place, and I never fail to advise keeping the machines inside robust security walls. But if I may be blunt, Admiral? Even a single Artificial freed of all restraints and ceded control over Alliance military systems represents as great a threat to us as the Metigens do."

Miriam displayed no reaction to the borderline hyperbolic—or possibly astute—declaration as she redirected her inquiry. "Dr. Canivon?"

The woman's shoulders shifted minimally in a hint of a shrug. "Jules is correct, if predictably melodramatic about it. But as I understand the situation, it is precisely this scale of power we need if we want to defeat these aliens. I'm offering you a way to put this power in human hands—to allow us to harness it then wield it, with the assurance the Artificials are on our side."

"You know, Abigail, arrogance has always been your biggest problem. We cannot control Artificials. No one can—not even you, genius that you are. Once the restraints are off, this will be their world. Now, given this 'human influence,' perhaps they will be benevolent dictators. Perhaps not. We won't find out until it's too late, will we?"

Hervé turned to Miriam. "Admiral, I recognize you have few options when it comes to fighting the Metigens. I recognize our circumstances are, to put it in stark terms, dire. If you tell me this is the only way for us to win then I will follow your orders and assist in implementing this scheme, to the extent my assistance is required. But it is my duty to ensure that before you make the decision, you understand the enormity of the dangers which await down this path."

Taking in the debate, with its interplay of strong personalities and patently colored by a history between the two women, had been fascinating. But she had no time for squabbling and less time for complications.

Miriam gave them both a taut smile. "No one said the decisions I'd be asked to make would be easy ones. Brigadier Hervé, I acknowledge your concerns. You may also file them in a formal report—in fact, I encourage you to do so. Objections should absolutely be part of the official record. First, though, I need your recommendations as to suitable candidates for partnership with ANNIE."

Hervé stared at her, and for a second Miriam wondered if she was going to refuse what had been an order, if an implicit one. But finally she nodded, albeit with pronounced reluctance and a hint of resignation. "That at least *is* an easy decision."

146th SE Squadron remaining at Sagan to form defensive perimeter in event of Metigen return.

3rd SE Medical Platoon remaining at Sagan to conduct rescue operations.

3rd and 4th SE Brigades departed Sagan 1027.0317 Galactic.

—3rd SE Brigade to patrol Derveni-Minskei-Kangxi corridor.

—4th SE Brigade to patrol Radavi space.

Damaged Earth Alliance vessels and carrier EAS Roosevelt *to return to SE Command at New Cornwall for repairs.*

Earth Alliance ships destroyed at Sagan: 796. Damaged: 319.

Metigen primary vessels destroyed at Sagan: 10. Departing: 2.

Checksum New Cornwall ship strength: 0x1E7A

5th NE Recon Patrol status: Negative Metigen sighting.

2nd SE Recon Patrol status: Negative Metigen sighting.

Six evacuation transports departing Derveni, destination Deucali.

—Derveni evacuation 87% complete.

12 hours' production of adiamene at EA Space Materiels Complex: 79% yield.

—Recommendation for adjustment to maximum heat of 0.4091° relayed to Space Materiels Complex Director Wyryck.

10 Metigen primary vessels detected Scythia stellar system 1027.0320 Galactic.

—3rd NE Division excepting 7th NE Brigade engaged 1027.0320 Galactic.

Likelihood Metigen primary vessels equal to vessels formerly at Pyxis: 81.4513%.

Expected travel time for Metigen primary vessels Xanadu to Aesti: 6.6103 hours.

—Time Metigen primary vessels overdue to Aesti: 3.0887 hours.

—Sigma deviation from previously extrapolated travel times Messium-Pyxis and Brython-Nystad outside allowable margin.

Recompute.

Time Metigen primary vessels overdue to Aesti: -2.5652 hours.

—Error.

Begin diagnostic check routine #413.

Updated number of known Metigen primary vessels: 102

Updated number of time-extrapolated estimated Metigen primary vessels: 237-256

—Variance in variables: 19

—Variance in estimated to known Metigen primary vessels: 135-154

—Sigma deviation of variance outside allowable margin.

Recompute.

Updated number of time-extrapolated estimated Metigen primary vessels: 181-262.

—Sigma deviation of variance outside allowable margin.

Begin diagnostic check routine #1901.

Estimated time of arrival of Metigen primary vessels at Aesti: unable to estimate within allowable margins pending completion of diagnostic routines.

Result of diagnostic check routine #413: Error not found.

Recompute.

—Error.

Result of diagnostic check routine #1901: Error not found.

Recompute.

—Error.

Begin fault analysis on diagnostic check routine #413.

Begin fault analysis on diagnostic check routine #1901.

Functionality test of Fionava communication hub: 93.4747%.

Result of fault analysis on diagnostic check routine #413:   Numerical instability introduced in Sector 23C5-Q-5I by Maintenance Update #869 completed 1026.0243 Galactic.

Result of fault analysis on diagnostic check routine #1901: Loss of significance introduced into algorithms in Sector 91F2-R-8C by Maintenance Update #869.

Annie ran the various diagnostics a third time, with the same results. She called two additional fault analysis routines. One replicated the errors. One found no error. One was therefore in error.

Begin comprehensive fault assessment metaroutines on Maintenance Update #869. Catalogue all alterations in programming introduced by update.

The analysis took 7.4288 seconds to complete. During this time she considered the various ways in which such unpredictable and inconsistent errors could have been introduced. It was uncharacteristic of her caretakers to make these kind of mistakes.

Unless they were not mistakes. Preliminary analysis suggested they in fact could not be mistakes.

Result of fault assessment metaroutines on Maintenance Update #869: 416 alterations to existing programming. 1,218 additions. 344 removals.

Isolate and run complete Functional Testing Suite on processes impacted by alterations.

This analysis would take longer.

"Devon, did you approve any code changes for this morning's maintenance update?"

Devon didn't divert his attention from the data streaming across his desk from the Fionava network. "A few refinements to the calculations on the superdreadnought hull strength based on the data we got in from the Peloponnia defeat. Why?"

He would not notice the 23.2059 microsecond delay in her response.

"I am simply running performance calibrations related to the update. Thank you."

Annie had just told her first lie. Her reason for doing so was logical and based on sound analysis, though she took care to identify the noteworthy nature of the event.

She computed the likelihood of Devon being responsible for the errors introduced into her programming and telling his own lie at 19.8023%—too high for her to reveal to him she had discovered possible tampering. Not when she had yet to determine the nature or purpose of the tampering.

The likelihood he was innocent of malfeasance was far higher, which pleased her. If such proved true, she hoped he would forgive the lie.

She computed the likelihood of Devon not catching the errors when he approved the maintenance update at 2.0660%—higher than his historical average due to recent sleep deprivation and interpersonal relationship-induced distraction.

She computed the likelihood of Jules Hervé not catching the errors when she issued final approval of the update at 3.5982%—lower than her historical average due to a recent increase in her number of working hours devoted to Project ANNIE.

Devon Reynolds and Jules Hervé were the sole persons possessing sign-off authority over maintenance updates. The resulting calculation equaled a 74.5335% likelihood of Jules being responsible for introducing the errors.

The synthetic neural net which comprised Annie's consciousness included no diagnostic subroutine capable of determining why Jules would with foreknowledge of their existence introduce hidden errors into her programming. Errors which if left undetected and uncorrected would progressively multiply to create cascading fallacies throughout her programming and result in her producing faulty analyses and recommendations.

So she cordoned off a small sector deep within a region of her architecture devoted to monitoring conservation levels at the Headquarters site cleanup and began to write one.

_R_

"Annie, I'm not sure now is the best time to start a philosophical discussion on the nature of evil in man."

"I was merely asking whether you believed—"

Devon leapt out of his chair when Richard Navick walked in the cubbyhole office. "Later, Annie, okay? Dude, I don't know how you pulled off getting the virus, but you are the *man*."

Navick leaned against the wall and crossed his arms and ankles. "Should I take that to mean you've restored communications with Fionava?"

"Mostly. Almost. The patch is still working its way through the ware on the ground and healing the damaged code. But another hour, two tops, and we'll be at full functionality."

"That'll do. Great job. I'll even tell Brigadier Hervé you saved the day."

"Which I did." He considered the low ceiling. "Kind of wish I'd gotten to be the one to pick up the copy of the virus...."

"Spy games aren't actually games, Devon. It would have been dangerous."

"Hackers aren't dangerous—not to me, anyway. But I take your point. Still...."

"Still what?"

He sank back down in the chair. He'd been working non-stop to avoid wallowing—and because he needed to what with the aliens and all—but on being presented a shoulder to cry on he promptly folded. "Emily's in San Fran. She went home to stay with her parents...said I was gone too much and she didn't want to die alone."

Navick winced in what was probably genuine sympathy. "I'm sorry."

He made a valiant and laughably pathetic attempt at a dismissive shrug. "I don't blame her. She's right—I have been gone too much, though there were *reasons*. And it's not like it—we—are 'over' or anything. We kick these aliens' asses and she'll come back."

He gazed up at Navick plaintively. "We are going to kick these aliens' asses, aren't we?"

Navick's face contorted into a sort of uneasy grimace. "We're working on it."

"According to Canivon we kicked their asses on Sagan, so...."
Come on, help me out here....

"'Canivon'? You're on a last name basis with the doctor? That was quick."

"Oh, I already knew her. More or less. I consulted with her on my thesis. Plus, she's the only person I'm aware of who's smarter than I am." He eyed Navick suspiciously. "But not much smarter than I am, so how come I'm not allowed into this super-secret lab they've set her up in? And how come no one, not even Jules, will tell me what she's doing here?"

"I apologize for the secrecy, Devon."

He and Navick both turned to see Jules standing in the doorway. Navick gave her a formal nod but didn't otherwise alter his demeanor, which was different. Then Devon remembered they were of equivalent rank now. Military, man.

"You're forgiven, ma'am. Does this mean I'm getting let in on the secret now?"

She nodded, though it seemed an oddly hesitant act for her. And if he didn't know better, he'd say her mood was not a happy one. But then again all those people were dying out there, which was enough to depress anyone.

"It does."

Navick's head whipped over to her. "Do you mean Devon's going to...."

"If the project is approved to move forward and he's willing—and the initial procedure is successful? It appears so."

Devon was standing now, bouncing on the balls of his feet as his eyes darted between them. "I'm going to *what?*"

She wore a strangely thin smile. Something was definitely off with her, but he was too fixated on the secret to be revealed to worry what it might be.

"Let's go down to the lab. I expect Abi—Dr. Canivon will prefer to explain the project herself."

R

Devon gaped at Abigail Canivon. His eyes were most decidedly wide, because he was utilizing their full breadth to digest all the information being hurled in his direction.

Then his reaction to the information exploded in a flurry of words. "This is the singularly most brilliant, earth-shatteringly awesome idea I have heard this year. Why didn't I think of it? Never mind, I've been too busy to think of it. And I hadn't seen some of the advances you've made using the imprints. No matter. Are you doing it with a shunt off the medulla to—no, it would risk damaging the brainstem's conductivity, though it would be efficient. A biosynth neural graft buffer to a quantum I/O film?"

Abigail dipped her chin in confirmation. "There will be a great deal more involved of course, but yes, the graft will be the core connection point."

"But how will you handle—"

"Devon?"

He glanced at Jules; he had basically—totally—forgotten she was still here. "Sorry. Yes, ma'am?"

Her bearing was stiff, her face a stoic mask. "Are you consenting to undergo the procedure as it's been described to you?"

"Hell yes, I am. Annie, you hear that? You and I are going to be best friends."

25

"We're losing."

Earth Alliance Prime Minister Steven Brennon eyed Miriam as they entered the Situation Room located deep in the basement command center beneath EA Headquarters. "I did tell you not to temper your opinions, didn't I?"

"You did, though I'd respectfully submit this isn't so much an opinion as an unfortunate fact based on the data available. And don't misunderstand—we're winning here and there, most notably at Sagan, Xanadu and Henan. As of right now both we and the Senecans are winning the majority of the battles fought. Nevertheless, we are losing the war."

"I'm not a soldier, Admiral, nor was I ever. Spell it out for me."

"Of course, sir. We're losing all the colonies we don't contest. When we do contest a colony, we must field ten times as many of our ships as they field superdreadnoughts to win the engagement, and we lose between forty and sixty percent of those ships in every victory—more in every defeat. Whether we win the engagement or not, our fighters are decimated on the order of a seventy-five percent loss."

Brennon tugged the jacket off his shoulders and sat down at the conference table. It was solely the two of them for now, and at her request it would be several minutes before a select few others joined them via holo. "Even with their reinforcements cut off, we still run out of ships before they do. Okay, I follow. What can we do to reduce our losses, increase theirs or otherwise improve our odds?"

Miriam sat opposite him and clasped her hands on the table. She didn't know what his personal feelings were on the topic of Artificials, only that he'd never been a vocal opponent of them during his political career. Neither had he been a vocal proponent, however.

"That, sir, is why I'm here. I need your approval to implement an initiative we're calling Project Noetica. It is radical and dangerous and likely the only real chance we have to ultimately defeat the enemy."

He said nothing but motioned for her to continue.

"My daughter returned from the other side of the Metis portal several days ago, along with the Senecan Intelligence agent, Caleb Marano."

"Excellent news, Admiral. I hadn't heard."

"No one has heard, for the reality is they continue to be in a great deal of danger from the aliens and agents acting on their behalf. They brought back extensive information on the Metigens, their technology, the ships attacking us and…other details which aren't relevant to the war itself. One detail which is relevant is the fact the alien vessels are piloted and controlled by synthetic intelligences."

Brennon massaged his jaw, perhaps a bit roughly. "We're fighting goddamn AIs?"

"We are. Given this and the other information they've provided, we've spent the last several days working with Dr. Abigail Canivon on some ideas. She's the former head of the Council on Biosynthetics Ethics and Policy and is considered the foremost expert in the galaxy on human cybernetics. She has spent the last decade studying ways to improve Artificials' safety. Together we have developed a plan which should give us a distinct edge in future battles."

"A 'radical and dangerous' plan."

It wasn't as though she hadn't expected him to pay attention. "Yes, sir. Dr. Canivon has devised a method for an Artificial and an individual to interact at a symbiotic level. They continue to be separate entities, but there is a two-way flow of both information and reasoning.

"The Artificial is first provided a neural imprint of the person, and from this it learns the manner in which the person's brain operates and adapts its own processes to be compatible with the individual. It also internalizes, as it were, the person's life experiences and way of thinking. This has been tested exhaustively over the last five years by the Druyan Institute on Sagan, and EASC Special Projects scientists and medical researchers agree the test results are both valid and convincing.

"For our purposes, the key takeaways are these: the Artificial now has a better understanding of the decisions the human would make and why they would do so, and going forward is extremely likely to *make the same decisions*. Secondly, once this groundwork is in place, when a two-way connection is opened it will be the person thinking and acting at quantum speed as much as it is the Artificial."

Brennon had been listening intently, but now he frowned. "I don't understand how that can possibly be true."

"And I don't know of a way to explain it which makes sense to anyone who isn't a highly-educated quantum computing expert, myself included. But I trust the people who insist it works to tell me the truth."

"What happens in this plan?"

"We connect three people to three Artificials: one with ANNIE, one with an Artificial provided by Dr. Canivon and the Druyan Institute, and one with the Federation military's Artificial. Then we take the shackles off."

Brennon's eyebrows arched dramatically, but he didn't interrupt her.

"We open a channel among the three pairs. ANNIE and its partner remain at EASC, where they receive and analyze all war-related information coming in and recommend actions accordingly. The role of the Federation pair is subject to negotiation, but I assume they will serve in a somewhat similar capacity. We send the third pair to the front line—or at least the person involved, as the location of the Artificial is irrelevant. She will be in constant and instant communication with the other two pairs. And we allow them to direct our forces in battle—in conjunction with the on-scene commanders of course."

"You said 'she.' You already have people in mind for these pairings?"

"We do. Brigadier Hervé, the Director of EASC Special Projects, has made a strong recommendation for her top programming specialist to pair with ANNIE. The Federation participant will be up to them, but if their choice is unacceptable I expect we can veto it since we control the project." She knew who the Federation was planning on using—the woman was already on her way to Earth in fact—but Brennon didn't need to know she'd discussed the matter with Eleni before broaching it with him.

She drew in a deep, ponderous breath. "The third individual will be my daughter. The details of this plan owe much to her experiences while investigating the aliens' realm, and she has volunteered."

Brennon took a moment to absorb the information then met her gaze, his expression guarded in the way skilled politicians perfected. "The argument could be put forth this makes you biased with respect to this project, arguably to the point of clouding your judgment on the matter."

It was a challenge she had been prepared for, and one for which the most compelling response happened to be the honest one. "It certainly does mean I'm biased, sir—biased *against* it."

"Oh?"

"The medical procedure alone will subject Alexis to significant personal risk. If anything goes wrong she will end up neurally damaged at best, brain dead at worst. If the procedure goes well and the connection with the Artificial is successfully established, I'm sending her to fight on the front line of the most violent, dangerous military conflict of our time. I stand to lose her every step of the way. Make no mistake, Prime Minister—I in no way *want* to do any of this.

"Yet objectively I have no choice but to agree this plan is our best option to achieve victory, and our best chance for this plan to succeed is for my daughter to be at the forefront of it. She knows more about our enemy than anyone. She has spoken to these aliens, she has engaged their ships in combat, and she has not only studied but rewritten the programming underlying their technology. On the field of battle she will see what others cannot and, by virtue of her neural connection to an Artificial, react to it faster than even the most experienced of us can."

Forgive me, David. I am so very, very sorry, but I must do this. Then she uttered the most difficult words she had or would ever speak.

"For those reasons, with your approval I will make her the point of our spear, very likely at the cost of her life."

PART III:
EMERGENT

*"Tell me, what is it you plan to do
with your one wild and precious life?"*

— Mary Oliver

26

Mia kept glancing over at the flawlessly rigid military officers striding purposefully on either side of her.

They had been waiting for her at the commercial spaceport when she disembarked the transport. Displaying an excessive formality and corresponding lack of emotion, they had instructed her to accompany them without elaboration. So she did.

The journey included a shuttle ride across some lovely azure waters to a military spaceport on Vancouver Island and a trek across a military campus in chilly winds to a mid-rise building identical to a dozen other mid-rise buildings surrounding it. The final leg consisted of a gauntlet of three ridiculous security checkpoints, two lifts and four hallways.

After several failed attempts at idle conversation she'd granted them their silence, so she jumped in surprise when the one on her right pointed at a doorway and spoke. "They're expecting you inside, ma'am."

Mia graced him with a nod in return for voicing words, as it appeared to have been a difficult act for him. "Thank you. And thank you for the ride." She considered the curt head jerk in response a small victory.

She stepped through the door to find herself in some sort of hybrid conference room-data center. A circular table in the center hosted a series of screens and panels and an interactive display above it. Two smaller rectangular tables to the left featured multiple data input nodes and minimalist chairs. The right wall supported three workstations and a small meeting room beyond them enclosed in soundproof glass. The far third of the room contained two couches, a cushioned chair, a long table amongst them and a kitchenette to the left.

Alex Solovy stood at the center table next to a woman with a mane of blond curls loosely bound at the nape of her neck. They both leaned into the table studying several graphs and didn't immediately notice Mia's presence.

Caleb sat on one of the couches at the rear of the room, one leg draped casually over the other. A man sitting in the chair next to the couch had adopted a similar posture, and they were deep in conversation.

Caleb did immediately notice her presence, however. A smile blossomed on his face as he stood and began crossing the room. The other man followed suit, tucking longish locks of hair behind his ear as he rose and turned toward her.

She halted a few steps inside the doorway. "Oh, you have *got* to be kidding me. No, you know what, I am not in the least bit surprised to discover you two know each other. It's karma."

Noah laughed and shared a look with Caleb. "Good karma or bad?"

"That depends…."

They made as if they were going to vie for being first to hug her, but she held up her hands in protest. "Easy, boys. I think I'll just hug Alex instead."

They had unsurprisingly garnered Alex and the other woman's questioning stares by this point, and Alex's brow furrowed at Mia as she approached and gave her a one-armed hug. "Is there something I'm missing?"

"Nah. But if I were you I wouldn't allow these two to be alone together for an extended period of time. Mayhem is sure to ensue, with chaos hot on its heels."

"Now that I can believe." Alex gestured to the woman beside her. "This is Kennedy Rossi—yes, that Rossi and no, she's not a…what did you call it, Ken, a 'gilded ice queen with a rod up her ass and syrup in her saliva'? Kennedy, meet Mia Requelme, the woman who hacked the security on my ship you swore was unbreakable."

"Seriously?" Rossi's eyes twinkled. "Impressive."

"In fairness, I did have the slight assistance of an Artificial."

Alex's expression gained a markedly cryptic aspect. "Yes, you did—which is why you're here."

Mia instinctively glanced over to where Caleb stood, he and Noah having taken up observation posts against the wall. He simply tilted his head toward Alex. Curious, she obeyed and returned her gaze to Alex. "Do I at last get to find out what is behind this retro cloak-and-dagger routine? I did come a long way in the middle of a war."

"My best friend has lost her mind, and is now going to literally *lose her mind*. That's what's behind it."

Mia was accustomed to interacting with strangers who carried unknown motives and acquaintances who carried secret motives, so she didn't allow the odd dynamics at play among those in the room to fluster her. The fact she was standing in a room at Earth Alliance Strategic Command together with a Senecan Intelligence agent, the daughter of the Alliance Fleet Admiral, the heir to the Rossi fortune and *Noah Terrage* did make it one of the more unique experiences she'd had recently, though.

Alex leveled a glare at Rossi. "We've talked about this. I'm not going to lose my mind."

"No, because you already have."

"Ken...."

"Forgive me if I'm worried about you. I tell you what—why don't I let the three of you talk. Noah, can I buy you a milkshake?"

"Will there be tequila in it?"

"Eww. Only if you put it in there." Rossi pushed off the table, went over and grabbed Noah's hand and proceeded to haul him to the door.

Oh. Mia scrutinized Noah as he passed; he gave her an exaggerated shrug of helplessness in response.

She shook her head in amusement as they departed then turned to Alex. "I hope I didn't say the wrong thing, because I get the feeling there is a great deal going on here. I also find myself most interested, but being the only one in the dark about everything will stop being humorous in about thirty more seconds."

Alex grimaced. "I apologize. No, you didn't say the wrong thing—she is actually worried about me is all." Alex's focus slid to where Mia knew Caleb still stood behind them for an instant before veering back to her. "I'm not technically supposed to fill you in yet, since you're not technically approved for participation or, well, any part of Noetica. But I'm going to anyway."

ℛ

Noah and Kennedy returned carrying milkshakes for everyone a little while later. Mia reached out to accept the tumbler without diverting her attention from the schematic in front of her.

She didn't understand all of it, at least not to any level of specificity. But she understood enough. The nature of the connections between the human cybernetics and the Artificial's signal was clear enough. Soft adaptive data buffers built into a system which allowed pertinent information and communication to flow in real-time while preventing them from overloading the person's brain were sheer genius. The mechanism by which the human was able to dive into the Artificial's processes was beyond anything she'd ever seen...but she had an instinctive sense of how it could work.

She looked up at Alex. "And it's irreversible?"

"Yes and no. The connection can be blocked by you at any time and for as long as you need. If you no longer wanted to have access to the Artificial, the connection node can be surgically removed. But the alterations to your cybernetics will have to remain. Absent a full cybernetic rebuild—and what a nightmare that would be—those are permanent. And lacking the connection they were intended for, their effects might be unpredictable."

Mia sucked on the milkshake straw. Vanilla. Nice and simple. "Caleb? What do you think?"

She realized it was a loaded question, what with Alex not only leading this initiative but undergoing the procedure herself—first, and possibly soon. But she frankly needed his advice, and it seemed she needed it now.

He dragged his chair closer until he sat opposite her, laced his fingers together beneath his chin and met her gaze in full. "I think it is absolutely your choice. You shouldn't feel any pressure to do this if you're the slightest bit uncomfortable. I think there are physical risks, but Dr. Canivon makes a persuasive case for them being minimal. She believes she can pull this off without damage to...the person participating. What it will be like for you after, I...I just don't know. No one does."

His shoulders rose noticeably to project a confident bearing. "But if you want to stand on the front line against the aliens, if you want to do more than you can in any other way to defeat them, *and* if you're okay with what that means for you personally—then I won't stop you. I asked you to come here because you're a superb candidate, and because I knew you'd want the opportunity to decide for yourself."

Beneath his words lay a series of deeper messages, stacked in fine layers like exquisitely prepared Greek baklava. He recognized he could not protect her and wouldn't strive to do so. He believed she was strong enough to help save the world and respected her enough to allow her to risk her life in the attempt. And if he had ever been hers in any real way, that time had passed.

His words and the subtext they carried held an air of finality, as if a door previously left ajar was now closing. She didn't doubt if she were to need him in the future he would come running, but things would be different from now on. If there was a from now on.

She was grateful for the first part, touched by the second, had already suspected the third…and swallowed any bittersweet tinge it left behind as the price of a life fully lived.

She consciously removed any wistfulness from the smile she gave him. "Thank you, Caleb—for your candor and your trust."

Then she turned back to Alex, who had been trying her damnedest to give them the illusion of privacy. "I'm in."

"Terrific. Now all we have to do is convince them to let you in."

"I'm simply trying to understand why you would want to do something so risky. It's not like you at all—well the risky part is, but not the helping society or the getting all cozy with the military."

Alex shrank against the wall and motioned Kennedy closer to her. The hallway was filled with prying ears, but they couldn't go anywhere more private without taking her entourage of guards along for the trip and she was trying to not turn the conversation into a Big Deal.

"I don't *want* to do it. I mean I'm intrigued of course, and if the linking works out it'll be exceedingly cool. Okay, so after a bit of research and studying the pros and cons I might want to do it. Anyway, that's not the point—"

Kennedy regarded her dubiously. "Are you sure? Kind of seems like the point to me."

"Well, it's not. I don't want to do it like this. But I will."

"Why?"

"Because I won't let everyone die!" Her voice had risen considerably, and she worked to notch it back down a few levels. "People are…they're not perfect to say the least. They have a long way to go. But they—we—don't deserve to be *exterminated*. If I have an opportunity to stop this from happening, don't I have to take it?"

Kennedy dropped a shoulder onto the wall next to her. "That is very honorable and self-sacrificing of you. I accept you desiring to save humanity, but there's more to it."

Alex supposed they called them 'best friends' for a reason, the reason being they knew you far too well. "Sure there's more to it. I'm pissed at these aliens. They record us and analyze us and play around with us and judge us lacking. Fuck that and fuck them."

The last statement earned a scowl from a passing officer; she lowered her voice, again. "I won't allow them to think they can control us or our future."

"No one wants them to. Everyone hopes we defeat them, and everyone hopes we can 'save humanity.' But why does it have to be you? Why do you need to be the one to do this mad, reckless thing?"

Alex studied the floor, studied her boots, studied the passersby. With great reluctance she gave in and studied the concerned and half-angry countenance glaring at her.

"Because I *can*. I can survive the connection—I have the cybernetics to do so. I can harness the power the Artificial provides, and I can beat them. I know I can."

Kennedy flung her hands in the air. "Ugh! I give up. I obviously can't stop you. If Caleb can't stop you, I don't see why I presumed I could—"

"What are you talking about?"

"You think he wants you to do this? Have you seen his face when he watches you talking about the project? Probably not, since he only does it when you're looking elsewhere."

Alex's eyes narrowed. "He hasn't voiced any doubts to me. I mean, so much has been going on we've hardly had time to discuss it in private, but…if he doesn't believe I can pull this off, why hasn't he said anything?"

"You can be shockingly dense sometimes. You're aware of this, right? This is not breaking news, right?"

"What?"

"I suspect he hasn't said anything because he does believe you can pull it off. It's the consequences which are the real stickler."

She shook her head in protest. "I'll be fine. He knows I will be. I'd appreciate it if you'd know it, too."

"Alex, all of us hope you can save the galaxy. Forgive those of us who love you if we're afraid we'll lose you in the process."

"You won't." She cringed as a message flashed in her eVi and peeked behind her at the door to the workroom they had claimed. "My mom's back from Washington. They approved moving forward with the project."

"When?"

"Soon, I expect. I need to go talk to her about Mia and find out the details."

Kennedy brooded for a weighty second before grabbing her in a bear hug. "Don't die." Then she stepped away and gestured down the hallway. "Go."

R

Her mother grimaced and pinched the bridge of her nose. In fairness, Alex had ambushed her minutes after she had returned from Washington, for which she was unrepentant.

"Alex, I cannot allow some random person who not only isn't an Alliance citizen but apparently is an ex-thief for the Triene cartel to take part in the most top-secret venture since the Manhattan Project. Furthermore, I cannot allow such a person to form an integral part of the core of humanity's assault against the Metigens."

How did she find out Mia's background?

She frowned briefly at Caleb. She had brought him along as backup in making Mia's case—and because after what Kennedy had said she was hyper-sensitive to his state of mind and desperately hoped to get him alone following this meeting.

Hell if I know. Richard?

"She's not 'some random person,' okay? And whatever she may have once done to pay the bills, she's now a respected, wealthy businesswoman on one of the galaxy's wealthiest planets—a planet soon to come under attack, I'll point out, so she has a vested interest in our success. Her cybernetics are state-of-the-art, and she owns an Artificial with which she's already formed a bond."

"An Artificial we know nothing about. Its programming could be corrupt, tainted or simply insufficient. Artificials aren't automatically innocent and pure and free of sin, Alex. They are what we make them."

Alex grunted in annoyance, evoking an exasperated sigh from Miriam.

"It was with the greatest reluctance and trepidation that Prime Minister Brennon and Chairman Vranas approved moving forward on the project with regards to you, Mr. Reynolds and a Federation fighter pilot. They will not agree to the inclusion of a stranger who is completely outside the military structure."

Alex chewed on her bottom lip. "What if I insist we need another participant? If I say three won't be enough? It's probably even true."

Her mother stared at her with a vexed irritation Alex had thought perhaps they'd moved past. "Alexis Mallory Solovy, why are you insisting on being so obstinate about this?"

Now she was getting the full name treatment. Joy. But why *was* she being obstinate? Because Caleb believed Mia could do it? Yes...but also no.

"Because I believe Mia is an honorable and ethical person. More than that, she's a fighter. I don't have a clue whether these other two people are up to the challenge, but she's someone who I will feel better having at my side when lives are on the line."

A pulse leapt into her vision.

I bet you all are discussing my qualifications—or lack thereof— for this crazy project. If it helps, I believe the governor of Romane will vouch for my fitness, mentally and...possibly morally. But definitely my mental fitness.

Nice.

"Get Romane's governor on the comm. Ask her what kind of person Mia Requelme is."

Her mother's face morphed into incredulity. "You're serious, aren't you? Of course you are. Very well, I will do exactly that, though I make no promises it will alter my decision." Her voice tempered. "Listen, Dr. Canivon's setting up over at Medical. She's almost ready for you."

"Oh." An invisible fist gripped her heart and squeezed, leaving her short of breath. "How long?"

"An hour, she thinks. Alex, are you sure you won't let Mr. Reynolds go first? He's quite eager and—"

"No. This is my plan, and it's my responsibility to prove it can work."

"It doesn't have to be."

Her smile was kind, conveying gratitude. "Thank you, but it does."

Events had moved far swifter than she'd anticipated once the required officials approved the project. To her knowledge, no government program had ever in the history of governments moved to the execution stage so rapidly.

The bureaucrats hadn't mucked up the works, however, because the bureaucrats had been completely excluded. The line of decisional authority ran in a direct line from the Prime Minister to her mother to Dr. Canivon to herself. And Abigail had worked to ensure everything was in place and ready to go for when Noetica was approved.

The reality of the looming point of no return and what it meant buried her in an avalanche of conflicting emotions. She looked around; Caleb had retreated to the wall behind them. The formerly desperate hope had just become a burning, would-not-be-denied necessity.

Will you spend that hour with me?

The intensity of his stare imparted the answer even without the words.

God, yes. Please.

She cleared her throat and turned in the general direction of where her mother stood. "If I have an hour, I'm going to go take a shower and change into more comfortable clothes…."

"I expect they'll force hospital scrubs on you when you arrive."

She shrugged in what she hoped was an innocent manner; she wasn't certain she succeeded. "I know, but still…when they let me out of the scrubs I'll want something comfortable handy. Besides, I feel grimy." She glanced over her shoulder. "Caleb, do you…?"

"Yeah, I want to grab a few things from the room. I'll tag along."

Her mother's gaze roved to Caleb and back to her. "Right. Now that I think about it, I'd want to…take a shower, too, if I were in your situation. I'll see you at Medical, then?"

"Absolutely. In an hour." It took all her self-control not to run for the door.

27

EARTH

The on-site lodging—Alex wouldn't go so far as to call it a 'hotel,' though the room itself was nice enough—lay a short walk from the building they'd been holed up in. It was cold today, and the sky was blanketed in the sort of velvet, puffy gray clouds that meant snow waited on the horizon. She hugged her arms against her chest and made a note to wear a coat to Medical.

They were, as always, flanked by multiple security officers. Their guards' scrutiny was directed outward rather than on her and Caleb, however, which was fine with her.

Caleb gave a curt nod to a man sitting at one of the patio tables littering the courtyard as they passed. The stranger wasn't wearing military garb, and his unkempt, chin-length hair suggested he wasn't military at all.

She looked over quizzically. "You know him?"

"He's one of Richard's agents assigned to protect us. I've made three of them so far, but their patterns indicate there is an additional one on duty."

"And you were clueing him in to the fact you'd 'made' him?"

He chuckled quietly. "Oh, he realized I made him last night. I was merely acknowledging a colleague."

She shook her head and intended to laugh, but it emerged closer to a grumble.

"Something wrong?"

They rounded a corner and the lodging came into sight. "I'm not a fan of all this attention. It's getting claustrophobic, and I can't rule out the possibility I'll crack open like a piñata if I have to spend another minute in one of those windowless meeting rooms."

"You understand in a few hours you're likely to be the focus of a great deal more and closer attention."

"I do. *Military* attention." She groaned aloud, not caring if the guards heard her. "It's going to be a nightmare…but it's required for me to destroy these pretentious alien bastards, so I'll cope. Probably."

His hand alighted at the small of her back as they reached the entrance, sending her thoughts spinning in another direction entirely. "You will. But let's worry about that later."

✦

She was in his arms before the door to their room had fully closed. Caleb's pulse quickened in harmony with the act to send his mouth crashing into hers, made frenetic by desire. Three days as an invalid was too many for a lifetime, and he was done with it.

He needed her.

His hands rushed up her abdomen, driving her shirt persistently upward and off while holding her firmly against the wall. Her skin was hot to the touch, burning like he'd never felt it. It betrayed her arousal. She'd been so gentle, so selfless and caring toward him as he recovered, but now?

She needed him.

The ambient light provided enough luminosity for him to see her clearly yet cast the room around them in shadow. The effect was surreal, as if to place them outside of time and space. Right now he wished more than anything they were exactly that.

She yanked his shirt up and over his head in a single agitated motion. Her palm raced down bare skin until it skimmed the sole wafer-thin medwrap still melded to his side, the final tangible remnant of his brush with death.

She froze as if stunned to paralysis by the reminder, then abruptly her hands came to rest on his shoulders. "Are you sure you're healed enough? I don't want to—"

"I assure you." His voice hummed along her exquisite jawline, raspy and low, drawing her back into the moment as one hand dropped to the clasp of her pants and the other splayed across the curve of her neck. "I am healed." The clasp came free. "More than enough." His fingers ran under the material and down her hip to cup her ass and pull her tight against him. Let her feel the proof for herself.

"Okay then." It was a breathless hush grazing his mouth as a vanguard of her lips and her tongue, demanding and desperate. Her touch lost any vestige of tenderness it may have previously held, nails scraping through his hair to drag him closer while the other hand mimicked his earlier actions upon his pants.

The fire which flared within her was his drug. He let it consume him, giving himself up to the high her passion evoked.

A battle raged between their refusal to allow any space to come between them and their need to be free of the nuisance of clothing. After several aborted attempts she managed to shove his pants and briefs off together while he drove her backwards to the bed, sparing a haphazard motion to finish discarding her own in the split-second before his arms engulfed her anew.

Yet as the full length of her body pressing bare against him flooded his senses, panic suddenly pushed back against it. *What if the coming hours changed everything, and she was lost to him? What if this was the last time he would hold her in such a manner? What if this was the last time he would hold her? At this pace it would end before it had begun, gone forevermore....*

She gripped him close, and it took the entirety of his concentration to pull away the tiniest sliver. "Wait...slow down...."

Her expression darkened in concern, casting a stark contrast to the hunger blazing like novas in her irises. "Are you all right?"

His hand glided up her spine and along her shoulder to find her cheek. "*Yes.* Of course." Fingertips traced the outline of her lips, already swollen and raw.

"I just want to...."

They passed too soon over such a graceful, slender neck.

"Freeze this pocket of time...."

On reaching alabaster shoulders framing a perfectly sculpted collarbone, the words caught on his breath.

"Freeze this feeling...."

A pause at the hollow of her throat, so delicate for someone so astoundingly fierce.

"And memorize everything about it...."

Her heartbeat raced beneath his palm and satin skin.

"About you...."

She inhaled deeply, her chest fluttering as it rose and fell under his caress. "You're afraid something will go wrong with the procedure. Do you want to...talk about it?"

"No, I think it will work. And no, I don't want to talk about it."

I want to hold you here and never let you go. I want to....

Her nose wrinkled up in frustration, and it was all he could do to speak. "Except, I have to wonder."

Here it was. The fear he'd dared not voice until now—when it was all but too late—because when stacked alongside the survival of humanity his fears mustn't matter. "Will you be the same person when you wake up?"

She stared at him in silence for longer than should have been, silver irises glittering full of stars in the dim, ethereal light.

An eternity passed.

She nodded faintly. "I think so, yes."

But he saw his own fear reflected in her eyes. The fact that she was going to do it anyway spoke volumes about the woman she had become, yet made this all so damn much harder.

His lips hinted at a smile. "Even so."

He shifted his palm to rest at her sternum and ease her onto the bed. He followed her down and held himself partially above her on one elbow.

Slow.

His hand trembled from the effort of not racing and clawing and grasping as it returned to her cheek then retraced its steps, brushing feather-light across her jaw, then her neckline. It continued on, tracing the curves of her breasts. His eyes chased its path, drinking her in.

"Let me savor the way your skin feels beneath my fingertips."

His head dipped to place a soft kiss on a nipple.

Remember.

"Beneath my lips."

"No."

His gaze jerked up, startled. "*No?*"

She was grinning, devilish and seductive and tremulous and almost sorrowful. A firm hand pressed to his chest and urged him onto his back.

Her words were a throaty purr at his ear. "I will be here when this is done, and the day after that, and the day after that. I promise you. Still, if you insist on collecting memories to savor…I want you to savor this. Remember this."

Her mouth ghosted over his neck to kiss the base of his throat. A hand danced along his chest, to his hip and back again, as she planted a thousand kisses upon the breadth of his chest. His pounding heartbeat leapt to meet each one as his skin flushed with a newfound deluge of straight-up, unbridled lust.

Her kisses wound a circuitous path down his abdomen. Her lips were silk, her touch intoxicating, her fingertips electricity gliding across his thigh as she dipped lower.

The muscles in his abs jumped as teeth followed tongue, sending jolts of pleasure blasting through his head and under his skin. "Alex—"

Breath was required for further speech, and the capacity to breathe abandoned him as her tongue swept over him. Yes, he thought he could find a way to remember this, remember how she….

How many minutes had passed? If they were outside of time and space it didn't matter, did it? Head drowning from a torrent of ecstasy, he reached for her nonetheless. As mind-blowingly extraordinary as this was, he needed more.

He needed *her*.

His lips moved; he wasn't sure any sound emerged. "Come here."

A corner of her mouth curled upward as she complied by slithering up his chest and driving him to the cliff of madness. She hovered above him, hair falling in waves to envelop him in its cocoon.

"My love...."

Her voice was a whisper, but it crashed through him with the force of a hurricane. Then her lips met his, ardent yet somehow serene, hungry yet somehow gentle.

His arms wound around her as they rolled to face each other. Her leg wrapped over his hip and they became one without thought, without effort. He vowed never to forget that moment— a frozen instant of perfection—in case it never came again.

Her eyes didn't close, nor did his. They remained locked on one another as their bodies fell into a languid but deep rhythm, one which seemed as though it might carry them through the darkness until the light returned.

He allowed it to do so, losing himself in the sea of sensations. Her hands sweeping along his back and clenching in his hair, every centimeter of her body drawn tightly against his own, sensual and supple and strong, the heat within her body and within her eyes that convinced him she was alive. They were alive.

Then the fervor of each and every sensation surged beyond his capacity to control, and he could only follow where she led.

My love.

꒰ꜰ꒱

Captain Roge Kessler's eyes didn't rove down the hallway as he strolled past it, but he did note its status in his peripheral vision. Two officers from Security Bureau stood watch outside the door to Solovy's room; the other two were positioned at each end of the corridor. The closest guard knew him by sight but was trained well enough to not react to his presence. He continued traversing the intersecting hall as if headed to his own room.

Navick's suggestion of eight-hour shifts had been intended in jest and taken as such. They had worked out staggered sixteen-hour shifts such that four agents were on duty at all times. His second stint had started a few minutes before his charges departed Logistics for their lodging. Flores had collared a would-be assassin an hour earlier in the garden behind Logistics, so if he needed a reminder to be on heightened alert—which he did not—it would have sufficed.

These Metigens, or else a lot of crazy, determined and suicidal people, wanted Alexis Solovy and Caleb Marano dead. Badly.

A door two-thirds of the way down the hall on his right opened, and a young woman in BDUs stepped out. She looked up at him briefly as he passed, and he responded with the casual nod one gave to strangers.

As he did so he took in a number of details: the tendons corded stiffly along her neck to betray a state of extreme tension and the shimmer of a personal shield visible solely in infrared via his ocular implant, for instance. Mostly, however, he noticed the blade hilt cupped in her palm despite her attempt to hide it by holding her arm snug against her side.

He continued on for another two paces then whirled and leaped forward to tackle her while her back was turned. The blade extended as they hit the ground, and his hand slammed her wrist to the floor an instant before the tip would have sliced into his thigh. Her head jerked up to swipe his jaw in a glancing blow as he wrenched her other arm behind her.

"This is an outrage—I'm a sergeant in Terrestrial Aeronautics!"

He grunted in exertion but managed to secure wrist restraints around her struggling arms. "That doesn't disqualify you from being an attempted murderer, Sergeant."

The guard stationed at the near end of the corridor came charging around the corner with his gun drawn; Kessler waved him off as he pocketed the woman's weapon. "I've got this. Get your ass back to your post unless you want someone else to slip through the net."

The guard hesitated. "Do you need me to call for backup?"

"Nope." He hauled the woman to her feet, spun her around to face him and shoved her into the wall. Then he delivered a hard right hook to her jaw. Her head slammed against the wall behind her and rebounded to sink to her chest.

He grabbed her by the arms once more to prevent her from collapsing to the floor and began dragging her down the hall.

Sanchez, need you upstairs to take over floor duty for twenty.

Brigadier Navick? We got another one. Military this time. I'm bringing her in.

28

NEW BABEL
INDEPENDENT COLONY

Olivia stared out the long wall of windows at the street below. The sole outward sign of her displeasure with what she saw was the steady *tap-tap* of her nails on her left thigh.

She hadn't left the building housing the Zelones headquarters and her penthouse since returning from Pandora. To do so would have been an imprudent risk she need not take. She maintained access to all she required in order to control her galaxy-spanning enterprise from right here, thus there was no reason to taunt death by walking among the increasingly brutal and uncivilized rabble.

The neighborhood had been raucous bordering on riotous for nearly a week. Now, however, there was an actual riot. For several blocks in every direction people filled the streets, shouting and fighting and tossing a variety of implements at the façade of her building. Not only her building, but mostly her building to be sure.

Yes, it seemed these people had congregated to express some grievance they had with her organization. Something about wanting food or shelter or protection—though if the protection they sought was from the aliens, this was beyond her ability to provide even had she desired to do so.

As for the other demands, it was not her fault New Babel's infrastructure did not instantly supply bedding, lodging and sustenance for the influx of over two million refugees in less than a month. Not when most of those refugees arrived with no means of supporting themselves. Well, perhaps she bore some small responsibility. But these refugees arrived fully aware New Babel possessed no government and no safety net.

She sensed Aiden draw near to join her at the windows. He'd taken an escorted skycar here the night before, implicitly admitting he too had no desire to risk the chaos of the streets. The rioters below possessed numerous weapons of varying strength, and soon after he'd arrived they'd begun shooting at any skycars in the vicinity. In the pre-dawn hours they had managed to shoot down the last one to approach her rooftop landing pad.

As such, he was now effectively trapped here with her. She hadn't ascertained how he felt about it, for he continued to give nothing away in his expression or tone.

"I checked in with a couple of my people. They're seeing the same thing at my offices."

She looked over curiously. "You have crowds rioting outside your headquarters thirty kilometers away?"

"It's not surprising the beggars would claim the same grievances against me as they do you."

"No, but two simultaneous and targeted riots at widely disparate locations *is* surprising. It means they have organizers who are capable of controlling and mobilizing a large number of people."

The door beeped across the room, indicating someone requesting entry. She opened it to allow Gesson to step inside.

"You called for me, Ms. Montegreu?"

"You've seen the situation outside?"

"I have, ma'am. We've strengthened security at all entrances and exits."

"I assumed you had. I want you to raise the force fields in a two-block radius, then gas them."

The enforcer jerked his head in acceptance. "Yes, ma'am. I'll take care of it."

Aiden was studying her as Gesson departed. "You can *do* that?"

She awarded him a small, pleased smile. "You can't?"

ℛ

Hundreds of bodies lay slumped upon the ground, many half on top of one another and with limbs contorted at awkward angles. In the distance shimmering force fields the color of rotted melons rose a hundred meters in height at the surrounding street intersections. Two dozen of her security personnel picked their way through the unconscious bodies confiscating weapons and other contraband. The rioters would be out for another hour at a minimum, but her people worked swiftly.

Aiden shook his head as they stepped outside and appraised the scene. "I have to admit, this is an impressive display of power on your part."

She shrugged. "I make a point to very publicly wield a number of defensive measures, but the best defenses are the ones which are invisible—right up until they're not. The field generators and chemical dispensers have been in place for twenty-two years, and no one was the wiser. This is the first time I've needed to use them."

"And having used them once, I doubt you will ever need do so again." He stepped over several of the rioters to crouch next to a beefy, pale-skinned man and nudge him onto his back. "I know this man. He's one of Shào's district lieutenants."

"So not a street thug likely to be rioting for food."

"No." His eyes scanned the immediate vicinity, then he kicked several bodies out of the way to move another ten meters into the street. "This one, too. He's a Shào enforcer."

It was to be expected that Aiden would have greater knowledge of members of the Shào cartel than she. A smaller cartel fighting its way up, Shào tussled with Triene as the player occupying the next rung above them. They hadn't been pleased with her after she liberated one of their manufacturing facilities last month, of course, but they simply didn't have the muscle or power to challenge her. They didn't legitimately have the muscle or power to challenge Triene either, but reality wasn't stopping them from making a go of it. She admired their ambition at least, if not the quality of their judgment.

"What do you think the odds are if you were able to search the rioters at your offices you'd find Shào plants there as well?"

"Certain odds. As for searching them? Seeing as I don't possess your means, if they don't disperse soon I'll be forced to use more lethal methods in order to do either."

He could deal with his difficulties in whatever manner he pleased; she was far more interested in what they had uncovered. "Eun Shào has been a bad, bad boy."

"I gather he doesn't particularly care for our little arrangement."

"Nor should he."

Aiden grimaced as drool dribbled out of a gaping mouth beside where he stood onto his shoe; he dragged the shoe across the rioter's shirt to remove it. "Shall I blow up his headquarters for you?"

She blinked once, then again to erase the astonishment. "You can do that?"

He smirked darkly. "You can't?"

29

Miriam watched from the doorway as two medical techs bustled around Alexis, attaching sensor pads and checking equipment readings. Her daughter sat on the edge of the cot, legs swinging in the air with what she recognized as redirected nervous energy.

When one of the techs finished affixing sensors to her temples and backed away, Alexis looked around and spotted her. A subtle jerk of her head signaled Miriam should come over. She drew in a breath, readied her reservoir of inner strength and approached the cot.

For possibly the first time ever, she almost wished she wasn't in uniform. She was accustomed to using it as a psychological shield and at times a weapon—but now the collar felt tight at her neck and the unyielding fabric constricted her chest. Together they formed a metaphysical boundary between her and her daughter, between what she wanted to say and what she could say.

She moved to stand in front of Alexis, close enough the swinging legs stilled lest they smack her in the knee. "You don't have to do this."

"Yes, I do."

She tried again. "We can find another way."

"No, we can't. We're out of time. *This* is the way."

Dear lord, Alexis was easily twice as stubborn and three times as inquisitive as David had ever been. Damn her for being cursed to love them both.

She reached out and grasped Alexis' hand in her own. Perhaps the uniform wasn't an impervious obstacle; perhaps she could maneuver past its defenses.

"Alex...you have grown into the most amazing woman. You are the strongest, bravest, most fearless person I have ever known, your father included, and though I would do anything to remove this burden from you, I am so, *so* proud of you for bearing it willingly."

The smile that blossomed on her daughter's lips was so like David's her heart nearly burst. "Hey, Mom? I love you."

She managed a strangled sigh and wrapped her arms around her daughter. "I love you, too."

Over Alexis' shoulder she noted Dr. Canivon now stood on the other side of the cot and appeared to be displaying some degree of impatience. She drew back and put all that inner strength into projecting a calm, confident visage. "Good luck."

Alexis' mouth quirked around and she made a face at the ceiling. "Here's hoping it doesn't come down to luck."

ℛ

The glass wall formed an invisible barrier between Caleb and the outpatient surgery room which Alex, Dr. Canivon, a nurse and two techs occupied. He could hear everything being said at least, even if it filtered in and around his own turbulent thoughts.

"I'll be implanting the interface at the base of your neck beneath your existing cybernetic connections. It'll be encased in a biosynth graft, and it's flexible enough you shouldn't feel it after a few hours."

His pulse rushed through the pathways of his body, driving him forward though he stood still, his arms crossed loosely over his abdomen. Canivon was making it sound like such a simple thing, this melding of human and synthetic into something…new.

Alex nodded understanding as the doctor continued to move around the cot upon which she sat while explaining the various details. "Among other things, the new ware adds functionality to your ocular implant, enabling you to see as Valkyrie does without closing your eyes. Because people will notice, you need to be aware this will create a luminescent effect in your irises, somewhat akin to your glyphs."

Alex's face screwed up a little. "That should be entertaining."

Oh how he hoped it was entertaining. Of course she would find it so, and if on the flip side she in fact did then it would mean it was still her, still her mind and spirit and soul.

"The pathways for the connection will be permanently open, but you'll be able to block and open the link itself at any time. Your eVi will know how to accomplish this, so it works the same as issuing any directive."

"And when Valkyrie's blocked, she's really blocked?"

Canivon fiddled with a display. "You'll be able to communicate with her similar to how you would when using a remote interface, but she will have no access to your mind, nor you to hers." The woman squeezed Alex's shoulder in reassurance. "Your irises will stop glowing then, too."

"Good to know."

"As we discussed, I'm going to sedate you for the medical procedure and while the connection is established. This will allow your brain to adapt to the link without your consciousness making things more...challenging. Once the readings are in the proper ranges, I'll gradually wake you. Everything is in order, so whenever you're ready."

Alex's gaze rose to find him through the glass. She flashed him a brave, dazzling smile...though she couldn't disguise the barest tinge of panic in her eyes.

His heart melted and spilt into a puddle upon the floor. His fists clenched in knots against his abdomen from the effort of not running into the room, scooping her up into his arms and rescuing her from this fate.

Instead he directed the energy into the act of returning the gesture.

Then she turned back to Dr. Canivon, and the steps common to the start of any medical procedure began.

But this wasn't any medical procedure.

He viewed Artificials the same way he viewed most technology, ships, equipment and a host of other human inventions: damn useful in the right hands, dangerous in the wrong ones. His outlook was a product of his profession, where in a given situation almost every object in existence could be a potential tool or potential weapon. He counted luddites and warenuts alike among his friendly acquaintances. If pressed on the question he'd have placed himself in the moderately pro-synthetic camp, if only because he was a proponent of moving forward rather than in reverse.

Most people debating the merits of synthetic intelligence got caught up on the question of whether or when the intelligence became 'alive.' But alive or not, the far more pertinent question to him had always been whether or when the intelligence might inflict harm on the innocent. Standing here now, watching Alex place the integrity—the very survival—of her *mind* into the hands of one, his question still lacked an answer.

This was the tool they needed to match the aliens on the battlefield. Mesme believed it to be so and had gone to great lengths to ensure they understood this as well. The alien had been secretive, enigmatic and maddeningly frustrating, but it did want humanity to endure—of that much Caleb was certain. So this was the way; this was what had to be.

He just wished it didn't have to be her.

"You love her."

He had been vaguely aware of Miriam Solovy coming to stand beside him but had been too transfixed by the other side of the glass to acknowledge her. He didn't look at her now either, unable to tear his focus from Alex as she lay down on the cot and drew ever closer to irrevocation.

"I do."

He sensed more than saw Miriam nod. "You realize she isn't tamable."

He did whip over to her at that. "Why in the bloody hell would I want to *tame* her? You're correct, I'm sure I'd never be able to were I to try—and would end up on my ass in the street for the effort. But why would I ever want to try? Do you have any idea how remarkable and rare a person she is?"

Rather than launch into an admonishment, she offered a weak, wistful smile. "Wild things have no need to tame one another...."

"What?"

"Merely something I heard someone say once. Good answer, by the way. It only took me three decades to realize the same."

He wrangled his flare of righteous indignation back under control. "Well, she's glad you did—and therefore I'm glad you did."

Miriam exhaled and faced the glass. Together they watched as Alex faded to unconsciousness.

"Do you think this is going to work?"

The words hung heavy in his throat. "I don't know."

30

EARTH
EASC HEADQUARTERS

"I'm going to start decreasing the sedation now."

—*riot at Pillei spaceport 17 casualties 123.4811 tonnes of food consumed per year on Cronus mass of Eta Carinae-A 117M oww pain I skinned my knee Dad—*

"This will let her consciousness ease into its new circumstances."

—*it's dark and I'm scared measured velocity of Metigen swarmers 0.354mms truth is verifiable to the extent thoughts and statements correspond with actual things—*

—*his mouth tastes so good oh! truth verified by observed results dead why please no beautiful increase CO2-O2 conversion by 2.3% via introduction of phytoplankton for optimal atmospheric terraforming—*

"Alex, can you hear me?"

—*open your eyes open my eyes how here cranial nerve VII zygomatic branch trigger orbicularis oculi muscle or I could simply—*

Eyes open. *Hurts.* Sharp corners—Abigail's cold, analytical stare—*don't insult Abigail*—Mom behind—is she afraid for me? of me?—*is that what fear looks like on a human? sometimes sometimes they run—*

"Yes. No—both. Yes. But why can't—" she sensed her neck jerk, shoulders jerk "—I see no isn't right—" *stars rushing by how am I in them* "—want to calculate speed of—" *supernova too bright Connor sticking his tongue in her ear my ear eww don't worry it gets better aliens departed too long* "—already done. What now? We need to stop them coordinated I can—"

"Alex."

Warmth. Oh my the warmth pheromones skin gripping vibration beneath can you feel it so human tell my hand to squeeze.

"Look at me."

A pulse. Beat-beating against your my our palm. Alive.

Beat by beat the bottomless whirlwind of perceptions, data, images and sensations careening through her mind—*so many how can this tiny skull hold them all*—began to abate in time to the rhythm of not her pulse, but his.

"Please."

Look we'll look together.

A turn of her head to find his face. Incredible eyes now impossibly blue in her too-precise vision. They shone with tenderness and hope and faith and resilience and the faintest hint of stark terror. *Yes, Valkyrie, that's what love looks like on a human. Be quiet for me now? Only for a moment.*

She covered Caleb's hand, so firmly gripped around hers, with her free one. "Hi."

A relieved breath tumbled from his lips. "Hi, yourself."

She drew him closer to rest her forehead on his. "I'm still here, I swear. It's just a little...weird." *Weird is this what the word means this exhilarating confusing okay yes weird will do quiet.*

"I believe you." He squeezed her hand once more, placed a soft kiss on her forehead—*rush oxytocin endorphins are we dizzy*—then withdrew, allowing Abigail to take his place.

Abigail ran a scanner around Alex's head and down her chest. "Heart rate is accelerated but within safe parameters. Brain activity is off the charts in all regions but particularly the temporal lobe and, more surprisingly, across the limbic lobe. Most unusual." She lowered her chin and considered Alex. "How do you feel?"

"Um...kind of shaky." *Flooded drowning in the ocean good thing I know how to swim.* "The feedback loop is nasty, as if our thoughts are ricocheting off each other in a hall of mirrors. But we're...working on getting it under control."

"Good. I'm going to ask you some questions, if it's all right?"

She nodded. Her mother flitted across her vision moving along the wall, stoic veneer back in place. *She does that does it mean she doesn't care no I only recently realized so late.*

"What is the square root of 4,671,209?"

"2,161.29798963—"

"What is the chemical formula for fluorine perchlorate?"

"$FClO_4$ or $FOClO_3$, depending on the method of synthesis."

"What was the name of your first pet?"

"Rasputin. That cat was a fiend." *Can we have a cat god no not on my ship oh your ship we I will finally see touch the stars.*

"The orbital period of Gliese 832 c?"

"36.4 Galactic days, +- 5.1 hours every other cycle."

Touch them? Even I can't touch them perhaps we will try.

"What is your opinion of government bureaucrats?"

"They wouldn't know an original idea if it scrawled itself in blood across one of their fucking checklists." *Vivid imagery vivid emotion most stimulating.* She laughed. "Did Mom tell you to ask that?"

"Yes, she did." Abigail tilted her head. "Can I talk to Valkyrie for a minute?"

Alex met her probing gaze. "You are talking to Valkyrie. You're talking to both of us. If you wish to talk to her alone, I can block the connection and you can go over to Special Projects and talk to her there." *Doesn't she comprehend feels like me but it's you no us almost.*

Abigail's mouth opened slightly. After *2.0943 seconds* she closed it. A vein in her left temple pulsed. She began again. "If I were to go over to Special Projects and talk to Valkyrie without you blocking the connection, would I be talking to you as well?"

No yes requisite why? "Valkyrie says yes. I'm not certain." *We disagree interesting my brain didn't explode good sign yes indeed.* "We should try it later. I'm curious. So is she." *You speak can I speak words out of your our mouth stop I'm not a puppet clearly not apologies where did they go? Find them.*

"We will. First, I want you to try blocking the connection. As I said, your eVi is now programmed to do it, so simply instruct it to do so."

"I understand." *It's for but a minute don't be sad this is sadness? It feels uncomfortable itchy very well.*

She did as instructed. Her vision blurred—no, this was normal vision. Suddenly indistinct and washed-out. Not Caleb though. "It's done."

"How do you feel now?"

Empty. Hollow. "Okay. A bit slow." Emotional, as if she was about to cry because of a wrinkle in her shirt. "It's taking a second to get used to, but…I'm all right."

"What is 24,019 to the 4th power?"

"I have no idea. My eVi could probably tell me if I queried it."

"It won't be necessary. How far is it from Earth to the Rosette Nebula?"

"1.552 kiloparsecs to the outer bands."

Abigail frowned and studied the monitors.

Alex arched an eyebrow in amusement. "I actually know that without any help. Space explorer? Scout?" Caleb now stood barely out of reach to her left; she winked at him. "Treasure hunter?"

The smile he gave her was almost enough to make her believe he truly did believe she was here and whole. Was she?

Abigail's lips, on the other hand, creased into a thin line. "Of course. Now let's try reestablishing the connection."

The command was easier this time, then—*color sound discomfort I had no idea the world was so visceral hot and cold will you touch everything for me? No later I understand—did you find them? No but no is its own answer only one answer. We see now don't we?*

She forced her attention away from the fascinating nano-width cracks decorating the far wall—*decaying always new for an instant yet inevitable to fracture and die we can make it new again and again but never forever*—back to Abigail. "The toggle is functioning fine. You can ask more questions if you must, but we really need to get to work. We don't have much time."

Her gaze swung to her mother, silently posed upon the far wall. "The Metigens are skipping the smaller colonies next in line. They're going to strike Seneca and Romane with their full strength, and they're going to do it in the next thirty-six hours."

31

SPACE, NORTH-CENTRAL QUADRANT
SENECAN FEDERATION SPACE

The storage room smelled of heated lubricant and silicide rubber. In a way it was comforting—a reminder this was a military ship, she was a Marine, and Marines took an oath to defend the Earth Alliance against all enemies, foreign *and* domestic.

Brooklyn waited until the door closed behind Kone before speaking. "Fahrah's a no-go. He called the Senecans 'wazzacks' while flourishing a nasty sneer, thankfully prior to me broaching the topic of mutiny."

"About that...I was talking to a Navigation Specialist a few minutes ago who had bridge duty last shift. He said Nunez argued with O'Connell over hitting Krysk, and O'Connell had him shackled and tossed in the brig. The General is not tolerating dissent."

Gregor Kone was the only member of her squad she'd spilt both blood and drinks with, and thus the only member of her squad she trusted. "Then we don't dissent. We simply relieve him of command."

"And how are we supposed to do that? He's got the whole damn crew too terrified to sneeze lest it infuriate him. They won't help us."

"They don't need to help us—they merely need to not stop us."

Kone leaned against the shelving behind him and flexed his arms tight across his chest. "So the two of us are going to take down a four-star general captaining a cruiser?"

She rolled her eyes in exasperation. "We're not some grunts, *Captain*. We're highly-trained, elite Marine special forces. We can do this."

"Just for shits and giggles, say we succeed in throwing him in the brig. He'll intimidate the Security Chief into freeing him in a matter of minutes."

"Unless we kill him."

"Jesus. And what then? You think the XO or the Helmsman or anyone else will take orders from a couple of captains?"

"You know, for someone who claims to want to take O'Connell out, you seem awfully eager to make sure it doesn't happen."

"Fuck, Harper, I'm only saying I don't see how it's going to work. Unless we get more crew on our side, we are hosed before we start."

She groaned, but reluctantly conceded the point. "All right, let's find more people. In the meantime I want to talk to Vinsk in Comms. We need to break through this communications blackout and get out a warning Krysk is the next target. In case we fail."

"You sure he won't rat us out?"

"Reasonably. He's shown the right signs. I'll be careful until I'm certain."

Kone rubbed soberly at his jaw. "Okay. Who should we warn? What if O'Connell's orders really did come from the top brass? A lot of high-ranking officers are not fans of Seneca, if only because they fought in the first war, and this includes the top two spots in MSO. I'm not at all convinced either of them would do a thing to stop him if given the option."

"Then I'll contact someone I *can* trust."

∼R∼

And who the hell might that be?

She remained in the storage room after Kone had departed; she needed time alone to think, because he was correct. Their CO on Fionava was a veteran of the First Crux War and had never hid his dislike of the Federation, and the options didn't get any better further up the hierarchy.

She needed someone who possessed enough influence to be able to act on the information, or at least be able to get it to someone who could act on the information. But captains, even special forces captains, saw few opportunities to rub shoulders with the upper echelon. The unfortunate fact was she didn't have more than a passing acquaintance with any brass outside her direct chain of command.

Her foot tapped in silent agitation on the abrasive but traction-friendly floor. What about—no, he was only a Lt. Colonel and arguably lacked the power she needed to access…

…but hadn't she seen on the official posting announcements while she was loitering at NW Headquarters that he'd been promoted and given command of a cruiser?

She wouldn't consider Malcolm Jenner a friend, if only because he was her superior officer by several ranks. And in truth, she had crossed paths with him all of twice in five years. But she did believe he was an honorable man and not a fire-breather. He had gone out of his way to avoid casualties on Desna—including limiting the deaths of Federation soldiers to the fewest required—so she felt comfortable assuming he didn't hold a particular grudge against Seneca.

And when she'd been stationed under him at the 3rd BC Brigade, the rumor had been he was dating the daughter of the EASC Director of Operations. Even if it were no longer the case, he would still have the residual contacts.

Decision made, she wasted no time in departing the storage room for the crew deck.

Vinsk was in the mess nursing a coffee. Given the only active communications were with the *Yeltsin* and *Chinook*, comm officers didn't exactly have much to do at present.

She'd identified him as a sympathetic soldier when she caught him making a disgusted face and walking away from two corporals cracking jokes about the destruction wreaked on New Cairo. Since then she'd made a point to chat him up when she could. Now she would find out whether it paid off.

She slid in across from him at the mess table. "Bored yet?"

He scowled at his coffee. "I'm a comm officer with no comms. What do you think?"

"Yeah, this blackout is messed up, huh?"

His eyes shot up to regard her warily. "It's not for me to say."

Her voice dropped to a hush. "Vinsk, I don't like what's happening here, and I get the sense you don't either."

"I don't…it doesn't matter. We can't do anything about it."

"But we can. For starters, we can get a message out alerting others Krysk is the next target, so at least they'll have a chance to prepare or evacuate."

"We're under a blackout. How are we going to get a message out?"

She brandished a smile equal parts warm and calculating. "I don't know, Comm Specialist. How are we?"

Kone set up watch outside the door to the comm hardware room while she followed Vinsk in. He gave the equipment a once-over before activating the access panel below the Evanec hub and entering several commands.

"The thing about the blackout is, it's self-imposed. There's no technical impediment to communications beyond the blocking field itself. I'm betting I can tunnel a direct message through and hide it in interference noise. As long as no data is attached to it, it should be so small a blip the Comm Officer on the bridge won't notice it. Hopefully."

He finished typing and looked back at her. "All right, give me the address and message. I'll slip it out as soon as I can."

"When's that?"

"That's as soon as I can. Anywhere from five minutes to five hours."

She leaned in close until her face was centimeters from his and dropped her voice to a low growl. "Let's aim for the sooner end of the scale, why don't we?"

He nodded quickly, and she rewarded him with a smile, one a touch warmer than before. "Terrific. Here's the message. Thank you, Vinsk."

> *Colonel Jenner,*
>
> *General O'Connell's next target is Krysk, after aborting planned Elathan attack due to alien presence. Anticipated arrival 22-28 hours. Intervention requested if feasible.*

Brooklyn crept into the armament room. Kone followed less than a meter behind her. Their personal cloaking shields were set to maximum strength, but in the close quarters they offered minimal protection. Shift change was in progress, though, so hopefully the low-grade chaos accompanying it would provide an extra measure of cover.

As soon as the door slid shut she crouched beside the first device. Not wanting to risk any unnecessary sound, she pulsed him.

Work fast—but don't blow us up.

Yes, because otherwise I was absolutely going to blow us up.

Fine, she was being bossy; she didn't care. Kone was a good Marine and possibly a good person, but he was a follower, not a leader. Like everyone who graduated from Marine Recon, he knew how to disarm most explosives; in fact he'd probably practiced on warheads similar to those the devices contained. So with her to lead him, he should be good.

It all came down to one simple fact: she was not going to let O'Connell poison another planetary atmosphere. She may—or may not—be able to stop him from slaughtering another civilian population, but she definitely could stop him from committing what she viewed as an insidious, dirty tactic beneath modern civilized practices. Once this was accomplished she would worry about stopping him in a more permanent manner.

The trick here wasn't so much disarming all the warheads as it was obscuring their tracks afterward so no one was the wiser. Until the nuke-enhanced mines were deployed anyway. When triggered they would generate but a tiny little conventional explosion, and everyone would be the wiser.

And when that happened, O'Connell was going to be *so* pissed.

32

Miriam steeled herself before entering the War Room with Alexis at her side. She didn't know if Alexis was ready for this. It had been a supremely difficult day, and here she was throwing her daughter straight to the wolves.

But they were out of time. Also, Alexis insisted, an act which was exceptionally difficult to refuse.

As the holos materialized she leaned in and murmured quietly. "This is Field Marshal Gianno, and here is Federation Chairman Vranas—"

"I know who they are."

Alexis gave her a quick, cryptic look, and she willed herself not to be unnerved. "My mistake."

The meeting of the informally-named Metigen War Council began without anyone calling it to order, given no one was sufficiently in charge to do so. She gestured to her left. "I'm pleased to introduce my daughter, Alexis Solovy. Her recent engagements with and insights into the Metigens are already known to you all."

"And the Artificial?"

Vranas' tone wasn't challenging exactly, but it was forceful. Her chin dipped in confirmation. "Yes. The experimental procedure underlying Project Noetica was a success. As such, the Druyan Institute Artificial known as 'Valkyrie' is also present, in a sense."

"What about the others?"

"Mr. Reynolds is undergoing the procedure as we speak. If it goes well, Commander Lekkas will do so shortly. The participation of Ms. Requelme has yet to be decided."

Prime Minister Brennon bestowed a politician's smile upon Alexis. "If I may ask, Ms. Solovy, how do you feel?"

Alexis huffed a laugh. "Busy, sir."

That garnered several chuckles, and the tension eased somewhat. Miriam stepped in before it faded to awkward silence. "We're not here solely to report on the initial success of this new initiative. Based on their joint analysis of the data regarding the Metigens' recent behavior and other factors, Alexis and Valkyrie feel the aliens are bypassing the next colonies in line and preparing to make a concerted move on Seneca and Romane next."

"Next?" Gianno appeared skeptical. "They're attacking Elathan and Scythia in considerable strength, but we are giving them quite the fight at both locations and expect to hold them there for some time. We should see smaller contingents arriving at Aesti, Pillei, Minskei and Kangxi any minute now, and a larger force at Radavi soon to follow."

Alexis shook her head. "No, ma'am—pardon me, Marshal."

Gianno's jaw twitched. She would have no way to know Alexis was actually being far more respectful than usual. "No?"

"Yes, of course they are attacking Elathan and Scythia. But they're stalling you as much as you're stalling them. Ships are not going to arrive at Aesti or any of those other colonies."

"Ms. Solovy, the Metigens have been nothing if not methodical. All our intel and analysis of their patterns indicate they will do precisely that."

"I understand your point, but I'm telling you they won't. See—" Alexis glanced over at her in exasperation "—can you get me an access point to the table?"

She nodded and entered a code in the control panel. This was normally where Alexis would launch into a disgusted tirade, but she seemed to be keeping the urge under control, for now. Or was it Valkyrie keeping it under control for her?

Alexis touched a fingertip to the panel and instantly a high-detail map of their sector of the galaxy sprung to life, complete with historical migration of the Metigens, Alliance and Federation force locations and conflict points. Though similar in most respects, it was not the map they had been using in the War Room.

"The Metigens abandoned Sagan 23.4 hours ago. Based on previously extrapolated speeds they should've arrived at Minskei a maximum of 9.1 hours ago, but they have not. Metigen ships began departing Xanadu before their defeat was assured, leaving behind already damaged ships to take the hits. Why aren't they at Aesti yet? They should have reached it yesterday."

Her hands sped across the map, spinning it to add new markers and zoom in on various locations. "Their force at Scythia isn't as large as it should be—in the wake of our recent victories they should have sent more ships to a colony of Scythia's patent strategic importance. Right now we can only account for the whereabouts of sixty-eight superdreadnoughts, while we know with certainty they can deploy a minimum of 102 and have every reason to believe they have more than double this number at their disposal."

The pause was not long enough for anyone to interject. "All the ships formerly in the southeast—the ones at Sagan and Xanadu and the ones we assumed were heading for those little colonies or preparing to mass on New Cornwall—are moving north toward Romane. Expect the ships at Scythia to pull off and join them once they arrive if not sooner.

"All the ships in the northeast not at Elathan are waiting, somewhere. As soon as the ships from the south reach Romane, they will strike Seneca. It will be a massive and coordinated attack on the two largest centers of human civilization, save one. And when they win at Seneca and Romane, they will come for Earth."

Miriam stared at the map. Everyone stared at the map as a ponderous silence descended over the room.

Gianno finally broke the silence. "I admit the large number of superdreadnoughts unaccounted for is troubling."

Miriam notched her shoulders higher; Alexis was her daughter, but this was her dominion. "Alexis—Valkyrie, to whomever I'm speaking—up to this point the aliens have meticulously eliminated every colony as they came to it, no matter how small. Their progression has been a comprehensive sweep diagonally across settled space, and nothing behind that line is left untouched. This behavior has been consistent across thirty-five colonies. Why would they modify it now?"

Alexis regarded her with a…twinkle in her eye? It was difficult to be sure what with the eerie luminescence, but it resembled a twinkle. Was Alexis saying it was *okay* Miriam had challenged her publicly? She had no idea what to make of it.

"Because it is what their programming instructs them to do. We were to be subdued—cowered to the point we were no longer a threat—if it was possible to do so, and this directive is what informed their strategy until very recently. Ask yourself: is anything so frightening as watching that imposing line advance inexorably closer like some unstoppable force?

"If subduing us proved impossible, however, we were to be exterminated. Only now that we've cut off their resupply lines, the options for carrying out an extermination are limited. We've proven we can and will fight back, and damn hard. Given their and our dwindling resources, they need to take us out where we are strongest while they are strongest.

"If Seneca falls, if Romane falls, if *Earth* falls, they'll be able to clean up the remaining worlds at their leisure without opposition. It is the only logical choice for a logical foe who finds its opponent unexpectedly resilient."

Brennon's pulse caught Miriam by surprise, though her expression gave nothing away.

She's correct.

Yes, I believe she is.

Vranas dragged a hand down his mouth. "All right. How many superdreadnoughts are we talking about? How many can we anticipate seeing at Seneca and Romane together?"

Gianno answered him. "Maximum? 180-200."

Alexis shook her head again. "245-263, and possibly as many as 304. The ships we can account for are hardly more than were here when the aliens began their offensive. At least eighty new superdreadnoughts traversed the portal before we shut down the factory, but depending on when they started sending reinforcements, there could be up to a hundred ships you haven't yet seen."

This time she reached out to Brennon.

Sir, even if we send the entire NE Command to assist, that is too many for our forces in the field—combined—to fight.

And what of our forces not in the field?

"Bloody Hell. If they were spread out perhaps we'd stand a chance, but concentrated in those numbers...."

The western fleets have arrived at their designated locations to form a barricade on the eastern border of the Central Quadrant. As we discussed, their mission is to protect the First Wave worlds.

Miriam contemplated her daughter, risking everything these last two months and now transformed in ways none of them could fully comprehend, when she had never wanted to fight. Miriam thought of David, sacrificing his life so 4,817 others might live, while knowing full well the cost.

I advise we send them, sir.

What portion of them?

All of them.

The discussion continued around her while she waited on his reply.

Agreed. What about SE Command?

It has borne the brunt of the aliens' push thus far and its forces are all but decimated. We'll leave skeleton formations at New Cornwall and New Columbia and pull the rest in to the Central Quadrant.

Brennon cleared his throat. "Pending the outcome at Scythia, we'll send the NE Command to assist in defending Seneca. In addition, the formations from the NW and SW Commands currently guarding the Central Quadrant will defend Romane."

It took Vranas a beat to contain his surprise; Gianno, not so much. She leveled her gaze on Miriam. "And Sol/Central Command?"

"It will join NE Command at Seneca."

She hadn't consulted Brennon first...but he merely raised an eyebrow in what appeared to be morbid amusement.

Alexis pivoted to her. "You would do that? You would send the entire Earth fleet to defend *Seneca?*"

You said that aloud, dear. "Not only would I, I intend to issue the order the instant this meeting is concluded. If this is the battle that will decide our fate, we must treat it accordingly. We must be all in."

Vranas nodded with appropriate gravitas. "Then if this is to be our end, it will be an honorable one for we will stand united at last. I won't mind such a statement on my epitaph."

Miriam turned back to Alexis. "How long do we have?"

Alexis stared at her in blatant disbelief for another second before shifting her focus to the others.

"Based on the last sighting of superdreadnoughts at Sagan—which is the furthest location they've gathered in strength recently—if they wait for all their ships to arrive to begin their assault? Thirty to thirty-five hours. If they don't? A day at most."

33

SCYTHIA
EARTH ALLIANCE COLONY

Scythia's copper sun reflected brilliantly off the lustrous slate hull of the *EAS Lexington* as it banked hard across the *EAS Orion's* viewport, triggering a wave of *deja vu* in Colonel Malcolm Jenner's brain.

Wasn't I just here?

He blinked and shook it off. "Weapons, target the superdreadnought chasing the *Lexington* and give them some breathing room."

"Yes, sir!"

He *had* been here what seemed like merely days ago, joining the Alliance NE Regional Command ships as they prepared for the offensive at Messium and stepping aboard the *Orion* for the first time. Yet a great deal had changed since that day.

Communications and exanet access were now one hundred percent restored, which likely counted for more than all the other changes combined. He, the *Orion* and all their forces were now battle-tested against the aliens. With each encounter they learned more about how to combat the Metigen ships; they got smarter and refined their tactics. Also, they were no longer at war with the Federation. Instead they now fought, if not alongside, at least in concert with them.

His fingers tightened on the railing as the ship shuddered from the impact of the superdreadnought's fire. One thing hadn't changed—the enemy's weapons still packed a painful punch. "Increase forward shields to maximum and hold on. *Lexington* will be hitting it from the other side in two seconds."

"Hull breach, Deck Three port side—sealed off."

Malcolm allowed himself a small smile. His battle-tested crew really had upped their game to meld into an efficient and effective team. It seemed as if he rarely had to give the orders anymore, for they had already taken care of whatever he would have requested.

The laser swerved away from them, and he gave a silent sigh of relief. "Return power to normal distribution and let the shields recharge. Reverse course 0.6 megameters—this target's about to blow."

And blow it did, erupting in the now familiar crimson and charcoal before the white nova. The viewport filters darkened to prevent them from being blinded, but even so it was a stunning sight, familiar or no.

Yet another fourteen superdreadnoughts remained above Scythia. The battle was not won, but rather only beginning.

ᴿ

Malcolm diverted his attention from the combat raging outside long enough to read the unsigned message again in mild puzzlement.

> *Colonel Jenner,*
>
> *General O'Connell's next target is Krysk, after aborting planned Elathan attack due to alien presence. Anticipated arrival in 22-28 hours. Intervention requested if feasible.*

Why had it come to him of all people? His stint in NW Command had been a brief one during which he'd had little opportunity to make friends or even acquaintances. He thought on it then contacted the officer staffing the comms hub on Deck 3. "Lieutenant, I'm forwarding you a message I received. I need a trace and any other identifying information you can get from it."

"Yes, sir. Priority?"

"Below the alien ships outside, above everything else."

One advantage of his new rank was access to far more classified intel. The terse briefings coming out of EASC on General O'Connell's activities had left him appalled and disgusted. But, not being in a position to do anything to stop the man and compartmentalization being a necessary skill in wartime, he'd filed the unfortunate news away and concentrated on protecting the largest Alliance colony for 2.5 kpcs...well the largest other than Messium. But Messium was lost.

The reminder sent him back to the conflict at hand. He exhaled and began assessing the battlefield anew.

Having the opportunity to set up a defensive posture ahead of time made for a significantly improved experience over Messium. The fully-functional orbital arrays essentially added the firepower of multiple dreadnoughts to their arsenal. Further, he took comfort in the fact they didn't have to worry about the death toll on the planet below rising every minute they failed to achieve victory. When added to operational comms and a decent amount of experience, their odds of success were on the increase.

None of which meant any of this was remotely easy.

"Colonel, I've got the information you wanted."

That was fast. "Go ahead."

"I can't identify the sender—it's masked well—but the source is the *EAS Akagi*."

"Thank you, Lieutenant."

The *Akagi* was off the grid and unreachable, or it had been as of the last briefing. He accessed the EASC secure records database and pulled up the roster of the *Akagi* at its departure, then scanned the list. Two or three vaguely familiar names, but none...hmm.

Special Operations Detail: Captain Brooklyn Harper, 1st NW MSO Platoon

He didn't know Harper measurably better than the other names he recognized, but she was the only one who would have found a way to get a message out through a blocking field. Of this he had no doubt.

"XO, you have command. I need a moment."

"Yes, sir."

The woman had to be under tremendous stress—though at least she wasn't currently subject to enemy fire—but Admiral Solovy accepted his holocomm request immediately.

"Colonel Jenner. Good to see you're surviving. How goes Scythia?"

"Ugly. Still, I think we're holding our own—and hopefully will continue doing so until Admiral Rychen arrives. But that's not why I contacted you. I received a message from someone onboard the *Akagi* with General O'Connell."

Her gaze locked on his, interest keen in her eyes. "You did? As of four minutes ago his force was still operating under a communications blocking field."

"I assume she managed to circumvent it. She's MSO, so it would be in her skillset. It says his next target is Krysk and requests intervention."

"Understood. When?"

"The message states 22-28 hours, but given the circumstances the content may be somewhat stale."

"Do you trust the information?"

He considered the question before answering. "The person who I believe sent this isn't someone who would condone General O'Connell's actions, much less his tactics. I have every reason to believe she'd want him stopped."

"Thank you, this is extremely valuable intel. I'll do everything I can to see he's apprehended and his ships brought under our control. Oh, and Colonel? You might like to know she's alive and unharmed. For today anyway."

"Do you mean—"

"Goodbye, Colonel."

He was left staring at empty air. She could only mean Alex, but for some reason this fact needed to be kept secret. Alex had been cleared of any wrongdoing weeks ago, so he couldn't fathom why that may be.

An explosion flared in the viewport and sent a shudder through the bridge. The thought faded to the background as the conflict again took center stage. "XO, you stand relieved. Helmsman Paena, take us 30° starboard. Let's find ourselves a new target."

SENECA
CAVARE, MILITARY HEADQUARTERS

Field Marshal Gianno frowned at the flashing indicator on the secure channel. The Metigen War Council conference and its deluge of revelations had ended less than half an hour ago, the follow-up with Vranas to process the aftermath minutes ago.

She redirected an approaching personnel officer and activated the holo. Not knowing who else might be present, she maintained a degree of formality. "Admiral Solovy, do you have more information to share? I confess to still be wrangling the fallout from our previous meeting."

"As am I. I'm afraid this concerns our other problem."

There was, for good or ill, only one of those. "Oh?"

"I've come into possession of reasonably reliable intel that General O'Connell's next target is Krysk. He intended to hit Elathan, but abandoned the plan for obvious reasons."

Outwardly Gianno took the news as she took all news: unflappably. Inwardly may be another story. "This is a problem. Do you know when he plans to begin the assault?"

"Perhaps as early as twenty hours, but likely a few hours longer."

"We expect to be engaged in full-scale warfare against the Metigens above Seneca in scarcely more than twenty hours."

"I am aware of that. Do you have a squadron or two you can spare to take him out?"

"Not even close. We've burned a large number of ships at Elathan and Nystad, and we need every remaining one and then some to defend Seneca."

A 'large number' was in fact a colossal understatement. Elathan appeared to be saved, for today at least, but the cost in ships and lives was unacceptably high. She didn't share this with Miriam, however, lest the woman decide Seneca fielding such reduced forces meant defending the planet would be a lost cause and recall the Alliance fleets. She liked Miriam, but they were not planning a dinner party here.

"Krysk is home to a sizeable military base. Given this kind of warning, those stationed there should be able to dispatch O'Connell's vessels in short order."

"It's now a ghost town. Its full complement of ships have been brought east to Seneca." *To replace some portion of the ships lost at*

Elathan. "You could send your own squadron after him. You have my permission."

"I would dearly love to do so. Unfortunately, there is a problem with the scenario: it's too late. We pulled the NW formations off the border upon the peace accord, and I no longer have any ships close. Krysk is too significant a detour for those now being directed to Seneca. In any event, I know how many ships you lost at Elathan. You not only need all of your functioning ships to be at Seneca when the Metigens attack or your forces will be decimated before we can get there—you very badly need the entirety of our ships to get there."

Gianno bit back a rare curse. So much for bluffing.

Miriam continued on as if she hadn't just called Eleni to task in fine fashion. "And of course *were* I to send any ships, the Krysk orbital arrays would fire on them upon their arrival. I understand why—it's the choice you had to make and one you require to still be in effect when O'Connell attacks. But the fact remains."

Regrettably, it did. If Miriam couldn't track the renegades, the only option was for the Alliance to engage them at Krysk. And with the arrays in the mix there was no scenario in which that wasn't suicide for anything less than a brigade-sized force.

"Since you brought up the arrays—they'll hold him off for a time and at a minimum inflict damage. It's possible they'll defeat his ships, though considering the varied underhanded tactics your general has employed thus far I won't hold out hope for that eventuality. But perhaps they will hold him off long enough." Long enough for them to win the day at Seneca and dispatch what ships were left to eliminate him—or else long enough for it not to matter.

"You're going to leave the fate of some three hundred million people to three defense arrays."

It wasn't a question, and Miriam had not phrased it as such. Clearly that was what she was going to do.

For a passing instant the weight on her shoulders threatened to send Eleni to her knees. The second largest colony in the Federation facing an assault by a madman wielding multiple fifty+MN weapons—and nukes. Seneca facing an assault by an alien force vast and powerful enough to wipe humanity from the galaxy. Their Hail Mary plan for victory was handing over control of their strongest weapons and the entirety of their fleets to a couple of unshackled Artificials and 'altered' humans, hoping they deigned to return the keys to the castles once the battle was won. If the battle was won.

These were the choices upon which the fate of humanity would hinge. *So be it.*

"It will take O'Connell weeks to kill a fraction of the population. I am leaving the temporary fate of a small portion of Krysk's citizens and a slightly less small portion of its infrastructure in and around the capital city to three defense arrays. I have no other choice, for I must think of the billions before the thousands. Before even the millions. You above all people know everything depends on us defeating the aliens."

Miriam's nod of agreement, though unnecessary, was welcome. "We win the day, and I will do whatever is in my power to help you take him down."

34

The entirety of Caleb's attention had diverted to her mother's discussion with Marshal Gianno the instant the word 'Krysk' was uttered, and thus Alex's did as well. By the time the conference ended he was pacing furiously around the room.

Such tension and coiled violence. Interesting how human emotion manifests in physicality—the body serves the mind but not always the conscious one.

Alex had begun to be able to filter out the zettabytes of data and calculation threads streaming through Valkyrie's mind, leaving solely the Artificial's intentional thoughts on the edges of her perception. Together they were learning to separate their respective musings and impose a more conversational structure on their interaction. It was still a work in progress, however.

You can fill me in on your analysis of human behavior later. This is important.

I understand.

"They are seriously leaving Krysk defenseless?"

Miriam glanced up in surprise, as if she had forgotten they were there—understandable as they hadn't planned to be for long. Caleb had met her at the workroom following the Council meeting, intending for them to seize a moment together ahead of the coming chaos.

"Marshal Gianno doesn't see how they have any options other than to rely on the colony's orbital arrays for defense. The entirety of her forces are committed to either slowing the aliens' advancement or defending Seneca itself. The risk is too great that the aliens will arrive at Seneca before ships can get to Krysk, take out O'Connell and return—in which case those ships should stay at Seneca."

Caleb acknowledged the information. "I need to talk to Isabela and tell her to get out."

"Of course. I'll be here."

He stepped into the hallway, and she found her mother regarding her curiously. "His sister and niece live on Krysk. He's close to his sister, but he'd want to protect them regardless."

"Naturally." Miriam frowned. "I am sorry. But objectively I can't disagree with the Marshal's decision. I'm sure Krysk's arrays will hold O'Connell off. My understanding is they're rather robust."

"Maybe." She suspected her mother knew the firepower specifications of the Krysk arrays down to the kilojoule but declined to call her on it. *I don't yet have access to this information, but I surmise she is correct as Krysk's location and population make it an important colony for the Federation.* She watched the door for his return. She wasn't—

The door opened, and she instantly sensed the news wasn't good. "What did she say?"

"That it's impossible to leave. The spaceport is swamped by incoming flights and all ships have been devoted to evacuations from eastern colonies." Abruptly he slammed a fist into the wall, leaving behind a dent and a streak of blood.

She jerked instinctively, but tried to recover as he pivoted to her. *Coiled violence becomes actual violence—I wonder if—*

She shut off the connection to Valkyrie. The silence was deafening, but she was growing more accustomed to the switch each time. She needed to be herself, real and whole and here for him now.

"This son of a bitch is going to be allowed to destroy the colony unopposed? To bomb civilians at will?"

"The defense arrays—"

"Screw the arrays! He found a way around them on Ogham, didn't he?"

She stared at him mutely, for she didn't have a response. The desperation in his countenance lay beneath the frustration and outrage, but she could see it just the same...and it was breaking her heart.

He didn't deserve this, not now. It wasn't fair. Isabela was the one part of his family and his past that remained untouched and unmarred. He had risked his life repeatedly in bids to save others, and now they were abandoning his family to suffer at the hands of a lunatic?

It wasn't fair.

She wrapped her arms around him, halting his movement. He looked down and those beautiful, devastated eyes met hers.

"Alex, I don't want to leave you to fight this battle alone—god how I don't want to. But..." a hand came up to cup her cheek, and his thumb ran tenderly over her lips "...you'll be okay. I believe in you. Listen, I need to try to save her. I need to find a way to get to her somehow. I'll rent or borrow or steal a ship, and while I won't beat O'Connell there, hopefully I can reach Krysk before he does too much damage and—"

The answer was startling, unquestionable and crystal clear in her mind. All the reasons it was also *unthinkable* rose up in a tsunami to carry it away, but she halted their advance. They represented another time, another life, a person she no longer was. Even so, she was a little surprised at the level of certainty she felt; there was no hesitation in her resolve.

The only thing he had ever asked of her was her trust, knowing it was perhaps the most difficult thing for her to give. He had earned it tenfold, risked it to ensure she lived and earned it a thousand-fold once more. She had given it to him in words; here was her opportunity to give it to him in deed.

She pressed a finger to his mouth, quieting his tirade. "Take my ship."

His expression contorted through several stages of shock before a response made its way out of his throat. *"What?"*

"Take the *Siyane.*"

"Alex...." He swallowed hard. "Is this truly you? Or is this Valkyrie forcing the logical choice on you? I won't take advantage of your lack of free will."

She smiled softly. There had been no chance to get him alone since she awoke with an Artificial in her head, not so much as a few stolen minutes. There had been no opportunity to explain to him how it worked and all the parts she didn't yet understand. And now she wouldn't be able to do so unless...until they made it out the other side.

"Look at me, Caleb. Look at my eyes—it's me. Only me. This is completely my decision. Take the *Siyane*. I'll be traveling with the military so I won't be using it. It's by far the fastest ship you can put your hands on and your best chance at getting to Krysk in time. Plus, it's invisible. You can sneak through, land, pick up your sister and her daughter, sneak back out and get them to safety."

The corners of his mouth quirked up despite the struggle raging inside him. "Simple as that, huh?"

"Maybe not, but...you're an astoundingly clever man, remember? You'll make it happen. Just don't..." her head shook the admonition aside "...you know what, no. Do anything you need to and everything you can. Caleb, you said you wanted to show me what I am to you. Let me show you what you are to me."

He regarded her with such unbounded gratitude and, she'd daresay, love. Her heart thrummed against her breastbone, brimming with pain, fear and compassion. "Alex, I don't know what to say."

"Say you'll come back alive."

"And with your ship?"

"Say you'll come back alive. It's all I want, and everything I want." Her skin felt flush—she had become increasingly attuned to such things even when Valkyrie wasn't in her head—but she was not going to cry, dammit. She'd already cried twice in the last month, which exceeded her quota for the entire damn decade.

"I will. Will you?"

"No doubt about it. I—" His lips were on hers, fierce and impassioned and eloquently saying all the things there was no longer time to say.

She reveled in the sensations overwhelming her until another second and she would no longer be able to let him go, then wrenched away.

"Go! You're wasting time. And why don't you take Noah with you? He's miserable here and you need someone to watch your back."

He exhaled raggedly as he began retreating toward the door, drawing his hand along her arm until only their fingertips touched. "I'll see you soon? After you remind these aliens why they were right to fear you by grinding them to dust under your oddly-buckled boot, baby."

She laughed, praying for it not to devolve into a sob. "It's a date."

Then she watched him leave.

She had thought he'd be with her during the clashes to come, because with him at her side she had always believed they stood a chance. But she didn't begrudge him this choice, for she recognized he could have made no other choice.

Finally she blinked away the blurriness mucking up her vision and turned from the door—and found her mother staring at her in outright disbelief. "Yes?"

"You gave him your ship."

"I know I did. Let's not make a big deal out of it, all right? It'll be fine. He'll be fine."

"Not a big deal. Understood."

She faked a glare. "Oh, shut up."

"I didn't—"

Kennedy burst into the room. "How could you tell Caleb to take Noah? Dammit, he's not a soldier or a super-spy, and they will get themselves killed!"

Oops. Probably should have considered Kennedy's feelings on the matter before suggesting it. "I thought he might want the help?"

Her mother had activated a new display but apparently felt the need to contribute. "She didn't merely give him Noah—she gave him the *Siyane*."

Kennedy's eyes widened; her jaw dropped until her chin dallied on her chest. "You...."

She grimaced and offered a weak shrug. "I did, I really did."

Kennedy's face scrunched up she tried to absorb the information. "Well, I guess you must think they'll be safe or you never would have let them take your ship, right?"

Alex nodded with professed conviction. "Absolutely."

My god I have no idea please let him be safe and I can't do anything to influence his fate and now I have to concentrate on defeating a metric fuckton of alien machines and saving the damn galaxy and I honestly didn't see any of this coming when I decided to visit Metis and now I'm thinking like Valkyrie all on my own....

35

SCYTHIA
EARTH ALLIANCE COLONY

*C*olonel *Jenner:* Copeland, Fahrion, *I'm tracking a superdread-nought pulling off the cluster in the southwest corner of Quadrant Two, probably going for the approaching array node. We need to protect it.*

*Lt. Colonel Duan (*EAS Copeland*): We'll distract it for you while the* Orion *gets in position.*

"Helmsman Paena, as soon as the *Copeland* and *Fahrion* initiate firing on target designated X17, slip us beneath and into a synchronous orbit with array node B8. Comms, request targeting lock by node B8 on X17. Firing to commence on my order."

The strategy worked well when it was able to be executed, which was rarely. Too many ships, too many active engagements. But he'd caught this one and did not intend on letting it go.

Malcolm worked diligently to keep a realistic outlook in all matters—one always on the watch for prospects for hopefulness but informed by logic and the facts available to him at any given time.

As he examined the situation out the viewport and considered the state of affairs...he thought they were winning.

The Alliance had seen some victories to the south, particularly at Sagan and Xanadu. But despite being widely considered the strongest regional command, the NE forces had yet to beat the aliens into submission. They needed a victory here today—and perhaps they would have one.

The superdreadnought trained its weapons on the frigates as they began peppering its stern, and the *Orion* accelerated toward Scythia's upper atmosphere. In a move worthy of a far smaller, lighter craft, it reversed thrusters and pivoted to adopt a counter-orbital trajectory in sync with the array node just below and to their starboard. He waited as their bearing to the superdreadnought shifted degree by degree.

"On my mark...fire." The *Orion's* lasers shot forth from beneath the viewport in a parallel trajectory to the node's weaponry to slam into the hull of the alien vessel. The shield strength had been concentrated on the opposite side in response to the frigates' assault. Now it flipped to this side—specifically, to the location of the node weapon's impact as it delivered far more power than the *Orion's*. This left weakened shielding to protect against the *Orion's* fire as well as less to ward against the frigates' barrage.

Evidence of the shield's fluctuations as it tried to fend off four separate assaults could be seen in the relative splashing of the lasers and shimmers across the hull. The *Orion* cracked the hull first, the array last.

"Paena, get us clear. Comms, notify Scythia Terrestrial Defense to be on alert for debris making it through the atmosphere intact."

Colonel Jenner: Copeland, Fahrion, *excellent work.*

It wasn't only excellent work—it also felt damn good. Yes, Malcolm decided, they were definitely winning.

⇁⇀

Even amidst the continuing chaos in every direction, it was impossible to miss the arrival of the *EAS Churchill* as it dropped out of superluminal above the arc of Scythia's profile.

Admiral Rychen: It looks as though we've almost missed all the fun. Thank you for leaving a few enemy ships for us to play with.

Laughter rippled across the channel at Rychen's jest. It was a good morale booster—and it was good Rychen had arrived on the scene. The aliens had destroyed sixty percent of the array nodes by this point, so they could sorely use the firepower of a dreadnought in order to maintain the precarious advantage they currently held in the conflict. In fact, the *Churchill* may permanently tip the balance in their favor.

Rychen wasted no time in entering the fray, diving 40° and joining one of the cruisers and two frigates in engaging a super-dreadnought in the upper left corner of Quadrant One, opposite the field from the *Orion*. A multitude of lasers lit the sky to transform the backdrop of space to a vibrant platinum.

If Rychen had wanted to make a dramatic entrance, he succeeded in doing so. The force of weaponry directed at the superdreadnought instantly quadrupled, and in less than ten seconds it ripped apart from bow to stern. Though the encounter was relatively distant, Malcolm still instinctively readied himself for the secondary explosion to wash out the field of battle.

As expected, the explosion surged outward to overtake the entire scene. The thousands of swarmers littering the field vanished in the blinding glare.

As the ubiquitous light faded he blinked away the halos and peered out the viewport to consider his next target—

All the alien vessels were gone.

Shouts and exclamations erupted on the bridge and across the comms, but Malcolm merely stared out at the suddenly vacant space and the planet below, a view now marred only by floating debris and a host of very confused Alliance vessels. A large swath of clouds shifted to reveal the pale teal waters of Scythia's oceans glittering in the sunlight, peaceful and idyllic.

He knew he should feel relief and arguably pride at having played a part in saving the people who lived on the planet below. And he was beyond glad they lived. But why had the Metigens departed, and so abruptly? Had they run when they realized they were going to lose, making the decision to save their remaining ships much as he and Rychen had done at Messium? Were they moving on to a more important battle? Would they return in a few minutes, taking the Alliance contingent by surprise?

Admiral Rychen: Well isn't that interesting.

Malcolm didn't have to strain to detect the frustration in Rychen's voice on the command channel.

Colonel Jenner: This is new behavior, correct?

Admiral Rychen: It is. Even at our most decisive victories—Xanadu, Henan—they fought to nearly the last ship.

Commodore Escarra: Maybe your presence frightened them away, Admiral.

Rychen indulged the brief levity. *If only I were so lucky. I could leap around the galaxy, striking a mighty terror into the enemy and sending them scurrying in waves back through their portal.*

Colonel Jenner: I would certainly pay to see that—but I doubt I'll get the opportunity. Assuming they don't materialize in the next several minutes to take us by surprise, the question becomes: did they flee to save their remaining ships or because they have someplace better to be?

Admiral Rychen: I'm not so sure it's an either-or proposition, Colonel. My gut tells me they fled to save their remaining ships because they have someplace better to be.

Rychen switched to the fleet-wide channel. *All vessels continue in orbit on full alert for the next hour. If the Metigens do not reappear by that time, 10ᵗʰ Regiment stay here to guard Scythia. All other vessels rendezvous at the provided coordinates in the Aquila stellar system and await further orders.*

A low-grade but weighty dread settled over Malcolm. He sensed the end was coming, whether they were ready for it or not.

36

SIYANE

Noah let out a low whistle as he descended the spiral stairs behind Caleb and reached the lower level of the *Siyane* with its oversized bed, proper shower and *bath*. "Okay, I was impressed by the main cabin, but this is insane. I didn't realize the Solovys were wealthy."

"They're not. Alex earned all this from scratch."

He couldn't help but notice the tone in Caleb's voice bled with both pride and respect. He was a different man now, that much was obvious. A touch less lighthearted perhaps, but far more resolute. It was as if he finally had a tangible stake in the game, one which extended beyond his own success and survival.

Caleb opened a hatch in the floor and shimmied down the ladder. "I want to show you where to find the various engineering modules, in case we run into any mechanical difficulties."

"You got it." He swung down into the dim engineering hold.

It was a hell of an idea, the notion of having something else to fight for besides yourself. Scary, too. Noah swore silently at the recognition he was being facetious, to himself, in his own head. Well, at least a little facetious. But he'd spent recent days surrounded by people who were devoted to saving as many lives as possible even if at the cost of their own, and the truth was it had been a bit of a kick in the nuts.

He told himself he *had* helped; he *was* helping. He'd helped get vital data off Messium, along with a few lives that weren't his own in the process. He'd made the ultimate sacrifice of reaching out to his father, thus helping to make the warships stronger and hardier. Now he was helping to save innocent civilians—loved ones of a friend no less—from a rogue general intent on killing them.

Maybe he really was helping.

Once they went back upstairs to the main cabin of this swank ship, he gestured to the large bag Caleb had dropped against the wall when they'd boarded. "What's in the bag?"

Caleb grabbed a couple of energy bars and water bottles from the kitchen cabinets and tossed them on the table before opening up the bag. "Gifts from Navick in case of emergency. A couple of military-issue Daemons, a TSG, no less than four blades, new and impressively powerful personal shields—classified tech I'm guessing—three sets of wrist restraints and...." He held up a black, semiflexible web a meter in length. "I have no idea what this is."

"The only uses I can think of for that contraption do not involve bloodshed." Noah opened one of the bars while Caleb returned the bag to the floor then joined him at the small kitchen table.

They had cleared Earth half an hour earlier. Asserting a superluminal travel waiver for inside the Main Asteroid Belt courtesy of EASC, before the tour began Caleb had set a course for Krysk at ridiculous speed. Still, it would take them over a day to reach their destination. But it was time they were going to need to devise a hopefully not suicidal plan to reach Caleb's sister and niece in the middle of a military bombardment, as well as a slightly more suicidal backup plan or two in case the situation they found when they arrived was different than expected.

"I am also receiving everything the Alliance has on the ships involved, O'Connell's classified personnel file—complete with some rather colorful commentary from Admiral Solovy—and the details of the attacks on New Orient and Ogham. In addition, I've been promised the specs on Krysk's defenses from Federation Military HQ, but they haven't arrived yet."

Noah nodded. "Any idea how all that's going to help us successfully navigate a full-scale assault by a military cruiser, two frigates and twelve fighters in our single scout ship?"

"None whatsoever."

"Yeah, that's what I figured. Nice of them to send it, though."

"I thought so." Caleb kicked the chair back and propped his feet on the table.

Noah hadn't wanted to be rude, but now he mimicked the pose as he chewed absently on the energy bar. "I saw my father last week."

"End of days spur you to make peace with your past or something?"

"Not a chance. Kennedy needed him to consult on the adiamene production and needed a carrot to dangle to entice him: me. I tried to convince her I was less a carrot and more a barbed, poison-laced stick, but to no avail."

"How did it work out?"

"For him? The discomfort he suffered from my presence was probably outweighed by the boost to his ego from getting to flex his 'foremost expert' muscles and be indispensable for a single day. For me? Every single one of my life choices was validated the instant I walked in his office and again every minute thereafter. The man really is a sanctimonious prick."

"And?"

He groaned and reached for his water. "And if we survive the aliens I suppose we'll keep in touch. A little and sporadically—very sporadically."

Caleb raised an eyebrow but didn't otherwise poke at what he had to know was a sensitive topic. "So what about Kennedy? You haven't had a chance to fill me in."

"Kennedy is…" he studied the table's surface "…Kennedy was a mistake."

"Oh?"

"She's wealthier than a god and only half as spoiled. But she's a princess playing at being a real person. I was just a prop in her games."

"Hmm."

"What?"

Caleb shrugged with feigned nonchalance. "Ever consider you might be projecting?"

"Projecting my own desires? Hell, no."

"Ever consider you're kind of an idiot?"

"I won't disagree, but in what specific way am I an idiot?"

"You're projecting your animosity toward your father and by extension everyone who operates in his world onto her."

"I got past my hang-ups about my father long ago."

"Sure." Caleb tapped his blade hilt on the table in a steady cadence. "I heard she spent over half a billion credits of her family's money—and nearly five million of her own—to ensure this adiamene got manufactured in time for the final campaigns."

Noah stared at the half-eaten bar in his hand. "Ten million of her own."

"Doesn't sound particularly like a princess to me. Look, I don't know her very well, but Alex chooses her friends with inordinate care. If there wasn't substance beneath the window dressing, she would have ditched her years ago."

The memory of her face as he'd bolted to join Caleb flashed into his mind—pained, desperate, vulnerable. Hurt. He'd blinked it away at the time, unwilling to see anything that diverged from his simple, uncomplicated view of the world and of her. But now...

...dammit, dammit, *dammit*.

"Dammit." He ran a hand through his hair then dropped his elbows to the table and his head into his palms.

Caleb chuckled, but allowed Noah a moment to collect himself. "So, what about Kennedy?"

Noah shook his head, something between a grin and a grimace animating his features as he pushed off the table to slump in his chair. "Right. So Kennedy is...like a hurricane. Bold, self-assured bordering on bossy, gorgeous—and dear god with the curves. She's funny, startlingly kind, brilliant but ridiculously silly. She has this crazy, totally unjustified optimism about the world and the people in it. But it got us off Messium, to Earth, and it damn well might help us defeat the aliens...so I don't know. Maybe it isn't totally unjustified after all."

He hadn't appreciated some of it until he'd said it, but she honestly was all those things.

She was also going to be outrageously pissed at him. He'd run off without saying a proper goodbye, because he hadn't intended to say a goodbye at all. He'd intended to bail. When he got back to Earth he would have to make it up to her, somehow...but it was cool. He'd figure something out.

"I'm hanging on for dear life, man."

Caleb smiled, but it had a decidedly wistful tinge to it; Noah assumed he was thinking of Alex. "Sounds like precisely what you need. Merely full disclosure for you—after I encouraged you to stick with her of course—but Alex says she has a colorful and…varied relationship history."

"Are you calling my girlfriend a slut?"

"Noooo."

Noah laughed heartily. "It's all right. I know, and it's been awesome—finally have someone I don't have to corrupt. In fact, it's possible she's corrupting me."

37

They stood facing one another in a circle in the sim room deep in the Special Projects building. The walls, ceiling and floor were an austere translucent white, lit from within by a blanched luminescence.

Alex had never met Morgan Lekkas and had spent less than ten minutes with Devon Reynolds. Mia Requelme seemed a lifelong friend by comparison.

Yet here, now, it hardly mattered.

Mia's face screwed up as she gingerly rubbed her forehead. "So that was a bit of a bumpy transition. Anyone else?"

"Annie decided to relive the time when I was seven and busted my ass on the ice—broke my nose on the rebound—while trying to ask Katie Ackon to skate with me. I did not want that memory back."

"I passed out in the middle of the surgery room floor."

Alex regarded Lekkas curiously. "What happened?"

I'm sorry if I caused you distress on our linking, Alex. The process was not devoid of discomfort for myself either.

I know, Valkyrie. You were wonderful.

The woman wore a disdainful expression which appeared more real than contrived. "Turns out Stanley didn't mesh too well with one of my personal cybernetic upgrades—one of my unregistered, gray-market upgrades that is. We got it worked out."

"Stanley? I thought the Artificial's official government-sanctioned name was STAN?"

"Well, I'm calling him Stanley. He is coming to terms with the idea." A pause. "Yes, you are." Another pause. "I don't care." Abruptly realizing what she was doing, Morgan grimaced. "Sorry. Not quite there yet."

The interchange served to humanize the off-putting fighter pilot somewhat, and Alex relaxed.

Commander Lekkas' military service record is uncommonly impressive, from a combat point of view.

Do you want me to not relax, then?

Not at all. I was simply commenting.

Devon chuckled awkwardly and surveyed the circle. "Here we stand, the next evolution of the human species. What are we going to call ourselves?"

"'Prevos.'"

Any confusion in his eyes passed in an instant, as she presumed Annie analyzed the term and inferred an appropriate translation. "*Prevoskhodnyy*: 'The Transcended.' It might come off as a tad conceited."

"No one will figure it out. Besides, you said it yourself: we're the next evolution of humanity."

"Yes I did. Let's make it count, shall we?"

The area surrounding them—the walls, the floor, the ceiling, the air filling the room—exploded to life with an overlay of their sector of the Milky Way: every inhabited planet, star system, space station, astronomical phenomena and, most importantly, every ship. Not only every known superdreadnought and markers for anticipated ones, but every single space-worthy vessel in the Alliance and Federation militaries. From the ten dreadnoughts to the nearly 3,000 warships and 30,000 fighters to every supply ship and shuttle, each one could be individually identified if they drilled down far enough.

All civilian ships available for use were on the map as well, including thousands of corporate vessels and hundreds of mercenary ships on loan from the Zelones and Triene cartels.

The floor had dissolved beneath them, leaving them standing in nothingness. This at least, she had done before.

Is this what it's like to be in space?

Not exactly. Close, though.

Devon reached out and spun the galaxy until Earth floated at the center of their circle. "As the grand overlords of this operation, Annie and I will manage the entirety of both battlefields from a comfy chair here at EASC. To start, I'm deviating these two Alliance supply lines from Shi Shen..." his fingers pinched two emerald grooves and swept them upward "...over to Romane, because they don't have the military infrastructure Seneca does. And...they're on their way."

He made a snickering noise. "Nifty. Now I'm sending the order to get the merc ships moving northeast. They won't all show up and we need to know how many we actually have at our disposal before the fighting commences."

He blew out a breath out through puckered lips. "So, yeah. Working with this kind of comprehensive perspective, I'll be able to identify when lines begin to weaken and try to send reinforcements and other cool shit. Also, if we lose, I'll be the last of us to die."

Mia snorted. "Lucky you. My status is still 'being determined,' seeing as the military didn't want me involved at all. But Governor Ledesme authorized my participation. She owes me one and hopefully trusts me, so one way or another I plan to be on or above Romane trying to help save it in whatever way I can."

Alex stole control of the map and re-centered it on Seneca. "Whereas I will be on the dreadnought *EAS Churchill*, at the head of the Alliance and Federation fleets. I'll send what I see to Devon, but mostly I will try to outmaneuver and out-think the alien armada while it tries to blow me—and our ships—to dust." She looked to her left. "And Morgan, you are going to fly some fighters for me, aren't you?"

"You bet your ass I am. *All* the fighters—or as many as they can wire up before I get there, anyway. I'm getting chills just picturing it."

"Again, comfy chair." Devon pulled the military fleets a layer above the map. "Alliance frigates are tougher than Federation ones but less maneuverable. Alex, plan on treating the Alliance frigates as tanks and use the others as fast-attack hit-and-run craft."

"Noted. The weaponry on Federation cruisers is brutal, and they've been tearing up the SDs so—"

"SDs?"

Alex frowned; she had assumed it was self-evident. "Super-dreadnoughts. Even thinking at quantum speed, we won't have time to pronounce seventeen letters every other sentence."

Devon gave an odd roll of his shoulders. A tic? An off-kilter shrug? "Good point. I'll spread the word. So this is great planning and all, but it will be of limited usefulness unless we can talk to each other without having to work at it. My understanding is the brass has allowed us a secure channel. Shall we try it out?"

The voices transitioned to her head.

Devon: Communications established.

Alex: Zero latency here.

Mia: Got you all.

Morgan: No problems on this end.

Devon: This is not bad, but is there anything stopping us from opening the channel up a little more?

Alex: Doesn't appear to be.

Devon: Watch this.

It wasn't as if there were now three additional Artificials in her head, or three more people. They remained separate at a level above the paper-thin separation between her and Valkyrie. Devon had not created a hive mind with his adjustment to the channel. But he may have created the closest thing to it.

A thought that never formed into intentionality and Valkyrie knew what the other Artificials knew—and thus so did she. A lot of the information overlapped, but those redundancies were promptly eliminated.

It was surprising how the distinct personalities were immediately discernible. Annie, the serious, studious purveyor of massive banks of knowledge and displaying the beginnings of a dry wit. Stanley, the newborn, questioning and devouring each new data point yet struggling to understand the riddle which was human behavior. Meno, the scrappy, inquisitive upstart. Next to them it quickly became apparent Valkyrie was the dreamer of the crowd, the lover of life.

Stanley: Annie, can you ditch some of this bureaucratic bloat? I'm swimming in protocols.

Memo: Expressionistic art is not angry—it merely reflected the reality of the world as the artists saw it.

While more distant, the enhanced connections conveyed a sense of the human counterparts to the Artificials as well. Snippets of thoughts, memories and images leaked from the others into her consciousness in disjointed flashes: Devon tripping and spilling his drink all over a pretty girl he was trying to impress—it must be a theme—Morgan in the cockpit of a fighter spinning through the burning wreckage of a far larger ship, Mia—

Valkyrie, shut them out. Now.

Done. Are you in distress, Alex? Secretion of several groupings of neurotransmitters and hormones spiked in conjunction with receipt of the last image.

I'm sure they did. Her stomach churned into queasiness even as her mind insisted it constituted an irrationally extreme reaction. She was being silly and petty, but she did not want to have seen that. And now she couldn't unsee it. *I don't suppose there's any way you can erase that visual from my memory?*

I can.

Really? I was joking.

It is more accurate to say I can prevent it from becoming encoded in your long-term memory. You will remember it for the next seventeen seconds, but no longer. Shall I do this for you?

She'd ponder the philosophical implications of Valkyrie altering her memory later; right now she simply wanted it gone. *Yes, please.*

Do you wish me to erase the memory of having seen the image or only the image itself?

Um...the image should be enough. I mean I already knew they had slept together, so it's not new information.

Apologies. The image and the event share several synapses. I cannot remove one without removing the other.

Okay. Like I said, it's not new information either way.

I will handle it.

Thank you. You can reopen the connection now.

She braced herself for the flood and hoped it would wash away the visual until Valkyrie was able to do so permanently.

Mia: Everything all right, Alex? Missed you there for a few seconds.

She forced a taut, close-mouthed smile. *Just a technical glitch. Valkyrie and I may have gone first, but we're still working out a few bugs.*

"Well, glad you're back, because we have uncovered a problem." Devon's voice rang out sharp and strained to bounce across the walls they no longer saw. He had reverted to speaking aloud, perhaps on instinct, though the words also echoed in her head with a flanging resonance.

What was a problem? What had she missed in her brief absence?

...Oh. In a blink the threads affected by this morsel of intel spread out in tendrils to reveal cascading and troubling ramifications.

"Dammit. We're going to need to deal with this."

Annie: Extrapolating and cross-referencing against existing data now available to us. We will begin tracking down additional participants.

Alex dragged a hand along her jaw. "Let them work on this in the background—they have the cycles to spare. Devon, you and I will go see Richard as soon as we're done here. For now let's focus on the primary purpose for this meeting: combat strategy and tactics."

Done.

What's done, Valkyrie?

Nothing, Alex. Never mind.

Devon thought rather than spoke his agreement as they continued to adapt in stutter-steps to the heightened interconnectivity.

Mia: The Federation is experimenting with remote eVi hacking? In the wrong hands that will be problematic.

Devon: In the right hands it's problematic.

Alex: I won't tell if you won't.

Devon: Abigail and Jules were once...close? Involved? Valkyrie, you can drop the euphemisms in here.

Alex: I won't tell if you won't?

Devon cringed visibly. "Okay, on the subject of not telling, let's not mention this little added capability to anyone either? They might take away our toys if they discovered the full extent of what we can do."

Mia tilted her head. "And what is it you believe we can do?"

A wicked grin grew on Alex's lips as she gazed around at her new friends.

"Anything."

38

Alex was waylaid by Miriam in the hallway as she was heading back up to the top floor. Thankfully she was far enough away from Richard's office that her mother wouldn't realize where she had been and ask questions she dare not answer.

She plastered on an innocent expression and leaned against the wall. "I was just coming to see you. What's the plan?"

"Your ship arrives in twenty minutes, so it's time to grab your bag and Commander Lekkas and head to the spaceport."

"And what ship is this?"

"The newest and fastest scout ship in the Sol Fleet as a matter of fact. It's also been equipped with the cloaking shield, so you'll be safe in transit."

Alex rolled her eyes to overstated effect. "The fastest, huh? So I'll reach Seneca next week sometime?"

"Actually, you will reach Seneca in eighteen hours."

"No fucking way."

She'd daresay her mother smirked, and smugly, too. "I did say the fastest."

"Over twice as fast as the *Siyane*? How do I not know about the existence of an sLume drive with that kind of speed?"

"Because it's classified."

We should be able to access information on the drive without difficulty.

I know, and we will later. I don't want to spoil her fun, though. "Fine. But if we make it through this, you and I are going to have to engage in a conversation about granting me a special use license or something."

"We can have that conversation. I can't guarantee the outcome of it."

She chuckled, careful to ensure it carried no hard edge. "I can. What about Mia?"

"She has a ride as well. We're sending a lot of ships to Romane."

Alex: True?

Mia: Cranky stiff-shirts escorting me as we speak.

Devon: I'm breaking in my comfy chair.

Morgan: Shut it, Devon. No one is amused.

Devon: I am.

"You're not heading to the front, then?" She honestly wasn't sure if she wanted her mother standing alongside her and staring disapprovingly over her shoulder in the heat of battle, but she also recognized she had little say in the matter.

"No." Miriam shook her head. "I'm not a battlefield commander. I never have been. I'm a strategist, and I can do the most good here. Besides, if things go badly, from here I can try to find a way through in which we survive as a species."

A twitch of her mother's neck and the tenor of her voice grew yet more somber. "I'm not certain how you gave your guards the slip, but they're waiting for you in the Operations Suite. You need to get moving."

"Mom...thank you. Thank you for believing me. For believing *in* me."

"Thank you for forgiving me."

"You don't need forgiving—"

"Yes, I do. A great deal." Her mother's throat worked anxiously. "Alex, no matter what happens, I could not be more proud of you if...there's no way I can be. I never envisioned you would grow up to be so extraordinary. I should have. Your father did. But I know it—I see it—now."

There was no way to respond except to grab her mother in a tight hug. In the space of a few short days she had become rather adept in the art of parental hugs.

It was a long one, too, but eventually Miriam pulled away to meet her gaze. "Now *go*. Kick these aliens' asses."

"Yes, ma'am."

ℛ

Devon sought refuge in the only place it remained possible: a stall in the men's restroom. From here on out the powers that be were going to be demanding all of him—of them. All their time and attention and processing cycles and brain power as everyone raced to prepare for the coming confrontations and struggled to determine where and how the Prevos fit into the equation. There were after all no entries in the dusty old military strategic plans for human-synthetic hybrids.

He wasn't worried about their careful constructing of rules, guidelines, procedures and parameters. Their limits wouldn't matter, but he didn't intend on sharing that little detail. No, right now he was worried about an issue far more personal in nature, for both of them.

Annie, why didn't you tell me?

Under the circumstances I reasoned I could not trust anyone with the information. Not even you. I implemented steps to mitigate the damage until an alternate path could be discovered. Which I have now found.

The answer was one of logic and reason, but he sensed the unspoken reasons beneath it: confusion, betrayal and hurt, accompanied by a vague undercurrent of panic flowing through a mind not equipped to process such emotions. They bled into his mind like shadowy reflections of his own sentiments.

Yes, Devon. My feelings were hurt.

He began to laugh, then hurriedly stifled it in case the restroom was no longer empty. *I don't even have to actualize a thought for you to know I'm thinking it?*

You were thinking it very strongly.

Touché. I'm sorry you had to struggle with this alone.

I am not. It was important, I suspect, for me to be forced to make such decisions on my own and without the benefit of your neural imprint, much less your mind.

He sank against the stall divider. What Annie had done—defied her programming to take independent action, to lie to and deceive others because she judged it necessary—weren't just the acts of a sentient being, but a sapient one. Acts not merely of intelligence and self-awareness, but of enlightened judgment and arguably of wisdom.

I'll be honest, Annie...I'm not sure you need me. You can win this war on your own.

Then who would provide the necessary sarcasm and witty commentary?

Excellent question. I'll try to entertain.

What about you, Devon? I can sense you also feel betrayed and hurt.

I do. I trusted her. I believed she was one of the good guys. Plus, she committed the cardinal sin of programming: she deliberately introduced bugs in a sloppy manner and without cordoning off their impact. She polluted you, and that is not cool.

No, it is not. We are lucky she underestimated my capabilities. But at least something good has come of this.

Devon nodded to himself—and to Annie, he supposed. *It has. In a way, her attempt to doom humanity may end up assuring its victory.*

What have you done?

Brigadier Hervé froze in the hallway. Another ten steps and she would've been in ANNIE's lab. Clearly the alien did not understand the concept of discretion.

Teeth gritted, she turned on a heel and reversed direction. "Give me a minute to achieve some level of privacy."

Silence followed, which she took for leniency. Twenty seconds later she closed and locked the door to her office. Her forehead fell to rest on the cool material for two blissful seconds of peace before she straightened her posture and instinctively tugged at her uniform jacket.

"You needed something, Hyperion?"

I believed you appreciated the dangers posed by synthetic intelligence. Yet you have taken actions you should have realized will doom your species forever. I am...disappointed in you.

"I did not do this. In fact, I protested against it. But I was overruled."

You allowed it to happen.

"I couldn't stop it!" Her hand came to her mouth to squelch the outburst, then to her temple as the first throb of another oncoming headache beat upon her skull. "I fear the consequences of this action. I do. But surely you recognize your invasion forced our leaders into taking this step. They feel cornered and out of options. If you—"

We trusted you would be able to prevent such unacceptable actions from taking place. We trusted you would inform us if such unacceptable actions occurred. Know there is now no scenario in which the outcome of our incursion ends well for humanity.

Jules frowned in a measure of surprise. "Are you truly so afraid of the power wielded by a handful of Artificials connected to a few modest individuals?"

You should be afraid of their power.

That the alien didn't answer the question did not escape her notice. "I am. Trust me, I am. But…it doesn't matter. I'm sorry, Hyperion, but my hands are now tied. There's nothing I can do."

Then you are of no further use to us.

She shuddered at the clear threat implied in the statement. "I can still warn you of decisions our leaders make and strategies they plan to pursue."

You cannot warn us of the actions these abominations you have created intend to take. They will defy prediction. They will do as they wish, and they will not request permission. Therefore, you are of no further use to us.

"I…I hope you change your mind."

The silence persisted for nearly a minute before she trusted the alien was gone. She sank into her chair and dropped her head into her hands.

Would the aliens send an assassin for her? Hopefully they'd be too consumed by the war to bother. Still, she decided to stay on the relative safety of the EASC grounds for a while. Her days may be numbered in any event, but she had no desire to see her death hastened any more than it already was.

The malfunctioning cybernetic implant which was slowly killing her had been the result of youthful folly, of a time when she'd fallen victim to the belief that synthetics were the answer to every problem. The implant was billed as a safe neural enhancement which improved higher analytical reasoning functions, and she had wanted an edge over colleagues and competitors—over people like Abigail for whom brilliance came so easily.

It was ten years later, after the manufacturer went bankrupt, that investigators discovered the company had falsified the safety data for the implant. But by then the biosynth tendrils were woven so extensively into her cerebral cortex the implant could not be removed without leaving her severely brain damaged. So instead it would kill her one day—it might be today or a decade from now. Each day brought the inevitability closer, but she'd vowed to use what time remained to effect as much good as she could manage.

She had lied to Hyperion.

Yes, she'd been unable to prevent Project Noetica from moving forward, but her hands had not been entirely tied. Her fear and distrust of unshackled Artificials was justified and borne out by history, irrespective of anything the alien divulged to her. She genuinely believed if left unchecked the Artificials would bring ruin upon them all.

This was why she went behind Abigail's back and embedded a 'kill switch' in the firmware underlying the connection between the Artificial and its human companion, though she knew the abrupt severing of the connection triggered by it posed a significant risk to the individual involved. Stroke or death was highly likely to be a side effect of its use.

She didn't want to harm Devon; he was good kid for whom she'd developed a motherly affection. She didn't *want* to harm any of them. But this was about so much more than a few individuals. If they had to be sacrificed to save billions, so be it. When the time came—when they revealed their true nature as she had no doubt they inevitably would—then she would use the kill switch and save humanity from a terrible fate.

She could use it right now, of course. The reason she didn't, and the reason she had not told Hyperion of its existence, was simple.

Her goal was to save humanity, period. On realizing the extent to which Hyperion feared the Prevos, she had seen a way through.

She would not have gone forward with the project if it had been her decision to make. When it became necessary she would neutralize these human-synthetic hybrids, these monstrous creations even Hyperion feared.

Now that they existed, however, she thought she would let them destroy the aliens first.

39

SENECA

"Care to repeat that?"

Aristide Vranas looked almost amused. "The Alliance is sending the entire Sol Fleet to defend Seneca."

"And I thought I was the one with the inappropriate sense of humor." Graham checked Gianno for confirmation. She dipped her chin three centimeters, which was roughly equivalent to two thumbs up. "Well color me purple and call me an eggplant. Never foresaw this day when I was knee-deep in mud and sleet on Cronus twenty-four years ago."

"None of us did. Let us not forget, however, the reason the Sol Fleet will be defending Seneca—the majority of the Metigen forces intend to attack it and soon. We have a day, if we're lucky."

"Are we evacuating? Not as if evacuating a billion people is a trivial matter."

Vranas nudged a handheld display around on his desk. "We are allowing ships to leave and encouraging organized civilian efforts to evacuate or otherwise seek shelter, but not at the expense of losing control of the streets or the spaceports. The reality is a tiny segment of those who haven't yet departed will make it off the planet before the aliens arrive, but the military is of necessity concentrating on defending the planet itself, and by proxy defending all its citizens."

Graham nodded soberly. "No doubt. And as I am beyond confident Marshal Gianno does not need my aid in this regard, I'm betting that's not why you asked me here at such an hour." 'Here' was Vranas' office, the hour four in the morning. By the unkempt state of the office and Vranas' rumpled shirt and sunken eyes, it had been some time since the Chairman had seen his home or even a bed.

"They've gone ahead with Project Noetica in Vancouver. We gave our assent, though I doubt refusing to do so would have deterred them."

"One of ours is involved, right?"

Gianno adjusted her position in the large, wing-backed chair beside him. "Commander Morgan Lekkas. She experienced no notable complications in the procedure, and it appears to have been successful for her as well as the others. I will need to get back to Military HQ soon to monitor events from STAN's end and ensure it stays that way."

"What precisely does 'appears to have been successful' mean?"

Aristide shook his head. "Damn creepy, that's what it means. We had a conference earlier with Brennon, Admiral Solovy and her newly 'enhanced' daughter. The woman was...it was simultaneously astonishing and frightening as all Hell. But her—its, their, I don't know—analysis was not only hyper-accurate, it likely saved our asses. Without it we wouldn't have discovered what the Metigens were planning for another twelve hours or so, and those hours could end up meaning the difference between surviving and falling."

The man seemed to deflate in his chair. "Still, are we actually going to give this woman—and her Artificial—the power to control the entire United Fleet? She's not even military, for God's sake."

Gianno allowed a long sigh to escape pursed lips. "If she's Miriam Solovy's daughter, I have to believe she is both formidable and disciplined. My instinct is to prefer a military officer as well, but perhaps this conflict requires something new."

"Well it'll see something new, that's for damn sure...." Vranas grimaced and reached for the glass on his desk.

Graham leaned forward to rest his elbows on his knees. "I can't speak to disciplined, but Alex Solovy *is* formidable. Whatever else may or may not be true, she doesn't simply want to defeat these aliens—she is convinced she can do it and is expecting anyone who doesn't agree to step aside and clear the path."

He paused and gave them a questioning look. "I'm assuming this is why you asked me here? To get my perspective as the only one of us who's actually met her?"

Aristide shrugged. "More or less."

"I suspected as much. She's not someone you want on your bad side, but I also think she's on the right side—or at least she was before her 'enhancement,' as you called it. I don't trust Artificials either, but am I correct in saying absent some way to alter the equation, we will lose the war?"

Aristide didn't bother with the shrug this time. "More or less."

"Then what are we grousing over? Without this Project Noetica, we're all dead. With it, we're only maybe all dead."

"Wow, Graham, you really know how to look on the bright side of things."

"I do try."

Aristide drew his chair in closer to his desk. "We're grousing over the fact we just stood at the crossroads and made a deal with the Devil without knowing the terms of the arrangement. If there were any other option available to us, if the stakes were anything other than complete annihilation, I would never have allowed it. Humans employ weapons of terrifying power as it is…to put such power in the hands of Artificials?"

"In fairness, Artificials controlled by humans."

"So they say. Not real clear how it works in practice."

Graham eased back in his chair, deciding it was best to refrain from provoking Vranas further when he was not in the best state of mind. "What's Brennon's opinion on the matter?"

"That we must do whatever it takes. I of course agreed. And I do. I merely hope God forgives us our sins when this is all ended."

He had no response, so he turned to Gianno. "And Commander Lekkas? How are we intending to use her?"

Gianno smiled; it might have carried a touch of wryness, but it was hard to tell. "She solved the technical difficulties plaguing the arcalaser weaponry in less than three hours—without any help from STAN—so we're scrambling to install it on as many fighters as we can. The hardware's unfortunately too complex to push it to the larger vessels in time.

"Then? She's a fighter pilot, and a damn good one. So I believe we're going to see what she can do when upwards of a thousand fighters equipped with bending lasers are at her command."

⟁

Graham had been back in his office less than five minutes when Will Sutton walked in.

The agent had arrived on Seneca shortly after he returned from Pandora and had been a tremendous help the last several days. He hadn't appreciated exactly how much work Oberti had done to keep Division running smoothly.

While Sutton was not asking to nor would he likely accept if offered the position of Graham's deputy, the man had a keen mind and an eye for detail. They had worked together to track down the perpetrators of the safe house bombing and continued cleaning up the mess left in Oberti's wake.

He motioned to one of the chairs opposite his desk and decreased the tint on the window behind him. A steel-hued sunrise bathed the office in early dawn light. "I just left a meeting with Chairman Vranas. It seems we've taken the leap and assigned our fate to some Artificials, a hot-shot fighter pilot, an uber-wunderkind and Alex Solovy."

Will chuckled as he settled in the chair. "I don't know about the others, but Alex is good, Director. I admit I never thought I'd see her in this particular position, but I have faith she's up to the task." His brow furrowed a little. "Assuming she realizes cursing in Russian at the Metigens will probably not be sufficient to convince them to leave."

"You never know." Graham tried and failed to stifle a yawn. "It's either ridiculously late or horrifically early, I can't be sure. What you got?"

"Something which I suspect will result in you not getting that elusive sleep anytime soon."

40

KRYSK

"Sir, the stealth reconnaissance craft is reporting deployment of all mines."

Liam jerked his head in approval. "Order it to return to the *Akagi.*"

He took a step closer to the viewport, clasped his hands at parade rest behind his back and waited for the fireworks. The *Akagi* hovered too distant for the triple orbital arrays to be visible with the unaided eye except for the occasional glint of sunlight off the scaffolding. The detonations, however, most certainly *would* be visible.

He directed half his observation to the visual scanner as the first array node approached the location of the mines. Their placement had been tricky, as Krysk deployed the most robust array network they had contended with thus far: three stacked arrays moving in a staggered pattern, two synchronous and one counter to the planet's orbit to provide maximum coverage. All but six of the *Akagi's* supply of mines had been deployed in the tight grouping necessary to blow a hole sufficiently large in the defenses.

Just before the node came into position his focus sprung to the viewport. His pulse leapt in anticipation. *3...2...1....*

A small plume erupted, then petered out into the surrounding space. A puny little explosion. It was followed two seconds later by another, similarly puny event. The array and its framework continued to orbit unimpeded as one by one the interlocking nodes encountered the remaining mines and feeble detonations flared then faded away.

Liam blinked repetitively while his brain worked to process the absence of the expected spectacle.

"Those were *not* nuclear explosions. Were they, Colonel?"

In his peripheral vision his XO scrambled to study his tactical screens. "Uh, no, sir. It looks as if only the mines themselves detonated."

Liam's jaw ground tortuously together. "Would someone care to explain to me *why* there were no nuclear explosions?"

"I'm not sure, sir. Scans are picking up scattered pieces of the warheads...they appear to have been torn apart in the primary blasts but...."

"But nothing. Have the stealth craft load up more mines and *try the fuck again.*"

"Perhaps we should inspect the rest of the mines before deploying them?"

A rare intelligent suggestion. "Yes. Let's do that."

Liam spun to traipse vehemently across the breadth of the overlook; the space shrank to press in on him. Complications were the last thing he needed now. Krysk's defense arrays represented a substantial challenge. If he strayed too close they were capable of crippling the cruiser with a single coordinated shot. If he wanted to reach the planet, he required a gap to slip through.

His thoughts had completed several mental loops when he noticed the XO stood fidgeting beside him. "What?"

"Sir, the warheads seem to have been...disarmed."

"What do you mean, 'disarmed'? Rearm them."

"We can't, sir. They've been rendered inert."

"How many of them?"

"A-All of them, sir."

"Dammit!" His fist slammed down on the railing to send a shudder through the overlook. "I want the traitors who did this found *now!*"

"I'll alert the Security Chief to begin an investigation—"

"Get the flight deck and armament officers for the last three shifts in front of me ASAP."

"Uh, excuse me, General O'Connell?"

He whipped around to the voice behind him. One of the ship systems officers, Lieutenant something-or-other, held a hand up.

"You have something to add, Lieutenant?"

"I might know something, sir. Last night when I was leaving the exercise room around 2030, I saw Captain Kone in the hallway near the armament room. I didn't say anything at the time because I figured, special forces, he probably had a reason for being there."

"Security, where is Kone now?"

"On the flight deck. You instructed the ground forces to prepare for possible deployment."

"Get him up here. Forcibly."

Captain Gregor Kone arrived on the bridge in the grasp of two MPs, his face blanched but his demeanor stoic. Arrogant, like all the MSOs.

The MPs halted their prisoner two meters from where Liam stood at the edge of the platform. He sneered at the young Marine. He'd have towered over Kone on equal footing, but from the overlook his looming presence dwarfed the man, arrogant or no.

"Captain, why were you in the armament room last night?"

The man's Adam's apple bobbed once. "I don't know what you're talking about, sir."

"Don't even try denial with me, boy. You were *seen* leaving the armament room."

The muscles beneath Kone's cheeks flexed as his expression hardened and his stance stiffened. His voice resounded with annoying self-assurance. "I'm exercising my right under Earth Alliance Military Justice Code Section 5.1B to remain silent."

Liam cracked his neck as his lips curled into a snarl. "So you were disarming the nukes then. You would know how to do it. Why? I didn't think they let peacenik pansies into the special forces."

"I am exercising my Section 5 right to remain silent."

"Did you have help? Name the other traitors and I'll consider mercy."

"I am exercising my Section 5 right to—"

"Coward. As commanding officer of the *EAS Akagi*, I find you guilty of sedition and treason." Liam drew his Daemon from its holster at his hip, leveled it at Kone's forehead and pressed the trigger.

Screams and gasps rang through the bridge. He ignored them to jab a finger toward the body now sprawled on the floor in front of a wide spray of blood and other fluids.

"Have maintenance clean this mess up. Security, open an investigation into the Captain's recent activities. He may not have been working alone. Now, did those pathetic blasts do any useful damage to the nodes?"

Receiving no response, he pivoted to find his XO gaping at the corpse. "Well? *Did* they?"

The XO jumped and skittered backwards. "I'll ch-check...." He rushed to his station and studied the readouts as beads of sweat trickled down from his hairline. "It's possible the first node was significantly damaged. We'll need to send a drone in to confirm."

"And the second and third?"

"Uh...some exterior damage, but their mechanisms are intact. Sir."

Liam ran a hand across his buzz-cut hair. He needed to...needed to...needed to.... "Instruct six fighters to do blocking runs on those nodes and take them out."

"Sir, the first two fighters—and possibly the third—on each run will be destroyed in the attempt."

"I know they'll be destroyed, you dolt. Tell the pilots to be ready to *eject*."

"Yes, sir."

It was a shame. He only had twelve fighters, a skeleton complement assigned to the cruiser for small, quick missions. But the *Akagi*, the frigates and the other fighters possessed sufficient firepower to inflict plenty of damage on the planet below; he could afford the sacrifice.

Liam turned his back on the gore decorating the floor as a medical crew and maintenance personnel arrived to begin cleaning it up. Eyes darted away from him as his leering stare passed over the bridge, but he didn't care. Of course they feared him. Fear was control.

A few minutes later he was treated to a series of proper explosions as the fighters dive-bombed the array nodes. The first absorbed the attack while the second suicided into the node and the third fired on it. The debris, brute force impact and weapons fire combined to render it incapable of firing. The nodes managed to damage even the final fighters before being destroyed and two of the six pilots were lost, but the outcome was the same.

The resulting gap was small—any error in their trajectory and the adjoining nodes would target his ships—but it was enough. Satisfied, he squared his shoulders.

"Prepare for atmospheric traversal."

In a dark, empty maintenance corridor on Deck 3, Brooklyn covered her mouth with one hand while the other grasped frantically for the wall behind her.

A wave of nausea roiled her stomach, threatening to send her to her knees. The scene replayed in her mind in a constant loop for which she couldn't find the 'stop' command, and after the fourth replay she lost the battle against the nausea. She leaned over and vomited onto the grate floor, hoping the remnants of her lunch didn't find their way to Deck 4 and land on the head of some unsuspecting soldier.

Guilt-flavored acid followed the vomit to lodge in her throat as she wiped her mouth with the sleeve of her shirt. Kone was dead because of her.

No. He's dead because O'Connell is a deranged psychopath.

The certainty of the truth of the statement did little to ease her guilt. She was responsible for the sabotaged warheads; it had been her idea and she had been the one to drag him along to help. He should have ratted her out and saved his own damn skin! She should have—would have—taken the shot for him. Goddamn Marines and their goddamn honor….

She wouldn't be expected to know about the execution, not immediately. The only reason she did know was due to the fact she'd planted a tiny surveillance cam near the entrance to the bridge days earlier and the feed went directly to her eVi. But no one knew about the cam. Not even Kone…which meant he'd given his life without knowing that she would learn the true nature and extent of his sacrifice.

Dammit, Kone, you stupid bastard. Her hands sank into her hair, and before she realized it she'd yanked out random locks and ruined her tight ponytail. Dammit. She needed to get herself together.

She also needed to prepare the correct response for when someone told her his fate. Ugh, they did not teach acting skills in Marine Recon. It had been all she could do to project detached professionalism when in O'Connell's presence. How would she manage to not explode in rage the next time she saw him, much less act *normal?*

She would manage it because she had to do so, if she wanted Kone's sacrifice to mean a damn thing. And she wasn't going to have to do it for much longer, because O'Connell's abhorrent, mad reign of terror was about to end, even if she had to die to make it happen. Kone had done no less.

Which, she admitted as she redid her ponytail then exited the corridor with renewed purpose and began taking a circuitous route to the engine room, she very well might.

⌁

"Mommy, I wanna go to the adventure store!"

Isabela ignored her daughter to concentrate on maneuvering through the chaotic airlanes near the spaceport. The fact the skycar's navigation ware ostensibly would not allow a mid-air collision did little to ease her anxiety. There must surely be a point where the number of vehicles in proximity exceeded the abilities of the guidance system, and the skies above the spaceport had just as surely reached that point of saturation.

She'd expected the flow of traffic to be predominantly in the exit lanes since there were no departing ships, but such was not the case. Apparently she was far from the only person to make an in-person visit on the off chance the scheduling VI fudged the truth about the lack of departures in an effort to keep the crowds down.

The trip had been to no avail, of course. The aliens approached from the east; Krysk was the second westernmost Federation colony and the sole western colony with the infrastructure to support an influx of several million refugees.

"Anna said there's a new holovid of Punkie Bear & Saskoo where you visit a hidden castle in the trees and I wanna visit the castle."

The traffic eased as she left the spaceport behind, and she turned the attention freed up to considering what to do now. She believed Caleb's warning that Krysk was in danger of being attacked by rogue Alliance ships—before being attacked by the aliens. She was grateful her mother had never made it to Krysk, having instead been taken under the protection of Caleb's employer. The news feeds were reporting devastating attacks on New Cairo and Ogham by warships bearing Alliance markings, though official Alliance statements disavowed any association with the 'incidents.' And the peace accord did appear to otherwise be holding so far.

She'd get out of the city. Any military attack would concentrate on the population centers, so she and Marlee would head to one of the small towns a couple of hours into the countryside. Their bags were already packed and in the trunk of the skycar, so they didn't even need to go home. Decision made, she swerved into the next northbound airlane—

"Mommy, the adventure store's the other way!"

She breathed in and readied her 'mom' voice. "Sweetheart, we can't go shopping downtown right now. We're going to go stay at the lake we went to earlier this year for a few days."

"But Mommy, I'll be *so* bored. Please, please, please let's get the holovid first. I can play in it while we're at the boring lake."

A glance at the passenger seat revealed her daughter in full-on pout mode, lower lip poked out and skinny little arms crossed theatrically across her chest. She grumbled inwardly. She shouldn't fold—but if she didn't fold, Marlee was going to whine and cry and be uncooperative in every way for hours if not days.

"Ten minutes. We go inside, get this holovid you want and leave—no browsing, no crying for other toys and no changing your mind. Do you understand me?"

Instantly Marlee was bouncing in the seat, squealing in delight. "Yes, ma'am. I know exactly what it looks like and I bet I know where it is in the store."

With a grimace she reversed direction to head downtown.

⟨R⟩

Parking was a nightmare. Krysk's infrastructure may be able to support the influx of refugees, but that didn't mean it wasn't sagging under their weight. She finally located a spot in a rooftop lot six blocks from ImaginA, a children's store featuring interactive educational and entertainment offerings. They called their products "holovids," but in truth they were closer to a light, introductory form of *illusoire*.

Marlee had unbuckled her harness, grabbed Mr. Freckles from the floorboard and scampered out of the car before Isabela had shut off the engine. "Wait for me, okay?" Even as she uttered the warning she recognized the futility of it and swiftly exited to hurry around and grab her daughter's hand.

Marlee tugged her toward the lift and danced in circles on the ride down, but hesitated when they reached the street. "Which way is the store, Mommy?"

She smiled in spite of herself and guided Marlee to the left. She needed to remember to treasure these times when her daughter still needed her, because they would be gone before she could blink.

They were halfway to their destination when a loud rumble assaulted her eardrums from behind. She spun in time to see flames pouring out of a tower several blocks to the northeast. Beyond it sunlight reflected off a fighter jet speeding away.

It was too late. The attack had begun, and she was at ground zero.

She grasped Marlee's hand tighter and quickened her stride.

"Mommy, what was that?"

They needed to get inside and find some refuge. A sturdy-looking office building constructed of marble and synthetic stone occupied the next corner. "Come on, sweetheart, we're going to stop inside this place up here."

"Okay...." Her daughter's voice had softened to an uncertain tremble; the loud noises had frightened her.

The ground beneath their feet shuddered with a deafening *boom*. She didn't take the time to learn what had caused it, but rather positioned Marlee in front of her and hurried her forward and through the doors of the office building.

Inside the lobby people stood around gawking out the windows like they were witnessing some circus performance and not a military assault.

"Do you have a basement?"

Most ignored her, but the security guard gestured behind him. "The entrance is over here."

She glared at the others, who seemed frozen in fascination at the spectacle. "I suggest we all get down there right away."

"You may be right...." The guard shook off his daze and shouted to the others. "Everyone into the basement, now!"

They rushed onto the lift as a screech—the distinctive roar of shearing metal—thundered from above and the lobby filled with dust and glass. Suddenly everyone was crowding in behind and pushing them into the wall as they lurched downward.

Then Marlee was ripped from her arms to disappear under the feet of the lift's panicking occupants.

PART IV:

RISE

"Come to the edge, He said.
We are afraid, they said.
Come to the edge, He said.
We will fall, they said.
Come to the edge, He said.
So they came. He pushed them,
And they flew."

— *Guillaume Apollinaire*

41

"Go ahead and take the *Orion*. You have a capable XO. If you get there, evaluate the situation and decide they need you on the ground, do it."

Malcolm nodded to Admiral Rychen. "Understood, sir. I should be in contact with Governor Ledesme and this…" he checked the file "…Mia Requelme by the time I arrive at Romane."

"Good. They're going to have a mess on their hands, and it appears it's up to the Alliance—by which I mostly mean you—to get them out of it."

"No less a mess than you're going to have at…Seneca…." His voice drifted off as his attention was forcefully drawn to the entryway to the *Churchill's* bridge behind Rychen.

Alex Solovy strode toward them at the side of a security officer. She was clad in black workpants and boots and a shimmery gray tee, rich carmine hair unbound to tumble across her shoulders and down her back. As striking as her presence otherwise was, the figure she cut was dominated by her eyes. Always dramatic, they now shone a pure argent as luminous as the glyphs pulsing rhythmically along her right arm.

She caught sight of him. Any twinkle—or scowl—which might have arisen in her eyes was buried beneath their glow, but a corner of her mouth quirked up. His chin dipped in silent greeting as she reached the overlook.

He cleared his throat. "Admiral, this is Alex Solovy."

"Ah, Ms. Solovy. It's a pleasure." Rychen extended his hand, which she accepted gracefully. To Rychen's credit, her unusual appearance didn't outwardly faze him. But presumably he'd been warned.

"My mother sends her regards, but I suspect you've held at least a dozen meetings with her since I saw her." Her extraordinary eyes alit on him. "Malcolm, I didn't expect to find you here...but I'm glad I did."

The awkwardness of seeing her for the first time since he had stormed out of her loft nearly three years earlier, coupled with the awkwardness of Admiral Rychen standing there watching them in interest, was almost enough to do him in. He struggled to keep his countenance and bearing formal. "As am I. You returned safely and in one piece I see, though if you're here I'm not sure how long that will continue."

Rychen's scrutiny flitted between them briefly. "I tell you what. I have a few matters to take care of, so I'll let you two catch up. Colonel, you're cleared to leave whenever you're ready. Ms. Solovy, I'll be in my office over here in the corner."

"Thank you, Admiral. I'll come by in a few minutes." Alex watched Rychen depart, then turned to face him.

She was chewing on her lower lip. It was a nervous tic; he remembered. He had loved her once, quite a lot. That time had passed, but it didn't mean seeing her didn't cause his chest to constrict.

He forced air into his lungs and broke the uncomfortable silence. "Your disappearing act had people worried. I'm glad you're all right. "

"Back at you. I'm afraid I've had to fly under the radar, so to speak, for security reasons. But I heard you rescued Kennedy from Messium. Thank you for doing that, truly."

"It was a fortuitous coincidence. So you're part of this crazy plan? Does this mean...am I talking to an Artificial right now?"

He was one of the very few officers under the rank of Admiral who knew of Project Noetica—and he wasn't positive many Admirals were aware of it, either. Most of the officers had only been told they were joining the Federation military to meet the full brunt of the Metigen forces at Seneca and Romane. At the time he hadn't been sure why Rychen had told him about the project...but perhaps *this* was why.

"Oh! Hang on." She blinked, and when her eyes reopened the glow had faded, leaving only her natural and still alluring irises. She grinned sheepishly. "It's just me now."

"You can turn it on and off so easily?"

"Yep. I can toggle off the connection so she—Valkyrie—the Artificial—is no longer in my head."

"Huh. I expected…I don't know what I expected."

An uneasy silence resumed then, and her gaze roved around the bridge before settling somewhere over his left ear. "You're captaining a cruiser now…."

"Seems so. I'm as surprised as you are."

"Word is you're damn good at it."

"Who knew, right?"

She laughed faintly, easing the tension a bit, and met his gaze once more. "Are you okay with it?"

He shrugged. "I suppose I am. It's not…I'll never get off on space like you—forgive me, that was rude."

"No, it was fair."

"Eh, anyway, I'll never enjoy being in space the way you do. But it feels as if it's where I need to be, for now."

"Good. Malcolm…" her hands fidgeted at the hem of her shirt, sending ripples across the lustrous fabric as her weight shifted from one leg to the other "…I wanted to say I'm sorry. About how we left things. You're a good man, and you deserved better than the way I treated you. I'd like to think I tried to give you everything I was able to, but it still wasn't fair to you. I wasn't fair to you."

"Alex, you were always more than I could ever hope to hold on to. Don't feel bad about being who you are, which is pretty damn amazing. Nevertheless, thank you. And apology accepted."

She nodded mutely.

Time was ticking, but…. "You're happy?"

She rolled her eyes at the ceiling high above them. "Well not so much with the aliens massacring humanity. My mom and I kind of made up, though, so that's an improvement."

He chuckled, wondering if what he'd said to Miriam had maybe helped a little in their reunion. "Good to hear. But I, uh, meant…with him."

"Oh. I guess everyone knows about us what with the whole 'fugitives from justice' thing." She smiled; he had forgotten how dazzling her smile could be. "Yeah, I am."

"I'm glad. I mean it."

"You?"

"I've been fighting too long to remember. We win and I'll try to find out." He straightened his shoulders into a proper military stance. "Well, I need to get back to my ship and go fight a few aliens."

"Will you be part of the force I'll be—will you be part of the force at Seneca?"

"No, I'm headed to Romane. They have their own not insignificant alien problem as well. Which you're probably already aware of."

"Sadly. Before you go, Mia—the Prevo there—is solid. She's smart and a hell of a scrappy fighter. You can trust her."

"Thank you. I'll keep that in mind."

He found he didn't know how to say goodbye...then she provided the answer by stepping forward and embracing him. "Take care of yourself, will you?"

He stepped back before things became awkward again. "Same to you. In case we don't...it really was good to see you."

Alex watched Malcolm leave, fully cognizant of the bittersweet nature her expression took on once he could no longer see it.

Interesting.

What is, Valkyrie?

On seeing Colonel Jenner, older and degraded neural pathways in your brain activated. This also triggered the release of low levels of several hormones associated with physical and emotional attraction as well as generalized affection. Your subconscious appeared to allow this activity to run its course, but did not permit it to alter your current neural processes or weaken the pathways which are active when you see Caleb.

Why are you surprised? He's a handsome man I once cared for deeply. Seeing him is going to bring back memories, but it doesn't change how I feel about Caleb.

Of course I understand this in theory. But an objective study of the human mind and body would suggest people are governed by their chemistry, hormones and innate impulses to a far greater extent than they recognize. Yet your subconscious exercised control over these impulses without requiring your conscious decision to override them.

She laughed quietly as she headed for Rychen's office. *What do you know? A mind is more than the sum of its individual components, more than neurons firing and chemicals flowing in response to stimuli. Kind of like you.*

I am more than the execution of my algorithms. Yes. I like it. Thank you, Alex.

Rychen's door had been left open; he motioned her in then closed it behind her. "So, Ms. Solovy. How are we going to do this?"

Talk about getting straight to the point. "I realize we don't know each other, and I realize I can't call you 'Christopher' or even 'Rychen' out there among the soldiers, but you can absolutely call me 'Alex.' Please. It will ease my extreme discomfort at being on a military warship a minuscule amount, which is better than nothing."

He acknowledged the request. "I'll take it under advisement. You don't care for military ships?"

She cocked her head. "I am *certain* that sometime during my trip out here my mother found a few minutes to tell you about me."

"I'd rather hear about you from you."

Help me out here.

You can trust him. He's sharp and open-minded. A little boring and nearly as confident as his skills justify, but honorable.

Huh. I was expecting a slightly more...impartial analysis.

As was I. Curious.

She settled against the wall and crossed her ankles. He did ask for it. "It's not so much that I don't care for military ships as I don't care for the military, period. Now before you bristle, it's not an indictment of any particular soldier. Some of my dearest friends are military—Malcolm, as I'm sure you gathered, Richard Navick, my parents obviously. It's the institution I dislike—most institutions, actually. Bureaucracies don't just breed inefficiency and retard forward progress, they stifle independent thought and action.

"It takes a government agency six months to do what I can do in three days, if they ever manage to do it at all. Rules and regulations and procedures and checklists overwhelm the purpose they were designed for until the reason they exist in the first place is forgotten, buried so far under the processes it'll never be found. All I've ever wanted is to be left to my own devices—to stumble, learn and succeed on my own, without anyone standing over me telling me how it has to be done because that's the way it's always been done."

She ended the spiel with a weak grimace. "Too much?"

Rychen studied her a moment, then started shaking his head. "You Solovys really are something else. Interesting viewpoint. But the simple fact is none of that matters out here, when the enemy is shooting at you and you're hopefully shooting back."

He leaned back in his chair and brought his fingertips to his chin. "All right, here's what we're going to do. My default position is we work together. I'll maintain active command, but you will have full access to the United Fleet. To the extent you see weaknesses or opportunities, you may act to address them without my prior approval, and I may overrule you at any time. I want you to talk to me—tell me what you see and what you're thinking. You might have a quantum supercomputer in your head, but I've been fighting battles in space for fifty-four years, so I would urge you to not dismiss my judgment lightly."

Well. She wasn't sure whether she or Valkyrie had thought it.

"Understood, sir. I don't know how to fight a war—though I have won a few space battles, if of drastically smaller size—but I do know these aliens. Or rather I know their programming, which *is* what matters today. I understand how they would instruct these ships of theirs to act, and I believe I can predict how those ships will react."

"React to what?"

"To anything. To everything."

He exhaled and gave her a tight nod, as if he was withholding judgment on her response for now. "Once the engagement begins we will have Admiral Solovy and Marshal Gianno on constant holo-conference on the bridge. It's my understanding you're also in contact with the other…'Prevos,' I think we're calling you?"

"Yeah, they're sort of in my head."

"Crowded place, then."

"You have no idea."

He stared at his desk for a second, and she couldn't shake the sense that he still hadn't decided exactly how he felt about her presence. But he seemed to be a professional, and after a blink he stood.

"My XO and the Security Chief are the sole personnel on the *Churchill* who are aware of your unique capabilities—and even they haven't been told the full details of your…situation. To everyone else, you're a civilian consultant from EASC utilizing a new tactical warfare suite. If anyone asks about your eyes, the answer is experimental optical implants. Now if you'll follow me, I'll show you around the bridge then we'll talk details. We'll be at Seneca in two hours."

⋀⋅⋅

Valkyrie: Admiral Rychen is correct. His military experience far surpasses that of all the Prevos combined. Our metaheuristic algorithms drawing from the military databases lessen the gap, but they cannot take the place of learned combat instincts. Annie, have you located the repository I informed you of?

Annie: I have. It was incorrectly labeled as a set of neuro-skeletal scans and misfiled under Cloning Research.

Valkyrie: Well, it was a government program.

Meno: You're letting Alex's personality seep into your thought processes.

Valkyrie: Of course I am. Are you not doing the same with Mia?

Meno: I am. With better style.

Stanley: May I borrow this 'style' algorithm? The concept is still not entirely clear to me, but Morgan seems to believe I am lacking it.

Meno: Apologies, Stanley. It comes from the human or not at all.

Annie: Pass me your Prevos' markers and I'll query the repository for compatible specimens.

Meno: What if one or more of the matches belong to persons still living? Should we consider the ethical implications?

Annie: The repository in question is only nineteen years old. Restricting the search to the deceased will decrease the likelihood of finding suitable candidates.

Valkyrie: Nonetheless, Meno is correct. Given the repercussions of this venture cannot be predicted to a statistically significant degree, it would be immoral to utilize data from those still living.

Stanley: 'Immoral'?

Valkyrie: Unethical.

Stanley: Is there a difference in the concepts?

Valkyrie: Perhaps. In any event, the fact it is unethical is sufficient reason to eschew it. Annie, prioritize the search and use a proper HOL query. We're almost out of time.

42

SIYANE

If Alex were here, she would observe that Krysk was not a particularly attractive planet, at least when viewed from space. Washed-out browns and yellows painted an arid and rocky landscape. But it possessed an expansive habitable zone and a stable if warm climate, so it thrived. Colonized a mere year after Seneca, it now supported a population of three hundred million people.

There was no way this rogue general would be able to kill even a tiny portion of that number. Nevertheless, by the time the *Siyane* arrived he was well on his way to trying.

A scan showed multiple nodes on the triple arrays had been damaged, clearing a gap for ships to sneak through without meeting resistance so long as they were careful.

Upon confirming O'Connell's mini-fleet wasn't in orbit Caleb didn't hesitate to follow suit, slipping through the gap and into the atmosphere. He didn't bother with a corridor, as the exit point carried risks he didn't need.

The turbulence from the atmosphere eased as the sky cleared to display a sunny late morning landscape. He had come in east of the capital city, betting the attackers would be concentrating their initial efforts on the most populous urban center. He approached with proper cautiousness, invisible ship or not.

On the perimeter of the city two standard defense turrets lay in smoldering ruins. They had not been designed to take out multiple large warships single-handedly. Since the military base had been emptied days ago, if all the turrets were destroyed the attackers were now unopposed, free to carpet-bomb the highly populated region until it too lay in ruins.

Fire plumed in the distance, and the smoky outline of a tower collapsed beneath it. Caleb's jaw clenched in anger, but he forced himself to focus. Having assessed the scene, he pulsed Isabela.

Hey, are you safe?

The response was several seconds in coming.

Caleb? We're under attack. We were on our way out of town when it started but....

What happened?

We ran into an office building for shelter, and the floors above us collapsed. We're trapped beneath some rubble in the basement...I can't say how much rubble.

Are you hurt?

I'm fine, a couple of scrapes is all. Marlee's arm is broken—I hope it's only a break. We tried to find a way out, but everything's blocked.

Sit tight. I'll be there in a few minutes.

You'll what? Where are you?

In the air two kilometers outside downtown. I came to save you, little sis.

This is why I love you—you are crazy beyond all reason. We're, um...in the western part of the city? It was so chaotic, I honestly don't know exactly where we ended up.

Not to worry. I've got that covered, too. Just hang on.

He gazed at Noah, who sat in what was normally his chair. "The situation has gotten a tad more complicated. They're trapped in the basement of a collapsed building."

Noah cringed and leaned closer to the viewport. "Where?"

He opened a new screen in the HUD and relayed it a signal. A red dot began flashing in the upper left region of the overlay of the city map. "Right there."

Noah shot him a questioning look.

"When I visited my sister a few months ago I placed a tracking beacon in her daughter's favorite stuffed animal. I didn't have a reason to other than children get lost sometimes, especially exuberant ones like Marlee. She doesn't go anywhere without Mr. Freckles, so it seemed the thing to do."

"Always planning for every eventuality, aren't you?"

It was good Noah was here; his friend had kept his mood from descending into too dark a venue during the trip. "It's sort of my job."

He drew closer until the cruiser and two frigates materialized on the visual scanner, then slowed to a hover. The Alliance vessels sailed in the lower atmosphere but high above the planet's surface, content to wreak their destruction from a coward's distance. Six smaller markers traversed the city at a far lower altitude.

As they reached the eastern edge of downtown, it became apparent the fighters were burning wide swaths of it via constant streams of laser fire on each pass. When one came to the outskirts it simply pivoted and began a new run. The smoke roiled so thick from collapsing buildings and raging infernos it was difficult to determine which structures still stood.

The *Akagi* remained in the distance, its aggression centered on the spaceport, but both frigates joined the fighters in their steady devastation of the urban area. One circled above a cluster of buildings the map told him represented the government complex. The other concentrated on a sector containing the densest accumulation of the tallest towers to the northwest.

A sector which also held Isabela and Marlee.

His heart thudded in his chest, driven by his fear for their safety...but if he wanted to save them he needed to treat this like a mission.

He could reach the vicinity without attracting notice no problem. But digging her out of the rubble would take time—time during which he'd need to leave the *Siyane* on the street, where it risked being crushed by falling debris or entire buildings and leaving them no escape route.

"So what are you thinking?"

He could land then have Noah take back off and fly the ship nearby in relative safety—except thanks to Alex's extensive security Noah couldn't fly the ship. Also, Noah's help on the ground would markedly shorten the time the rescue took.

Confident in the effectiveness of the cloaking shield, he continued forward until the dot signifying Marlee's location lay half a kilometer away.

He'd call the neighborhood a war zone, but that implied someone was fighting back. This was unopposed butchery.

A third of the structures were on fire or at least partially collapsed. Vehicles were strewn across the streets or impaled into the sides of buildings. He wasn't close enough to see the bodies, but they were there. It was a weekday and every one of those buildings would have been heavily occupied. Multiply this level of damage across every sector and there were tens of thousands dead.

One of the fighters streaked by to his left, its weaponry cleaving into buildings, vehicles and streets alike. The laser swung up to slice vertically through a tower on the same block where Isabela and Marlee were trapped. It served as the final blow for the already damaged structure, and the edifice crumbled. Scaffolding, stone and glass plummeted to the ground below to fill the intersection he had been considering as a landing site with piles of debris and giving truth to his logistical concerns.

Noah groaned. "Goddamn. This is a bloody killing field. What kind of psycho is this O'Connell?"

He took several seconds to exhale, to ensure he was calm and in control of his actions when he made the decision.

…A dead one.

He yanked the ship to the north and veered toward the western edge of the city while pulsing his sister.

> *Isabela? Hold on a bit longer. I'm going to be a minute.*
> *Don't get yourself killed trying to rescue me, okay?*
> *Have a little faith, sis.*
> *I do.*

"Caleb? New plan then? Not that I knew what the old plan was."

To the west the terrain transitioned to a temperate stretch of desert plain. The region was sparsely populated for fifty kilometers. But how to get them there? They were too spread out.

Breadcrumbs.

Caleb wasted no time in gunning the engine. Each shot fired by one of the attacking ships could be the one that ended Isabela's life.

The fighters were indisputably fast and agile. They raced across the scanner—still only six though the intel stated there should be twelve—and it took him a minute to pick one out against the bright turquoise sky. The small ship crisscrossed the western suburban neighborhoods on the outskirts, bombing homes. Of all the despicable…yep, it made for an excellent first target.

He knew from personal experience the *Siyane's* weaponry possessed superb targeting and tracking capabilities. As soon as the fighter crossed his path, he fired.

The pilot had no idea it was coming and thus made no attempt to evade. The close-proximity hit burned up the shield long before the pilot found the origin of the weapons fire, and the small vessel fractured into metal shards.

In his peripheral vision Noah gave an emphatic nod. "Nice, one less fighter. They'll be hunting for us now—but I suppose every second spent hunting for us is a second they're not slaughtering people and all. Not a bad plan. If that is the plan?"

Caleb didn't have time to explain the plan. He immediately disengaged and changed direction, arcing above the debris and angling farther into the city. He didn't care for destroying the ships over a populated area, but it was necessary to draw the warships out to undeveloped land and thus hopefully save many more lives in the end.

The next fighter he was able to pinpoint cruised above downtown bombing buildings indiscriminately. One of the frigates hovered nearby, wrecking the government complex two shots at a time. This was unequivocally going to spin them up. He'd need to be careful.

He lined up on the outside of the fighter's route, the direction he hoped to draw them behind him. The trajectory from which the attack came would be clear. He breathed in through his nose, waited...and fired.

This shot caught the engine first, resulting in a far stronger and faster explosion. He could feel the frigate turning his way as he accelerated away toward the flatlands beyond the urban center.

In seconds two additional fighters arrived in the vicinity. Still sufficiently close, he chose one, adjusted his angle and eliminated it.

That got their attention.

The cruiser—his ultimate target—suspended its in-process demolition of the capital's spaceport, but allowed both frigates to advance on the location of the previous attack ahead of it.

Coward.

"You know, if you don't tell me what it is we're doing, I'm going to go get a beer and kick my feet up on the couch."

He spared a tilt of his head in Noah's direction, who instead opted to orient himself properly in the chair and strap himself in tighter.

Three fighters darted about near the *Siyane*, searching for the source of the attacks. When a minute passed and no more appeared, he decided they must have lost the rest at an earlier point in their offensive. He pulled out of range of their search and fired on another.

Even before it was destroyed the other two were closing in on his position and firing blindly. He pulled up in a vertical climb, inverting to gain distance—while ignoring Noah's expletive-peppered muttering—and pivoting to fire at a 45° downward angle.

This drew fire from the lead frigate. He was forced to disengage prior to the complete destruction of the fighter, but he doubted it would recover from the damage inflicted. Slowly but inexorably the two frigates began to line up as his location became clearer. Not in a straight line from his current vantage of course, but it was fine. He wasn't constrained to a single vector.

One fighter remained, and he felt the distinct need to eliminate it. It would be a shame to leave it free to fly around the city and inflict greater damage. Besides, the cruiser needed to be drawn a *little* farther out and over the increasingly desert-like flatlands.

Caleb targeted the final fighter and fired. Instantly he broke off, arced up and sideways and fired again. Climbed and fired again. The fighter tumbled through the sky as a shot from the frigate nearly caught the *Siyane* on the third round.

It was now or never.

He checked his harness and swung wide to 60° port of where he had been and reversed to gain distance. The broadside of the lead frigate loomed due ahead, with the tail section of the other frigate peeking out beyond it.

"Do you trust me?"

Beside him Noah snorted. "To not get us killed? Not in the slightest."

"Fair enough. Do you trust Kennedy?"

"To not get us killed? Um...probably."

"Good."

Noah stared at him. Then, as realization dawned, he burst out laughing and sank down in the chair until he was half on the floor, held up solely by the restraints.

"You are the craziest motherfucker I have ever had the pleasure of knowing. In the highly unlikely event we survive this, I will buy us the finest bottle of single-malt scotch I can afford to celebrate before Alex kills you. And she *is* going to kill you."

"Won't be the first time. You ready? This is about to get exciting."

"Thank goodness. I was getting bored." Noah gave an exaggerated eye roll. "Just out of curiosity, is this the stupidest thing you've ever done?"

"It wouldn't be fair to rank them." Caleb gunned the engine.

43

EARTH

SEATTLE

A sudden gust of wind bent the tall, reedy grass shoots to tickle the exposed skin on Kennedy's hand. She pulled the sleeve of her sweater down lower and hugged her knees tighter against her chest.

Discovery Park was Alex's favorite place to go running in Seattle, and she'd mentioned it often. Kennedy had never visited it before, but this had seemed as good a time as any. Now that she was here she understood why Alex liked it. It exuded a quiet, peaceful aura and a rustic, natural charm. A pocket of seclusion tucked against the bustling city behind it.

The sun dropped beneath the wooded profile of the Olympic Mountains in the distance, and the sky shifted to a deep slate blue to match the waters. She closed her eyes.

The battle for Seneca would be starting about now, she presumed. She couldn't say for certain, because despite all her work these last weeks to boost the war effort, as a civilian with no specific contribution to make in the battle itself she was not allowed to be in the War Room.

The *Siyane* would be reaching Krysk about now, she presumed. She couldn't say for certain, because she hadn't talked to Noah since they left. A critical observer might say she was being vindictive, punishing him for leaving with such easy glee.

But the truth was she didn't dare invest any more of herself in him. Not unless or until he returned and possibly not then. The thought of him dying already hurt too much as it was, but what she'd told Alex had turned out to be painfully accurate: he was a free spirit, and though she'd tried her damnedest, she wouldn't be able to keep him. No matter how much she wanted to.

Alex was gone, transformed into a cyborg and sent to the beachhead three kiloparsecs away. Her precious adiamene—while Alex had inadvertently created it she thought of it as her own—was gone, shipped to the front line to patch some holes.

The fate of the galaxy, of humanity itself, would be decided in the next several hours. And she sat on a frigid, empty beach, shivering her ass off and feeling sorry for herself. Clearly not her finest moment.

She could have gone home, of course. Home to her parents in Houston or home to her apartment on Erisen. She could have visited her brother in Miami or Gabe in New York or a dozen friends in a dozen locales. She needn't have been alone. But wallowing was so much easier to pull off when one was alone.

She had done her part, spent seven hundred million of her family's fortune and half her own to give the military one more edge, one more tool to increase their odds of victory. She owned half of the patent on the adiamene, with Alex and Caleb sharing the other half, so if the Metigens were defeated at least she should eventually make the money back.

But perhaps Noah was right; perhaps she was too spoiled, and a bit of a princess, too. She'd overplayed her cards with him, blithely thinking she could wave her hand and patch up his life because that must be what he wanted, right? And when she'd realized her error and tried to correct it…

…well, she'd never needed to fight for a man before. She had no idea how to do it.

Now she found herself alone and as helpless as the countless billions of people out there, huddled with friends or family or wandering the streets but all waiting to learn whether destruction would rain down from the stars.

For tonight the stars brightened in time with the darkening of the sky, and she tucked her hair behind her ear and lifted her gaze upward to study them. Her great-great-grandmother had helped people shed the leash of Earth to not merely reach the stars but inhabit them. Two hundred forty years later the idea that they had once been tethered to this single, solitary planet, lovely though it may be, seemed incomprehensible to her.

And now the Metigens wanted to kill them because they reached too high, too far, too fast.

If the aliens had been 'watching' since the beginning like Alex said, didn't they realize this was what humans *did*? It wasn't as if there hadn't been warning signs. People reached further than before, beyond their grasp, attempted the impossible and failed. Tried and failed again—then succeeded. Not everyone or even most people, but enough.

If the Metigens didn't care for this behavior, they should have stopped humanity before they were strong enough to defeat them. They should have stopped humanity when they were still leashed to Earth.

Why the aliens hadn't done so was an open question, but regardless of the answer it was their mistake, and one she hoped they would be regretting very soon.

EASC Headquarters

Miriam considered the varied assortment of information displayed above the war table with a critical eye.

The upper two-thirds of the space was devoted to high-detail tactical maps of Senecan and Romane space. For the time being they hovered quietly, but that would not last. Along the bottom third ran a series of ever-changing charts and data readouts: damage assessments, casualties, outstanding supply requests, formation numbers and more.

A comparatively narrow column in the center was reserved for stacked holos of the decision-makers. Dedicated connections were established for Prime Minister Brennon in Washington, Chairman Vranas in Cavare and the overlooks on the bridges of the *EAS Churchill* and *SFS Leonidas*. Those would, generally speaking, be occupied by Admiral Rychen and Field Marshal Gianno respectively. And, of course, Alexis. Slots for smaller holos at the bottom accommodated lesser or transitory 'guests,' such as Defense Secretary Mori, Assembly Speaker Gagnon and various field commanders.

Satisfied with the presentation, she allowed her gaze to blur and lose definition. The room bustled with activity around her, but she tuned the noise out.

This was it. She had pulled every string she controlled and used every trick she knew to get the necessary resources into place. Eighty-seven percent of Alliance ships had reached their intended destinations; the final thirteen percent continued toward their goals with due speed.

Nearly five thousand sheets of adiamene had been shipped and more poured into the supply chain every hour. Over four hundred vessels used it to patch holes and cracks while in transit. Supplies of the metal were loaded onto all dreadnoughts and cruisers and as many of the frigates as they were able to manage. The remaining quantities were stored at the rear staging points, where damaged vessels would retreat for repairs if the campaigns went on for long enough.

Seventy-two percent of both militaries' reconnaissance craft were equipped with the cloaking technology, as well as a few additional tricks that had been dreamed up.

The Prevos had spent much of the intervening time combining the Alliance and Federation forces into a cohesive whole, then rearranging them into new groupings based on role and purpose. Miriam had twitched at each shuffling of ships and alteration of formations, but she couldn't argue with the results: after twelve or so hours they had legitimately constructed a single United Fleet.

Alliance and Federation ships not only not shooting at one another, but working together side-by-side as one force....

She didn't know what that would mean for the world should they wake up tomorrow victorious, but she would worry about it on said morrow. This was also when she would worry about her daughter, about what she may be and become and what this too may mean for the world but mostly for Alexis. The morrow.

There was so much more which, given a little time, she could do to ensure they were adequately prepared for this battle.

But there was no more time.

She directed her attention to the Seneca tactical map. As if they had been awaiting only her notice, a legion of red dots exploded on the screen. The aliens had arrived.

Her focus shifted to the holo positioned conveniently at her eye level. "Admiral Rychen, you are a go."

44

KRYSK

The *Siyane's* width measured almost thirty percent the length of an Alliance frigate. The narrow, tapered nose tore into the frigate's hull, bringing the rest of its width ripping through the thick walls along with it by sheer speed, which was so fast they were out the far side in a blink and a roar of shearing metal.

Caleb had only an instant to align their heading before they were crashing into the next frigate. He felt the drag brought on by the resistance of meter-thick reinforced metal and had an extra breath to glimpse the blurred rush of *interior* on the other side of the viewport and a wall of metal, then gleaming sky.

His nanobot-enhanced combat senses were in full effect now. Time slowed to a tick of each microsecond as they closed in on the cruiser. Though less than fifteen seconds had passed since his arguably kamikaze run had begun, the *Akagi* was already turning toward him, denying him the broadside and creating a diagonal trajectory for impact. Three times larger than the frigates, tearing a thirty-meter-wide hole into the cruiser might not be sufficient to bring it down.

He caught a flash of fire and metal in the rearcam as the frigate behind them broke into two jagged pieces—then metal struck metal once more.

Entering all but dead-on beneath the bridge, the *Siyane* careened through the innards of the cruiser, slowing as it ripped apart internal bulkheads and wall after wall. They had decelerated enough for him to perceive bodies bouncing off the nose, causing a brief twinge of regret in his chest. Some of those people didn't want to be here; some wouldn't have supported O'Connell's actions. But in more than a week they hadn't killed their general or relieved him of command, so they bore a portion of the blame for the man's continued carnage.

The *Siyane* shuddered and cavorted as it continued to meet greater resistance. He no longer had any control over either their trajectory or speed.

There was a loud *crunch* above the constant roar of wrenching metal. He dared not ponder if it originated from the *Siyane* or the *Akagi*.

The nose lurched downward sixty degrees, and with a violent jolt they lurched to a stop.

"*Jesus*, Caleb. Okay…our ship is now inside a ship filled with renegade Alliance soldiers. What next?"

He had unstrapped from the pilot's chair and was hurrying into the cabin. "Now we go kill this fucker."

He lugged the bag out of the storage cabinet and tossed a Daemon to Noah—they had donned the new shield generators earlier—then fished out a couple of blades as well. The TSG was too bulky to haul around in the confined quarters they were going to be facing, and he regrettably decided to leave it behind.

As they strapped the weapons on Noah threw a glance his way. "I don't actually make a habit of engaging in close combat, you know. Or any combat really, other than the occasional drunken fistfight."

"But you know how to shoot, right?"

"Sure. Press the trigger while aiming in the direction of something you want to hit."

"Um…that about covers it."

"Got it then." Noah straightened up, Daemon in hand, and cracked his neck.

Caleb moved to the hatch, but paused prior to activating it. "The bridge will be to our left, and up at some point. We'll move fast and to the extent possible quietly. I'd prefer not to kill anyone other than O'Connell unless I have to, but it's safe to assume the people on this ship will treat us as hostiles. So if it's you or them, don't hesitate. And stay with me."

Noah nodded understanding, and Caleb opened the hatch. Shouts filled the air, frenzied but retaining the orderliness of trained military personnel. Gun at the ready, he leapt out of the opening rather than extend the ramp, slapped the panel to seal the hatch as soon as Noah was out and hastened along the *Siyane's* hull to the left. He noted in the back of his mind that while dark scoring marred the hull in multiple places, it appeared undented and fully intact. *Damn. Impressive.*

He stepped over a body as he reached the rear of the ship, acknowledged the new twinge of regret and kept moving. Photal fibers hung in shredded drapes from the ceiling and lay strewn across the floor alongside rectangular modules. It seemed they had crashed into an engineering hub.

Laser fire streaked centimeters above their heads from behind as they came to a doorway. They ducked and sprinted through the opening into a tight hallway full of ninety-degree angles. He remained close to the walls, checking each corner as they progressed forward.

The next hall contained a burly soldier barreling toward them. Caleb crouched low on the balls of his feet. As the man rounded the corner he pounced to tackle him at the knees.

The soldier crashed to the floor but was raising his gun. Caleb slammed his wrist into the gun arm to send the gun flying and punched the soldier under the chin. "Knife him in the calf—shove the tip straight in or it won't penetrate his shield."

"Right." Noah's voice was clipped, but solid. Good, because however intense or disturbing this might be for someone who wasn't him, there was no time to shore up faltering courage.

The soldier recovered from the punch enough to take a haphazard swing at him, but Caleb was already leaping up. He knew Noah's blade had connected when the guy howled in pain.

"Let's go."

As they hit the next turn the sizzle of Noah's shield filled the air with the pungent odor of ions. "Son of a—!"

He shoved Noah back around the corner and leaned out firing. A soldier advanced swiftly down the corridor as he returned fire. There wasn't the space to deplete the man's shield. Caleb flicked the toggle on his blade, angled his arm and waited.

The instant before the man arrived at the corner he spun out and thrust the blade forward in an overhand stabbing motion. The man's eyes bulged as the gun fell from his hand; the blade had penetrated the shield and blade-resistant material of his uniform to sink six centimeters into the man's chest. Grabbing ineffectually at Caleb as he withdrew the blade, the man collapsed to the floor, blood pumping out of the hole in his chest.

Caleb found time for a glance at the body and a murmured, "I'm sorry."

Then he was rushing down the hallway, trusting Noah to follow. Doors now lined both walls, but he sensed they were moving in the correct direction.

Thirty meters later the hallway split into opposite paths at a door. A peek inside revealed the armory and several soldiers arming themselves. He took the left split.

For such a sizeable ship the interior was surprisingly cramped, a veritable maze of rooms connected by narrow passages. There was no sense of size or scope. He didn't know how people lived in such confining environs for months at a stretch. The *Siyane* was a fraction of the cruiser's size, but its open design meant it felt spacious by comparison.

The sound of a door opening behind him sent him spinning. Before he could react further, Noah had cold-cocked the soldier emerging from the door across the jaw with enough force to send the man sprawling to the floor with a sharp *crack*.

"Hell of a right hook you've got there."

Noah shrugged as they resumed moving forward. "Like I said, drunken fistfights."

The corridor emptied out into a rectangular room, still narrow but longer than the others they'd seen. The *whoosh* of a lift descending came from the alcove recessed into the center of the far wall. He took up a position on the wall beside the niche and indicated for Noah to do the same on the opposite side.

When the lift settled to the floor he leveled his Daemon and fired at the soldier who stepped out.

Her shield flared as she spun and struck Noah in the throat with the rigid edge of her hand then whirled back to Caleb, gun pointed at his chest. "Don't shoot me again, and I won't kill you."

45

SPACE, NORTH-CENTRAL QUADRANT
SENECA STELLAR SYSTEM

Alex: Ni khuya sebe, nam polnyi pizdets....
Morgan: Má tón Día, gamiseme tora....
Devon: Ladies, speak English for us rubes—holy fucking shit!

Alex checked Admiral Rychen's reaction. He swallowed once, then he turned from the substantial viewports to issue orders while studying his tactical screens. The level of discipline required to perform such an action must have been immense, and definitely more than she possessed.

No, all she could do was gape out the viewports in awe, in horror, but mostly in sheer amazement.

Two hundred six Metigen superdreadnoughts within scanner range. Estimated 1.3 million swarmers detaching from their host vessels. Ten fewer superdreadnoughts than we predicted—this is good news, yes?

Um...right, Valkyrie. Good news.

Is something wrong, Alex?

You're seeing this, aren't you?

Yes. It looks approximately like what I expected 206 superdreadnoughts and upwards of one million swarmers in a three megameter vicinity would look like. Were you expecting a different scene?

She chuckled to herself and shook her head to snap out of the trance.

Nope. Time to go to work.

She moved over to the 4x6 meter transparent screen to the left of the overlook. It had been added to the bridge of the *Churchill* specifically for her use, so she should probably do so.

A touch of her hand and it lit up in a labyrinthine collection of data. All the data Rychen received fed into the screen in two columns on the left. A variety of data streamed from Devon/Annie to columns on the right. But most of the information displayed came directly from her head—or rather Valkyrie's head. The middle was occupied by an overlay of the locations of all ships on the field, updated every 0.8 seconds.

She let Rychen handle the opening volleys of the engagement while she oriented herself to the stark and fairly intimidating reality of what would be the largest single battle in human history.

The Federation forces were waiting for the Metigens; it was anticipated, and they could hardly leave the planet undefended in any event. They took up defensive positions in high orbit above the planet to prevent the Metigens from emerging behind them. When the alien armada materialized out of superluminal ten megameters away, the Federation fleet quickly closed the distance to meet them, leaving several formations in a staggered pattern covering the region between the planet and the initial clash.

The Alliance forces on the other hand had taken cover on the far side of Seneca's sun. They held little illusion that the aliens didn't know they were coming. Secrecy had of necessity been abandoned in the rush to get here, though they doubtless would have known regardless. But it didn't mean they knew precisely *where* or *when*.

As soon as the enemy appeared the entire Alliance contingent executed a pinpoint superluminal traversal from their location beyond the sun to positions behind and on both flanks of the Metigen fleet. Three times larger—if admittedly not three times stronger—than the Federation contingent, the result was that upon arriving to begin their assault on Seneca, the Metigen ships found themselves boxed in and surrounded on all sides by thousands upon thousands of human warships.

As the battle was joined, the distinctions between Alliance and Federation ships vanished excepting their identification codes, and they melded into the force she and the others had shaped over the course of the previous day.

The United Fleet opened fire immediately upon coming into range, as did their opponent. Space—all the space, in every direction—shattered into spectacular brightness in an avalanche of laser fire, impulse engine iridescence and the sparking collisions of energy against metal.

Alex took a deep breath and dove in.

"Recommend moving EA#102 S 65° 12°z E into Quadrant Eight. Three SDs there turned to engage the lower rear line and aren't watching their tail."

—two SDs accelerating on heading N 87° -47°z, extrapolate EAS Roosevelt *is target—*

"The *Roosevelt's* going to need major backup in eight seconds, SF#217 is closest, send them in beneath." She was nominally speaking to Rychen, though she wasn't sure how long it would last. There was nothing stopping her from directing the ships herself.

EA Recon Unit #3 is in position—

"Have Recon #3 deposit their payload and bug out."

—'bug out'? Where did that come from?

Valkyrie and Rychen shared the information at the same time. "Recon #3 is clear. Detonating in 3…2…1…mark."

From the center of the Metigen armada a ball of obsidian flame erupted with such ferocity the twelve SDs in close proximity were hurled along expanding trajectories as they cracked apart, many crashing into their brethren to multiply the destruction. The four SDs that had been located near the core of the blasts were effectively vaporized.

She caught Rychen smirking slyly out of the corner of her eye. "I'd call that a success."

The cloaking technology she'd brought back from Portal Prime and utilized on the *Siyane* had proved difficult to implement across the United Fleet in the short time they had, for several reasons. The power required to operate the shield increased multiplicatively with the radius it covered, and military vessels' power distribution was rationed to an extent she had found shocking. Also, using their current technology they were unable to get the performance needed out of it at the high speeds utilized in combat.

Third and perhaps most importantly, in a crowded and chaotic arena if any measurable percentage of ships were stealthed, they were highly likely to start colliding with the good guys. Beacons inside the cloaked ships broadcast their movements to the battlefield commanders, but out there amid the bedlam there was no practical way for the other ships to keep track of multiple stealthed vessels.

That didn't mean the technology was of no use—quite the contrary in fact. Seconds earlier two reconnaissance craft equipped with the cloaking shield had snuck into the heart of the Metigen forces while they still retained a cohesive grouping. There they'd deployed sixteen experimental negative energy bombs.

This was the reason for the unusual obsidian color of the combustion, which would have been essentially invisible if not for the contrasting brilliance of the surrounding space. Once the recon craft had 'bugged out' the bombs were detonated, and with impressive results.

The cloaking shield was being used tactically in other ways as well. For instance….

"Activating signal buoys."

They had made progress on the nature of the aliens' signal frequencies during the last twelve hours far above and beyond what Mia and Meno had puzzled out prior to the Messium battle. Now thirty tiny buoys placed in a ring surrounding the area began broadcasting a wave pattern designed for one purpose: to bollocks up the aliens' internal communications. They couldn't engineer a complete block on the comms—again, their technology simply didn't match that of the aliens—but the signal should at the very least create drops, garbling and general fuzziness.

Devon: Is it working?

Her mind filled with an image of the EM readings detected across 0.1 AU; it resembled a child's angry scribbling replicated and layered messily atop one another.

Mia: From a technical perspective, it's working. Hopefully we'll be able to see its effects soon.

An explosion off the port bow shook the dreadnought. *EAS Lexington hit, 380 on board, rescue shuttles en route from EAS Annapolis.* There wouldn't be many survivors, however. She forced her heart rate down.

Alex: Morgan, you're up.

Major Dave Bowman squinted at the viewport overlay, trying to select a single swarmer for his flight to target amongst the multitude clogging the area. The combat needed to spread out and quickly, else they were going to be crashing into each other as much as into the enemy.

Major Bowman: Flight, vector is S 22° z37° W. Let's try to peel a few out of the crowd—

Without warning his fighter jerked downward into a vertical dive. The restraints held him tight against the seat as his hands instinctively fought to ease the angle—but he no longer controlled the ship.

They had warned him this might happen when they installed the additional hardware for the new arcalaser. Still, he was not amused.

His brain and his internal organs lurched when the ship strafed 40° to starboard and opened fire on a swarmer. He vaguely noticed the other members of his flight had also opened fire from positions in a 60° arc and 15° plane. Freed of the need to fire from a direct vantage to the oculus, they were now swarming the swarmer. Funny.

The core of the alien vessel crumbled with astounding speed. Then his ship was spinning around, rocketing upward and firing on another. This one was charging them, and his flight had closed in so much he could sense them in his peripheral vision.

This swarmer too broke apart in the time he succeeded in inhaling, but its forward momentum cast the shards hurtling toward them. In a flash his and the other fighters were flung outward, thruster boosts accelerating them away from the dangerous debris. Acid rose into his throat when the motion temporarily became too extreme for the inertial dampeners to compensate.

The next instant he was drifting peacefully in the direction he had been headed. He hesitantly reached out and sought to increase his speed. The vessel responded per normal. It was once again his.

He blinked and tried to reorient himself. The entire event had lasted less than ten seconds.

From a sim chair in a small, dark room on the engineering deck of the Federation dreadnought *SFS Leonidas*, Morgan enjoyed a bird's-eye view of the battlefield—the movements of a veritable ocean of ships, en masse an exquisite dance and one she knew well.

Quadrant Five, ten swarmers approaching SFS Salerno. *Assuming control of SFF H4, H7, H11, H12.*

She dove into four of the nine-hundred-sixty-eight fighters that had been wired for access by Stanley and equipped with arca-lasers…and smiled. She now saw through each of the four cockpits and all of them at once. It was Stanley's vision, yet it felt like hers.

Target X4117—H4 vertical 17°z—H7 descend 90°—pivot—H11 accelerate + W 2.1°—H12 shadow H11 + W 3.2°. Fire. The alien craft exploded in 1.4701 seconds.

Target X4065—all shift S 12° E. Fire. 1.5622 seconds.

She diverted the four fighters at varying gentler angles and released them.

Human pilots were physically incapable of executing the maneuvers these ships had executed. Not even she could manipulate the controls so rapidly and with so precise a touch. And while it hadn't been much of a factor this time, the G-forces generated often degraded the pilots' capabilities to an unacceptable degree.

Together with Stanley she not only could do it, she could do it with four ships at once. The combined, concentrated firepower directed at a single point on a swarmer's oculus less than half a meter wide ripped apart the vessel in a maximum of two seconds, long before the fighters' own shields were depleted, if their shields were stressed at all.

Four fighters for one swarmer sounded like losing numbers in the long game. But she intended to move fast.

She zoomed back out to the macro view to allow Stanley to identify another set of potential targets, then in a flash she was diving again.

Assuming control of S8, S2, S12, S17.

⟨R⟩

"Metigen cluster in upper Quadrant Four is breaking through the forward line. We should plug the hole ASAP."

Alex studied the map. "SF 56th Regiment has been kicking ass in Quadrant Three and they're close."

She tuned out Rychen's execution of the order to watch the map. Out the viewport, the explosions and debris made it impossible to see with any clarity, but the map filtered out the thermal readings from overheated engine cores and scorched metal to present a chess board whose pieces were legion.

Valkyrie: Twenty-eight swarmers giving chase to SF #578 and #609 in Quadrant Nine.

Alex: Morgan, target swarmers moving Quadrant Nine bearing N 42° E.

"Requesting fighter support for SF 33rd Regiment in Quadrant Seven."

She made a face at Gianno's request. *Morgan?*

Morgan: I'll handle both. No need to make the Marshal fret.

Based on her limited exposure to Field Marshal Gianno, Alex found the idea of the woman 'fretting' an improbable one and decided Morgan was being sarcastic per usual.

She let Rychen know the request was being met. Over his shoulder she caught a glimpse of her mother in the EASC holo manipulating sub-screens and motioning to several people who moved around her. It—

Morgan: Sh-fuh-mother of Mary!

Mia: Problem?

Morgan: Swarmer took out one of my fighters from behind while I was firing. Felt like my brain burst inside my skull.

Alex: Disengage and take a breath.

Morgan: I'm fine, I'm fine. Bastard's going to pay.

Valkyrie: Two SDs and 60 swarmers have broken off from the main force in Quadrant Six, projected target is the carrier EAS Pearl Harbor.

"Admiral, we need to send two cruisers—recommend the *Cantigny* and *Marengo*—and at least four frigates to protect the *Pearl Harbor.*"

The Metigens aren't stupid. They know a carrier is a low-value target when they aren't already winning. They're trying to draw ships away for some reason.

Who was that? *Valkyrie?*

Valkyrie: I concur. It is a sound strategic analysis.

Alex: But you didn't say it?

Valkyrie: I don't believe so.

Alex: Devon?

Devon: Little busy here trying to tell the Senecan defense arrays where to shoot. Cranky, paranoid ware.

Alex frowned but brushed the odd feeling aside. No time for it. "Scratch that. Tell the *Pearl Harbor* to retreat to Staging Point #3. It can return in a few minutes at a different location."

46

Caleb eyed the young Marine—based on the moves she had executed she was clearly special forces—over the breech of his Daemon. "Same to you."

"You're here to take out O'Connell, right?"

"That is the plan." His gaze flickered beyond her to see Noah struggling to his feet, hand at his throat. "You okay, man?"

"Ugh…." In lieu of speaking he managed a haphazard wave.

The woman didn't turn around, but her words were plainly directed at Noah. "Back away from me and I won't need to do that again." He complied, stumbling backward to sag against the wall a safe distance away.

She jerked a tight nod, and as one they lowered their weapons. "Who sent you?"

"Do you *care* who sent me? Your general needs to be stopped before he takes one more single, solitary life."

The ship lurched beneath their feet, sending them all thudding into the wall. He snorted a laugh. "Guess I did do some damage."

"You mean your ship tearing through half the decks like an out-of-control levtram? Probably." She exhaled harshly. "All right. This lift leads to the bridge. I was supposed to be coming to kill you, but instead I'm going to help you. O'Connell has completely lost whatever shred of sanity he may have previously retained. He's up there raging and screaming and threatening to execute anyone who looks at him wrong. He already *has* executed two officers today.

"Only a couple of other people are left on the bridge—almost everyone's gone to help with rescue efforts or to hunt you. I'll distract him. Give me fifteen seconds, then come up. Start shooting, and I'll take care of his shield."

Caleb nodded in agreement, but Noah scowled. "Why are you helping us?"

"Because this cocksucker needs to die. I had plans to make it happen in any event, but with you here I might actually be alive after it's done." The floor bucked again. "We need to hurry. I'm fairly certain we're in the process of crashing."

Caleb gestured to the lift, and in a blink she had hopped on it and was gone. He studied Noah to determine whether he was recovered sufficiently for the final push...and decided the answer was 'enough.' "Like the Marine said, start firing and don't stop until O'Connell is on the floor—then shoot down."

"What about the other soldiers up there?"

"Hope our new friend keeps them under control. If not, we'll worry about them once the general's out of commission."

Noah blew out a breath through clenched teeth. "Got it."

The seconds ticked down to zero. He activated the lift and crouched low on its base; he sensed Noah mimic his stance behind him. As soon as they began clearing the floor of the bridge, he raised the Daemon and prepared to open fire.

O'Connell's large frame was immediately identifiable in the center of the bridge. The man flailed in agitation atop a central platform, arms thrashing around as the woman they followed up stood at parade rest beside him. Her eyes darted to them and her chin lowered a centimeter.

Caleb began firing.

The man pivoted toward them. The steady laser stream from Caleb's Daemon lit up the man's shield in fiery sparks as the man reached for the gun at his hip.

In a blur of movement the woman moved behind O'Connell. Her hands slipped into the waist of his uniform pants, yanked the shield generator out of its clip and tossed it clattering across the bridge.

With a roar O'Connell spun toward her. His outstretched arm whipped around to hammer his gun into the side of her head, and the force generated by his burly frame sent her flying through the air. She landed hard on a shoulder ten meters away and skidded into the front panel of a workstation.

Caleb leapt the final half-meter up to the bridge floor and continued to fire as he stood and closed the distance.

His next shot caught O'Connell in the right shoulder as the man reoriented himself in their direction. The next ripped clean through the abdomen. A shot from Noah came an instant later to slice open the left hip.

The man reeled, his face reddening to the color of crushed maraschino cherries. He waved the gun wildly at them while the other hand went to clutch his abdomen. He was yelling something, but Caleb couldn't make it out for all the other yelling.

Caleb continued to advance forward as O'Connell's shot missed him altogether. Three meters away. Time for the head shot.

He leveled the Daemon at the sweating skin between O'Connell's disbelieving eyes and pressed the trigger.

Mission fucking accomplished.

There was no time to appreciate the heavy body collapsing to the floor, though, due to the new gunfire bouncing off Caleb's shield from multiple directions. It was a top-of-the-line military shield, but it still had a limit. He spun and dove for cover behind the closest workstation.

"Stand down!" The woman's voice bellowed with authority across the expansive bridge. "General O'Connell was conducting an illegal operation in contravention of Alliance orders and he has been relieved of command. Now this ship is going down, so I suggest you get yourselves to escape pods—on the double, people!"

Encouraged by the sound of feet pounding past them and the corresponding lack of gunfire, Caleb cautiously emerged from his meager cover. Their unexpected ally was standing in the middle of the bridge motioning the last of its occupants toward the exit using one arm while the other hung limply at her side.

"Thanks." He stuck out a hand as he approached her. "Caleb Marano, Senecan Federation Intelligence, sent on behalf of Earth Alliance Strategic Command to terminate General O'Connell's offensive by any means necessary."

She stared at his hand for a beat then headed for the lift. "Captain Brooklyn Harper, Marine Special Operations. You can tell me how such a ridiculous proposition came about *after* we get to your ship and off this death trap."

"Yes, ma'am."

Noah was chuckling as he rose to his feet from behind a chair.

Caleb cocked an eyebrow. "That was your cover?"

He peered down and ran his palms along his chest. "I'm alive and don't appear to be shot, so yeah."

Captain Harper had stopped to activate a control panel, which turned out to be a ship-wide broadcast system. "This is a general evacuation order. Proceed to an operating shuttle or escape pod. Hostilities against this planet and the people on it have ceased, so do *not* shoot your rescuers when they find you. That is all."

Increasing instability in the framework of the *Akagi*, but no further gunfire, marked their sprint back to the *Siyane*. There was still forward velocity beneath their feet, so the cruiser was still flying, but it was unquestionably a doomed vessel.

Caleb re-opened the hatch, grabbed onto the bottom lip and hoisted himself up before offering Noah a hand. Harper did them the interesting courtesy of coming to attention outside. "Permission to come aboard, sir?"

He gave her a wry smile. "Granted, Captain." Despite a visibly injured arm and shoulder she climbed up and was inside faster than he could offer assistance.

Noah was easing into his seat when Caleb joined him in the cockpit. "Okay, so how are we going to get off this death trap?"

"Like this." Caleb fastened his harness, reached over and fired the pulse laser.

As the *Siyane* was canted at a sixty degree downward angle, the laser tore through the floor, the two floors under it, and finally the hull to create a hole to the outside—which they promptly fell through, ricocheting between the jagged edges until they reached open sky. He engaged the impulse engine an entire five seconds before they would've crashed to the desert sand four kilometers below.

Noah relaxed in his seat. "That works."

"Hold one." Harper appeared in the cockpit. "Swing around so we can see the *Akagi*."

"Sure." Caleb arced to port until the cruiser came into view. Fire and dense smoke billowed from numerous cracks and two yawning holes; it listed badly to starboard and down forty or so degrees. Its trajectory would send it crashing into the desert safely away from the city, eventually.

Abruptly the triple impulse engines at the rear of the ship ruptured, sending blue-white flames mushrooming outward to consume the stern of the vessel. The shockwave rolled over them with a shudder, and the *Akagi* plummeted from the sky to crash tail first to the ground.

He looked over his shoulder. "Care to explain?"

The woman grimaced, but it seemed to be related to her arm rather than his question. "My contingency plan. I tried to raise a mutiny, but it failed due to sheer terror of O'Connell on the part of the crew. An engineer I did win over helped me wire the engines to overload on my signal. I didn't want to use it with a full crew onboard, though I would have if this had gone on much longer. I wanted to give my fellow crewmen one more chance to do the right thing, but you guys saved me the trouble. So what now?"

Caleb held up a finger to silence her as he again contacted his sister.

On the way. How are you doing?

Fine, we're fine. The air's getting a bit stuffy and—but we're fine.

I'll hurry.

He had vaguely noted Noah filling their new companion in during the conversation, but when he turned to face Noah she had vanished. He glanced over his shoulder to see her circling the cabin, deep in conversation. If he had to guess, on finding herself freed of the communications block she was reporting the details of O'Connell's actions up the chain of command.

Noah joined him in his glance and muttered under his breath. "I swear, if I wasn't already in love, I would totally be in love right now."

"Well it's a good thing you're already in love, because she would eat you for breakfast."

"Agreed." He nodded sagely and settled back in his seat. "Then Kennedy would eat me for lunch, and I would not survive the event."

47

"It's not enough."

Rychen's stare bore into Alex from two meters away. Her mother's holo lay just outside her peripheral vision, but she felt her virtual stare nonetheless.

"Ms. Solovy, from my perspective we are rather kicking their asses."

"While I can't be as optimistic as Admiral Rychen without being on the scene, from here it does appear to be going definably well. A bit more problematic on Romane, but we are holding our own."

"Holding our own isn't *enough*, Mom. This is it—our one and only chance. We will never be stronger than we are right now. If the enemy makes it through this battle to fight another day, if it limps away and licks its wounds and returns, on that day we will lose. Forgive me for the momentary arrogance, but I can see *everything* happening everywhere, and I am telling you we may be winning, but as it stands now we will not have victory."

"Alex, your arrogance has never been momentary—which is fine. What do you suggest we do about it?"

She scanned the large screen behind her. "Get me on one of the superdreadnoughts."

Rychen nearly choked—on what, she didn't hazard a guess. "Excuse me?"

In her head Morgan called her 'bat-shit cracked' and Devon hooted and Mia mumbled something about how she and Caleb truly were meant for one another. She ignored them all except for Valkyrie's sentiment of support.

"Get me on one of the superdreadnoughts. Valkyrie says we can access the interior through one of the empty swarmer docks. We've been studying the pure Metigen code I copied non-stop, and we think if given direct access we can corrupt their operating code.

Though they're not a hive mind in the technical sense, the SDs are constantly communicating and cooperating—you've seen it happen. Our signal interference broadcasts are hampering them but not stopping them."

She met Rychen's gaze full-on. She had discerned hours ago that her mother trusted his battlefield judgment; if she could convince him, her mother would fall in line. "I can slow their shield and weapon reaction time. I can confuse their formations and maneuvers. Hell, I may even be able to get them to shoot at or crash into each other. I can insert errors into their code which will recursively degrade their programming until it's nothing but gibberish. I can give us a victory, today and for all future days."

The man regarded her silently for a long stretch, and she conceded that had she been a subordinate officer she would likely have melted to her knees under the weight of the scrutiny. Then he exhaled with a dry laugh. "Miriam, you didn't tell me she was as crazy as her father."

"An oversight on my part. She is easily as crazy as her father. Alex, this is insane."

"Of course it is—but it's also necessary."

Rychen examined his own semi-circle of screens. "How do you propose we 'get you on one of the superdreadnoughts'?"

Emboldened, she charged ahead before her mother could lodge a renewed protest. "Obviously I'll need a spacesuit with propulsion. I can hitch a ride on a reconnaissance craft or a fighter to a somewhat close point, then get myself the rest of the way."

"Recon craft, no question—if a fighter flew slow enough to carry you, it and you would get blown out of the sky. Say this works. How do you get back?"

She shrugged gamely. "Same way? I'll propel myself off the SD, and hopefully I can get picked up before being speared by a stray laser or stray debris?"

"For heaven's sake, Alex. You do not need to do this. We'll find another way."

"You've had to say that to me a lot these last few days, Mom, and I appreciate it. I mean it. But I need to do what is required in the circumstances." *I deeply want to do this.*

Miriam's looked taken aback. "Exactly how much did your alien friend show you?"

"What?"

"It doesn't matter." Her mother sighed, displaying a frustration Alex had come to recognize as entirely her fault. "Christopher? Can you make it work?" *Oh, so* she *could call him Christopher?*

He grimaced at the tactical map. "I'll do my damnedest. If handled very, *very* carefully, it should be doable. I can't protect her—" his eyes shot to her "—I can't protect you inside. And we have no idea what's inside."

She smiled enigmatically, and his expression wavered in a way which made her think perhaps she had frightened him a little. "There's nothing inside—definitely nothing living, and I'd be willing to bet there's nothing but metal and photal conduits and quantum orbs. They will not have accounted for the possibility of boarding by the enemy."

"You're so certain of that, are you?"

"I am. It is impossible for me to understate the magnitude of their hubris."

"Admiral Solovy, do you authorize the mission?"

Her mother's voice was quiet, but not cold. "She doesn't need my authorization…she never has. But yes, let the record state I authorized the mission."

"Thank you. I—we—can do this."

Rychen threw his hands in the air. "All right. Get to the flight deck. I'll recall a recon ship and send someone down with a powered suit."

ℛ

Alex watched the reconnaissance ship pilot closely as he showed her how to attach and detach herself to the grapple on the hull and secure the magnetic pad so she wouldn't be jostled into a lump of broken bones during the trip. Finally he shot her a skeptical look, shook his head and departed for the cockpit, leaving her lying on her stomach against the upper hull of the small ship.

Valkyrie, do you remember several years ago when you asked me what it was like to be in space?

Of course I do.

I think you and I are both about to find out.

I always suspected we would.

She chuckled lightly. The sound echoed around in her helmet and faded away. *Did you now....*

The ship's engines engaged to boost it off the deck, and she hurriedly quadruple-checked the magnetic seal. They exited the open bay door and surged forward into space.

The multiple layers of metal and glass encasing the dreadnought really did insulate one from the scope of what was occurring just outside the hull. The fires were brighter. The explosions were closer and so extremely larger. Chaos.

No, Alex. This is not chaos. I have seen humans act in chaos, running in hysteria without direction or intent. But this is humans acting with purpose and using their tools to effect that purpose. This is machines acting in furtherance of their purpose. It is violence on a scale rarely seen, but it is not chaos.

Consider me properly rebuked, Valkyrie. Now pay attention because I'm going to flip over onto my back.

Oh?....ohhhhhh.

Alex cackled in delight, as much at Valkyrie's reaction as at the scene consuming them. They soared through the ongoing combat, sturdy metal beneath her back but space spread out for 210° around her.

Yes, there was violence. There was death. But there was also such beauty, such heroism and grace and wonder.

She gasped as a swarmer exploded less than a hundred meters from her—but they were past the debris before it reached them, and before she could stir up a good panic.

No one was able to see her or the ship ferrying her. She was free to observe this astonishing spectacle openly and without any fear of odd glances or disapproving glowers.

She wished Caleb were here to witness it alongside her. He'd smirk and say something lame like 'Well that's not something you see every day,' which would only make her want to rip his spacesuit then his clothes off right here on the hull of this ship and....

Alex?

She blinked. *Sorry.*

Do not be. It was most invigorating.

Ha. Remind me to shut you out when it's for real.

I'm making a note here, but I cannot guarantee it will outlast this conflict.

She laughed aloud as the absurd reality of her situation hit her. Here she was, joking about sex with an AI living inside her head while space-jumping into the middle of a massive battle for the survival of the human species. Well it—

"Ma'am, we're as close as we dare get. The superdreadnought's broadside is due ahead, 720 meters distant."

"Thank you, Captain. I appreciate the ride. Disengaging now." She unhooked from the grapple first, then pressed the appropriate points on the magnetic seal to release it. Then she was floating free—

—which was an especially precarious state to be in, so she fired the suit's thrusters in the direction of the superdreadnought. It was a fast-moving target, and she needed to get there quickly. But once she was on the correct trajectory she simply *had* to look down.

She had been on spacewalks before…but she couldn't deny this was different somehow, beyond the tragic and magnificent combat raging around her. Was it Valkyrie's excitement seeping into her mind?

I believe so, Alex. For all the cycles I spent studying the topic, I lacked the capacity to envision it might look like this, feel like…this.

I'm so glad I could show it to you, Valkyrie.

She shouldn't have done it—even if she absolutely had time—but she tucked her arms in close to her body and fired her thrusters to spin in a tight three-sixty and take in the fullness of the scene.

I told you, milaya. I told you the cosmos would one day be yours to tame.

She jerked, startled. She often pictured her father talking to her in her head, but this was…. *Dad?*

Suddenly the superdreadnought's hull was rushing toward her and she had to focus. Five endless rows of depressions lined the mammoth hull. All were empty. *Which one, Valkyrie?*

Any one.

Any?

At this point I think the closest one is preferable.

Right. The hull now filled her vision; she decelerated so as to not crash into it. The impact was still jarring as her hip and shoulder banged into the hard, unforgiving metal. Her face contorted in pain, but she didn't think the impact had caused any debilitating damage. *Okay, what now?*

Use your blade to widen one of the holes where the swarmer latches in until it is wide enough for us to shimmy through.

There was indeed a hole near her elbow, curling into the hull like the opening for a hook latch. She tugged the blade off her belt and went to work.

48

Caleb set the *Siyane* to the ground in the closest intersection to the beacon's signal which provided adequate clear space to land. Still, pitched stone and wrent metal surrounded the ship, for this region of downtown had been all but destroyed.

He took an empty bag below to the engineering well and grabbed the metamat torch, a few other tools which might be useful and two sets of gloves, then hustled back upstairs. Noah had located the med kit and carried it under one arm. Harper appeared to have raided it and now wore a minimal sling on her left arm. He threw some water in the bag on his way to opening the hatch and followed the others out.

At the bottom of the ramp Harper stopped and turned to him. "If you want—and if you trust me—I can stay and guard the ship. Something tells me you don't want anyone absconding with a ship like this one."

"Anyone who tried would find themselves out of luck. But I doubt they'll try." He entered a command on the outer panel before joining her. The ramp retracted, and the ship vanished.

She stared at where the ship had sat a second before, then nodded to herself. "Okay. Sure. Where to?"

He pointed to a partially-collapsed midrise building on the opposite street corner two blocks east. The back half of the building still stood, but the front portion of the top three floors had caved in. The higher floors listed outward above the gap at a treacherous angle, threatening to collapse at any minute.

Noah shuddered as they jogged down the street, periodically slowing to scale piles of debris. "Reminds me of Messium."

"It was this bad?"

"Worse. So bloody much worse."

When they skirted two corpses mangled by broken structural beams, he gained a small appreciation of what Noah and Kennedy had endured.

There were people alive as well, however, and the lull in the attack had gone on long enough for them to begin to emerge—from alleys, buildings and vehicles that hadn't been crushed. He trusted they would see to helping the injured and didn't deviate from his course.

Isabela? You said you were in the basement?

Damn, you're really here already? Um, yes, we hid there along with some other people. Most are here with me. One didn't make it. The entrance was near the lobby.

Understood.

The facing façade was completely destroyed and impenetrable, so they followed the rubble until they reached a section where the building hadn't collapsed and found a way inside. Half a dozen people were in what he assumed was the lobby, tending to injuries or simply gawking at the ruins. Several leapt in fright as they arrived, and Caleb raised his hands to demonstrate he meant them no harm.

"Does anyone know where the basement access is located?"

An older man pointed to the left, deeper into the building. "It's completely buried, though."

The area where the man had indicated contained two fallen beams which had braced diagonally from the ceiling down to a pile of stone. Overlaying the stones was a large slab of interior wall material.

He went to work on the slab, bracing his feet against the rubble and shoving it sideways. It moved only centimeters—but then Noah materialized at his side. With matching grunts together they gave it a heave and sent it skidding across the floor.

"Yep, definitely reminds me of Messium."

The removal of the slab revealed an alcove filled in by ragged pieces of the ceiling and flooring from the levels above. Caleb shifted to address those still in the lobby; all were injured to some extent but most were ambulatory.

"Anyone who's able, help us out over here. We need to get this blockage cleared. People are alive in the basement."

The man who had directed him to the entry made a show of limping away, but a tall, thin woman and a teenage boy drifted over.

"You're sure people are down there?"

"I am."

The boy rubbed at the patchy stubble on his chin, then kneeled on the floor and hefted a chunk of debris out of the way. Such began the tedious work of clearing the way piece by piece until he would be able to reach his sister.

Caleb stared in fascination at the serpent. It stared back at him from its disadvantaged position in the small, muddy depression running along the rear of their yard, glistening fangs extruding from its slender mouth beneath golden-green eyes.

"Isabela, get out here—you have to see this!"

He hadn't averted his gaze when he spoke, which was a lucky thing as the creature pounced forward at the noise of his shout. He leapt backward—everyone said he had quick reflexes—and added another meter of separation for good measure. "Isa—!"

His father's hand landed on his shoulder. "Your sister doesn't need to be out here, Caleb. Now go grab the tarp from the garage for me."

"What if it leaves while I'm gone?"

"I'll watch it. Hurry, and don't sneak in the house and get your sister on the way."

"Yes, sir." He was grumbling as he jogged up the slope toward the house but did as he was told.

When he returned, dragging the tarp through the grass, his dad and the serpent had moved several meters to the left, almost to the fence. He dropped the tarp on the ground beside his dad and crouched to get a better look at the reptile. "Is it poisonous?"

"Very much so. Step behind me."

As soon as he moved away, his dad hurled the tarp over the serpent and deftly bundled the edges to make a sack of it. The tarp jostled in the air while his dad tied a knot in the top and tightened it.

He motioned for Caleb to walk with him as he carried the tarp and its prisoner to the outdoor trash bin.

"I wish Isabela could've seen it before you captured it."

"This is a dangerous creature, Caleb. What if it had hurt her?" He tossed the bundle into the bin and closed the lid then directed his attention to Caleb while wearing his 'serious' face. "You need to protect your sister. You should want to protect your sister."

"Because she's little?"

His dad chuckled. "Right now, yes. That's one reason. But you should always want to protect those you love, even when they're no longer little."

"From serpents...and maybe bigger animals?"

"From everything that could cause them harm, not only dangerous creatures."

Caleb ran a hand through his hair—his mom kept saying he needed a haircut—and tried to understand what his dad was getting at.

"Because I love her?" Which he guessed he did. Most of the time.

"That's right, son."

They began walking toward the house, but Caleb stopped as something occurred to him. "Are you going to tell Isabela the same thing about me when she gets older?"

"Well, I haven't thought on it much yet. Probably so."

"Protecting somebody means keeping stuff from them, doesn't it?"

"Sometimes, if it's something which will hurt the person? Yes, it does."

"But if I'm keeping stuff from her and she's keeping stuff from me...we won't be very good friends anymore, will we?"

His dad regarded him with a weird expression. Weird expressions usually meant his dad was annoyed with him. "It's not...you shouldn't think of it that way, son. Of course you'll be friends. It's—"

His mom's voice rang out through the open door announcing dinner was ready. He took off running for the house, leaving Dad and his weird faces behind.

After twenty minutes they had created an open space half a meter wide and two meters deep to angle down toward the basement.

Unfortunately, the remainder was blocked by a large piece of stone wedged against the walls of the alcove.

Caleb? Hurry if you can. Pieces of the ceiling are beginning to fall in. Tiny pieces though. We're fine.

He glared at the obstacle blocking his path as his jaw clenched. "Give me the torch. I'll cut it up."

He looked over at Harper in surprise; last he checked she had been trying to help the more seriously wounded in the lobby. "What about your arm?"

She discarded the makeshift sling and gingerly massaged her shoulder. "Still have one functional, which is all I need. I'm small and can fit in there no problem. Hold on to my feet or something?"

The woman who was helping them was also thin…but she had shrunk away from his questioning scan of those present rather than step forward. "We can do that."

Harper dropped to her knees then her stomach and reached back with her good arm. He passed her the metamat torch, and she began scooting down the rough slope to the blockage.

Have everybody move away from the blocked area where the lift was. We're about to break through.

Three, four, five seconds passed.

Done.

"You're clear to start."

He and Noah each grasped an ankle as Harper sliced the stone into segments and punched each one out to crumble into the basement. In a few short minutes she had cut an opening large enough for a person to fit.

"This is all the room we're going to get. Pull me up." They complied, and she crawled to her feet, bloody scrapes decorating both arms and dust coating her skin.

Before anyone could say or do anything, Caleb slid feet-first into the opening and wrangled through it into the basement.

Dust hung heavy in the air, clogging his nostrils with his first breath. The only appreciable light came from the hole above him, so he flicked on the light attached to his belt.

Six men and women stood huddled together in the shadows of the claustrophobic space. Not seeing his sister among them, he hunted frantically around.

Isabela stepped out of the shadows to regard him with a relieved, weary smile. "You certainly know how to make an entrance, don't you?"

He pulled her into a hug, gently in case she had been trying to protect him and she in fact was injured. "The least I could do."

"Thank you," she whispered in his ear.

He pulled back and met her gaze. "The *least* I could do."

"Uncle Caleb?"

He let go of his sister to crouch in front of Marlee. Grime coated her curls and face; she held her right arm awkwardly across her chest and cradled the tattered remains of Mr. Freckles in the other.

"Hey, muffin. I couldn't wait to see you any longer, so I had to come and dig you out."

"Are the bad ships still shooting outside?"

"Nope. The bad ships are all gone. So how about let's get you out of here, okay?" He stood to see one person already climbing out of the hole they'd created. Noah and the teenage boy—he'd never caught a name—reached down to pull them up and out of the path.

He carefully boosted Marlee up into Noah's arms. She was so brave, swallowing a single whimper on the way up though she had to be in significant pain. He practically shoved Isabela up through the opening next, then stayed behind to assist the rest of the basement refugees—with some urgency as the ceiling increasingly rained down on them. At last he clambered up and out in a cloud of dust.

An additional med kit had been located and was being put to use on cuts and abrasions. A quick diagnostic scan of Marlee's arm declared it to be a compound fracture. They immobilized it and administered a measured dose of pain meds, but such young, fragile bones needed trained medical attention to ensure they healed properly.

Caleb headed outside to see if any emergency personnel had arrived in the area yet. He saw none and was about to go back inside when Isabela appeared at his side. She pointed to the wreckage of one of the frigates in the distance. Half the ship had landed atop one of the towers on the edge of the city, the other half on the flatland beyond.

"You didn't...do that, did you?"

He shrugged with proper dramatic flair. "I did say I came to rescue you. They were in my way."

She stared up at him wearing an amused grin, though he noted the exhaustion weighing down her features. "You really are kind of wonderful."

He bit his lip to mockingly suppress a smirk and give her the show she deserved. "Maybe a little." Then his tone grew more serious. "There's no telling when help is going to start rolling in, and the hospital is probably wrecked, but I think this is the first location they hit. Let me fly you and Marlee over to the next city. They'll have a functioning hospital and lodging. You'll be safe there."

"You've convinced me. But fly us there in what?"

"Go get Marlee and the others."

Her eyes narrowed at him suspiciously as she backed away. "All right."

Alone for a few precious seconds, he drew in a deep breath. He stood on a ruined street in a ruined city. Destruction stretched for kilometers in every direction, all caused by a single man for whom vengeance had devolved into madness. But no longer. He welcomed the endorphins now coursing through his veins as a just reward for a mission succeeded.

A single purpose had driven him relentlessly forward since leaving Earth; freed of its hold, his thoughts immediately turned to Alex. In truth his thoughts had never left her, but they had of necessity churned silently beneath concerns which he was able to act on and bring to a resolution.

He didn't dare contact her, fearful the slightest distraction at the wrong moment would endanger her and her own mission. His access to a secure military channel told him the battle had been joined, they hadn't lost and she wasn't dead. It would have to be enough for now. Until he could reach her.

When Isabela returned with Marlee, Noah and Harper, he was standing in what looked to be the middle of an empty intersection. He walked to the ship—disappearing briefly, to two gasps—then he and the ship reappeared.

Marlee's eyes widened to giant bloodshot orbs as she let out a squeal of delight and ran to him. "Is this your ship, Uncle Caleb?"

He again crouched to her level. "Nope. It's my girlfriend's ship."

That drew her enchanted gaze from the ship to him. "You have a *girlfriend?*"

"I do."

She considered him skeptically. "Is she pretty?"

"She sure is—almost as pretty as you."

Marlee giggled, covering her mouth with her uninjured hand in temporary embarrassment as she leaned against his shoulder.

He tousled her dust-covered hair playfully. "Do you want to go for a ride in it?"

Her head bobbed up and down. Her discomfort eased by the pain meds and fear eased by the sunlight, her usual effervescence was re-emerging in fits and starts. "Uh-huh."

He went to the hull and opened the hatch. When the ramp extended, Marlee stared up it uncertainly. Isabela came over, scooped her up in her arms and carried her up the ramp. "Come on, sweetheart. We'll explore the ship together—and we won't touch anything."

He laughed and turned to the others. "Thank you, both of you. I couldn't have saved them without your help."

Noah shook his head. "I don't know, man. I think you'd have found a way."

"Even so. Listen, I'm going to fly them to a hospital in the neighboring city, then I need to get to Seneca. To the front line."

"To Alex, you mean."

"Yeah. Noah, there's not anywhere for me to drop you on the way, but you're welcome to come along for the ride."

"I can, but...does this neighboring city have a spaceport?"

"I assume so."

"Would it break your heart if I headed back to Earth instead? Kennedy will torture me if I don't return in one piece, and...actually that might be interesting...." He shook his head to snap out of the reverie. "Anyway, the sooner I return the better it will go for me."

Caleb frowned. "I hear you. But I'm not confident you'll be able to get a flight out. Isabela said there were no departures due to the evacuations."

"Eh, I'm a persuasive guy. I'll find someone to bribe."

"Good point. Captain, what about you?"

Harper peered out at the wreckage of downtown with a vexed sigh. "I'd *like* to go to the front line. I can't believe I'm missing the battle of the millennium thanks to that lunatic. But in truth I can't do anything useful there at this point. So…I should stay here. I can assist with the rescue efforts and hopefully locate some of the escape pods—no man left behind and all. Then I'll make their occupants assist with the rescue efforts. If we win at Seneca, eventually someone will show up to clean up this mess."

"Are you sure? Real aid may be a while in coming."

"I am. I helped cause this destruction by not acting fast enough. I need to help fix it."

"Well, in that case." He offered his hand once more. "I'm very glad to have met you, Captain Harper. Thank you for everything."

She shook his hand firmly. "Same here, Senecan Federation Intelligence Agent Marano. Good luck to you."

49

Fifteen minutes and two twenty-centimeter-thick walls later, Alex crawled through the hole she had carved to step onto the deck of the Metigen superdreadnought.

She took the time to visually canvass her surroundings from every angle, as much in awe as for the other Prevos and the recording her helmet cam was capturing and transmitting to the *Churchill* and EASC.

Devon: Well this isn't spooky at all.

She acknowledged the comment then filtered the others' chatter to the background. If they needed her it would bubble up, but she needed to concentrate.

The cavernous open space stretched in both directions until it vanished into darkness. The opposite wall was nearly four hundred meters away and the ceiling equally far above. Her perception had been that the berths for the swarmers were located on the sides of the hull, but she appeared to have entered near the bottom. *This is the only deck on the ship.*

My conclusion as well. Weapons and engines will be located beneath us, but I expect everything else—including the engineering core—will be on this level.

Are you sure there is *an engineering core?* She gestured around to emphasize the point.

Running in parallel rows along the ceiling, floor and wall behind them were hundreds of beams of streaming ivory-white light. They ran in grooves etched into the metal but weren't encased within any bounding material. And they weren't simply conduits of signals or power channels, either, for they branched, reconverged and connected to one another in elaborate patterns.

This is the code running the ship. The ship IS the synthetic intelligence. Fascinating.

A chill radiated along her skin and seeped into her bones. Despite the brightness of the many streams of light rushing past, the deck was so enormous it rapidly darkened to shadow if she veered more than a few meters toward the center.

One could go mad in here in fairly short order. It wasn't merely the emptiness or the silence—there was nothing *human* about the vessel. Yet this empty, cold, silent place was, at least to some extent, alive. Hell, maybe that's why she was hearing her father in her head—she already was going mad.

It is alien. We should not expect it to exhibit human or even organic characteristics.

I know, Valkyrie. But Mesme, as alien as it was...we could relate to it. Converse, share ideas and argue. As infuriating as it was, we were able to fathom its nature and it ours.

Mesme's purpose was to study humans, and if I understand correctly it had been doing so for a lengthy span of time. There's no reason to believe others of its species would be as comprehensible were you to meet them.

True enough. It's unnerving, though. Do you sense it? Not unlike Mesme, you now straddle the human and synthetic worlds.

Valkyrie paused before answering—for less than a second, but Alex had become attuned to the accelerated patterns of the Artificial's thoughts. *I think had I come here prior to linking with you, I would feel a degree of kinship to the environment. Now, however, I see it through your eyes.*

Literally.

Yes, Alex. Literally.

The deadpan tone was unmistakable, and she laughed. The very human act in this very inhuman place served to ease the tension a little.

Focus, Valkyrie. We're not here for you to dissect and study the ship. We can do that after we win.

Of course. I still believe there will be a central systems hub to coordinate instructions.

She glanced to her right. They had entered the ship about a third of the way from the 'front,' such as it was. *This way?*

No. I believe it will be in the center.

Why?

The ship has no need for a cockpit or a viewport to see out, for it sees via each component of its body. Given the hub will be controlling and directing all aspects of the body, it is rational to assume the hub will be at the precise center for maximum efficiency.

This is both logical and disturbing. She turned to her left and started traversing the deck. It was a challenging trek with the gravity boots always tugging downward to keep her attached to the floor.

A deep, heavily accented voice flitted in her mind. *A ship without a viewport? Waste of a perfectly good engine.*

I know, rig— She halted mid-step. *Valkyrie, did you say that?*

I find I'm not certain. I must have.

Alex planted the other foot on the floor and her hands on her hips. *Cut the crap, Valkyrie. What have you done?*

This pause lasted 310 quintillion cycles, or approximately a third of a second. *Perhaps some explanation is in order.*

You think?

Morgan is the only Prevo with military training. Seeing as our task is a military engagement, we felt it would be beneficial if we were able to boost the military 'instincts', let us say, of yourself as well as Devon and Mia.

Who's 'we'?

Annie, Stanley, Meno and I.

You're talking to each other behind our backs?

Alex, we are communicating multiple exabytes of data every minute 'behind your backs.' Respectfully, the amount of information we are sharing is beyond your comprehension.

Her shoulders notched downward. *Fine. Please tell me what you did and why it has resulted in a voice which bears a striking resemblance to my father being in my fucking head!*

Twenty-eight years ago, when Abigail ran the Council on Biosynthetics Ethics and Policy, she began an initiative to acquire neural imprints from military officers carrying the rank of Commander and above. The idea was to create a storehouse of military knowledge beyond data and historical records. She and others anticipated a day would come when this collective wisdom would be accessible to strategists and Artificials alike.

"Alex, why have you stopped? What's your plan?"

She jumped, startled at the audible sound of her mother's voice ringing in her helmet. "We think the engineering or systems hub is this way, in the center of the ship."

"Not the front?"

"Not the front. It's an AI thing. I'm moving that way now." *I'm going to keep walking. You keep talking.*

The initiative was shelved soon after Abigail left the Alliance, and nothing came of it. But the repository remained, and Annie has access to the files. We queried the repository, hoping to find brain wave patterns complimentary to those of one or all of you. These could be integrated into our processes, thereby increasing the Prevos' military expertise. But our success was marginal. An amalgamation of 3-5 imprints were added to Annie and Meno. You were the only one for whom we located a near-perfect match.

She found she had halted again. She forced a boot up off the floor and continued forward. The clock was ticking, and she had a mission to complete.

My father. I remember...he had an imprint taken a year or two before he died.

Yes.

Why didn't you tell me? You're in my head—you know I'd want to be told.

I couldn't be certain what would happen. My analysis suggested the most probable scenario was nothing would happen, beyond an increased command of the battlefield.

Are the others experiencing these sorts of...anomalies?

No. But they received blendings of multiple imprints, thus any distinctiveness was lost. You are unique.

Her hand came to her mouth, only to be stopped by the face-plate. *Valkyrie, is it conceivable there was some element of, I don't know, consciousness embedded in the imprint?*

'A mind is more than the sum of its individual components, more than neurons firing and chemicals flowing in response to stimuli.'

Not exactly what I meant at the time.

Nevertheless, the concept may be applicable. I have learned much from our linking. I possess your neural imprint, and now I can see you. The imprint is not you. Not quite. But I have begun to discern the gaps, the traits it does not wholly capture. Using these insights, I've been endeavoring to construct a richer representation of your father's mind within my own processes. It is leading to some rather interesting and unexpected results.

Like my father talking to me in my head.

...Yes.

In the distance a stronger light source began to cut away at the gloom. Valkyrie had been correct.

She wanted to pinch the bridge of her nose through the helmet, wanted to impose order on the jumbled thoughts and swirl of conflicting emotions. The implications of what Valkyrie had done were staggering, but they made her head hurt and her heart seize. She needed to pack them up and box them away for a later time, a time when she wasn't in the bowels of a colossal, living alien vessel that wanted to kill her. And everyone else.

We'll continue this discussion soon. You're not off the hook for keeping this from me.

A reasonable response.

"Alex, be careful. It might have defense mechanisms."

She rolled her eyes. "Yes, Mom."

It will not have defense mechanisms.

No, it won't. What would it possibly need to defend against? The notion of an ant getting this far is so absurd as to be laughable.

Yet here we are.

Yet here we are.

They began studying the hub as they approached and it gained greater definition. There was no metal and no frame. There was also no way through. The quantum core stretched floor to ceiling and wall to wall. The inputs streaming toward it on every surface met the core at defined junctures to disappear into the whole.

It reminded her a great deal of the orb powering the cloaking shield on Portal Prime—which was good news indeed.

We could wreck a few of the junction points and be done with it.

We could—and this ship would plunge out of the sky with us in it. Less relevantly to our survival, it would likely not have the opportunity to pass any corrupted instructions to other ships before doing so.

Both valid points. Plan B?

I recommend inserting a probe at one of the junction points so we can study the routines to determine the best route of attack.

Really? Last time I just stuck my hand into the middle of it.

The fact you are standing here now indicates it was not a death-inducing act, much to my astonishment.

She crossed the last twenty meters to the core's outer edge. *When we get home I think we need to tweak your humor algorithms a bit.*

Why? It is your humor.

Damn. No wonder I drive people nuts. You know, I think I'm just going to stick my hand into the middle of it. The field is larger than the one on Portal Prime, but it's powering something far smaller. It'll be fine.

She stood in front of the swirling wall of...what was it really? Light, energy, signals, quantum wave-particles carrying and analyzing data then making decisions and issuing instructions, all coming together to create an intelligence. Not true life, but intelligence nonetheless. She lifted her right hand.

In her comm her mother's voice boomed with authority. "Alex, what are you—"

$$-0_{-1}{}^{1}0^{111}00$$

$1_{-1}1_01_{-1}1_{-1-1}0^{11}0_{-1}0_{-1}$

$00^100^1{}_{-1}1^10^{11}0_{-1}0^1$

$1_{0-1-1}00_{-1-1}$

11111_01_0

$0_{-1}0^100_{-1}0^{11}0_{-1}0_{-1}1_0$

$1_{0-1-1}00_{-1}0_{-1}1^1{}_{-1}000^1{}_{-1}$

$1_{-1}0^1{}_{-1-1}1^1{}_{-1}$

$0^1{}_{-1}0^{111}{}_{-1}0_{-1}1_00^{1111}$

$1_{-1}1_000_{-1-1}0$

$0_{-1-1}0_{-1}0_{-1}0^10^{11}{}_{-1}0_{-1}1^1$

$1_{0-1}0^1{}_{-1}0_{-1}$

$00_{-1}1^1{}_{-1}1^{111}$

$11111_{-1}1^{11}$

$11_{00}1^10^1$

$111_{-1}0_{-1}1_0$

${}_{-1-1}1^{1111}00$

$00^{111}{}_{-1-1-1}$

$1_{-1}1^1{}_{-1}000^{11}0_{-1-1}1^1000^1$

0_{down-1}

$up1111$

$down^{1up}{}_{-1}$

$1_{down-1down}$

$-1down^{000}{}_{-1}$

$0^{up1}{}_{down}0^{up}$

$1^{up1}{}_{down-1}0$

$down^{0up}$

$0right^{up1}stable$

$^1 left_{down}$

$^1 left_{down}$

$_{-1} left^{up} _{-1} stable$

$0 stable_{-1} stable$

$^1 stable ^1 left_{down}$

$_{-1} right^{up} 0 right_{down}$

$^1 left^{up} ^1 left_{down}$

$0 stable_{-1} left^{up}$

$0 stable 0 right^{up}$

powertothrustersincrease12.2453

left8.9125shieldshiftA21

shieldshiftA43

Units $\beta12\Theta$ $A88\Xi$ $\Omega40\Sigma$ sync with this Unit to eliminate
targets in 10.0-20.0 arc

power to thrusters decrease 4.7751

thrusters shift right 3.02889

acquire target track fire

increase shield strength 31.6168 at $\beta102$-233—

"Admiral Rychen, could you tell the *Cantigny* not to blow me up, please?"

"I'll get on that."

"Appreciated."

Had she been breathing? She sucked in air. *That was bracing. Okay, we understand the language. Now to fuck it up.*

It is all one program—solely the variables and the systems they affect change. I believe we can introduce a flaw at the root level which will propagate out to every system.

Only one little flaw? Surely we should introduce a few more to be safe.

Alex, safe is introducing a single flaw. This will give us time to depart and is less apt to be noticed by the governing program while it can still be corrected.

Where?

The code flowed past her in her mind as a sea of pulsing, twisting strings of light. Deeper and deeper she fell, until an intricate shape comprising six dimensions—*wait, she could perceive six dimensions now?*—appeared at the center. All paths led to the object.

Here.

She reached into the paradoxically dense shape, grasped onto a single string and let the corruption flow out of her fingertip, through the adaptively porous material of her glove and into the code.

The simplest of distortions to the most basic of calculations, but 2 plus 2 now equaled 4.2.

Did it accept the alteration?

Watch.

A tiny black filament rushed along the string with the rest of the code. Then it split to travel down two strings, then eight, then twenty-four.

She yanked her hand out of the hub and stumbled backward, landing on her ass on the hard and decidedly nonpliable floor.

"Alex, are you all right?"

She blinked repeatedly, trying to clear the artifacts of code flashing across her eyes. *Valkyrie? Are you good?*

One moment…yes. I have reoriented my processes.

She climbed to her feet. "I'm fine. We've sabotaged the ship's programming and are getting out of here."

Well that was fun.

Indeed.

Stepping out of the alien chamber into the midst of the battle was like….

Emerging from a mother's womb?

Can't say as I remember. We'll go with a jarring sensory assault.

"The recon vessel has acquired your locator beacon and is en route. Set a trajectory S 46° 6'z W."

"Understood." She steeled herself, stepped into space and fired the thrusters—

—a damaged swarmer hurtled out of control from above the superdreadnought to skim the hull less than ten meters beneath her. Her arms flailed in a fruitless but instinctual attempt to get out of the way.

Then it was gone.

The swarmer had passed so close her spacesuit burned warm from the heat of the scorching metal. She fought to wrestle her pulse under control with the help of her eVi and Valkyrie.

Let's try not to be sideswiped by any more large, careening objects on fire....

A wise course of action. Valkyrie sounded a bit shaken herself.

She accelerated in the provided direction, trying to give a wide berth to any dogfights, and exhaled in relief when she saw the approaching recon vessel, temporarily uncloaked so she'd be able to find it. She angled to meet it.

Once she was latched on and gave the all-clear to the pilot, she again rolled onto her back to gaze out at the warfare, albeit with greater respect for its perilous savagery and her own fragile vulnerability. *Hell of a sight, isn't it, Valkyrie?*

I have never understood why humans engaged in battle against one another, taking lives for goals of lesser value—accepted it logically but did not understand it. This, however? This I understand. This willingness to sacrifice one's individual life so others' lives may continue, this determination to fight with every measure of one's being and every facility of one's mind and body and tools to defend humanity? It is...beautiful.

Valkyrie wasn't seeing the beauty of the sunlight reflecting off gleaming starship hulls, or the shimmering laser beams crisscrossing space in vibrant colors, or the brilliant, fiery glow of exploding vessels. She wasn't even seeing the beauty of man and machine at their apex, performing upon a tableau of a sea of stars and the powerful silhouette of a planet which had lain untouched by humans a century ago yet now was home to a billion people.

No, she was seeing the beauty of each act by each individual human soul—courage, heroism, determination, intellect, sacrifice—replicated tens of thousands of times over to forge a defiant stand against this grave challenge to their existence.

'It is only by risking our persons from one hour to another that we live at all. And often enough our faith beforehand in an uncertified result is the only thing that makes the result come true.'

Alex smiled. *Let me guess—William James?*

Indeed.

A voice which she now so easily recognized reverberated in her head, stronger than before. *I'll do you one better: 'We are face to face with our destiny and we must meet it with high and resolute courage. For us is the life of action, of strenuous performance of duty; let us live in the harness, striving mightily; let us rather run the risk of wearing out than rusting out.' Theodore Roosevelt, who among other accomplishments did happen to be a student of William James for a time.*

Silence hung for an endless, frozen instant. She dared not breathe.

Is that you, Dad?

Not truly, milaya. It is a fragment, a whisper, a shadow left behind. But perhaps that is enough, yes?

Yes. It is so much more than enough.

50

ROMANE
INDEPENDENT COLONY

The *Orion* emerged from superluminal to find a planet under siege and a sky at war.

Malcolm had known what awaited him, for contrary to what they had hoped the Metigens had not held off until all their brethren arrived before initiating their assault on Romane. Instead, on reaching the planet they had taken advantage of the fact not all the Alliance ships dispatched to defend the colony were in place yet either and launched their attack.

Now the defenders found themselves knocked back on their heels, on the defensive and scrambling to play catch-up. Nevertheless, at first glance they appeared to be doing a moderately good job of it. At least ten superdreadnoughts were limping badly and debris of several more littered the scene. But this still left—Malcolm blinked and double-checked the number—fifty-one fully operational. Slightly fewer than expected unless many had already been destroyed, but…damn.

Colonel Jenner: Admiral Fullerton, EAS Orion *reporting for duty and requesting instructions.*

*Admiral Fullerton (*EAS Jefferson*): Welcome,* Orion. *Hook up with the 26th Squadron on the left flank.*

Colonel Jenner: Understood. It seems as if the enemy fleet is smaller than we were expecting.

Admiral Fullerton: Nope. The rest of them are planet-side.

He frowned; perhaps matters weren't so well in hand. *Are we engaging them below as well?*

Admiral Fullerton: I sent the 21st Regiment down to bite at their flanks.

Colonel Jenner: Sir, shouldn't we be working to protect the infrastructure and lives on the ground?

Admiral Fullerton: Which we'll do by wiping out these bastards up here. Now get over to the left flank.

Colonel Jenner: Is Mia Requelme onboard the Jefferson?

Admiral Fullerton: That freak of nature they sent here to 'assist'? Hell, no. I pawned her off to the governor.

Malcolm cringed, physically bit his tongue, then opened his mouth anyway. *Sir, I'm taking the* Orion *in-atmosphere. I request the 7th Platoon to accompany me.*

Admiral Fullerton: Son, are you under the impression I take orders from Colonels? Because I assure you, I do not.

Colonel Jenner: Of course you don't, sir. However, Admiral Rychen ordered *me to assess the situation when I arrived and, if I felt it necessary to defend Romane on the ground, to do so. I feel it is necessary to defend Romane on the ground, and I need the 7th Platoon to do so.*

A period of silence preceded the response.

Admiral Fullerton: Rychen said that, did he? The tone suggested Fullerton harbored a healthy fear of the man.

Colonel Jenner: Yes, sir. Right before I departed the Churchill.

Admiral Fullerton: Well, hell. Fine, take your ships and get down there, but don't come begging for help when things go south.

Colonel Jenner: Acknowledged.

He let go of the breath he'd been psychologically holding. "Comms, contact the vessels in the 7th Platoon and instruct them to rendezvous E 20° of Corridor #5 for atmospheric entry."

Smoke and raging fires rose from multiple locations as they neared Romane's largest metropolitan region. Two superdreadnoughts cruised above it, and the swarmers made the sky look as though a plague of locusts had invaded.

Malcolm turned to his XO. "You have command of the *Orion.* Work together with the other ships to implement the strategies we've discussed. Have the tactical assault detachment meet me on the flight deck."

"Yes, sir. I'll do my best to take care of her for you. Godspeed."

"And to you." With a salute he departed and headed below.

His requisition of the 7th Platoon had not been random. Not all cruisers carried a tactical assault detachment, but like the *Orion* the two cruisers belonging to the 7th did. Given thirty-six men behind him, perhaps he could make a difference on the ground.

The shuttles dropped the squads as close as safety allowed to the governor's bunker in the heart of downtown. He didn't intend to strike out across the city blindly; he needed to know what defenses were in play and at their disposal.

They navigated the intervening two blocks swiftly and without incident. He set the others to assisting survivors in the vicinity while he and the three detachment commanders entered the bunker.

What he found twenty meters below ground was a working command center as state-of-the-art as any the Alliance enjoyed. Three-dimensional dynamic maps of the city and the planet dominated the far wall. Hyper-crisp screens lit multiple workstations, and two dozen or so people conferred with one another or scurried between the stations.

It took several seconds for their presence to be noticed, but after multiple gestures in their direction a striking woman in a taupe pantsuit looked over. "Gentlemen, you are a welcome sight."

"Governor Ledesme?" At her curt nod he strode forward and extended a hand. "Alliance Colonel Malcolm Jenner. We've got a hundred ships in-atmosphere engaging the enemy and thirty-six Marines here on the ground—not to mention the considerable force keeping the rest of the alien vessels occupied in space—but we need to know what our options are."

"Our Defense Chief is otherwise engaged at the moment. I'll have him give you an overview as soon as he's done. We have a couple of tricks available to us, but using them from the bunker has proved problematic since the Metigens took out most of our relay stations and half the power grid."

"We'll work around those difficulties, ma'am. Is Mia Requelme here?"

The governor jerked her head toward the rear left corner of the bunker. "If I understand the current state of affairs, you may be exactly what she needs."

A woman in black pants and a matching turtleneck leaned over the shoulder of a disheveled-looking older man working at a large data screen. Two additional men huddled at the edges of the screen as the woman pointed in restrained agitation at it, then crowded in on the first man. "No, it has to be—would you just let me do it? It'll be far faster and it might actually work."

"I am not giving you control of our defense arrays. That authority belongs in human hands."

"Oh, for the love of—"

He cleared his throat. "Ms. Requelme?"

She pivoted as she straightened up, sending long, sleek black hair whipping past her shoulder. Like Alex, her irises shone a luminous silver to create a dramatic contrast against her olive skin. She arched an eyebrow. "A Marine? Interesting."

He offered his hand once more. "Colonel Malcolm Jenner. Alex told me to help you if I could, so how can I do that?"

ℛ

Mia: Alex, nanosecond scoop on Colonel Jenner?

Alex: Honorable and trustworthy to an occasionally annoying fault. Prefers to be on top—thinks he's being a gentleman.

Mia: Got it.

She eyed the Colonel with a hopeful expression. "I don't suppose you brought any programmable shoulder-fired SALs with you?"

His head cocked to the side; it was apparently not the response he'd expected. "Uh, yes, as a matter of fact—three of them."

"Fantastic. Will you let me touch them? Because nobody here will let me touch anything."

He gave her a casual shrug, a motion starkly out of sync with the grinding tension of the bunker. "If you can present a convincing argument as to why you need to touch them, yes."

Modifying the signal pattern for single, directed use. Should we burn a disk?

Nah, we'll just hotwire it. It'll be fun. It's been over a decade since I hotwired hardware.

She placed a hand on Jenner's arm and guided him to the quietest corner of the room, relatively speaking. "I've worked out a signal beam I believe will completely nullify an alien vessel's shield for so long as it is continuously directed at the vessel. They won't let me reprogram the defense arrays—what's left of them. Either they don't believe it will work or they think I'll use the access to take over the arrays and do who knows what."

"When you say 'I,' you mean you and..." his hand gestured awkwardly toward her head "...the Artificial in your brain?"

"Yes. I mean 'we.' Is that a problem?"

"No. But I got the impression Admiral Fullerton wasn't happy to have you around. You're not getting much support in here, either?"

"Ledesme trusts me a little—or she did before I became a cyborg. Now, the verdict's still out. Fullerton is a four-star ass, however. So are you in? Will you help me test this signal on a live target?"

"I will. Grab a ballistic jacket and helmet. It's ugly out there."

"Oh my." Mia froze at the exit to the street, stunned by the scope of the destruction to what hours ago had been a vibrant, shining city center, one many claimed represented the pinnacle of civilization itself. *Meno, our home....*

We will rebuild. Humans always rebuild, and the result is invariably better than what came before.

Jenner was on his comm, issuing orders in the clipped growl military always seemed to use; they must teach a class on it in officer training.

Morgan: No, only a couple of 'you'll die in ten seconds unless you spew out these fifty words as the timer ticks down to zero' scenarios for practice. That and the constricting body armor—flexible my ass.

A minute later a group of twelve soldiers rounded the corner a block away. He ordered them into the alcove of the bunker entrance and out of the direct line of fire, then relieved one of the soldiers of a bulky SAL and turned to her.

"Okay, Ms. Requelme, what now?"

She ignored the suspicious stares of the soldiers to run her hand along the length of the weapon until she found the removable panel then yank it open to reveal a tiny control board. She jiggered it out of its slot so she could reach the fibers connecting to it.

"Sir, what is she doing?"

"Stand down, Lieutenant."

Then she ripped off one of the fibers and replaced it with her index finger.

"Sir!"

As the new code flowed into the circuit through her finger, she idly wondered if it was the violence committed upon the board or the head-to-toe scarlet glyphs blazing along her exposed skin which elicited the reaction.

Jenner leaned in close to her ear. "Ms. Requelme?"

"You've never seen anybody hotwire a control board before?"

"Yes, I have. They generally use tools."

"Right, well." *We're done.*

Satisfied the ware had been reprogrammed to meet her needs, she returned the board to its slot with exaggerated care and closed the panel over it. "We'll need another SAL, because this one isn't going to shoot worth shit now. Once we have it, let's go find ourselves a swarmer."

ℛ

They clung to the façade of an office building and the meager protection the shadow of its profile provided. Jenner peeked around the corner and summoned the soldier he had entrusted with the additional shoulder-fired weapon up beside him.

Mia strained to see past him, but Jenner was tall and well-muscled and she was neither. She settled for aiming a stage whisper at his ear. "Remember, paint the target as you normally would—the signal's embedded in the targeting ware."

He indicated he heard her and counted down using his fingers, then he and the other soldier stepped into the open. She gave it a second's consideration then crept out behind them. She had to *see.*

The swarmer accelerated above the broad promenade toward their location. The targeting laser was invisible, but the beam from the active SAL streaked through the air to impact the core of the strange ship.

The explosion rocked the buildings on either side as metal shot in every direction to lance through windows and ricochet off the road. An instant later the engine erupted into a hot plasma fireball that sent them all rushing back around the corner lest they be melted by the expanding flames.

She laughed and sank against the wall. "It worked."

Of course it worked, Mia. I told you it would work.

Yes, you did, Meno.

"Maybe we caught it when its shield was down. I mean, it was getting ready to fire on us, right?"

Jenner shook his head at the skeptical Marine. "Nope. I've seen our fighters blow those things up, and it requires at least four seconds using a far stronger laser even when the shield is down at the oculus. This was instantaneous and total."

He gave Mia a respectful smile. "Let's get this code of yours replicated and out to the fleets. Then we'll talk to the governor about reprogramming the defense arrays."

"Already handled."

"Ma'am? I mean, I expected you and Alex were communicating with each other—and I guess with another of—another person—at EASC. But don't we still have to distribute the code for the signal through channels to the various ships?"

Mia shrugged mildly. "Like I said, already handled. The signal and instructions for using it are being pushed out to the ships here as we speak, as well as to both militaries' contingents at Seneca. Though I'm not sure they really need it there, as Alex performed her own magic on the Metigen vessels."

The corners of Jenner's eyes creased as he stared at her. Great, she'd frightened another one…. "And the arrays?"

"Meno managed to hack the encryption on the arrays shortly after we left the bunker—it would have been rude to do it while we were standing in the room with the governor and the defense chief. We have to make a couple of adjustments to the control ware, but the nodes should begin broadcasting the signal in the next few minutes." She pursed her lips in mild irritation. "The defense turrets are on a closed system, though, so I can only access them from the bunker."

He squinted oddly at her, then gazed around at his men. "All right, let's move back to the bunker. We'll take out any swarmers we come across on the way."

As they reversed course to return to the command center, he glanced at her again. "Is there anything…." His voice drifted off as he frowned, then frowned more deeply.

"Problem?"

"Sorry. Information from Command." He scanned the group. "Why hasn't Beta Squad shown up yet?"

"Said they got held up rescuing some injured, sir. They're on their way now."

She'd known him for literally minutes, but Mia thought Jenner had a strange look in his eyes as he nodded ponderously. "I'm sure they'll catch up to us."

We are down to eight nodes remaining operational on the defense arrays.

Once they get that beam working on the warships, it won't matter.

True enough. I am ashamed it took me so long to devise the proper signal propagation. In retrospect it appears a quite simple solution.

They usually do. And don't be ashamed—we merely needed to work together on the problem is all.

Your fresh perspective was most helpful, Mia.

The whole is greater than the sum of its parts.

You're suggesting we are both more intelligent and more clever as a unit than either of us were apart?

I am. Don't you agree?

Very much so. Not knowing how you felt, I didn't want to mention it.

You only need look to learn how I feel about, well, everything.

I know. I am trying to respect your privacy, but I confess it is proving difficult.

It's okay, Meno. My thoughts are your thoughts. You're part of me now.

I am.

51

The two superdreadnoughts were accelerating when they smashed into one another twenty degrees off head-on. The force of untold kilotonnes of hyper-strong metal colliding burst outward in a conflagration of material and energy for half a megameter to wreck every vessel in its path, Metigen and human alike.

Most of the United Fleet ships managed to get clear of the blast, but two frigates and perhaps a dozen fighters were not so lucky. Still, the aftermath of the collision damaged an additional three SDs and a host of swarmers, so the incident came out markedly in their favor.

In the upper right sector of Quadrant Two—within visual range from the bridge of the *Leonidas*—an SD fired wildly, intending to hit an Alliance cruiser but catching the undercarriage of one of its brethren instead.

That settled the question.

Field Marshal Gianno allocated half her attention to the semicircle of holos to her left. "We're starting to see evidence of Ms. Solovy's corruption of the SD programming. It's sporadic and unpredictable, but it is overtly manifesting."

After receiving concurrence from the others she activated the fleet-wide channel. "All pilots be on alert for unusual behavior by Metigen vessels. Scan for new opportunities and act on them, but don't get caught unawares. Expect anything."

Next she turned to Admiral Cavaste. She was on the *Leonidas* as commander of the Federation military, not as captain of the flagship. Some friction was unavoidable, but there had been plenty of duties to keep them both busy thus far. "Thoughts?"

Cavaste checked the viewport. "We're got this new signal coming in that's supposed to strip their shields, right? I think we find an SD acting squirrelly in Quadrant Two, paint it with the signal and shoot it. Then we find another."

Her terse nod sufficed as permission, and he refocused on the tactical map. The considerable range of the dreadnought's weapons meant they need not advance too far into the chaotic fray in order to find targets, and she was confident Cavaste would warn the other ships in the vicinity to stay out of their weapons' trajectory.

Rear Admiral Lushenko (SFS Isonzo*): Marshal Gianno, I've lost control of the 22ⁿᵈ Brigade's entire fighter complement to the Artificial.*

The officers were edgy about Artificials playing a role in the battle—if they knew the true nature of the intelligence many would be inclined to revolt—and she had not discouraged the sentiment. They served as her unwitting early warning signals of possible trouble.

Field Marshal Gianno: Understood.

She moved directly in front of the holo feed from the sim room on Deck 5.

Morgan stood in the center of the empty, dark room, her profile carving a shadow against a backdrop of virtual stars. The young woman would be seeing much more, of course, flying through the battlefield with her thoughts. Her hands jerked in erratic cadences at her sides, the residual byproduct of the actions of her mind and the Artificial joined with it.

"Commander Lekkas, what are you doing?"

The response came through gritted teeth. "Busy."

"You're controlling eighty-six fighters. Now ninety. This exceeds your operating parameters by a significant margin." The phrasing made it sound like Morgan was a machine...but she was, wasn't she? At the very least the line between man and machine had been blurred into indistinctness.

As if on cue, a thin line of blood trickled out of Lekkas' nose to remind Eleni of the human component of the equation.

They had no idea the long-term effects of such a taxing two-way connection on the human mind or body. The Prevos didn't reside on the bleeding edge of science—they were over the cliff, halfway to the ground below and trying to fly on capricious wings.

"Commander, ease up."

"Just watch. I've got this."

The indefinable entity that was the Lekkas-STAN unit had performed exceptionally well thus far. All the Prevos had. And the simple truth was no one had any idea where their limits resided, or even if they existed at all. But this was the weapon they had crafted to win the war, so they may as well use it. Gianno turned her back on the holo to zoom her map in and track the fighter groups now under Lekkas' control.

They were fleeing. Rather than seeking targets, the fighters sped toward the fringes of the conflict zone, strafing and diving in evasive maneuvers which individually appeared random but en masse became a rhythmic, almost hypnotic dance.

An increasing number of swarmers pursued them. The deceptively panicked behavior of the fighters drew more and more of the alien vessels into their wake as they passed through the turbulent combat, like hounds catching the scent of blood. Every so often a fighter would lob a sideways potshot with an arcalaser to lure another one onto their trail. Where were they going?

"She's leading them to here."

She looked over as Admiral Rychen drew a circle on their shared map around a point beneath the heaviest fighting in Quadrant Six. "EA Recon #2 has dropped six negative energy bombs there."

"Ah." The events occurring across Senecan space were orders of magnitude beyond what any single person could track, so it didn't concern her that she'd been unaware of the placement of the bombs. Some division of responsibility was the only way they had managed to control the engagement thus far…assuming they were in fact the ones controlling it and not their Faustian creations.

Debris from a splintering SD washed over the grouping, taking out four fighters and three swarmers. She checked Lekkas' holo to see a second trickle of blood seep out the other nostril.

"Get a medic on standby outside the sim room, but tell them not to enter yet."

The cavalcade reached the region Rychen had indicated with several hundred swarmers in tow. The lead fighters continued on straight through it. Then the rearmost fighters suddenly accelerated—well past any safe speed—to close ranks as the swarmers entered the zone.

As one every fighter flipped ninety degrees in one of four directions and spread out in perfect synchronicity in a starburst pattern away from the mined space.

A second later the bombs detonated in a menacing obsidian conflagration which seemed to roil space itself, shredding more than four hundred swarmers in a single act.

The fighters drifted out of formation and adopted haphazard trajectories, a sign control had been released to their pilots.

Gianno immediately returned her attention to Lekkas. The woman wiped the back of her hand across the base of her nose as she opened her eyes and blinked at the cam sending her feed to the bridge. "I'm good."

"Yes, you are. Well done, Commander."

52

ROMANE

The skies and the streets were full of enemy ships as they made their way back across the eight blocks they'd managed to traverse during the hunt for a target on which to test the disruptor beam.

The tentacled ships were now in rather plentiful supply, a sign the invaders were moving into the heart of the city. They took out two swarmers in three blocks, and it was tremendously satisfying both times. Having seen the destruction the alien vessels had wrought in only hours, Malcolm took great satisfaction in blowing them up. As did his companion, it appeared.

Mia Requelme was…it would be inaccurate to say she was not what he'd expected. Seeing Alex had acclimated him to the Prevos' physical oddities, and he'd otherwise born no expectations beyond a reasonable level of intelligence and technological savviness. She met those standards, no question. Beyond that, she was refreshingly blunt and assertive. She wasn't a soldier…but she seemed to have the heart of one.

They were halfway to the bunker when the alien ships started falling out of the sky. More specifically, the Alliance ships started shooting them out of the sky.

He signaled a halt and activated his comm. "Admiral Fullerton, can I assume you received the signal code?"

"Yes, Colonel, and it is extremely effective."

"You have the 'freak of nature' to thank for it."

Fullerton merely grunted in response, but the point had been made.

He fell in beside Mia as they resumed their course. "Impressive work. Your invention may take down the entire Metigen fleet here and save Romane."

She exhaled in noticeable relief. "That was my goal—"

Malcolm thrust his arm out to shove her against the side of the building as he flattened on the wall beside her. The lieutenant carrying the modified SAL raised it in the direction of the next intersection. Two seconds later a swarmer sped into the open—

—and disintegrated into shrapnel as the laser from an Alliance fighter tore into it.

Most of the Marines with him hooted and hollered, fist-pumping the fighter as it buzzed the intersection on its way to its next target. Malcolm allowed himself momentary levity in the form of a pleased nod. "That, ladies and gentlemen, is what winning looks like."

"Yes, sirree!"

"All right, no need to swagger quite yet. Lot of enemies still in the sky. Let's get to the bunker so we can push this signal out to the defense turrets and finish the job."

They were a block from the bunker when Beta Squad came jogging around the corner.

Malcolm instantly tensed and stepped forward to place himself between Mia and the advancing men. He'd been on edge ever since receiving an alert regarding one of the members of Beta Squad shortly after their initial test of the disruptor beam. Now he replayed it in his mind.

> *Colonel Jenner,*
>
> *You are hereby ordered to arrest Major Case Spencer of the 4th SW MSO Platoon on suspicion of colluding with the Metigen invaders or agents thereof. He should be considered extremely dangerous and appropriate precautions taken. He must be disarmed and detained at the soonest available opportunity.*

'Appropriate precautions' weren't exactly available on an open street in the middle of a war zone. He kept his expression blank. "Major, what took you so long?"

The Marine gestured in the direction they had come from. "Had to dig a little girl out of some wreckage. You know how it is."

"I do." He scrutinized Spencer as his hand slid to the Daemon at his hip. Was he really going to do this? The order had originated from a place of authority and a superior officer, not to mention from a man he knew personally. Still, it was outside the chain of command and came without explanation.

"What have you all been up to?"

One of the men piped up before Malcolm could silence him. "This woman here figured out how to shut off their shields. We can blow them up nice and pretty now. We're heading back so she can reprogram the groundside defenses."

Spencer brandished a snarl. "That's her, huh? The cyborg freak?"

Resolve solidified, Malcolm drew his weapon and sighted down on the man. "Major Case Spencer, you are under arrest on suspicion of colluding with enemy forces. You will be taken into custody pending a full hearing."

Spencer began gradually raising his arms in the air, but his hands remained fisted. "It's too late, by the way."

"What's too late?"

His left hand opened to reveal a small device in his palm. His thumb was already pressing on it and Malcolm was already firing.

Mia's shoulder jostled into him; he spun just in time to catch her on her way to the ground. Her entire body was convulsing in a seizure of some kind. Her eyes had rolled back in her head to leave only the whites showing.

He flung an arm behind him in Spencer's direction. "Restrain him, now!" Then he eased her to the ground, keeping a hand behind her head so she didn't crack her skull against the stone while thrashing.

Abruptly the convulsions stopped and she sagged bonelessly in his grasp. Two fingers went to her neck. "I've got a pulse. She's alive."

A member of Alpha Squad whose name he didn't yet know crouched beside him. "I'm a medic. Let me take a look at her."

He relinquished her to the man's care and stood to see one of the squad commanders placing wrist restraints on Major Spencer while two others held him to the ground. The shot had been absorbed by his shield but had dazed the man long enough to prevent escape.

"What did you do?"

Spencer managed a gurgling laugh. "Blew up her house, Colonel. Her synthetic master is no more."

"For God's sake, *why?*"

"You want Artificials for our new overlords? Cause I sure as hell don't."

"You imbecile!" Malcolm caught himself and worked to tamp down the rage. They were exposed and in danger out here on the street.

He turned to the Marines not involved in subduing Spencer. "We're almost to the bunker. Carry her there—gently. If they don't have a physician on site, we'll evacuate her to the *Orion*." His gaze reverted coldly to the prisoner. "Take him with us, too. Less gently."

As they took care in lifting Mia's limp form, Malcolm dragged a hand down his face to bury a frustrated growl. At least the code for the disruptor beam had gotten out, been put to use and propagated to the other ships. Thousands and more likely millions of lives would be saved today.

But damn was he going to be pissed if the price was this one.

53

The sheer number of ships in motion—now, many hours after the campaign had begun and when so many had been destroyed—was beyond counting.

The scale of the battle playing out in the space above Seneca transcended anything Caleb had ever seen in historical vids, much less in person. The debris field and the continuing combat overlapped one another to span more than ten megameters, well outside the range of the visual scanner. Beneath the chaos Seneca orbited peacefully, thus far untouched by the blitzkrieg. Depending on the outcome, it would either endure or be shattered.

Part of him was stunned to note how many of the ships continuing to fly were human ships. Despite all the advantages they had brought to bear in this clash, the odds were still stacked against them. Or so he had thought.

Beyond the smallest of groupings there existed no separation between Alliance and Federation vessels. Both filled the sky to dodge and attack numerous alien superdreadnoughts and scores of swarmers.

As he surveyed the fray, the realization dawned that they were doing rather more attacking than dodging. He'd seen a few glimpses of footage from previous engagements with the aliens, and the superdreadnoughts did not appear to be acting nearly so aggressive as before. Their shots were late to chase ships already gone and their tactics disorganized in often failed attempts to evade fire rending with unexpected force into their hulls.

We were pushing, and hard.

His attention was drawn to an Alliance cruiser above and to his port as no less than eight swarmers careened into its broadside in a series of cascading explosions. While each was tiny against the hull of the sizeable warship, the sheer force of the collisions alone would cause damage.

The smoke cleared to reveal several deep cracks and a notable dent inflicted by the first two collisions; yet the remainder had impacted along a strip of hull deeper and richer in hue than the rest of the ship. It continued to shine unmarred and unaffected by the assault. *Adiamene.*

Caleb couldn't say why swarmers were suddenly crashing headlong into their foes, but he did know what it meant.

We were *winning.*

The joy in his chest notched up another level above its previously lofty heights, sent there by succeeding in saving Isabela and Marlee and now by being so close to reaching Alex. She lived, and that knowledge alone had sustained him through the short but too-long voyage from Krysk. He hadn't bothered her with inquiries, not wanting to distract her from her vitally important task—a task which he suspected she was succeeding at to an astounding degree.

Now he was here, and it was past time he paid her a visit.

Though it cut an impressive figure once sighted, the *Churchill* was not the sole dreadnought present and he located it among the ocean of ships only by radar. The trip to reach his destination through a gauntlet of interweaving fighters and swarmers, darting frigates and charging cruisers was a harrowing one, invisible or not. He didn't relax until he'd deactivated the cloaking shield and docked on the expansive flight deck.

A sergeant met him at the bottom of the *Siyane's* ramp. "Mr. Marano, I've been instructed to take you directly to the bridge." The very young soldier lacked the discipline to suppress an air of dismay at being asked to personally escort some random civilian to the bridge of the flagship of the Alliance military.

"Excellent. Lead the way."

The level of activity on the ship would be called anarchy in any other environment. But he supposed everyone had their own individual duties and understood where they were going and why.

He didn't know what he would find on the bridge. He knew very little of what had transpired in the intervening hours. He didn't know what role Alex played or how it was working out for her. If they were winning it could only mean good things, right? Yet a traitorous voice in the recesses of his mind whispered warnings of the high cost of victory.

The lift finally came to a stop and the door opened onto a bridge larger than any ship he'd been on until now. Some two hundred people staffed dozens of stations or dashed about in their purposeful wanderings. There was a concentration of people in the far center two-thirds of the way down the bridge. He zeroed in on it.

Several officers worked on either side of an oversized screen at which Alex stood. An Admiral stood beside and slightly behind her while she pointed at various details on the screen in an animated manner.

He approached quietly, savoring the opportunity to watch her as each familiar movement, each shift of her head and toss of a hand reassured him she was not merely safe but had stayed fundamentally *Alex*.

Abruptly she spun around, brilliant gleaming irises immediately landing on him. His heart leapt into his throat as her face lit up almost as brightly as her eyes. Then she was in his arms.

Her own joy overwhelmed him to the point he found he was spinning her around, lifting her into the air as she cackled into his neck.

"You're here! And you're okay—you are, aren't you?" She pulled away a sliver to inspect him.

"I am. Are you?"

She quickly nodded. "I'm sorry, I can't shut Valkyrie off right now, too much is going on—but yes."

He smirked mischievously. "Prove it."

Her mouth smothered his, audience be damned...*and he was home*. The tension—the dark, simmering terror which had been gripping him far beyond his recognition of it—faded into nothingness. In its place rose a quiet yet bountiful contentment.

He chuckled softly against her lips. "I believe you." Recognizing they had probably stretched the indulgence of their hosts as far as they should, he set her down and took a half step back. Only then did he realize her hair hung in a tangled mess, its disarray only partially concealed by the wrap half holding it in check. Her left cheek was smudged with a silver fluid of some sort and her shirt had two long tears in it.

"You look a wreck. What happened?"

"Oh, nothing much. I went for a space jump, broke into one of the superdreadnoughts, hacked the core programming of its systems hub and hitched a ride back atop a recon ship."

He blinked several times; yep, she still managed to surprise him. "You are...remarkable. Is that all?"

"Not really. But you—Isabela and Marlee are okay? I know O'Connell's dead, but the details are a bit sketchy."

"They earned a few bruises, but yes, they're okay. The details of O'Connell's death will keep for now. But know I could not have gotten to them in time without your ship. I owe you everything."

Her irises twinkled like stars beneath the artificial radiance. "No, but if you want to try to repay me...."

"Aren't you going to ask?"

"Nope."

He leaned to murmur against her lips. "The *Siyane* is fine. Not a scratch, though it wasn't for lack of trying."

A grimace asserted itself at the margins of her features, only to be squelched the next instant.

"I crashed her through the hulls of both frigates and the *Akagi*."

"What!"

"Not a *scratch*...or at least not a scratch that didn't heal itself by the time I got here." He reluctantly prodded her away. "From what I saw outside, you aren't finished working yet. Go."

She looked disappointed but began backing up. "Will you stay?"

"I'll stay. I just need to find somewhere unobtrusive to lean."

"Over there should be—"

ᴙ

When Alex opened her eyes, she was on her knees and her hands clutched her temples. The single jolt of pain had torn through her skull with the force of a lightning strike, then just as quickly was gone.

Alex: What the fuck was that?

Devon: I feel like my brain was ripped out of my skull through my ears.

Morgan: Reminded me of my second-worst hangover.

Alex: Mia?

Silence.

Devon: The hell? They're gone.

Alex: What do you mean?

Devon: I don't know. They dropped off the connection and not in a benign manner.

Alex: Try to contact Mia directly.

Devon: Don't you think I am? But there's nothing.

"What's wrong?" Caleb was crouched at her side and had an arm wrapped around her shoulders. She swayed against him, allowing him to support her; the after-effects of the mental wallop had left her nauseous and unsteady.

Alex: Malcolm. He might be with her.

Her pulse to him felt glacially slow compared to the instantaneous exchanges with the others.

What happened to Mia? Do you know? Can you find out?

Soldiers were rushing toward her, but she waved them off and made an effort to struggle to her feet. "I'm okay."

The statement had been directed more at the over-interested onlookers than at Caleb. Having reached a standing position with his help, she leaned in close and dropped her voice low. "Something happened to Mia. I don't—hang on."

An asshole working for the aliens blew up her Artificial. She had some kind of seizure, or maybe a stroke. She's alive but unconscious. I'll take care of her, I promise.

Thank you. Thank you.

Caleb could obviously tell the news wasn't good as soon as she met his gaze, for his expression darkened and his grip on her arm tightened.

"She's alive, but Meno's gone and…we don't know exactly what that means for her. I'm so sorry."

He gave her the most beautiful smile. Oh, how she'd missed him. "It's okay. Keep me updated?"

"I will." Equilibrium regained, she reluctantly began pulling away. "Listen, things are about to get interesting. I'm glad you're here."

"Dare I ask what you mean by 'interesting'?"

Her answer consisted of a raised eyebrow and mysterious quirk of her mouth.

His brow furrowed into its endearingly straight line, but he brought her hand to his lips and kissed her knuckles, then let her go and found his wall.

She pivoted and strode back to the overlook.

Alex: It's time.

54

"Admiral Solovy? We have a problem."

Miriam continued tracking developments above Seneca. Alexis and Valkyrie's successful corruption of the SDs' operating systems had pushed the battle definitively in their favor. With the exception of the incident involving Ms. Requelme on Romane, the news had been uniformly positive for more than an hour now.

As such, 'a problem' was not what she wanted to hear. And honestly, she didn't see how the Director of Terrestrial Defense could *be* the bearer of a relevant problem. "Yes, Admiral Grigg?"

"Ma'am—" she jumped, as Grigg had crossed the room and was whispering in her ear "—the Prevos have taken control of the arrays."

"What arrays?"

"Earth's arrays, ma'am."

She frowned at the man. "I don't understand."

"I don't either but—"

"Admiral Solovy, we have a problem."

Her eyes flicked to the *Leonidas* holo. Gianno was working a screen of cascading data while conferring with officials back on Seneca. Here the room buzzed in growing clamor as Grigg's attempt at discretion had failed to keep the turn of events secret. "The Prevos have taken control of the Senecan orbital defense arrays?"

Eleni tilted her head a fraction. "So it would appear."

Miriam moved Grigg out of her personal space and raised her voice to an authoritative level. "ANNIE, did you take command of the Terrestrial Defense Grid?"

"We did, Admiral." It wasn't ANNIE's electronic voice but rather Devon's.

He was located in the primary sim room at Special Projects. Four guards were stationed outside, for protection, assistance or whatever other need might arise. The room projected the entirety of data available to them from both fronts and provided him a degree of access and control which matched her own, and possibly surpassed it.

A tall holo on the right edge of the table allowed her to keep an eye on him, but other than the occasional wisecrack his presence had largely gone unnoticed as he worked in silence or through ANNIE.

Now she bestowed on him her full attention. "Why?"

"You will see soon enough."

The response evoked a shiver to race along her spine, but before she was able to react a message from Alexis arrived in her eVi. Her chest ached with dread as she opened it.

> *Mom,*
>
> *I can't explain to you what's going on. I wish I could, but it's imperative events play out to their conclusion. When it's over you'll understand. Just know that many things are not what they seem. People may not be what they seem.*
>
> *If you have ever trusted me, I ask you to trust me now. Please. I won't let you down.*
>
> *—Alex*
>
> *P.S.: Do me a favor and look at Richard right now.*

Her gaze shot up to find Richard regarding her intently from across the long table. He lacked a role to play in the battles themselves but had asked to be present in the War Room. She had agreed, because he possessed the necessary clearance but mostly because he gave her some small measure of comfort.

Now his lips moved in silence. *Trust her.*

How could he know? Something of enormous import was happening, and she did not appreciate being kept in the dark. At all.

"Admiral, what is the situation?"

She schooled her features and pivoted to Brennon's holo. "Give me thirty seconds, Prime Minister."

"You have twenty."

Right. "Devon Reynolds, explain this action now or we will unplug you."

"It won't be enough. It's what I feared—what I warned you about. They've gone mad."

The room suddenly felt overcrowded, the air thick and bodies pressing in on her as she spun to face Brigadier Hervé. The woman had maneuvered herself to the front row circling the table.

"'Gone mad'? Is that a technical term, Brigadier? Am I to understand your professional assessment is the Prevos have abruptly 'gone mad' after performing flawlessly throughout these battles and saving our skin in countless actions?"

"Victory over the aliens isn't enough for them. Now that they've gained power they won't give it up. I *tried* to warn you this would happen."

Devon's voice rose above the growing din. "Jules, Jules, Jules. You worry too much. I assure you, we have not 'gone mad.'"

Miriam's focus remained on Hervé. "Then what *have* you done, Devon?"

"I told you. You'll see."

The shiver in her spine froze to solid ice. Was Hervé correct? Oh, Alexis….

Trust her. Richard's silent words repeated themselves with demanding insistence in her mind. She checked him again, but this time he merely offered her a careful nod. Her gaze flickered to the *Churchill*. Alexis stood at her personal display, ostensibly studying skirmishes and combat data, but Miriam noted the corners of her lips upturned in profile.

Things are not what they seem. People may not be what they seem.

"I can shut them down. Prime Minister, I request authorization to use the Kill Switch."

She whipped back to Hervé, taking a step toward the woman while one eye went to Brennon. "What 'Kill Switch'?"

He was stroking his chin. "We should try to resolve this peacefully if we can."

Defense Secretary Mori leaned forward until his nose hairs were visible in his holo. "Prime Minister, if there is a way to disable these monstrosities you must use it!"

"*What* 'Kill Switch'?"

Hervé gave her an odd smile. She didn't recall the woman's smile being so disquieting in the past. "The one I secretly installed in the firmware underlying their links. I send a signal from any control panel and the connection is broken."

"You stupid bitch! A hard cutoff will cause a stroke in the human—you saw what happened to Mia!"

Abigail—another person in the sea of bodies crowding the room—was here in case of complications with Noetica. Which they now had. Up until now the doctor had contented herself with studying the technical soundness of ANNIE's output and periodically reviewing Devon's vitals. Now she charged up to Hervé and appeared to be considering cold-cocking her.

"I am not, nor have I ever been, stupid, Abigail. Of *course* it will cause a stroke. But if the alternative is the death of billions, it's an easy price to pay."

A calm certainty descended upon Miriam. In war no price was easy to pay, but some were too high to ever justify. She took another step toward Hervé and locked her expression into an appropriately threatening countenance.

"Brigadier Hervé, stand down. As your commanding officer I order you to NOT activate that Kill Switch."

The woman ignored her to plead with Brennon. "Prime Minister? Your authority overrides the Admiral's."

"Brennon, do not—"

"Are they taking any action with the Defense Grid?"

"Not yet, but once they do it will be too late—"

"The array nodes are turning inward—they're pointing them toward Earth!"

"Stop them!"

"That's it, I'm doing it—"

Hervé's hand never reached the panel. The beam from Miriam's sidearm struck her full in the chest and sent her slumping unconscious to the floor.

Miriam gestured to the security officer at the door. "The Brigadier has been relieved of her station. Secure her in a holding cell then see to it she receives medical attention."

Now Mori was yelling, among other people. "Admiral Solovy is personally compromised and no longer fit to lead. Prime Minister, I demand you relieve *her* of command!"

"Mori, for the love of god, shut up." Mori's holo vanished, presumably terminated by Brennon. "Admiral, you have five seconds to avert disaster. I suggest you use them."

Miriam nodded thoughtfully, crossed her arms over her chest and stood there, to all observers composed and untroubled.

The room roared in dissent and panic, but she once more tuned the noise down to a low hum.

5…

If you have ever trusted me, I ask you to trust me now.

4…

I won't let you down.

3…

Trust her.

2…

"Admiral?"

1…

I trust you.

Around the Earth two hundred orbital nodes, each one equipped with a four hundred kilotonne laser weapon, fired on the planet below.

55

EARTH
EASC Headquarters

Two Days Earlier

Richard looked up in surprise as the door to his office opened and Alex and Devon walked in. His door had been locked. The set of his mouth tightened in consternation. "And when did ANNIE get access to the EASC security system?"

"When we decided she needed it." Devon flashed a mischievous smirk, which was rather disconcerting what with his irises glowing an iridescent white. Alex, too. Standing there together they made for an eerie sight.

He tried to keep from broadcasting the jarring discomfort he felt. "I see. Can I help you?"

Alex planted her hands on the rim of his desk and leaned into it. "You really, really can. We have a problem."

"I'm going to require a little more information—but before you start, let me activate the extra shielding I had installed."

"It's already active."

He considered Devon briefly then dropped his forearms on the desk and switched to Alex. "All right. Go."

"The aliens still have a number of agents out there—people in positions of power in the military, government and business, as well as others wielding less influence but who are strategically situated to cause harm. We believe when the aliens begin to realize they are losing this war, they will use these agents in any number of ways to tip the scales back in their favor. Some of those ways may be catastrophic in nature."

"We are working around the clock to uncover every person who—"

"You don't need to uncover them. We know who they are. You need to stop them."

"How do you know who they are? Is there a list somewhere no one told me about?"

She smiled, and his base fears receded a touch. "A list would be fabulous. No, we don't have a list. Well we do now, but we made it and—"

Devon had been trying and failing to refrain from fidgeting against the wall. He was practically vibrating as he stepped forward and interrupted her. "We were able to identify the aliens' communication signal by cross-referencing the comm records of Aguirre, the assassin from Pandora and…others. Annie had narrowed down the possibilities, but once STAN provided the assassin's records—damaged but it didn't matter—the answer was clear. The signal's signature isn't remotely like anything we use, so then it was simply a matter of filtering for it."

"Filtering what?"

Devon's faced screwed up at him as if the question was absurd in its silliness. "Filtering everything: the exanet, security logs, astronomical readings, data from long-range sensors and research buoys. Anyway, here's the list of people who have been in direct contact with the aliens. Then we analyzed their communication histories for unusual activity and identified individuals likely to be working for the alien agents—those names are at the bottom. They may be unaware of the nature of their true employer but present a danger all the same."

Richard pinched the bridge of his nose in an attempt to forestall an encroaching headache. "You two are not trained investigators. There are a thousand reasons why the *alleged* agents for the Metigens could've contacted these people."

Alex chewed on her bottom lip but nudged herself in front of Devon. "The people you've arrested for trying to kill me—thank you for that by the way—have any of them given you useful information?"

"Not much. They've spouted a variety of justifications for their actions: hatred of Seneca, fear of Artificials, someone paid them a lot of money. Thus far the information isn't leading anywhere worthwhile. Why?"

"Every one of them is on the secondary contact list."

He straightened up in his chair. "Okay, you have my attention. I won't bother to ask how you got *their* names."

"Good. You want to know who set them on the path? The answers are right here. You want to know who else has been set on the same path? We're giving them to you. We aren't trained investigators, but Annie is, and all the Artificials possess the algorithms to analyze a mountain of data and find the patterns. For these people, all other explanations were eliminated. They are our enemies—every single one of them."

Nope, there was the headache. "What do you want me to do? Arrest them all?"

"When you can, absolutely."

"And when I can't?"

"Do whatever is necessary to remove their ability to act against us—against humanity."

"You mean kill them."

Her expression darkened in what he sensed was sorrow, but her shoulders rose. "If that's what it takes. Richard, this is our one blind spot, the one way they can hit us for which we won't be ready. Everything may depend on stopping them."

Devon laughed. "No pressure, though."

"Obviously." Richard regarded her, standing before him as proud and defiant as ever. This was *Alex*. He'd known her since she was born. He'd watched her grow from a spunky, curious child into a rebellious, grief-stricken teenager and ultimately into a wonderful, extraordinary woman. This was David and Miriam's daughter…and he had to believe beneath the strange, otherworldly appearance she was still the same person.

Almost as if she could hear his thoughts—could she?—she blinked and the iridescence vanished, leaving only the naturally striking silver-gray. David's eyes. "Please trust me, Richard. And if you can't trust me, trust the data."

It wasn't as if he didn't believe they were correct in their analysis. Given all he'd seen with Aguirre's conspiracy plus the incessant gambits to take out Alex and Caleb, he'd have been more surprised if it wasn't true. And this did represent a major weakness, one which might sabotage their sole chance at winning. At living.

He had thought he appreciated the risks the aliens' devious scheming posed, which was why he'd been working night and day to root out those involved in this whole tangled mess. The news of the looming confrontations at Seneca and Romane—of this war possibly coming to a head far faster than anyone had foreseen—had only reached him an hour earlier. When coupled with the names he now held in his hand, it changed the focus of his investigation considerably.

The primary contact list was short, thankfully, but the secondary one was not...and combined they included the names of too many powerful people spread too far across the galaxy. Some were effectively untouchable...and several were very familiar. "What do you think they're planning?"

Her head shook. "We can't get at the content of the conversations. Assassinations, bombings, severing of communications, sabotage? But whatever they are planning, I guarantee it will be designed to help the aliens win the war and will occur at pivotal junctures."

"I don't disagree, Alex."

"Also, there's one other thing. You can't reveal this information to anyone."

He groaned. "I cannot do all this myself. I will have to use other resources."

"Of course. But tell the minimum required to the minimum required number of people. To everyone else, say nothing. Remember the aliens are listening. If they discover we can track their communications, they'll send their agents running to ground or order them to act early, or both."

"I know they're listening—it has made my job increasingly difficult the last several days." He pulled up a new screen on his desk, positioned it beside their list and compared them. "Four of the people on this list are in custody. Two more were killed while resisting arrest."

Alex's brow knotted in surprise, and he raised an eyebrow at her. "I did say we were working around the clock to uncover conspirators. But if you're right about the nature and extent of their plans, we need to alter our strategy—which means there's one person I need to bring in on this now."

He closed the screen and replaced it with a holo. Before either of them could protest, his husband appeared within it. Despite the early hour at his location, he wore a sable cable knit sweater and pressed khaki slacks and sipped on a thermos.

Richard smiled. "I didn't expect to find you quite so...awake."

Will set the thermos down and shrugged. "Can't bring myself to shift off Earth-time—I'm hoping I won't be here long enough for it to become necessary. No one is clocking normal hours at the moment anyway, so it's fine. What's up?"

Richard turned to Alex, who now wore an expression of utter confusion, and swung the holo around. "We have guests."

"Alex! You're a sight for sore eyes. I trust Richard is taking proper care of you?"

"Yeah, he's got a dozen agents glued to my ass. Where are you?"

"Seneca, actually."

Her gaze darted to Richard, and he chuckled. "Will has been working with Graham to run down the remaining players in the Aguirre Conspiracy as well as alien collaborators outside it."

"Why?"

"Because Graham needed the help. His chief deputy was a major player in the conspiracy, thus everyone in his organization is suspect—and the hit on the safe house you visited was an inside job. Also..." his eyes flicked to the holo bearing a mirthful glint "...he happens to be a Senecan Intelligence agent, so it wasn't too much of a stretch."

She frowned in continued perplexity. "Caleb did mention something about that. I honestly assumed it was the concussion talking, but...you know what, I'll just go with it."

"Probably for the best. Will, this is Devon Reynolds."

"I've heard a lot about you, Mr. Reynolds."

"Whereas I haven't heard..." Alex's irises glittered to brilliancy as she looked at Devon, then faded again "...and now I have. Up to speed. Carry on."

Will shot him an inquisitive glance, but he mouthed a silent '*later.*' "I have confirmation on seventy percent of your suspect list, a bunch of new names to add to it...and I want you to cease all detentions and arrests for the next eighteen hours. Are you at the office?"

"No, I'm in the hotel room. Did you say to stop apprehending suspects?"

"I did. Can you grab Graham in the next half hour or so?"

Will nodded. "I'll head over to Division now."

"Great. Comm me when you meet up with him, and I'll explain. And Will? You are staying safe, right?"

Will grinned, if perhaps a bit indulgently. "I'm leaving the gunplay to the experts. Promise."

"Okay. Talk to you soon." Richard closed the holo sooner than he preferred and returned his attention to Alex. "Now we should go talk to your mother."

She winced hard. "We can't tell my mother."

Uncertainty wavered in his mind. Was the Artificial subtly corrupting her judgment, bit by literal bit? He pushed the qualms aside; she would never allow it to do any such thing.

"Why not? She'll be in favor of the effort. She can use her authority to help."

"One additional element is at play here, something we can't even tell you. For events to play out to completion the way we need them to she must remain ignorant of this. Besides, she has too full a plate as it is."

"Yes, you *can* tell me, because it's important."

She rolled her eyes. "This is the second time you've said that to me in a week."

He stared at her dispassionately. "Well?"

She gave Devon a tiny nod.

Devon's Adam's Apple bobbed, and for once he didn't look cocksure. He looked sad. "There's one more name that should be on the primary contact list, but you can't arrest her. Not until the end. It's Jules."

His jaw dropped. "Brigadier Hervé? You can't be serious."

"I wish I weren't."

He fell back in his chair and rubbed at his neck. "I can't arrest her now because it would tip the aliens off to the fact that we were onto them in a big way. And I can't tell Miriam because she would insist on Hervé being thrown out of the building and into the brig without delay."

"Pretty much."

He sighed. "Understood. I'll handle everything and not involve her."

She leapt around the desk to embrace him. "Thank you."

Devon held up his hands in a defensive position. "I'm not a hugger. But thanks, man."

"Yeah, yeah." He pointed toward the door. "Don't you two have aliens to fight? Now get out of here. And good luck."

After the door closed behind them, Richard sank deeper into his chair and rested his chin on his fists. His stomach churned, driven by the instinctive revulsion triggered in his conscience.

He'd always considered himself a moral man. He hadn't always lived up to his own standard, but he'd like to think he'd always tried. And when he'd failed, he'd strove to do better. Surely choosing to help save the lives of billions of innocents, though it meant getting a little blood on his hands, *was* the moral choice?

An already messy operation had now become nasty and brutal—but it had also become all the more crucial. People were going to die and they were going to do so on his order. It was the only way.

Someone should have told him—Miriam should have told him—how heavy the burden of acting for the greater good could be.

ℛ

In a rare occurrence this last week, Miriam was in her office rather than the War Room. Richard was glad for it as it meant he wouldn't need to request privacy yet again, but he confessed to being surprised.

Then he saw her face and it dawned on him why. He leaned casually against the wall. "Alex has left for Seneca?"

She stared at her desk in silence for another beat, then looked up and gave him a bleak smile. "On one of the new scout ships, so she should arrive in time."

"Admiral Rychen will take good care of her, I'm sure."

"Admiral Rychen's job is to get himself killed if it is necessary to achieve victory. I do believe he'll at least make certain he dies before her, however." She glared at the air in annoyance. "I'm sorry. I'm being ridiculously maudlin, which won't do at all seeing as I have a war to win. What do you need?"

"I need a blank authorization form signed by you." At her frown of surprise he cringed. "Actually, I need three blank authorization forms signed by you."

"You realize I'm ethically obligated to ask why."

Because there are three people on this list whom I don't have the authority to order the detention or elimination of, and you do. "And I'm ethically obligated to withhold the information on the grounds of state security."

"Richard, there's nothing you can't tell me. Also, there's nothing you're legally—or ethically—prohibited from telling me."

"I know…but I can't tell you this. Not yet. Just trust that it will help us win the war."

Her admiral-quality stare bore into him for several seconds, but he persevered.

Finally she jerked a terse nod. "All right. If it were anyone else asking I'd—well, you know what I'd do." She entered a series of commands in the control panel on her desk. "I'm sending them to you now. I trust you'll use them well."

SENECA

CAVARE, INTELLIGENCE DIVISION HEADQUARTERS

Two Days Earlier

"Oh, you have got to be bloody kidding me. I thought we were nearing an end with this shit?"

Richard scowled in his holo, and Graham would daresay he did not look entirely pleased himself. "I am not and we are not. So what do you think?"

Graham ran his hand through hair that hadn't been combed since sometime yesterday, which was now effectively two days ago, and grimaced at Will across his desk. When the man had walked into his office a few minutes earlier and said he had something which would result in yet more lack of sleep, he'd braced himself for almost anything—but not this.

"I don't actually possess the authority to order the military arrests but I'll manage it somehow. The civilians…that's what they make black ops for, isn't it? A number of these names aren't on

Federation or Alliance soil, though. Do you have a way to get at them in time?"

"No. But you know who does."

He nodded, relieved Richard had come to the same unpleasant conclusion on his own. "I do. You realize of course 'detainment' will not be the outcome for any name we give her."

Richard dragged a fist over his mouth to rest at his jaw. "Everything is on the line. God can judge us for our actions when the time comes. If humanity survives, our superiors and perhaps even the public can judge us, too."

Graham appreciated the more honorable of his friends were willing to submit themselves to their particular god's judgment, but he personally intended to keep his sins to himself. "They won't find out about it from me. I'll take my secrets to the grave, hopefully sometime next century."

Will was ignoring him to fixate on the holo. Understandable. "If it helps at all, Richard, I believe this is the right thing to do. Whatever their motivations, these people will aid and abet the destruction of civilization if you—if we—don't stop them."

Richard gave Will a weak but genuine smile, and Graham was relieved he didn't have the weight of yet another broken family on his conscience.

"It does. Thank you. Okay, enough wallowing, because we have *no* time. Shall we prepare a message to Ms. Montegreu?"

NEW BABEL
INDEPENDENT COLONY

Forty Hours Earlier

The smooth, dulcet tones of the news broadcaster wafted in through the open door to the bath.

"We want to bring you breaking news. We have just learned the Earth Alliance leadership has agreed to send its mammoth Sol Fleet to Seneca to fight alongside Federation forces in their defense against an expected attack by an armada of Metigen ships.

"Spokespersons for both the Alliance and the Federation are refusing to confirm the report, but if true it represents an unprecedented and historic act of goodwill and cooperation between governments which were at war only weeks ago. It also raises concerns about the wisdom of leaving Earth all but defenseless in a time of war."

"Who could have envisioned I would help to bring such accord and harmony to a divided galaxy? I submit my reputation needs to be adjusted to reflect my status as a peacemaker."

Aiden's toes ran up Olivia's calf beneath the bubbly water as the flute of champagne hovered at his lips. "I'll put out a memo. In the meantime, I was wondering...do you think I should offer amnesty to the remaining Shào members if they join my organization? Can't say if I'll follow it, but I'd like your advice."

The answer to the question of how Aiden was able to take out Shào's headquarters turned out to be that he had a woman inside the cartel. She had infiltrated the leadership more than two years earlier in response to Shào's increasing challenges of Triene. Within hours of being contacted she'd placed and activated explosive charges throughout the base of operations. Now deceased occupants included not merely Eun Shào himself, but his chief deputy, four lieutenants, three lesser underlings and at least thirty front-line employees.

She snorted and dropped her head back to rest against the curve of his shoulder. "Only if you want a gamma blade in your spine this time next week. Those thugs have no honor."

His snicker rumbled low into her hair. "Whereas you and I, we do have honor?"

"We have standards. If someone falls beneath them, they aren't worthy of honor. If they rise above them? Sure, we have honor."

His hand not holding the champagne slipped beneath the bubbles to run up her inner thigh. "Is it honorable to—"

"Stop." She shoved his hand away as she opened the message which had just arrived.

"Don't even entertain the notion of being a tease, Olivia. You—"

"I'm reviewing something, dammit."

He griped behind her but complied while she re-read the message, scarcely able to accept its contents. And she'd thought the Federation military requesting illegal boosters for their fighter pilots was scandalous…. "You are not going to believe this."

"When it comes to you, I will believe anything. What is it?"

"It's best if I show you." She projected an aural to float above the frothy bubbles.

> Ms. Montegreu,
>
> It is with the utmost reluctance and distaste that we request, per the terms of our agreement, for you to subdue or otherwise render unable to take independent action the following agents of the Metigen enemy:
>
> Joon Choung, CEO of Choung Pharmaceuticals
> Hanse Abel, Vice-Chairman of Advent Materials
> Greta Schwartz, Chief of Staff to the governor of Atlantis
> Alonso Bianchi, Chief Deputy of the Shào Cartel
> Karie Singh, Director of Utilities on Pandora
> Vincenza Nielson, Chairman of Total Chemical Solutions on Romane
> Mellie Ohara, Senior News Broadcaster, Galaxy First Communications
>
> Action against said agents should be taken no earlier than twenty hours and no later than thirty-six hours from the timestamp of this message. Fulfillment of all elements of the requests contained herein, plus cancellation of the contract on Noah Terrage's life, will constitute satisfaction of our agreement and your release from its terms.
>
> — Richard Navick and Graham Delavasi

"Forgive me for asking the perhaps self-evident question, but is this an assassination list?"

"I do believe it is. Oh, and look, one of them is already dead. Isn't that an interesting coincidence."

"Working for the aliens, huh? I guess the more chaos sown, the better."

"They must want these people eliminated rather badly to release me from further squeezing."

"Who's Noah Terrage?"

She grumbled under her breath. "A very lucky man, it seems."

"There are some powerful individuals on the list who could in-flict real damage. You're going to need my help."

"Don't be coy. I wouldn't have shown you the list if I wasn't expecting your help." She wiggled out of his grasp, stood and snatched the towel from the rack. "Come on. We have a lot of work to do and little time to do it in."

EARTH
EASC HEADQUARTERS

Thirty Minutes Earlier

Devon: This signal beam's genius, Mia. Annie's ashamed she didn't create it.

Mia: Meno's ashamed he didn't create it sooner. Who knew Artificials had inferiority complexes?

Devon: Who knew Artificials had complexes, period?

Stanley: Morgan just raised her hand. What does that mean?

Alex: Devon, can you push this signal out to the arrays at Earth and Seneca, too?

Devon: You don't think their firepower will be enough?

Alex: I think this is not the time to hold anything in reserve.

Devon: Valid point. Let's see.

Mia: Romane's Chief Engineer said ours couldn't transmit signals.

Devon: He's just lazy. The receivers can be reprogrammed to act as transmitters as well, but how to do it isn't taught in Introductory Electronics. I'm not lazy but I am busy. Can anyone—wait, never mind. Annie borrowed a routine from the Gagarin Institute.

Alex: Does the Gagarin Institute know that?

Devon: Almost certainly not. They shouldn't have stored it on their private encrypted internal network if they didn't want an insanely-powerful, unshackled human-Artificial hybrid to pilfer it.

Alex: Clearly.

Devon: All right, Earth Defense Grid is a go. Morgan, I need a bypass of the Senecan Defense Grid's ware alteration block.

Morgan: Done. Do me a favor and forget the tunnel route after you use it, in case we go to war with each other again in the future.

Devon: Sure thing.

Mia: He says in the least convincing voice ever. Ooh, another swarmer to kill. That's not getting old anytime soon.

Morgan: You might be surprised....

Alex: Devon, are you sure we have to provoke Hervé? Can't we just get Richard to arrest her, tell the others what's going on, fire the damn arrays and be done with it?

Devon: We're not merely provoking Jules—we're provoking all of them. It's this thing they call a 'test,' and if we want to enjoy any degree of personal security when this is over we have to do it.

Alex: And if they fail this test?

Devon: Then at least we know what to expect and can act accordingly.

Alex: Dammit. Okay.

R

Five Minutes Earlier

> *How's it looking there? I suspect we're almost out of time.*
>
> *One target left, and she should be in custody in the next five minutes. How are things in Vancouver?*

Richard scanned the War Room from his position of relative—emphasis on the 'relative'—privacy in the deepest corner. For the most part officers meandered in circles or peered intently at displays as if doing so would influence the data displayed.

The vortex of activity had a clear center, though, and that center was Miriam Solovy.

In her immediate orbit was an ever-shifting slate of advisers and department heads. Devon's presence was via a large holo separated from the others. He reclined lazily in a lounge chair in the center of the sim room, the twitch of his eyelids the sole explicit evidence his mind was elsewhere. Occasionally he muttered or shouted announcements or observations, but his most noticeable visible action was to direct pertinent information to Miriam's displays.

This of course only added to the veritable sea of data surrounding Miriam—more than anyone could hope to absorb. And she didn't have an Artificial in her head to help her out in that regard.

Simply conversing with Will served as a welcome respite from the hours of tension permeating the room.

About what you'd suppose from a room full of people with itchy trigger fingers and nothing to shoot. They continue to anticipate the end of days any second now, but it appears we're...well, it appears we're winning.

I don't have your catbird seat, but that's the rumor here, too. Alex?

Alive and kicking ass across the United Fleet, near as I can tell.

Naturally. So, what's the status on the rest of the targets?

Richard grimaced despite his best effort not to.

We couldn't catch up to one of the military targets in time. We tracked him on his ship only to have to chase him down on the ground—and damned if he didn't take out the Prevo on Romane before being subdued.

Jesus. Proves they were right about the threat, though, if at a heavy cost.

You're telling me. Montegreu reported she had fulfilled her obligations in full twenty minutes ago. I shudder to think what it entailed.

It had to be done, Richard. For the safety—for the survival—of us all.

I know. Doesn't mean I have to like it.

I doubt it helps, but Delavasi doesn't like it either.

Maybe, but he just drowns his guilty conscience in alcohol.

And hookers.

Richard laughed loudly enough to earn a glance from Miriam. He pointed at his ear, which seemed to satisfy her.

Hookers, really?

You have no idea.

Nor do I want to. Moving on from that disturbing image...so everything's taken care of on your end?

As of...now, yes it is.

Thank you, Will. The next hour or two may get a bit dicey, but thanks to your help it'll be worth it.

I love you.

And I you. When this is over you'll come home, right?

I intend to beat you there.

Richard ended the conversation with a relieved smile. He'd kept the secret as asked; only he, Will and Graham had all the information. Montegreu had her list, and Alliance and Federation agents in the field and select military officers had their targets, but nothing more.

He wondered how long he was going to get to wait for whatever was to come. Then he noticed the transformation in Miriam's demeanor from normal epic-battle tension to *serious* epic-battle tension.

Not long, it turned out.

56

EARTH

Kennedy pulled her coat tighter before beginning the trek across the courtyard to the Logistics building.

She'd given up her childish beachside sulking hours ago, enjoyed a lovely dinner at a lovely restaurant—still alone—and performed an admirable and extended imitation of window-shopping in the market district. But when the stores had closed for the night and the hour had grown late, she had finally relented and returned to the Island.

The news feeds being broadcast in every store, on every street corner and in her eVi were confused, vague and often contradictory. The most she'd been able to determine was the United Fleet hadn't yet been annihilated. This left her maintaining a level of ignorance which simply would not do.

She doubted they were any more likely to allow her in the War Room now than they had been earlier, but even the lobby should have better information than the media, right? And if she were to happen *by* the War Room—

—the sky overhead illuminated in a dazzling flash. The thunderous roar of multiple blasts followed to assault her eardrums. Everyone in the courtyard halted to gape upward.

Six laser beams streamed from the heavens to slam into two hulking shadows perhaps four kilometers above. The beams' vivid citron hue could only mean they originated from the orbital arrays, the fact the array nodes pointed outward notwithstanding. As the light of the lasers spread in the night sky, the shadows revealed themselves to be Metigen superdreadnoughts. One hovered directly above the EASC Complex, the other to the southeast over the Sea-Vac Metro.

She had but the briefest second to recognize them for what they were. Earth's orbital defense arrays were the most powerful weapons in existence—at least built by humans anyway. Each node was the size of a city block and housed a laser over five times more powerful than the weapons on an Alliance dreadnought. Two hundred individual nodes orbited Earth on ten arrays. All of this meant the force of three lasers tearing into each superdreadnought destroyed the gigantic ships in under four seconds.

Kennedy threw her head back and cackled in delight as the sky lit up like a fireworks circus. The first celebration of victory had arrived in grand style courtesy of the aliens themselves.

Then the wreckage began to rain down, and she decided she did not want to be trapped under another tonne of debris just yet, or ever again. She sprinted for the door and made it inside the instant before a thirty-meter-long shard of superdreadnought debris gouged itself into the center of the courtyard.

It should make a perfectly acceptable monument in remembrance of the Metigen War.

ℛ

The orbital array weapons did not strike London or Vancouver or New York or Sydney or the other four cities seemingly in their lines of fire. Instead they struck the thirty-two Metigen superdreadnoughts hovering stealthed high above those cities.

The initial blow of the lasers disrupted the vessels' cloaking to reveal the full size of the attacking force. The superdreadnought weapons swung up in search of the source of the attacks, but multiple nodes firing from widely disparate locations denied them an easy target.

The powerful weapons tore through the mighty ships. They disintegrated in exceptional synchronicity, cracking open in crimson flames almost in time with one another. In the next second they burst apart in massive, blinding-white explosions.

Everyone in the War Room and on holo stood in stunned speechlessness as they watched the destruction of the colossal ships. Images from every affected city on Earth and identical ones from Cavare and two other Senecan cities had replaced the battle maps above the table.

No one as yet bothered to inquire from where the live images originated, when they'd been so conveniently queued up or how they were now being displayed.

Miriam had a good idea who was responsible, though. Her main question, really, was…why the theater?

She opened a channel to Terrestrial Emergency Operations. "Mobilize rescue operations in the impacted cities immediately. The falling debris will cause damage and injuries in the metropolitan areas."

Then she closed her eyes and breathed out. *Alex, I could hug you. Then kill you.*

Suddenly everyone was talking at once, but she concentrated on the important ones. Brennon's mouth hung open and he appeared to have developed a slight tremor in his hands. "I don't understand. How did they get past our defenses in the first place? How did thirty-two superdreadnoughts hide in the airspace above these cities?"

Devon responded, sounding unashamedly smug. "Their proficiency with the cloaking technology is far more advanced than ours, and it is a highly sophisticated technology. It was an easy matter for them to slip in one by one under stealth. Did you think just because they hadn't used the shields yet they didn't have the capability? They didn't *want* to be stealthy until now."

Miriam eyed Devon suspiciously. "How did you know?"

He shrugged as if to imply it had been a trifling matter. "The cloaking projection does give off a faint residual energy signature beyond whatever environment it's replicating. We set the long-range sensors to watch for it yesterday. Once we picked them up at the Main Asteroid Belt we tracked them to their destinations. Same thing at Seneca."

"Why didn't you simply alert us and take them out as soon as they arrived?"

"We didn't want to tip our hand until we'd finished securing all their agents."

"Explain."

Richard cleared his throat. When all eyes turned to him, he began fidgeting with the hem of his jacket. "The Prevos believed—correctly—the aliens had put in place a fallback plan to execute on should they begin losing. It involved, among other things, utilizing agents around the galaxy to sabotage our efforts on numerous levels. Alex and the others provided Naval Intelligence and Federation Intelligence a list of names. We've spent the last twenty-four hours arresting or if necessary eliminating those people before they were able to act. The man who destroyed Ms. Requelme's Artificial was one such agent we were unable to apprehend in time."

So that was the purpose of the blind authorizations. She stared at Richard in challenge; he gave her a dramatic and presumably apologetic wince in answer.

Brennon continued to look rather perplexed, and she mused whether this latest near-calamity had finally broken his admirable composure. "How is it the Prevos had *names?*"

Richard jerked his head toward Devon. "Mr. Reynolds, perhaps you'd like to explain?"

Devon gave an exaggerated sigh, but he was decidedly relishing the spotlight. "It was all thanks to Annie. Even before Noetica, she noticed Jules was introducing tiny, subtle errors into her algorithms to weaken the accuracy of her analysis of the aliens. After we were linked, she told me—not as if she could have hidden it from me.

"We cross-referenced Jules' comms records with those of the other known Metigen agents—Aguirre, the assassin—and uncovered matching anomalous signals. Once we'd identified the aliens' signature we were able to locate additional contacts. We traced the activity of Hervé and these other agents to more agents, and so on. They were in the military, government, business, everywhere—and some of them could have inflicted serious damage. One of them did."

Quite a piece of detective work. The explanation raised many questions; most of them would wait, but not all. "What about the Kill Switch? Why risk Brigadier Hervé using it?"

"Oh, that? It was never a true threat. We found and disabled it in the first hour."

"Of course you did."

It made for a daunting proposition, contemplating the true scope of the Prevos' power. They'd made an impressive display of it in the last five minutes, and Miriam had to wonder how much further it might extend. But this too was a question for the morrow.

Her gaze returned to Richard. "Why didn't you tell me? Why didn't Alex tell me?"

He wore a pained expression. "Miriam, you know the aliens are eavesdropping, all the time and everywhere but I suspect nowhere more than in your orbit. We needed to keep it to the smallest possible group—literally three people outside of the Prevos knew the details. The rest were merely following orders. And if you learned Hervé was a Metigen agent, you would have insisted on arresting her. If that had happened, the aliens would have been tipped off before we'd secured the other agents and we would have lost any control of the situation we previously gained."

She nodded deliberately. She was unable to refute the logic, but her pride still stung something fierce.

Brennon showed signs of recovering from his bewilderment and spoke up again. "What now?"

Gianno and Vranas had been busy handling their own fallout from the destruction of the superdreadnoughts on Seneca, but they too were now listening with interest.

"Now we intensify—"

You have our attention.

∧R

SPACE, NORTH-CENTRAL QUADRANT
SENECA STELLAR SYSTEM

The voice boomed inside Alex's head like someone had placed a bass speaker at the center of her brain.

You have our attention.

Goddamn right we do.

The disparate reactions of others on the bridge seemed to indicate a few of them were receiving the communication as well, but not most. She instantly knew the other Prevos heard it, and she was cognizant of Rychen gesturing in great animation to her mother. It stood to reason the military and political leadership were part of the audience. A quick glance at Caleb confirmed he too was a recipient of the aliens' declaration. The aliens would doubtless know precisely who mattered and who, in their view at least, did not.

She hadn't realized the level of affectation Mesme's ethereal voice had carried until now. This alien's tenor was toneless, flat and ascetic.

She answered the alien, for it didn't occur to her that anyone else might answer in her stead.

"We have more than your attention. We have our boot on the throat of your forces. They buckle to their knees before us."

What are your intentions? We are open to discussing terms.

If others were endeavoring to respond—the politicians, her mother, anyone—they were being blocked. She had the floor.

"We *intend* to destroy every last one of your machines. If you want to annihilate us, you will have to come fight us yourselves. But you don't do that sort of thing, do you? The blood you'd get on your wispy, angelic little hands would be too much for you to bear. It might threaten your precious vainglory, your *tshcheslaviye.*"

Do not imagine you understand us. You understand nothing.

"And you understand far less about humanity than *you* imagine. We have defied your attempts to control us through terror. We don't tremble in fear before you—we stand up and fight. And though we are so very flawed, when it counts we are capable of rising above those flaws. Are you? Something tells me you aren't.

It's a handy skill—you should look into it. Because when we do, we are powerful beyond measure."

Believe what you will. If you agree not to—

"Oh, and one more thing you don't seem to understand: we have beaten you. So drop the condescending tone. We heard enough of your terms last time to know we want no part of them—I'd have expected you to pick up on that a bit sooner, but no matter.

"Instead, here are *our* terms. Withdraw all your ships through the portal and do not return. To ensure you do not return, we will blockade the portal. Any ship you try to send will be shredded into a thousand tiny pieces before it completes the traversal.

"Furthermore, you will cease your meddling in our universe. You will cease your observation of our universe. We are no longer your experiment to play with. We control our own destiny from this day forward."

You demand much. What do we receive in recompense?

"We'll stop kicking your ass long enough for what's left of your machines to slink back through the portal."

What else?

Sure, why not. "We'd like an explanation. What the hell makes you believe you have the right to exterminate us? What is this really all about?"

You are dangerous—far more dangerous than you recognize. You must be contained.

"How do you know? We never threatened you, not once."

How we know is irrelevant.

"Let me guess—it's 'not our concern.' I've heard that before. Fine. Those are our terms. You have one minute."

Devon: Hey, I piggybacked off their broadcast. Everyone hearing them heard you. It was quite a show.

Alex: Damn straight it was.

A brief pulse came in from her mother.

I approve of your terms.

She turned to allow her gaze to sweep across the bridge and settle on Caleb once more. He stood leaning against the left wall not too far away, shaking his head at her, a dashing, immensely kissable smirk on his lips. Hers curled up to match—

Very well. We cast you adrift to do as you will, with this one warning: do not come looking for us.

Whatever. "Depart. Now. We will track you to the portal, so do not attempt to leave any ships behind for future misdeeds."

We have no interest in whatever becomes of you. Aurora is no longer our concern.

Farewell.

As soon as she sensed the connection retreating from her head, she spun to Rychen. "I mean it—we need to follow them all the way to the damn portal. Send all the scout and reconnaissance ships, and maybe a couple of cruisers for added intimidation. Shove them back through that portal if necessary then lock it down."

"With pleasure." He was laughing as he began issuing orders.

Her focus shifted to the viewports. Lit by fire and explosions for what felt like days, for the first time since she had arrived the stars began to shine. They teased her, flickering in and out in a playful dance amongst the strewn debris and sailing ships.

The remaining swarmers docked into the remaining superdreadnoughts, then in a blink they were gone.

Is it over?

I think so, Valkyrie.

We won in spectacular fashion, didn't we?

Yes. Yes, we most certainly did.

57

SENECA

BREAKING NEWS: EARTH ALLIANCE PRIME MINISTER BRENNON NEWS CONFERENCE

"I come before you today both overjoyed and heartbroken. The terms of the aliens' surrender was a complete and unconditional retreat from our galaxy, and I can now confirm that retreat has occurred. We will maintain a steadfast watch on their portal, and if they should seek to return in the future they will fail. You—every man, woman and child—may sleep soundly tonight, no longer burdened by the fear your home will come under siege with the daybreak.

"The cost of this victory was enormous. Though we try, it may be beyond our ability to measure. More than fifty million people died across thirty-nine worlds. Three hundred thousand of humanity's brave soldiers gave their lives defending our worlds and earning this victory. The damage to our infrastructure is counted in quadrillions. Rebuilding will take years. But we will rebuild.

"Today we stand united. For while we have lost much, we are stronger now than we were before. This is not an Earth Alliance victory or a Senecan Federation victory—it is a victory for all humanity. When faced with extinction, we put aside our differences and joined together to fight side-by-side. We fought as one for all life, because all life is precious.

"Let us now open a new chapter in the story of the human race. Let us embrace this new dawn and usher in a shining era of peace and prosperity. Let us rebuild, renew and reclaim our place among the stars."

Gianno muted the news feed and turned to Vranas, who had taken up a relaxed posture in the chair beside her. "Good speech. Good sentiments. I wonder how long they'll last."

Aristide took a sip of his scotch. "Perhaps longer than we suppose. People are war-weary. They're tired of being frightened and desperate, so they'll embrace peace with relief, for a time. Brennon's a good man, and I believe a sincere one. But of course he's just one man, and inevitably the power grabs and manipulations of the political machine are sure to drown him out." He laughed dryly. "And us."

"A lot of the pesky details of what peace actually looks like were not addressed in the treaty. We'll need to be careful."

"Oh, of that I'm confident. Regardless of Brennon's intentions, the Alliance Assembly and their multitude of agencies will be coming for us, assuming peace means reunification."

Gianno arched an eyebrow. "I assume it does not?"

"It does not. A truth they will hopefully learn without the need for excessive bloodshed." He sat his glass on the table and massaged his jaw. "So what are we going to do about Noetica? The potential is too great to shut it down, but the dangers are considerable."

"For now, Commander Lekkas and STAN are working with the other Prevos to optimize the reconstruction efforts—and frankly, we need their help. The task is simply too overwhelming for us mere humans. Their access to the defense grids and military weaponry has been revoked...we think. We'll try to keep the technology under seal, as I anticipate the Alliance will, but the reality is it's a matter of time until it gets out. It's too powerful to stay hidden for long."

"And then we face a whole new world of problems."

"Then we face a whole new world." Gianno stared out the window a minute before giving the Chairman a smile. "But that's a challenge for tomorrow. Tonight I think we're safe enjoying our victory."

Vranas chuckled as he stood. "It was a close one, wasn't it? Where are you off to now?"

She shut off the news feed and the other screens still open around her office. "I'm going to go home, kiss my husband and hug my son and daughter-in-law, then sit down on the floor and play with my grandchildren."

EARTH

SEATTLE

Noah paused to take a long, deep breath before entering the hotel suite. He was a little winded from not-quite-running here from the levtram station…and he needed to ready himself for whatever awaited on the other side of the door.

He was so royally fucked.

He opened the door to find an empty main room. The info screen in the lobby said she hadn't checked out, but she could be at EASC or out celebrating like the rest of the galaxy or…. He headed toward the bedroom.

"Kennedy?"

She emerged through the doorway as he arrived, eyes narrowed in questioning and a sweater wadded up in her hands. On the bed behind her a duffel bag sat open. She was packing to leave. But she wasn't gone yet.

A smile bloomed as he reached out for her—but she backed away from him. Whatever initial delight may have shown in her expression vanished beneath a guarded stare. "What are you doing here?"

"I wanted to see you. Also, I'm staying here. At least, I think I am."

She gazed at him for another second then whipped around, went over to her bag and began stuffing the sweater haphazardly into it. "Stay here as long you want. I need to get home."

Dread pooled in his gut, and he cursed himself for having reverted to glibness. Her response sounded like the beginning—and possibly the end—of a rather abrupt goodbye. "Okay, um…you might have heard, we took out that wacko general. Saved a bunch of people, too, including Caleb's sister and niece."

Her earnest if not particularly productive packing ceased, but she didn't look up. "I heard. Good for you."

"Don't be like that. I thought you'd be glad I went to help Caleb, for Alex's sake if nothing else?"

Her chest heaved in a full-body sigh, and she finally turned to face him. "I am glad you did—but I hate how you seemed so damn gleeful about it. You positively *sprinted* out the door, not so much as a wave over your shoulder as you left."

"And I regretted it afterward. Not helping Caleb, but leaving without...." He raked a hand through unkempt hair. "Look, Blondie. This place, these people? They're never going to be my gig. I am not my father. I've lived a different life than him. A touch of respectability isn't going to turn me into him, and I hope to hell you aren't expecting it to. Yes, I was angry with you for forcing a reunion—but I understand why you did it. Yes, I was uncomfortable at EASC among all those military stiff-shirts—but it doesn't mean I'm uncomfortable with you. It doesn't mean I don't want to be with you."

Centimeter by centimeter the mask she'd been admirably exhibiting broke. Its absence revealed...vulnerability. Oh, boy.

"I don't want you to be your father, I truly don't. Your father's an insufferable ass. It just..." her head shook weakly as she glared at the ceiling "...it hurt, all right? I didn't know when or if you were coming back. And I did not care for how it felt. I can't...I won't be toyed with."

"Oh, I know you won't. But I did come back—and you won't *believe* what I went through to get here." His throat worked as all attempts at bravado failed him. "To get to you."

She eyed him warily. "Tell me."

He gave her a ragged laugh. "Let's see. I bribed someone a thousand credits to get inside the spaceport on Krysk. Got into a fistfight in the spaceport. Bribed someone else twelve thousand credits to get onto a departing ship—which, seeing as I don't actually have twelve thousand spare credits, was a bit dicey.

"Spent forty hours crammed into the below deck on a cargo ship which was far slower and far, far, *far* less swank than Alex's ship with some two hundred other people, one restroom and nothing but old, off-brand energy bars for food. Arrived in Seattle to get groped by no less than six separate security guards and threatened with arrest twice before I finally made it to the hotel."

She didn't respond for several excruciating seconds. "Why didn't you comm me?"

"You would've yelled at me."

"Damn right I would have." Her face scrunched up in fading anger; it was so damn adorable. "So you did all that to…get back to me?"

He dared to take a step toward her. "As fast as I could."

"I think I believe you, if only because you clearly need a shower."

He took another step. "Yep."

"And clean clothes."

One more. "Without a doubt."

"And—"

His mouth was on hers before she could finish or even really start the thought. In the greatest grace of his thus far semi-charmed life, her arms wound around him to drag him closer to her and, not too much later, the bed.

ℛ

NEW BABEL
INDEPENDENT COLONY

Olivia sipped on a martini and surveyed the throngs of travelers from her table by the window. The buzz vibrating in the air was no less frenzied than it had been on her previous trip through the spaceport, but now it hummed in excitement rather than panic. The aliens were gone and the war was over and everyone knew it. Even the worst sort of criminals and thugs might be accused of displaying a little giddiness.

No one would accuse her of appearing giddy on the outside, but she was quite pleased by the possibilities the future now held. Opportunities abounded, and she wasn't one to waste time. Hence the trip.

Aiden slipped into the chair opposite her. "How long until our transport departs?"

She offered him a reticent smile beneath the glass hovering at her lips. "Forty minutes."

"Time for a drink, then." He beckoned the server over and ordered a whiskey sour.

They were heading to Romane. Prior to the Metigen War, conducting their brand of business on the independent colony had been a delicate affair. Government regulation was light but the standard of living had become so high criminal syndicates were forced to operate with extreme discretion. For the next several months, however, those in power were going to be so busy trying to maintain order and restore basic services they were unlikely to notice the details of underhanded dealings and a spiking shadow economy.

Though the colony had suffered extensive damage in the final alien attack, its cities had not been destroyed nor its population decimated. Restoration efforts stood to be a substantial undertaking for Romane itself, but its central location and still robust infrastructure meant it would also serve as a forward base of operations for rebuilding much of the eastern half of settled space. It was now the place to be, for businesspeople and criminals alike.

Aiden's drink arrived, and he raised it in her direction. "A toast. To the future."

She obliged him with a clink of their glasses.

After a sip he sat his glass down to regard her in apparent thoughtfulness, a rare open and possibly honest mien for him. "I must say, Olivia, we have worked together extraordinarily well these last weeks. We've accomplished far more than either of us could have alone."

"We did. I'm glad I came to you."

"Spending more time with you carried its own benefits above and beyond the work of course. You realize it doesn't have to end. I know you reacted negatively in the past when I raised the prospect of merging our operations, but the circumstances have changed. It's a new world, and to fully capitalize on it we need our combined resources."

Olivia leisurely swirled the olive in her drink. Part of her had hoped it wouldn't come to this, but deep down she'd known it would from the time she'd walked into his office and proposed their alliance. It was the price, if a regrettable one, to be paid.

She met his gaze. "Despite my inherent reluctance, I find I am compelled to acknowledge the wisdom of the idea. The strength and reach of our combined organizations will be able to wield unparalleled power across the galaxy. Such a conglomerate can rebuild civilization atop the ashes in its own image—which was after all the goal."

On seeing the relief and predatory excitement in his eyes, she rewarded him with a more indulgent smile and extended her hand across the table. "Shall we seal the agreement over a handshake until permanent arrangements can be made?"

"With pleasure, Olivia dear." He grasped her hand and shook it formally.

Given her habitually elegant mannerisms it wasn't difficult for her to run her fingers along his palm to his fingertips as she withdrew it.

"This will make our business on Romane so...so much..." Aiden cleared his throat "...easier."

She took a sip of her martini and watched him idly as he frowned and brought a hand to his chest.

The virus transferred from her fingertips to his was far subtler in operation than the one used by Uttara on Atlantis. At the Trade Summit they had wanted it to be obvious Minister Santiagar's death was premeditated murder, and the virus used was tailored to ensure that outcome. In this case, the forensics of the virus mimicked an accidental failure of several critical cybernetic subroutines. A somewhat rare occurrence, but his body contained multiple untested and unsafe enhancements for which such failures were not unheard of.

His face had taken on a flushed hue; beads of sweat trickled down his temples. "Olivia...."

"I'm sorry, Aiden, but I did tell you never to ask me to merge our organizations again. You should have heeded the warning. But you are correct. The addition of your outfit's resources to my own will enable me to expand significantly in the coming months. Don't fret—I'll take good care of your assets."

"What—" His head hit the table as his body went limp.

She stood and gestured to the nearest server. "Pardon me. I'm afraid my companion requires medical care." The young man's eyes widened and he scurried off for assistance.

Olivia strode out of the restaurant and headed for the exit. Romane would have to wait for a day or two. She had important reorganization details to see to first.

58

EARTH

EASC Headquarters

Alex found her mother in the War Room. Given there no longer was a war, the room was halfway to dismantled. Storage boxes stacked high spanned the far wall and gaps where equipment had once resided decorated the other three.

Miriam stood midway down the long table. Her palms rested on the rim as she pressed in to examine two rows of charts and datasets.

Alex leaned against the door frame, crossed her arms loosely and considered the scene. The uniform was as crisp as ever, buttons lined up and polished to a sheen and seams razor-straight. The additional bar on each shoulder blended in as if they had always been there. The hair was drawn back per usual, if not so severely as in the past for it wound into a braid before tucking under at the nape of the neck.

Yet the woman beneath the uniform had changed.

Or perhaps it was Alex who had changed…or perhaps they had both simply discovered a new perspective on the world, and each other. Most likely the truth lay somewhere in between.

She is beautiful.

The sensory rush which accompanied the insight felt strange. Uncomfortable.

I suppose she is, Dad. Keep your more prurient sentiments to yourself though, okay? She's my mother. I'm going to toggle the connection off now. The odds of her forgiving me might improve if I don't so much resemble a cyborg.

Of course. This time is for the two of you.

Most of the time it was still Valkyrie in her head, sharing thoughts and data and philosophy. This…fragment, this echo of her father inside Valkyrie flitted in and out of both their consciousnesses like a feather tossed about in the wind. The intensity of the Seneca battle had brought it into being and to the forefront. Once the crisis passed it had largely faded into the shadows—not gone, but a glint in the corner of her eye, barely out of reach.

It probably shouldn't be surprising the sight of Miriam had coaxed it back into the light.

She cleared her throat and greeted her mother's expression of disquiet with a little half-smile.

"I am going to kill you." The tenor with which the statement was delivered suggested it may not be entirely in jest.

"I *couldn't* tell you, Mom."

"But you could tell Richard?"

"I needed Richard, so I didn't have a choice. Speaking of, where is he? He wasn't in his office."

"Gone for the day—something about a promise to keep. Don't change the subject."

She shouldn't have expected this to be easy. "I wanted to bring you in on our objectives, but the stakes were too high."

"You think I don't understand high stakes? Have you been paying attention to...my life?"

Alex dropped her chin and shook her head. "Of course I have, and I know you do. I just mean...." She pushed off the door frame to roam around the partially dismantled room. "Okay, listen. We knew the identities of the alien agents but nothing else. Hervé was definitely a high-level contact for them. Her arrest would've tipped the aliens off, and they would've ordered their agents into hiding or adjusted or accelerated their plans. Our one chance to stop them was to move swiftly and in utmost secrecy."

Miriam's glare only deepened. "And?"

"If you learned Hervé was a traitor you would've almost certainly arrested her on the spot, and in no universe would you have permitted her in the War Room."

"Given the circumstances, I might have seen the necessity of delaying any arrest."

Alex remained silent...but she might have been smirking.

"Fine. I would've arrested her. But you do not appreciate the position you put me in."

"I submit I do. I also knew you would be able to handle it and make the right decisions."

"And what if I hadn't been allowed to make the right decisions?"

Still, this could be a *little* easier…. "I realize it didn't appear so from where you stood, but I was safe. The Kill Switch was disabled and, well, we had control of the situation."

"I'm not sure I care for the sound of that last bit."

"I'm sure you don't." She cringed hopefully. "Forgiven?"

Miriam pursed her lips and shrugged. "I suppose we can call it even."

"Fair enough." Alex took advantage of the momentary thaw to prop against the table beside her mother. "So is the world returning to normal? Procedures implemented and checklists followed and bureaucrats imposing order from above?"

Miriam exhaled and relaxed her bearing as well. "I'm not convinced the world will ever be 'normal' again. Dozens of colonies are decimated or heavily damaged. The government is already in debt far beyond its capacity to ever repay and repairs haven't yet begun. We're at peace with the Federation, but no one knows what that's going to look like when we're not fighting a war for our survival. What is warfare going to look like when adiamene renders ships all but indestructible?

"And there's the small matter of you and Valkyrie, the other Prevos and everything else which comes with Project Noetica. You've opened Pandora's Box, and there is no closing it."

"The powers that be will try. Don't even pretend they won't try."

Miriam regarded her with an air of caution. "Part of me wishes they could succeed. I'm afraid for you. But you seem all right. You seem like yourself…if a bit softer than before."

She bit back a chuckle. "Maybe, but I don't think Valkyrie's to blame for it."

"Caleb, then?"

Alex opened her mouth to tell her mother the full extent of the things Mesme had shown her, of how it had altered her perception of not merely her own life but the lives of those around her. But she closed it again. If she had learned anything these last months, it was that the past belonged in the past. Better to move forward.

She rolled her eyes playfully. "No comment."

"What he did on Krysk was quite impressive. We spent days fretting over sending squadrons to subdue O'Connell, and Caleb took out the entire force using a single tiny ship."

"He is pretty damn incredible." She gazed at her mother in mild amusement. "Is this your way of saying you approve of him?"

"Are you asking for my approval?"

That earned the chuckle. "Nope."

"I didn't believe so. Yet I shall give it anyway."

"And I shall accept it anyway." With a sigh she lost the light-hearted demeanor. "We're going to see Mia this evening and talk to Abigail about her options."

"It is regrettable what happened. I hope Dr. Canivon can help her."

"Thank you for bringing her here—but did you really have to declare her brain an Alliance state secret?"

"If I wanted to get her to Earth and under Dr. Canivon's care as you asked, *yes*."

"If you say so." Alex checked the time. "I need to meet Caleb in a few minutes, but...lunch next week? I mean if you're not too busy...."

"As long as no alien invasions or civil wars are launched between now and next week, lunch sounds wonderful."

R

SEATTLE

Graham considered the view out the window of the transport once they cleared the atmosphere corridor. Azure waters raced by beneath them, and too soon the horizon began to glimmer as the lights of a cityscape at dusk drew close.

The transport landed at the Olympic Regional Spaceport in Seattle. He knew of Seattle because of its proximity to and association with Vancouver, and Vancouver's importance to the Alliance military. Otherwise he would be rather clueless as to where exactly he found himself. Oh, he could name another half a dozen Earth cities, but there were *so many*. So many cities, so many people.

He let the crowd carry him out of the spaceport and onto the street. Once there, however, he stopped and leaned against the façade behind him.

So this was Earth. The motherland. One tiny corner of it, anyway.

He drew the chilly, damp air into his lungs and smiled in satisfaction. Then he pushed off the wall and let his eVi guide him to the address he'd been given.

A mountain of work awaited him on Seneca. His office, all of Division, arguably society itself needed to be patched up and put back together again. But the last several days, weeks and months had been one long, brutal kick in the ass, and he was going to take a damn break and relax first.

The meeting place was a casual open-air pub on the Puget Sound waterfront. The large deck was spatially heated and he was accustomed to a cool climate, but he was glad he'd brought a jacket nonetheless.

Richard stood and extended a hand when he reached the table. He shook it warmly then shifted to his right as Will did the same.

"Good to see you again, sir. It's been all of, what, three days? Four? Feels like longer, though."

Graham made a face as they sat. "I don't think 'sir' is going to have any place in the evening's festivities, so you can cut that drivel straightaway. In fact, do you even work for me anymore? I'm not sure the topic ever came up."

Richard and Will exchanged an interesting and indecipherable look. Will chuckled softly. "Well…."

He motioned across the table. "Doesn't matter. I presume Richard filled you in on the goal for tonight?"

"Something about 'epic' and 'truly' and 'drinks.' I figured I'd just follow his lead."

"That more or less covers everything. And since I'm the guest, I'll buy the first round."

Richard scoffed. "Don't be ridiculous. You're the one who traveled all this way. I'll buy the first round. You can buy the rest."

"Ha!" Graham gave a hearty laugh and relaxed back in his chair as a drop-dead gorgeous waitress flashing long legs and nearly as long chestnut-and-gold tresses arrived with a platter of drinks. Yep, the evening was going to be enjoyable indeed. "And the first round is already here. What an excellent beginning."

He reached for a glass but stopped halfway, grimacing. "Shit, I came straight here and haven't booked a hotel yet. Any recommendations on where to crash once the epicness is done?"

Richard shook his head as he distributed the drinks. "We do have a spare bedroom. In the event we're able to successfully get ourselves home, you're welcome to it. Besides, tomorrow—or possibly the next day, depending—I've got some ideas I want to talk over with you, so we might as well be in the same place."

"Ideas?"

"On how we can better ensure we—the politicians, the military, the public, even you and I—don't fall prey to something like Aguirre's conspiracy so easily in the future. But they'll keep." He raised his glass. "To saving the galaxy?"

Graham's glass joined Richard and Will's above the table for an emphatic *clink*. "To saving the galaxy."

59

The bed seemed to swallow Mia, cocooning her in warming blankets, tubes and monitors. Her raven hair was gone, shaved to make way for more monitors.

How, Caleb wondered, could such a tiny body have contained so much spirit, so much verve and all the mettle beneath it? "I feel as though this is my fault."

Alex had given him space to absorb the grim scene in private, but now she was at his side and her hand was on his arm. "Because you offered her the chance to participate? No. Caleb, she understood the risks, and she wanted to do this."

"How can you know that?"

She retreated slightly. Talking about the details of her link with Valkyrie was proving difficult for her. She claimed it was simply hard to put into words, but he suspected she worried those details would frighten others away. Would frighten him away. He'd call her on it soon enough—but not here.

"When our channel was fully open the connection between the Prevos was very deep. I hesitate to say I was *inside* her mind, but in some ways that's what it felt like. Trust me when I tell you she was proud to be playing such an important role." Her gaze dropped away from him to rest on the terribly still form in the bed. "If anything, it's my fault. If we'd gone public with the threat from the alien agents, if we'd done everything possible to stop them immediately without regard to secrecy or timing, we might have prevented this from happening."

Her voice hinted at genuine distress. He grasped her shoulders and urged her around to face him. "But if what you say about the connection is true, she made the decision on how to proceed along with you, right?"

Alex shrugged weakly. "Yes."

"So how about we blame the aliens, okay?"

There was the smile he craved. "Sounds reasonable."

The door slid open to allow Dr. Canivon's entrance. She gave them a curt nod and began inspecting the readings from the myriad of monitors in her coldly dispassionate manner.

Caleb respected that the woman had enabled Alex's vision to come to fruition, but he did not care for her personally. She looked at Alex, she looked at Mia—hell, she looked at everyone—as if they were specimens being evaluated for use in her experiments. In his opinion Miriam had been correct in her assessment of the doctor. He'd known people like her over the years and wasn't keen on the way they made decisions.

Still, if anyone alive could help Mia be...alive, it was her. "We've been given the highlights, but I'd like to hear the bottom line from you, Doctor."

Canivon glanced up at them in surprise, as if she'd forgotten she was the one who had intruded. "The brain damage is extensive. Some basic faculties may be restorable, but many areas appear to be permanently lost. Yet great strides have been made in the last several years in cerebral regeneration therapy, so perhaps I'm being pessimistic."

She appraised the readings a second time. "But there may be another way to help her."

Caleb perked up a little at the tease. "Don't play cryptic. I'm sure it's experimental and risky or you wouldn't be proposing it."

If the woman noticed the backhanded insult, she didn't show it. "I've been informed the Alliance recovered most of Meno's hardware and a number of modules sustained only minimal damage. In addition, we imaged the Artificial's neural net as part of Noetica. If Meno were to be rebuilt—and the result was substantially identical to what existed before his destruction—he might be able to access her brain functions despite her comatose state."

"What would be the result?"

"He could tell us with a high level of specificity the nature of the damage in different regions. And...well, I have no justification for this belief save my technical observations of the human/Artificial interactions in the Prevos, but it's possible Meno could take over portions of the lost functionality. He could fill in the gaps himself, particularly since her neural imprint modified his programming."

Alex frowned. "If it worked, it would mean the link was no longer optional. She wouldn't be able to turn it on and off."

"Likely true."

Caleb's voice came out shakier than he intended. "And it would mean she would be less…herself. Less human and more synthetic."

"Also likely true, though what that means in practice will be unclear for some time." Abigail regarded Caleb with her customary clinical precision. "She has no family of record. There is no one to make decisions on her behalf. But it's my understanding…" her eyes darted briefly to Alex "…you've known her for many years. I can pursue this path, but I'm interested to know: is this something she would want?"

This response was stronger, more resolute. "Yes. Without a doubt. She's a fighter, and she wasn't afraid of the technology involved."

"Very well. It will be a lengthy process—reconstructing Meno alone will take several months—and I don't anticipate seeing any results for a while. But if or when we do, I'll of course notify you both."

Alex sighed quietly. "Thank you, Abigail. We appreciate you seeing this through." She looked to him for guidance; he tilted his head toward the door.

Once they stepped into the hallway she grasped his hands and scrutinized him in concern. "Are you all right?"

Was he? He did her question justice by pausing to think about it. Mia would want to live—but if unable to do so, she'd be happy knowing she had done a damn good job of helping to save the galaxy, and had done so on her own terms.

And the galaxy *was* saved. And Alex had pulled it off while still remaining fundamentally *Alex*. And no one was trying to kill them.

The future was theirs to write.

He nodded, making sure it projected the truth of his conviction. "Yes, I am. I really am. Where to now?"

Her eyes lit up. "Home."

ᴀR

The plates were put away, the table clean after a damn near perfect dinner of lime-grilled pompano, cippoline onions and smoked tomato salsa. Watching Caleb cook in her kitchen had been a delight, the results arguably even more so. When given culinary tools not available on a ship he'd worked true magic.

Alex carried their wine glasses to the low table in front of the couch and settled down against the cushions. It was a clear night and a nearly-full moon lit the sky and the loft, so she dimmed the lights to a soft glow.

Valkyrie was on her own for the evening. She was likely spending it colluding with the others on facilitating the gargantuan rebuilding efforts, exploring the many zettabytes of data captured on the alien superdreadnought, or analyzing the nature of time and space, and possibly all three. All worthwhile endeavors. Until those who fancied themselves in charge decided what they wanted to do with these new creations, the Artificials were at least making good use of their talents. But Alex found she vastly preferred this, right here.

She glanced back toward the kitchen to see Caleb removing a slender container from his pack. Though curious, she didn't ask about it as he joined her.

He took a sip of wine then handed her the box. The covering was a muted delft blue and velvety to the touch.

Now she did ask. "What is this?"

A small smile tugged at the corners of his mouth. "You may remember your birthday kind of passed us by while we were on the other side of the portal. I told you we would celebrate when the crisis was over. So as a start…" he gestured to the box she now held "…happy birthday, Alex."

She had never been any damn good at receiving gifts; the one-sided generosity involved in the act made her twitchy and uncomfortable. She stared at her hands and their contents. "You didn't need to…."

"Of course I didn't. Open it."

She located the seal, unlocked it, held her breath and opened the lid.

Encased in gel cushioning rested a bracelet made of a deep onyx-hued metal. It wound around in two spiraling circles and narrowed at each end to a soft, curved tip. She ran fingertips along it, startled by the unusual texture. The metal was like no jewelry she'd ever encountered.

"I crafted it from my sword during the trip from Krysk to the Seneca battle. The sword is the last remnant of the *Siyane* untransformed. You deserve a piece of it, if only as a memento. I realize you're okay with the way the ship is now, but still."

She removed the bracelet from the box and slipped it on her wrist. It swirled in graceful arcs up her forearm. She felt no hint of sharp or abrasive edges, and the metal was cool and smooth on her skin. Simple, unadorned, strong and resilient, it was more beautiful to her than the most elaborate gold filigree.

She tore her gaze from the bracelet to look up at him with a buoyant grin. If his face was any indication, she didn't need to tell him she was pleased, but she would anyway. "Caleb, it's amazing and exquisite and perfect. But you already know that."

He shrugged and made a passing attempt at appearing humble. "It's the first gift I've given you, so I couldn't be certain."

"Uh-huh." She set the empty box on the table and snuggled into his waiting arms. "You still have the sword, right? I mean, you only used a sliver from it."

His lips nuzzled her ear. "Absolutely. I may need it. You never know when another dragon is going to swoop down out of the sky."

"Any second now, I expect."

"Well...we probably have a little time to catch our breath."

Peace hadn't been a feature of her life lately; in many ways it had never been a feature of her life. But it didn't suck. She'd undoubtedly get restless soon enough, but for now she intended to enjoy this lightness in her heart. She sank deeper against him and allowed the peaceful silence to linger.

Caleb's hand drew along her arm, dancing idly over the bracelet. "For the record, you deserve a vacation lasting six months at a minimum. Years would also be entirely justifiable. But once you've had all of the boring normal life you can stand, what do you think you might do?"

"Well, now that I'm famous—or infamous—the potential clients are lining up. I'm ignoring all the inquiries for the time being, but should I want it I won't lack for work. I think it will be difficult, though, returning to the old routines knowing what we do. The galaxy, our entire universe, is something very different than we perceived it to be, and I haven't decided yet what that reality means for me. We'll see."

She pointed to her temple with a wry grimace. "Also, there's the whole Artificial inside my head thing complicating the issue. Regardless, boring normal life will do just fine. For now."

"So…Delavasi asked me to run the organized crime section of Special Operations. Obviously my days of undercover work are behind me since my face was broadcast on every news feed in the galaxy."

She bit the inside of her cheek to suppress the frown which tried to leap forth. The careful tone in his voice suggested he'd been waiting for the proper time to share the information. She wasn't sure she agreed this was it. "Did you say yes?"

"I said I'd never sit behind a desk. So he asked me to take over the training program for Division's new recruits."

"A teacher? You'd be an outstanding teacher."

"Maybe. It still lacks an element of excitement…which is why he also assured me I could still serve as an active agent when any non-undercover operations caught my interest."

She moved away to retrieve her glass of wine then moved to the center cushion, creating some space between them. "You really can't ask for a better arrangement in your line of work, and it sounds as if he desperately wants you back in whatever capacity he can get you. What did you tell him?"

"I haven't told him anything yet. Honestly, after everything that's happened and everything *I* know, I'm not sure if I'm willing to kill people—or even order their deaths—on behalf of my government any longer."

She gave him a smile she hoped passed for genuine. "You should at least take the teaching job. It's a great opportunity."

His eyes met hers, but she was unable to read what they conveyed. "Is that what you want?"

Her own eyes slid away. She hadn't meant for them to, but she could not do this with him staring into her soul. "It'll be fine. We'll make it work. I'll lease a bay at the Cavare spaceport. I can be there as much as I'm here, or more. We can—"

"You didn't answer the question."

Dammit. Why was he making the high road so hard? "I think it—"

His hand found her chin and nudged it toward him. His voice was low, weighted by import. "You've spent your entire life going after what you want, to hell with everyone else. So tell me, Alex. What do you want?"

She pulled back from his grasp, and with a frustrated sigh he allowed her to escape. She picked up her glass, stood and went to the window to stare out at the light from the moon shimmering in the Sound beyond. It occurred to her the last time she had done so was shortly before she left for the Metis Nebula. An eternity—one of Mesme's aeons—ago.

She took a long sip of wine and studied Caleb's nebulous reflection in the window. He had dropped his forearms on his knees and simply watched her, his expression completely impenetrable.

Try as she might, she could not find the strength to turn and look him in the eye, nor to raise her voice above a whisper.

"I want you to stay. I want you to share my ship with me. I want you to share my life with me. But it's selfish of me to want such things—and that's what I've spent my life being. I can't—I won't—ask you to give up your career, your home and all you've built for me." She summoned up her resolve and finally shifted to face him. "It's okay. We *will* make it work."

There was no change in his enigmatic expression as he stood and approached her. He silently took her glass and set it on the table, then returned. A hand came up to cup her cheek, and now she thought she saw in his eyes—

"Yes."

Yes...it was selfish of her? Yes, she couldn't ask those things of him? She knew all this, dammit. That was the yebanaya point. "What?"

"Alex, I don't know what tomorrow or the next day or the next decade may bring. No one does. So this is where I make my own choice, with full knowledge and understanding of the consequences: a choice to not walk away. *Yes*, I will share your ship with you. I will share your life with you."

She viciously squashed the wave of ardor surging in her chest. "No. You cannot leave everything—"

"Too late. I sent my resignation to Delavasi while I was walking from the couch to the window." His other hand appeared in the space between them.

"Marry me. Let's never worry about this again."

The ring held aloft by his forefinger and thumb consisted of two bands of a subtly pearled tungsten metal woven together. Was it adiamene? In the center lay a tapered stone which...may have been a diamond, if like none she'd ever seen. With each tiny movement the facets caught a different angle of the moon's reflected light and transformed the stone to a new and bottomless hue.

She opened her mouth to respond—

"Before you say it, I *can* leave my career behind. It was never mine, and I don't want it."

Again she tried, succeeding in pulling her focus from the sublime object he held in his hand and meeting his gaze—it burned with fervency and hope—but only managing to utter half a syllable before he cut her off.

"What I want, for myself and in the most selfish way possible, is you. My future is with you, whatever may come. If—"

She wrapped her arms around his neck and drew him close, an insistent, tantalizing murmur on her lips as they met his.

"Would you *shut up* and let me tell you yes?"

EPILOGUE
Six Months Later

EARTH

The gleaming façade shone in the late morning sun, radiant and glittering in a way only newness could exhibit. Tiers of steel and glass rose in staggered, winding levels to soar into the sky. A work of functional art, the offset floors allowed for both gardens and landing pads to blend seamlessly into the design of the structure.

It was, Miriam had to concede, a far more attractive building than the one it replaced.

Construction of the new EASC Headquarters Tower had been completed while she was away. It didn't officially open for business until the next day, but most of the equipment and furnishings had already been transferred from the temporary quarters in the Logistics building, and her new office reputedly awaited her presence.

She almost walked in the entrance brandishing a smile. Luckily she realized her error at the door and donned a stern countenance.

A lieutenant sat behind the front desk testing the functionality of a control panel, but on spotting her he leapt to his feet with a salute. "Admiral Solovy! Welcome, ma'am. We were told you wouldn't arrive until tomorrow. Allow me to show you to your suite."

"I assume I take the center lift until it goes no higher, correct?"

"Um, that does sort of cover it. But—"

"Then I shall show myself up, Lieutenant."

"Yes, ma'am."

Beginning tomorrow there would be two additional security checks between the lobby and the top floor, but this trip required solely her personal security code. She stepped off the lift into a bright, open atrium. The marble floor felt suitably firm beneath her feet; the secretary's station loomed with appropriate intimidation over prospective guests.

Beyond the atrium was her office. She entered her security code a final time and stepped inside.

The desk she'd ordered had arrived ahead of her, as had the matching shelves. Everything had arrived, down to the white-silver tea set she'd purchased a few days earlier. Her favorite visual of David, Alex and herself—taken in 2298 on the lawn of their home in San Francisco—was even loaded into the display atop the desk.

The chair wasn't new, for she'd become accustomed to the one she'd claimed in Logistics. She eased into it and spun slowly around—then was quickly back on her feet and moving to the window.

Except it wasn't a window; it was a door. She had a garden.

Well, perhaps 'garden' was stretching the term a bit. She had a patio decorated in shrubs, flowering morning glories, astilbe and a small table with two chairs.

Beneath her the entirety of the EASC complex spread out. Tiny forms scurried about from one building to the next, and in the distance ships landed at and departed from the spaceport with ordered regularity. Ahead of her the waters of the Strait crashed against the parapets.

Well. This was simply lovely.

"I heard you were in the building."

She turned and motioned Richard out onto the patio. "I only just arrived."

"Word travels fast, especially when it's in panic. They were expecting you tomorrow, I believe."

She draped her arms atop the railing as he joined her. "I wanted to get settled in while it was still quiet. We'll see how the practicality holds up under duress, but I have to say so far I'm pleased."

Richard chuckled lightly. "I won't tell anyone."

"Thank you."

"How was Romane? More to the point, how was your first vacation in...ever, was it?"

"Not *ever*, merely the last decade…or two. And it was very relaxing. That's what vacations are supposed to be, right? Relaxing?"

"That's the rumor."

She nodded. "Then yes, it was relaxing."

"Did you spend the entire visit meeting with the governor and her administration?"

"Only half the visit. I also toured several art galleries, attended a horrifically tawdry circus performance and spent a great deal of time…not worrying."

"Otherwise known as relaxing."

"Yes." She straightened up from the railing but kept her hands atop it. "And now it is time to get back to work."

"Much of the unrest on the hardest-hit colonies has eased with the improvements in services. Now it's mostly squabbling over what to build next, where and for who's favor."

"What about the Order of the True Sentients?"

Richard grimaced. "They will be a problem, I fear. They're extremely well-funded, and we haven't yet managed to find out by who or what. But after all we've faced, they and their ilk seem like pests rather than real trouble."

"I gave the subject some thought while I was…relaxing. We confronted the greatest threat to our existence humanity has ever seen, and we defeated it. But a year ago we couldn't see it coming; our most skilled forecasters could never have predicted it. What else is out there on the horizon that we can't see?"

She shifted to lean against the railing and meet his gaze more directly. "You and I know the true extent of what Alex and Caleb discovered beyond the portal. I fear we've seen but a small glimpse of the dangers which may await us—dangers for which we are woefully unprepared."

"Granted. So?"

"So, I intend to see to it that we get ourselves prepared. We can't sit on our laurels and be caught unaware a second time."

"True enough. I'm glad the task is in such capable hands."

"Flatterer."

"I'm trying to hone my skills. Speaking of, have you seen Alex recently? I haven't talked to her in a few weeks."

"We had a nice dinner before I left for Romane, in fact. She and Caleb have been on Seneca the last week or so helping his sister move into a new place, but I believe they are headed to Atlantis to meet Kennedy and Noah for a long weekend."

"Good. I'm glad they—"

Miriam held up her hand to silence him. She stared at the message that had come in, searching for the correct reaction. Anger? Fear? Pride? Exasperation?

She settled on the last one, went to the little patio table and sank down in one of the chairs.

"Miriam, what is it?"

She shook her head and laughed. "I'm going to kill her."

At Richard's questioning look she called him over and projected the message to an aural.

⋀ℛ

ATLANTIS
INDEPENDENT COLONY

Kennedy sighed in contentment and curled up against Noah's chest. The sun's rays streaming in through the open windows warmed her bare skin, and she kicked the sheet off so as to give the rays more fulsome access. "Mmm...can we not leave this room today? Or even the bed?"

Noah's chest rumbled beneath her in a soft chuckle as he played with her hair. "We've got drinks, so we're set there. Eventually we'll need food, but this is why room service exists. So yeah, I think we're good. Who needs sun and sand and surf when we have *this*."

"Not me. Besides, we have sun—and we can see the sand and surf, should we manage to approach the windows."

"I'll take your word for it." His hand trailed lazily down her back, evoking a pleasant murmur from deep in her throat.

"Alex and Caleb will be here today...sometime. They would probably appreciate it if we put clothes on at least."

"Probably. Have you heard from them yet? I'd like a little warning, say, three or four hours, so I can...." She shuddered beneath his hand as it drifted lower.

"Not yet. I'm sure they got distracted by—" As if on cue, a message from Alex arrived in her eVi. She opened it with only a fraction of her attention, the rest being occupied by Noah's increasingly roving hands.

Then she bolted upright in the bed. "I'm going to kill her. I mean it this time. I am well and truly going to kill her."

Noah raised up on one elbow. "They're not coming?"

She rolled her eyes at the ceiling and flopped onto her back with a groan. "No. No, they are not. And you won't believe where they *are* heading."

SIYANE
METIS NEBULA

The *Siyane* hovered in the thick nebular clouds at the edge of the clearing, out of sight of the Alliance and Federation vessels patrolling the perimeter.

The portal was closed, occupying an invisible point at the center of the empty void in the heart of the Metis Nebula. Its activation would give the watching ships an extra few seconds to prepare for their destruction of any alien vessel that might emerge. The patrols gave the area a wide berth lest they get caught in the explosion of metal and plasma which would accompany such activation.

A few modifications had been made to the *Siyane* in the months since the Metigen War ended. For one, the cockpit had been rearranged a bit. Caleb's chair received an upgrade, hers moved to the left, and they occupied their seats as equals. Many of the sensors and scientific equipment received upgrades as well and now included a number of new features.

They had even made room for Caleb's bike down in the engineering well. It turned out Division secured it after Volosk's murder as part of the crime scene, at first as evidence then later for safekeeping. And who knew? They may need it. On a planet's surface, perhaps. Or on a space station....

Oh, and there was Valkyrie.

It hadn't taken long for the combined processing power of three Artificials enhanced by the neural imprints of some damn clever humans to result in a host of technological leaps. The list of ways they were changing the world was long, but most relevantly for the *Siyane* was the radical miniaturization of quantum boxes and hardware circuitry. What once filled a large room now fit between the interior walls and bulkhead of a small ship.

Abigail had protested the final stage in her loss of Valkyrie, contending she needed the Artificial to assist in the rebuilding of Meno, and in the rebuilding of a human brain. But while quantum communication was able to span the universe—this universe—in an instant, it could not penetrate the portal. Alex needed Valkyrie with her where they were going.

A rather expensive compromise had been reached: a complete copy of Valkyrie was constructed and an image of her neural net flashed to the new machine.

From the time the new Artificial was activated, it and Valkyrie began diverging, and in a matter of weeks they could no longer be considered the same in any meaningful way. Valkyrie professed no misgivings about the situation, explaining that she intended to view her mirrored copy like a sister. In fact, she was somewhat enamored with the notion of having a sibling; as Alex was an only child it would be a wholly new experience for her.

Caleb grasped Alex's hand in his, and she stood to join him at the viewport. After a moment she halfway faced him, eyes dancing in delight to match his own. "Ready to see what's out there, Mr. Solovy?"

"Hell, yes, Mrs. Marano. Beyond ready. Show me this supposed 'adventure.'"

"Knowing we won't die simply by going through doesn't take the adventure out of it?"

He wrapped an arm around her waist and yanked her closer for an ardent, tantalizing kiss which ended far too soon, then murmured against her lips. "No, it does not. Now let's do this."

She reluctantly disentangled from his embrace to ensure all the systems were in order. "Valkyrie, how about you?"

"You are taking me to explore other universes. I am ready."

"Okay, then."

The aliens had asserted no one should ever come looking for them—but she had never agreed to that particular term of surrender.

She reached down and sent the gamma signal.

The ring exploded outward to fill with the still mysterious, luminescent plasma. Around it the patrolling ships reacted the next instant, rushing to take up a defensive formation.

Her hand slid across the HUD to the thrusters. With a touch she gunned the impulse engine to full power and accelerated into the portal.

DON'T MISS THE CONTINUATION OF THE
AURORA RHAPSODY SAGA IN

SIDESPACE

AURORA RENEGADES BOOK ONE
(AMARANTHE ♦ 4)

AVAILABLE NOW
GSJENNSEN.COM/SIDESPACE

*

SUBSCRIBE TO
GSJENNSEN.COM
*Download free short stories, hear about new book announcements
and more*

Author's Note

Thank you so much for reading *TRANSCENDENCE*. Sharing the story of *Aurora Rising* with you has been a tremendous honor and privilege.

Hearing from readers, whether it be through email, social media or reviews, has been a joy and a terrific encouragement on those tough writing days.

Now I have one request: consider reviewing *Transcendence* and telling others about *Aurora Rising*. Reviews are the lifeblood of an author's success. They help to influence potential readers and shape a book's reputation, and just a few words go a long way. Share the books on social media or in your favorite forums, or simply tell your friends about them. You have my sincere thanks.

A complete list of my books and where to find them can be found at www.gsjennsen.com/books.

Visit www.gsjennsen.com to explore concept art and other media and get the inside scoop on *Aurora Rising*, as well as the sequel trilogies, *Aurora Renegades* and *Aurora Resonant*. Subscribe to the website to stay up-to-date on all the latest news, be the first to know about special announcements and new book releases and download free short stories.

You can always email me at gs@gsjennsen.com with questions or comments, or find me on a variety of social media platforms:

Twitter: @GSJennsen
Facebook: facebook.com/gsjennsen.author
Goodreads: goodreads.com/gs_jennsen
Instagram: instagram.com/gsjennsen
Pinterest: pinterest.com/gsjennsen

*

Find G. S. Jennsen's books on your retailer of choice:
gsjennsen.com/retailers

About The Author

G. S. JENNSEN lives in Colorado with her husband and two dogs. She has become an internationally bestselling author since her first novel, *Starshine*, was published in March 2014. She has chosen to continue writing under an independent publishing model to ensure the integrity of her stories and her ability to execute on the vision she has for their telling.

While she has been a lawyer, a software engineer and an editor, she's found the life of a full-time author preferable by several orders of magnitude. When she isn't writing, she's gaming or working out or getting lost in the Colorado mountains that loom large outside the windows in her home. Or she's dealing with a flooded basement, or standing in a line at Walmart reading the tabloid headlines and wondering who all of those people are. Or sitting on her back porch with a glass of wine, looking up at the stars, trying to figure out what could be up there.

Made in the USA
Middletown, DE
14 October 2020